WELL OF DREAMS

Praise for Well of Dreams

"The bonds of sisterhood are not easily broken, with neither time nor circumstance hindering their devotion. Norse mythology punctuates this moving tale of loss and acceptance in a way that will leave you wanting more!"

- Britt Cooper & Erin Dulin, authors of Queen of Shadows

"This book is a must-read! If you love the dystopian feel of books like Divergent and The Hunger Games, but also love fantasy elements like royalty and magic, you'll love Well of Dreams! The two genres are masterfully woven together to create a unique story that will have you obsessively turning pages to find out what happens next! Definitely pick this one up! You won't be disappointed!"

- Emily Schneider, author of Scales of Ash & Smoke

"Combining ancient powers and modern times, secrets and political intrigue, Ann delivers heart-pumping action in this young adult dystopian fantasy. Brimming with Nordic lore, ancient magic, and secrets to discover; Well of Dreams sets the stage for an exciting series ahead!"

- Amanda Auler, author of Daughter of the Sun

"Well of Dreams is everything I expect a YA Dystopian Fantasy to be. Kayla Ann has crafted a beautiful tale of forgotten pasts and discovering who you are, full of action and suspense that will leave you on the edge of your seat!"

- Angela Morse, author of The Thief's Relic

THE RUNIC SAGA

BOOK ONE

WELL OF DREAMS

KAYLA ANN

Kayla Ann Books

979-8-9884385-2-6 (ebook)
979-8-9884385-0-2 (paperback)
979-8-9884385-1-9 (hardback)
979-8-9884385-3-3 (limited edition)

Library of Congress Control Number: 2023912228

Ebook, Paperback, & Dust Jacket Cover Art by Etheric Tales

Hard Case Laminate Cover Art by Nemaiza Rhayne

Illustrations by Efa-finearts

Mapwork by Aaguirreart

Edited by Addison Horner

First Edition 2023

10 9 8 7 6 5 4 3 2

For my son.
Chase your dreams.

IYSTHEIM
1. THE WALL
2. INTAKE YARD
3. MARKETPLACE
4. COURT OF ARISTOCRACY
5. THE PALACE

1
3
4
3
1

N
RANN'S SEAS
RANN'S SEAS
RANN'S SEAS
RANN'S SEAS
DIAMANT
Gjoll River
ISHJEM
TREHEIM
Undarbrunnk Lake
Nordryggen Mountains
RUBIN
SMARAGD
BRANNSIDEN
VIÐNÁM
Karalven River
PERLE
SAFIR
LYSTHEIM
HAVSIDEN
EVROPA

Part One

Vakna

"Under the mighty tree Yggdrasil
A child, a woman, and a crone dwell
Discussing the fate of mankind,
Determining destiny, and
Spinning their ultimate design."

-Urðr, *Book of the Past*

Prologue: The Norn

Verðandi

IN THE DAYS BEFORE *the end, mankind dwelled in madness.*

Focused on fabricated satisfaction and marred by manufactured wars, nation battled nation, convinced of their own righteousness. Technology dismissed belief, and hatred replaced compassion. They'd been told the world would succumb to demons, but they never suspected the birth of monsters would originate within their own hearts.

Mankind forgot the gods, but the gods had not forgotten them. Summoned by the calloused hearts of men, demons and giants infested the world. Only the Æsir, deities of wit, strength, and valor, could rise against them. The golden blood of the gods and the black ichor of demons covered the Earth. Then Sutr, the giant of fire and darkness, burned the world to ash.

This was Ragnarok, *the beginning of the end.*

Nations sank beneath the waters. All was silent.

Yet Yggdrasil, *the tree of life, endured.*

With branches clinging onto the darkened heavens, its roots sheltered the last nation, cradling it above the waves. That nation, Evrópa, was all that remained of the Earth.

Sheltered by the tree, humanity survived. Awakened by the Norn—those three goddesses of fate who had survived Ragnarok—mankind was reborn from the ashes. For what are gods without mankind to worship them?

When the waters receded, the humans rebuilt, forming communities around ancestral bloodlines. In rediscovering lost technology, mankind grew and flourished. But when extinction threatened once again, the Norn imbued within humanity a bit of their own galdr, *the power of the gods.*

ᚾᛁᛗᚱᛋᚾᛁᛗᚱᛋᚾᛁᛗᚱᛋᚾᛁᛗᚱᛋᚾᛁᛗᚱᛋ

VERÐANDI SHUT THE BOOK, not minding the puff of dust it exhaled into her face, then looked into the faces of her sleepers. The boy and girl appeared to be approaching adulthood, with a hint of youth rounding out their faces. They slumbered at the base of the stone well, their hands separated by only a width of grass.

The young goddess' pale fingers brushed aside a lock of flame-red hair and traced the runes on Urðr's *Book of the Past.* The old crone would scold Verðandi for taking it, but she didn't care. Her sleepers liked to hear her tales of old, even if Urðr said they couldn't hear her in their suspended state. Besides, the stories reminded Verðandi of the golden era, when mankind had truly revered the gods.

As they should. As they would again one day.

Verðandi rose, balancing bare feet on the well's edge and grasping the book in both arms. Urðr might actually kill her if she dropped it into the still waters that *dripped, dripped, dripped* from the deep stone walls. As always, Verðandi's eyes were drawn to the runes etched deep into the rocks. With delicate yet sturdy fingers, she'd carved them there herself. They glowed at her touch, warming at her presence.

For all of Urðr's grand stories, it was Verðandi who held the power of the runes.

As light as air, she leapt, her feet brushing the bark of the roots that nearly strangled the well within their grasp. More of Verðandi's runes decorated the gnarled roots that snaked away from the well, leading to the enormous trunk of the ash tree, *Yggdrasil*. From the top of the tree, endless branches reached up to block the sky, casting half of the clearing into shadow.

In that shade, Verðandi's sleepers lay unaware as the humming child-goddess settled beside them, the book still clutched against her chest. Although there was no wind, her vibrant red hair twirled and twisted about her face like tendrils of flame. She gazed at the bodies with eyes older than her size implied, then sprang to her feet, clambering back onto the edge of the well.

"And now," she announced, "the wondrous Verðandi will perform her famous balancing act!"

She strutted along the well's uneven edge, teetering every so often on the crumbling stone, looking as though she might fall and plummet into the depths of the bottomless well. Making a great show of it, Verðandi squealed loudly, flailing her arms with every slip before regaining her balance and directing deep curtsies to the bodies in the grass.

A deep voice echoed from within the well. "They cannot see you, Verðandi."

Verðandi squeaked and nearly toppled over the side. "Urðr! I didn't see you coming."

Age-spotted fingers with thick nails cut down to squared tips curled around the stone. With deceptive ease that belied her age, an old goddess pulled herself from the depths and sat on the edge of the well. A loose, graying cloak hid her slight frame and hooded her wrinkled face. Strands of fading auburn hair hung like dying embers within the hood. She ignored Verðandi and the sleepers in the grass, instead locking her gaze on the water deep in the well.

"That is because you are too focused on your present," Urðr said. Her eyes narrowed on the book in the girl's hands. "That doesn't belong to you."

Verðandi stuck out her tongue but handed over the book. "They can't see me *now*, Urðr, but when we wake them they will remember that I was their friend in their darkest hour. It will be just like the old times!" She clapped her hands in delight at the thought. Was it not a wondrous thing to be involved in such a momentous occasion?

Urðr only listened to the *drip, drip, drip* of the well. Moments passed. The sleepers neither tossed nor turned. The only proof that they lived at all was the slight rise and fall of their chests.

"Do you hear that, Verðandi?" Urðr asked. "That is the sound of time passing away. Remember Ask and Embla. Soon, these mortals you are so fond of will be gone from us, forgetting us just as before."

Verðandi huffed, springing to a nearby tree root. She ran a small hand along its bark, her thin fingers finding the grooves of runes that yearned for her touch. "You say I live too much in the present. I say you focus too much on the past. Why can't we make our own future?"

She leapt from the root, landing next to the two bodies. With a quick glance back at Urðr, convinced the clearing was otherwise empty, she snatched the sleepers' hands in hers. They did not resist as Verðandi wove their fingers together. From within the folds of her cloak, Urðr pulled out yards of tangled, multicolored string that dripped from her fingers as she watched.

Satisfied with her work, Verðandi returned the sleepers' hands, now properly intertwined. "There, they look much happier now."

A scolding voice shook the clearing. "Do not touch the mortals, Verðandi."

The girl shrank from the voice and stepped away from the sleepers, folding her hands behind her back. Urðr shifted on top of the well but otherwise ignored the interruption, continuing to untangle her mass of strings.

From the depths of the well, the voice spoke again, this time no louder than a sigh. "We must send them back. Let us see if they can change Fate's design."

Inspection

Larissa

THE *MARA* ALWAYS STRUCK at night, feeding on nightmares and fears.

Larissa bit her pillow. The taste of cotton muffled her scream. One glance revealed her sister, Halla, sleeping peacefully in the bed next to her. Twice, shudders ran through Larissa's body, lingering in the muscles between her shoulders and neck, leaving her weak and shaky.

It was always the same. Those monsters called *mara* would come, and Larissa would free herself from the prison of sleep. But each time, the struggle took longer than before.

She forced her throbbing jaw to unclench and counted her breaths. Mamma had taught her how to ease the pounding of the blood in her ears, to slow the racing of the blood in her veins. But even those tricks couldn't stop the trembling in her hands.

Those would have to run their course.

Though the *mara* was always the same, the nightmares changed every night. Pappa encouraged her to try and remember. Dreams held meanings, especially nightmares. Even as Larissa chalked up the pain in her chest to Pappa's ever-growing superstitions, she couldn't ignore the pressure that squeezed the air from her lungs.

Fighting the weight of her arms, Larissa swept her hands through the air above her chest as if brushing away cobwebs to banish the creature of the night. The pressure remained, as she knew it would. Experience taught Larissa that the feeling would only dissipate with time. There would be no more sleep tonight.

Careful to not disturb Halla, Larissa sat up from beneath the covers and rested her back against the headboard. The well-worn bed creaked in protest against her movement. She shoved her head between her knees at the familiar onslaught of dizziness. The shock of chilled air seeping in through her damp shirt quickly chased away the remnants of sleep.

Morning air flowed in from the screen-covered window beside her bed; dark blue hues colored the black of the night. With dawn still on its way, Larissa needed light, something to chase away the remnants of her nightmares. Stretching up, she felt for the cold metallic chain hanging from the ceiling and yanked on it. The bulb flickered twice, swaying. Shadows danced along the wall before the light's brilliance chased them away.

A small, annoyed voice broke the silence. "Lara, why?"

The side of Larissa's mouth tilted up. On the bed beside her, the pile of blankets shifted. Bright green eyes appeared, peeking between the layers of cotton. Squinting against the light, they glared at Larissa.

"Sorry, *bebe*," Larissa said, rubbing her sister's back through the thick blankets.

"Don't call me that." Halla huffed, but Larissa knew she didn't mean it. Halla must have noticed the remnants of the nightmare in

Larissa's eyes because her next words had lost all trace of irritation. "Was it the *mara* again?"

Larissa's smile vanished. "Just a dream."

Blankets rustled as Halla settled next to Larissa. Their legs stretched out before them, although Halla's were much shorter than her sister's. Her small frame was swallowed by the blankets pulled up to her chin. Although she would be thirteen soon, others would guess Halla was nine or ten based on her size. Not that anyone ever saw Halla.

Technically, she didn't exist.

Halla leaned forward. "That's what the *mara* cause, Lara. They sit on your chest at night and feed off your bad dreams."

"That's just one of Pappa's stories, Halla." In the yellow electric light, it was easier to believe that the *mara* weren't real, that the pain in Larissa's chest was all in her mind. Besides, Halla already believed in Pappa's stories too easily, and Pappa's stories made Halla brave.

Too brave for a second-born.

Larissa rose from the bed, her bare feet protesting against the freezing floor. She searched for the boots under her bed, then yanked out the socks tucked in the toes. "We're both up; might as well get this day started."

Produce Day.

Every harvest, Dal's Berry Farm made regular deliveries of their produce within the walls of the city. These deliveries were the only thing that allowed Larissa's family the smallest bit of freedom in living outside the Wall. That freedom was necessary to keep Halla safe. She wouldn't make it a day within the Wall without being caught by the sentries or, worse, by the *thræll*, slavers whose business thrived off of second-borns.

Halla's head turned toward the window, her eyes watching the rising sun. "I want to go."

"You know you can't." Larissa paused, regretting the fear that bled through and sharpened her words. Softening her voice, she tried again. "I can try and bring you something back."

Halla piled the blankets high on her lap. "Like what? Another pebble?"

Larissa's eyes glanced at the rocks lined up across their dresser. Smooth and polished by waves, they nearly glowed in the early morning light. Years ago, Pappa would stop by the shore after his dropoff to the Wall and bring back a pebble from its rocky beaches. Larissa had continued the tradition only recently, but she'd spent hours searching for the perfect addition to Halla's collection.

"If you'd like."

Halla snorted. "Pass."

Larissa bit down her own retort. She was simply the target of Halla's frustration, not the cause. Every Produce Day, Halla grew more and more restless.

Larissa dressed in silence, pulling on worn jeans and shoving the thick work gloves into her back pocket. The morning air wafting through the screen sent goosebumps running along the exposed skin of her neck. It signaled the change of seasons and the coming of fall.

Ignoring the blanketed bundle of indignation on the bed behind her, Larissa tugged her brush through her own tangled hair. Strands of pale, white hair floated to the floor. With practiced fingers, Larissa braided her hair closely on each side of her head. All the while, Halla's resentment seeped into the air.

Larissa opened the door, wishing beyond anything that she could take Halla with her.

Then Halla's hand shot up, yanking the light's chain and plunging the room into gray darkness. Larissa stepped out and closed the door behind her. There was no use repeating to Halla what she already knew.

It wasn't safe for her to leave the house.

It wasn't safe for any second-born child to be seen in public, especially not within sight of the Wall.

In the main room, Mamma was already awake, washing vegetables in the cracking porcelain sink with her worn apron tied around her waist. A stool sat beside her, ready should Mamma need to grab anything from the shelves. Halla had clearly gotten her height from Mamma. Both girls had Mamma's pale coloring. Though Halla often wished for Pappa's olive skin that protected him from the sun in the summers, she was every bit a replica of Mamma.

"Morning, *bebe*," Mamma called over her shoulder, removing the kettle from where it whistled on the stove. Some residents within the Wall were blessed with electric kettles, while Larissa's family made do with scalding tongues. "Did you sleep well?"

Larissa shrugged. "Well enough."

Mamma dried her hands, surveying Larissa. "Is Halla still asleep?"

Grabbing an apple from the basket on the table, Larissa joined her at the counter. "No, she's awake and pouting. She wants to come with me today."

Mamma nodded, still drying her hands on the damp wash rag. Although she said nothing, her silence unlocked the words from Larissa like a well-cut key.

"She lives like a prisoner," Larissa continued, picking at the apple and leaving crescent-shaped wounds in its green skin. "It's hard on her. Produce Days make it worse. It doesn't help that Pappa fills her head with the *mara* and *Æsir*."

"Bad dream, again?"

"That's not the point." Larissa knew Mamma wouldn't understand. Like Pappa, Halla, and all of those in the commonwealth of Safír, Mamma loved the stories of old. The runes carved into their home and the amulet of Njörðr sitting between Mamma's collarbones only emphasized their faith. To believe in the gods was one thing, Larissa supposed, but it was another to trust in them so blindly.

Even before the wars, diseases, and natural disasters that crippled mankind long ago, the people had stopped believing in things like *mara*, Norn, and the *Æsir*. Those ideas belonged to an old mythology from a long-dead culture, and yet society's fascination with them grew every day. Even from her brief visits within the Wall, Larissa had seen charms of the gods—symbols of luck, wealth, and prosperity—hanging around the necks of farmers, citizens, slaves, and sentry alike. Some had gone so far as to tattoo runes on their skin.

Larissa imagined the city was a lot like home, where Pappa's stories were an additional member of their family. Halla's faith rivaled Pappa's, but then again, so had Larissa's. That was before she'd realized just how useless the gods truly were. Perhaps they were out there, but Larissa knew the truth. Every Inspection only solidified Larissa's opinion. The gods didn't listen to prayers. It wasn't the gods that kept Halla safely hidden. It wasn't the gods that held Halla when she woke up shaking from her nightmares. No, Larissa could not rely on the *Æsir*.

Mamma grabbed the apple from Larissa's hands, slicing it into eight pieces and wrapping those in a napkin. "Halla will be alright. I'll see if she can help me in the garden. Some dirt on her hands ought to cheer her up."

"Is Pappa already outside?" Larissa asked.

"He was up before the sun." Mamma's smile was strained, drawing tight lines around her hazel eyes. "He wants to make sure your delivery goes well."

Larissa bent down, lightly kissing Mamma on the forehead before accepting the apple slices offered to her. "It'll be fine."

The screen door slammed as Pappa's heavy footsteps thudded across the wood. Sweat pooled at his graying hairline as his broad figure filled up the doorway. His eyes were grim and his mouth pulled tight as he spat out one word. "Inspection."

The kitchen erupted into a frenzy as Pappa darted out the front door. They had been due for an Inspection, but Larissa never would have guessed the sentries would arrive on Produce Day.

"Kings and Queens," Larissa cursed, but Mamma's rebuke did not come. She was already rushing into her daughters' room. Larissa followed, darting after her as Mamma shook Halla from her doze.

"Inspection," Mamma said.

Halla froze at the word, then bound into motion, shoving on her shoes. With practiced movements, Mamma wrapped an arm around Halla and pulled her from the room. Mamma would take

Halla out the back door before joining Pappa on the dirt drive. Larissa remained, remaking the bed, organizing the dresser, and hiding any evidence of a second child. Within moments, the room was spotless. It would be enough to fool the sentries.

It always was.

Motors from the sentries' trucks grew louder. Larissa could only hope that Halla had made it to the barn under the cover of morning's dim light, tucked away beneath the trapdoor in the last stall. Mamma's footsteps pattered across the wooden floors, signaling her return.

"Larissa, hurry!" Mamma called.

Larissa gave the room one last glance then bolted through the house. As she passed the front screen door, her eyes caught on the rune for luck Pappa had etched into the frame. She rubbed it, willing it to work.

Even *she* believed in the *Æsir* on Inspection Days.

Taking her place beside Mamma and Pappa, Larissa forced herself to remain still as three sentries parked and exited their armored trucks. Guns and knives hung on their belts. With their black armor and helmets, Larissa struggled to distinguish one sentry from the other. She never knew if the same sentries performed each Inspection or if new ones came each time. Larissa never attempted to look too closely under their visors to check. Not that it mattered if they were the same or different sentries, as long as they didn't find Halla.

The tallest of the sentries approached Pappa, extending his hand. Pappa wordlessly supplied him with the requisite paperwork that detailed their latest product quotas. The sentries would check their production, inspect their lands, and search for any contraband within their home. As long as their family passed, they were allowed to continue their work of providing food for those within the Walls. If they failed for any reason, they would be sold into slavery.

Of course, if the sentries discovered Halla, execution was more probable.

One of the Empress' initial mandates after her rise to power was the population law. All families were permitted the conception of one child, but additional children had to be requested and recorded. Most of these requests went unanswered, and unapproved children were stripped from their families and sent north to become servants for the Empress. Some of the unregistered children were merely taken by the *thræll*, who seized and sold the children within and between the five commonwealths. The children were never heard from by their families again.

As the sentry continued reading, his two partners drifted away. One went into the house, while the other entered the barn. Larissa forced her eyes away. The trapdoor was well hidden. It had never failed them yet.

"State your name," said the remaining sentry.

"Dal Oginson," Pappa answered.

"How many farm hands do you have?"

"Myself, my wife, my daughter, and Tucker. He's out in the fields."

The sentry's eyes narrowed. "Only one field hand?"

Pappa met his gaze. "My family works hard."

Pappa didn't mention that he'd turned down other potential farm hands in the past. Besides Tucker, whom could they trust to keep Halla's secret? The sentries had never bothered to find out why Pappa turned down the extra help. As long as the produce quota was made, the sentries didn't care.

The sentry moved to stand before Mamma. "Name."

"Vern Askdóttir."

The sentry turned his visor toward Larissa. "Name."

She gulped, swallowing her nerves. "Larissa Daldóttir."

He perused the pages further. "You will be making the delivery today?"

"Yes, sir."

"A bit young to be doing deliveries."

"I'm seventeen, sir."

The sentry nodded, boredom creeping into his expression. He split the pile of papers and handed half of them to Pappa before shoving the other half at Larissa. "Your papers are in order. Take them and leave."

Larissa's eyes swung to Pappa. She'd never left mid-Inspection before.

Clenching his hat in tight fingers, Pappa nodded in her direction. "Truck's ready." His tight eyes spoke the words he couldn't. *Get in, get out, and get home.*

Mamma squeezed Larissa's hand, both as a comfort and a warning. It wouldn't do to ignore the sentry's order.

Their family truck idled where it sat between the house and the barn. No doubt Pappa had left it running out of fear it would break down again should he turn it off. It had been painted blue in some distant past. Now it sat rust-colored with spots of peeling, blue paint. Some dents had been banged out, while others remained. Pappa spent many an evening fixing it and cursing at it in equal measure. The truck was a beast and a menace, but Larissa found its enduring presence reassuring.

She and Halla had named it Helga.

Larissa forced herself toward Helga now, knowing that any deviation from the norm would only lead the sentries to investigate further.

Helga sat low, especially toward the bed where crates and boxes of produce had been packed by Pappa and Tucker earlier that morning. Surprised to find the tailgate still down, Larissa slammed it up before continuing on. Once inside Helga's cab, Larissa risked one glance back to where Pappa and Mamma stood at the sentry's mercy. From the corner of her eye, she caught a sentry leaving the barn. The pain in Larissa's chest rivaled the pressure her nightmare had brought. The thought of the sentry discovering the trapdoor with Halla beneath it was enough to tempt Larissa to pray to the unanswering *Æsir*.

She shoved the truck into gear, guiding Helga down their dirt drive while her eyes remained locked on her family growing smaller in the rearview mirror.

The Stowaway

Larissa

THE WAIL OF HELGA'S engine rose to an indignant moan. She had held the last several hours of the drive, but Larissa was starting to worry if they would reach the Wall.

"Come on, old girl," she muttered, rubbing her hand against the opened window-sill. "You can do it."

Minutes passed, and the moan died into a familiar grumble. Larissa sighed in relief, her hands patting the ripped and stained seats. Helga would make it. She always did. Or, at least, she had since Larissa had taken over the deliveries this season. At first, Pappa refused to let Larissa take the dropoffs, but there was always work to be done in the fields, and he hated the mandatory visits to the Wall that surrounded Havsiden, the city of the Safírian commonwealth.

Larissa had offered—begged, really—to let her take over the deliveries. Call it a seventeenth birthday gift, she'd told him. Larissa would never tell Halla that she also wanted to explore beyond the boundaries of their fields. Eventually, Pappa gave in, as Larissa knew he would.

He couldn't stand the sight of the Wall. "An unnatural blight placed there by the Empress' hands," Pappa would say.

"Don't," Mamma would respond, leaving the rest unsaid. *We don't speak of the Empress, not even within our own homes.*

The thought of the Empress turned Larissa's stomach. Although the Empress was a vague figure in the back of her mind, the Empire and its effect on her family were an everyday reality. The Empress reigned over the five commonwealths of Evrópa from her northern palace within Diamant. From Pappa's stories, Larissa knew only that Diamant was a frozen wasteland, as cold as its mistress.

The other four commonwealths consisted of Smaragd, nestled in the western forests of Myrkviðr; Rubin, settled amidst the volcanoes of the eastern seas; Perle, situated just south of Smaragd; and Safír, stretched along the cliffs of the southeast shores of Rán's seas. It was Safír that Larissa called home, although living out on her farm, she saw little to nothing of the famous shoreline.

Fifty years ago, the Empress had overthrown the other kingdoms, killing or imprisoning their monarchs and replacing them with her own chosen regents. Although the Empress held more power, it was the regents, with their firing squads and gallows, that scared Larissa most. It was the regents who would take Halla and kill her family for violating the Empress' policies.

Halla is safe.

Larissa repeated this phrase again and again as if it would form a prayer that the gods might actually hear. She blew air from her mouth, forcing her thoughts away from the farm. The sooner she reached the Wall, the sooner she could return home to see what had become of the Inspection.

Distracted by her thoughts, Larissa swerved just in time to avoid a tree branch lying in the road. In the bed of the truck, crates shifted. Larissa checked her rear view mirror, scanning for any lost produce. Those crates would be counted once she reached the Wall. The quota had to be met.

Produce Day will go perfectly. It has to.

Salty air drifted in through the open windows; she was close. Larissa shifted in her seat to waken long-sleeping limbs. The road—once asphalt, now a poor mix of dirt and rock—would pain her body for days after a delivery, but even the brief respite from her daily farm life was worth it.

The world hadn't always been like this, Pappa told her. Before *Ragnarok*, the world had been beautiful, civilized, and safe. Larissa snorted as the truck bounced out of a particularly deep pothole. The world before was just another one of Pappa's stories.

Again, she heard the crates shift in the bed and frowned. It wasn't like Pappa to loosely pack the crates. Larissa pulled at one of her braids while keeping her other hand on the wheel. She needed to focus on doing what Pappa always said.

Get in, get out, and get home.

The sun reached its peak just as the Wall came into sight. The sheer size of the Wall caused Larissa's heart to thump against her ribcage. Pappa was right; it was unnatural, the way the Wall blotted out the sky and land. Although she knew the innermost part of the city sat on a cliff overlooking the sea, Larissa couldn't see it due to the trees and the great Wall.

The city of Havsiden, the only city of Safír, was built in concentric half circles. The outer section encapsulated the majority of the land's population with separately tiered communities. Within each segment lay residences, shops, and markets. In the higher levels, there were even schools, or so Larissa had been told. She'd never been beyond the produce Intake Yard.

Looking at the Wall, Larissa couldn't comprehend the power it must have taken the Empress to overtake not only this land, but three others as well. Each of the commonwealths' central cities were similarly enclosed by their own Wall, placed there by the Empress' decrees. In hissed whispers, Larissa had heard rumors of the Empress' *galdr*. It was said to be some magical force bestowed upon her by the Norn, those three fickle goddesses of fate, that gave her the right to rule and have a long-lasting life.

Larissa scoffed at the thought. If that were true, it was only another reason to distrust the gods.

A mile from the Wall, the tree line broke and opened into a vast field that had been cleared in every direction, ensuring the sentries could see anyone approaching or leaving. Larissa took her spot in the line of trucks waiting to enter the city and reached for the papers on the dash. They listed how much produce was to be expected, where it was coming from, and most importantly, her credentials as Larissa Daldóttir, the first-born and only daughter of Dal, stamped with the royal seal.

It was for this reason that Halla could never leave her farm and never enter the city. Children born within the Wall were not easily concealed. Pappa and Mamma would talk in hushed tones about how such children were ripped from their homes and sold on the auction block. That is, until they realized Larissa was listening. Larissa vowed she would never let that happen to Halla.

The truck ahead of her crawled forward. Larissa released the brake ever so slightly, but a thump from the bed of the truck caused her to slam the pedal down again. Spinning to look out the back window, Larissa expected to see produce tumbling about in the truck bed. What she found was far worse.

Staring back at her were two wide green eyes set above a familiar freckled nose.

A curse slipped through Larissa's lips. "Kings and Queens!"

Halla's green eyes disappeared. Larissa's foot slipped; boxes shifted. Halla yelped as a box collided against her. What in Mimir's name was Halla doing in the truck?

"Move it along, *slápr*!"

Larissa's eyes swung back to the growing gap in front of Helga. A sentry stood there, beckoning her forward with his other hand resting near his holster. With numb fingers, Larissa clenched the steering wheel and closed the gap between her and the truck. The Wall loomed closer, five stories tall, with sentries surveying the incoming trucks from their positions on top.

Sweat gathered at the base of Larissa's hairline and beaded down her neck. Her thoughts raced as she considered her options. Halla couldn't run. The tree line had been cut back miles ago, leaving nothing but open fields. Halla would be spotted if she fled the truck.

Larissa's fingers twitched in her gloves against the steering wheel. She couldn't flee any more than Halla could. Any deviation from the line would draw unwanted attention from the sentries. They would want to know why she was veering from her normal course. They would stop her and search her.

They would take Halla.

She glanced in the rear view mirror again and sent a silent prayer that Halla would have the sense to remain hidden. This day was determined to make a believer of Larissa after all.

The line surged forward, leaving only two trucks ahead of her. The gates of the Wall hung open, allowing a big enough gap for trucks to move both in and out at the same time. Sentries on each side of the gate checked those who were coming in and made sure that only those approved were going out.

There was no other choice. Larissa would have to enter the city and figure out what to do once inside. But first, she had to calm down. If the sentries noticed her unease, they would not hesitate to investigate it further.

Halla's safety depended on her.

Only one truck remained ahead of her. Larissa grabbed the paperwork, shifting it to line up the edges, and dropping them when they sliced through her skin.

"Njörðr's beard," she muttered Pappa's favorite phrase, the one he never used in front of Mamma.

The truck in front of her pulled through the open gates. This was her last chance to try and flee. She sucked at the cut finger, weighing each option and its consequences.

The sentry beckoned her forward. Did she dare flee?

They would never make it.

Larissa breathed out, releasing her finger and the brake simultaneously.

She waited for the sentry to approach the opened window. Dressed in all black, the sentry pushed back his visor, revealing dark eyes that peered into Helga's cab.

"Identification."

She handed it to him without a word, praying that the sweat running down her back wouldn't show through the shirt, or that the sentry would attribute it to the rising warmth of a late-summer day.

"Where are you coming from?" the sentry asked, his voice cold and demanding.

Larissa swallowed, determined to keep her voice from shaking. "Dal's Berry Farm."

"Name."

"Larissa Daldóttir."

"Is this your first trip inside the Wall?"

Larissa tried to swallow, but her throat was too dry. She coughed at the attempt. "No, sir, my sixth."

"Then you know the procedure." He shoved the papers back through the window. "Follow the previous truck into the unloading area. Once you are finished, you may collect your family's rations at the next station."

"Thank you." Larissa released the brake.

"Wait."

Her foot collided with the brake. Another thump sounded from the bed. Larissa could only hope the sentry would think it was the fruit shifting. "Yes, sir?"

He wasn't looking at Larissa. He was standing next to the bed of the truck, peering in between the slatted wooden walls. Had he seen something? A flash of green eyes? Halla's golden hair?

The sentry's arm shot through one of the slats. Larissa tensed, wishing for a knife, something from home to protect Halla, but weapons were strictly forbidden. Anyone carrying one was immediately sentenced to death, but that didn't stop Larissa from daydreaming about running him over with Helga.

The sentry withdrew a handful of strawberries. He bit into the largest one, tossing the stem into the dirt. "You may go."

Not trusting herself to speak, Larissa pulled through the gates. On the other side of the Wall, the Intake Yard was filled with trucks and the overwhelming sound of voices shouting, talking, and overlapping with one another. More sentries walked between trucks, facilitating the unloading of produce and the reloading of family rations. More often than not, the cracks of their whips snapped in the air, hurrying the slaves that rushed from truck to truck, their backs bent under submission and shame. Metal bracelets wrapped around their wrists identified the slaves for what they were: someone else's property. A young boy with shorn hair ran past Helga's cab, his metal bracelets glinting in the sunlight.

A glance in the mirror reassured Larissa that Halla had hidden herself well.

They had made it in.

But Larissa wasn't sure how they would make it out.

A Rescue

Darien

THE INTAKE YARD WAS a riot of noise. Darien coughed to clear the thick dust settling in his throat as the truck in front of him pulled out of the yard.

"Load up your rations," the sentry's voice bellowed in his ear. "Make way for the next truck."

Darien heaved the last box up into the truck bed with too little effort. Five boxes wouldn't be enough for Farmer Aagen and Darien's fellow field hands, but the Regent of Safír believed that the farmers' own produce could make up for their lack of basic toiletries and supplies. Not that farmers could keep much of their own crop anyway. Even if they could, how could apples substitute for flour or soap?

Messy, black strands stuck up at odd angles as Darien ran his hand through his hair. His tanned olive-colored arms and neck were sticky, his leather jacket safely stowed in the cab of his truck. Sentries dressed in black padded armor contrasted sharply against the flannel-clad field hands and farmers that surrounded them. Darien dismissed the notion of asking for more supplies. The sentries were not known for their empathy. Aagen and the others would just have to make do until next Produce Day.

"Hurry up, girl!" Another sentry's voice cracked across the Intake Yard, silencing every other voice around it.

The farmers quickened their pace, hurrying to unload or load so they could get out of the way. Farmers and laborers alike kept their heads down and eyes on their work, studiously avoiding the brewing confrontation in the unloading bay.

Knowing he shouldn't, Darien sought out the voice and found a sentry yelling at the light-haired girl in the bed of a rusted blue pickup. Upon seeing the girl, an odd sense of familiarity washed over Darien, though he was certain he'd never seen her before. He would have remembered a face like that.

She looked about his age and stood in the midst of pallets and crates, trying to unload her produce. The sentry shouted something Darien couldn't hear over the increased noise of the crowd. He could see the way the girl's shoulders tensed up closer to her ears as she turned to grab another crate.

The smart choice was to turn away. Before he could, Darien saw the sentry step toward her, one hand pointing directly at her back and the other resting just above his gun.

His blood crashed in his ears. Smart choices were overrated anyway.

Darien slammed the tailgate, leapt down, and headed for the girl.

"Leave it, boy," an older farmer near him muttered.

Darien kept walking even as he called himself every kind of name for his own stupidity. Perhaps it was the gods' interference or his own imagination, but Darien was drawn to her. Even knowing that Aagen, Darien's adoptive father, would scold him later for his recklessness did not alter Darien's path. For if Aagen was honest, he would've done the same.

Darien had crossed most of the space between them when the sentry spotted his approach. The sentry spun, facing Darien, his fingers curling around the grip of his gun. "Stop right there."

Darien froze, a lump hardening in his throat. From his peripheral, he watched the girl in the truck bed pause, half-bent in the process of picking up another box. Her eyes flashed toward the sentry's gun hand, and Darien's eyes returned there as well. He had not yet done anything to deserve execution, but he knew he was at the mercy of the sentry. They all were.

Darien swallowed, ignoring the tension in his body. His mind recited the prayers Aagen had taught him. Freyr, god of Harvest and protector of farmers, would not let him die here. Such a death would not be heroic enough to be sung alongside the great *Volsungs*, and Darien had already determined he was destined for greatness.

With meticulous caution, he raised empty hands. "I was just going to offer to help unload the truck."

"Get back to your place," the sentry said. When Darien did not obey, the man's hand tightened on his gun.

"You want this truck unloaded and out of your way. I can help with that." Darien's voice was low and calm, as though Freyr was filling him with the words to say. "You don't want the trucks getting backed up, right? I'm just offering to move things along."

The sentry paused then loosened his grip. "Fine. Hurry it up."

Darien lowered his hands, proud to find them steady. He stepped up into the truck bed, nearly colliding with the girl, and found himself staring into the most extraordinarily golden eyes he'd ever seen. They were like pure honey dripping from the bee-hive he'd found in one of his apple trees. However, the bees had been far friendlier than these glaring eyes.

"What are you doing?" the girl hissed.

The sharpness of her voice snapped Darien from his thoughts. "Excuse me?"

"I don't need your help, and I really don't need you in my truck."

Darien's mouth fell open. He expected quiet gratitude, maybe, or even an uneasy acceptance, but this outright hostility was astonishing. His bravado slipped from his grasp.

"I, um..." *Kings and Queens, I'm blowing this.* She may be a damsel, but perhaps not quite as in distress as he imagined.

"What are you doing up there?" The sentry snapped his fingers. "Either help or get out."

Spurred into motion at the sentry's voice, the girl heaved a box of strawberries into Darien's arms. Darien passed them along to the unloading laborer who waited at the end of the truck. As she lifted crate after crate, the girl's loose shirt pulled against her back and shoulders, revealing the toned muscles of her body. Clearly she worked as hard on her land as Darien did on his orchard.

As time passed, Darien's appreciation of her strength blurred into confusion over her movements. Every time he reached for a crate, she was there. Her hands beat him to the next, and then the next, only allowing him to handle the boxes she picked up herself.

She's intentionally getting in the way, he thought.

The idea that she was obstructing his advance as they went further back into the truck bed only piqued Darien's interest. Every block, every hedge was intentional. For whatever reason, she did not want him in her truck. Even more curious, she continued stacking the pallets only on one side, even as the pile grew danger-ously tall. Had this girl ever run a delivery before?

"My name is Darien, by the way," he said, hoping to thaw her hostility.

Her gaze flashed to meet his, and he was struck by the light splattering of freckles across her nose. He smiled, but her only response was to reach for the next box. Darien let the smile fall from his face, transferring that box to the laborer who went to stack it with the rest.

So much for coming to the rescue.

With the unloading process moving smoothly, the sentry moved on to harass another field hand further down the line. Seeing that they were nearly finished, Darien figured if his devilish charms weren't working, he might as well try for some honesty. "Look, I'm sorry if I overstepped. You looked like you needed some help."

She said nothing, her hands occupied with the last box wedged behind the towering stack of pallets. If she'd distributed the pallets more evenly, she wouldn't have been in this predicament. Darien's frustration grew. If she would just let him help, they would be done by now, and he could get out of the hot sun. Besides, if they didn't get these trucks moving soon, the sentry was bound to return in an even worse mood than before.

Before she could scold him again with those startling eyes, Darien snuck past her guard and yanked out the remaining crate. He froze at the sight of the child before him.

Curled up in the corner of the truck, hiding behind the last of the boxes, the small girl stared at him in horror. Her eyes fled to the girl standing behind Darien, who was wearing the same fearful expression.

The towering pallets, the intentional blocking, the girl's cautious movements, even her frustration at Darien's help—it all made sense. There was only one reason to hide a child like this.

She was an unregistered second-born.

The white-haired girl slipped past Darien, wedging herself in front of the child. Darien couldn't help but notice the way her body moved with flexible grace. He sucked in a slow breath, then glanced toward the back of the truck. The unloading laborer would be back at any minute, and the sentries were never far away.

Legally, Darien was duty-bound to reveal the girl, to turn her over to the sentries. That was the logical choice. But the fear on the child's face was enough to prompt Darien to do something *illogical*.

He did not speak—he couldn't trust himself to. Instead, he handed the girl the crate, then swiftly moved the pallets to create towers of equal height that blocked the back of the truck.

"Lay down," he whispered.

The child stretched herself out in the crevice between the truck and the pallets. Darien grabbed another pallet and lay it on top of the others, pushing it up against the truck cab covering the pale-faced child. Just as the pallet slid into place, the laborer returned with ill-concealed impatience, motioning for the girl to pass over the remaining boxes. She paused, then hefted them to the back of the truck where the laborer waited. Darien continued his stacking. Hopefully, he would appear to be evening out the weight, making sure the pallets wouldn't break during the drive home. As long as the child kept low, she would be hidden, if she could handle the claustrophobic space and the pressure of the wood all around her.

Darien had heard of stowaways trying to slip out of the city. Was this girl a courier? No, she'd clearly never done this before. Were the girls sisters? There was a story here, and he was determined to learn it if only to confirm the child's safety.

With the last of the crates cleared out and the pallets secured, Darien and the girl hopped down into the dirt. The girl closed the back of the truck so hard that the wood wobbled. Her hands shook as she clasped the lock.

"Thank you," she murmured, not meeting Darien's eyes. The sound of her voice played an odd harmony in his mind.

"Alright, move it!"

The sentry was back. Pointing at Darien, he said, "You, your truck is already loaded with rations. Get it out of the way. And you"—he pointed to the girl—"hurry up and load. You've wasted enough of our time today."

The two farm hands shared a stolen glance. The girl's eyes lost their aggression, growing in curiosity. Then, with one glance at the sentry and another toward the truck bed, she opened the cab door and hopped in, pulling the truck forward to the next station.

The sentry shoved Darien hard in the back, knocking him forward into the dirt. "Did you not hear me, *slápr*? I said move it!"

Darien ground his teeth; only a sentry would use such an insult. "Alright, I'm going."

The sentry's rough hand yanked him up by the collar. "What did you say, *slápr*?"

Darien bit his tongue. Aagen was always reminding him to watch his mouth. "Nothing."

The sentry released him, dropping him to the ground once again. "It is only by the Empress' generosity that you are allowed to serve outside the Wall. Don't test me."

Darien did not look back when he picked himself off the ground, brushing the dirt from his hands. He walked obediently toward his truck, knowing that the sentry was watching, waiting for a reason to heap on more abuse. These sentries were all the same, looking to earn glory before the gods in a war that had ended with the Empress' victory years ago.

Nearby, the girl had parked her truck and was in the middle of quickly loading up her rations. The concern in her eyes made it clear she had seen the sentry's abuse.

Darien's face flamed. *So much for the heroic rescue.*

He kept his head down until he was back in the driver seat. Turning the key, Darien navigated his truck toward the outer gate. In his rear view mirror, he could see the girl swing shut her tailgate.

No one had noticed the child during the loading; the pallets were doing their job. As long as the child remained quiet and still, they might actually make it out of there. Darien resisted the wild urge to laugh. The sentries didn't have the slightest idea.

At the gate, a sentry searched Darien's truck for runaways while another demanded his identification papers. Darien knew the words on the paper, labeling him Darien Aagenson. He also knew that the words were a lie. He forced his hands to tap slowly against the steering wheel as he waited for his papers. The sentries didn't need to know that Darien was Aagen's son only by name and not by blood.

His leg bounced with tension at the sight of the rusted blue truck pulling in two trucks behind him. Darien's prayers echoed in his mind, asking that the girl and the child would make it through the gate.

"You may leave," the sentry barked. "The Empress thanks you for your service."

Darien accepted the papers offered by the sentry and pulled forward before he could tell the sentry where the Empress could stick her appreciation. Just outside the gate, the carved icon of Njörðr, Safír's patron god of the sea, watched Darien as he drove away. It was said that Njörðr had died in the great battle of *Ragnarok*, but that his soul still watched over those of Safirian blood, imbuing the royal bloodline with his own powers.

Of course, the Empress had killed the entire royal line decades ago, leaving none of Njörðr's line to remain.

Darien tore his eyes from the icon. A fluttering of black wings drew his attention to where a raven soared overhead, dipping into the Intake Yard. In his rearview, the rusted blue truck approached the sentry's checkpoint, growing smaller until Darien could no longer see it at all. There was only one road that led from the city toward the farms and fields of the Safír land. All other roads had either been reclaimed by nature or destroyed during the Empress' upheaval and subsequent reign. If the girl made it past the sentries, she would have to follow the same road.

Reaching the tree cover, Darien drove a bit further before peeling off onto a stretch of dirt that ran parallel to the deteriorating asphalt. He parked in such a manner as to block enough of the road. Any oncoming traffic would be forced to either stop or swerve. He would wait to see if they made it out.

One way or another, Darien would get his answers.

4

Deceived

Darien

MINUTES DRAGGED ON. TWO trucks passed, their owners waving angry hands as they swerved around Darien's truck.

Finally, the rusted blue pickup came clanking down the road, slowing before the obstruction of Darien's truck. The pickup's engine protested loudly at the sudden stop, whining as Darien threw open his own door. He raised his hands in a show of surrender. He had not forgotten the fierce look on the girl's face when she'd stepped in between him and the child. She would run him over if she thought that he was a threat. He admired her for it.

She sat in the driver seat, both hands gripped around the wheel, eyeing his approach.

Darien smiled. "I thought you might need some help moving those pallets before she's squashed."

An exaggeration, but it did the trick. With a loud squeal, the emergency brakes popped into place as the girl threw open the door. Dust swirled under her boots when they hit the ground. Outside the Intake Yard she stood taller, no longer hiding herself from the sentry's gaze. She strode to the back of the truck, her hair catching the light flickering in through the branches.

"Are you going to help or what?" she asked. From the raise of her eyebrow, she'd clearly caught him staring.

Darien grinned at the ground as he joined her at the tailgate.

Short strands of sun-bleached hair fell from the girl's braids, hanging around her face. A bright red smear on her cheek traveled to the bottom of her ear, most likely from one of the strawberries. He considered mentioning it, but chose otherwise.

"You said your name was Darien?"

"Darien Aagenson." The lie stumbled through his lips before he could stop it. It tasted sour in his mouth; after all, she'd been forced to share her own secret with him. It seemed wrong to not reveal his own. That he was only Aagenson in name, but not in blood.

Pounding erupted from the bed of the truck, accompanied by an angry, muffled voice. The girl rolled her eyes in amusement and clicked her tongue. "Well, Darien Aagenson, I would appreciate your help freeing my *hálfviti* sister from the pallets."

Sisters? The child was definitely a second-born.

Darien glanced down the road, knowing another truck would be along shortly, but he had to make sure that the child was okay.

They made short work of removing the pallets, revealing the tiny child who stood from her cramped position. The smear on the older sister's cheek was nothing compared to the child. From head to toe, she was splattered with various stains of reds, purples, and blues. The frizzled yellow hair at the nape of her neck looked more like a bird's nest than anything else. Sweat clung to her clothes. Her cheeks were flushed so red they could have been painted with strawberries.

Darien grinned at the sight. So often there was nothing he could do about the sentries' brutality, but this time was different. The child was unharmed and free, thanks to him.

The girl pulled her younger sister into a hug, ignoring the sticky mess. "Halla," she said, her voice laced with worry, "what in Mimir's name were you doing back there?"

"Lara, too—tight—" Halla gasped, her voice muffled as her mouth was still squished tight in her sister's arms. She wriggled her face free. "I couldn't make it to the barn, the sentries—" Noticing Darien's presence, Halla's mouth clamped shut.

Darien waved. "Hey, kiddo."

Halla's eyes rounded, but her hand seemed to wave back of its own accord.

Lara's eyes moved to Darien, as if she too were worried Halla had said too much. Darien considered telling her his secret, if only to ease her fear. There were so many questions he wanted to ask, but time was passing too quickly. They would not be alone much longer.

Darien cleared his throat. "Not that this isn't heartwarming, but another truck will be coming down this road any minute now."

Lara nodded. "Halla, get in the passenger seat and stay below the dash line."

Halla nodded, climbing over the pallets, which Lara then shifted back into place. Darien hopped down and turned to offer a hand to Halla.

"Need some help? It's a far jump for a little thing like you."

The pink in Halla's nose traveled up to her forehead. "I'm not a child. I can do it myself."

Behind her, Lara rolled her eyes as if to say, *Welcome to my world*. Amused, Darien stepped aside.

Halla lowered herself from the bed, but her foot caught the edge. She plummeted toward the ground face-first, only to be caught in Darien's waiting arms. He righted her and stepped back, tightening his lips to keep from laughing. With a dignity befitting one of the Queens of Old, Halla straightened her shoulders and walked past him without another word, taking her place in the passenger seat of the truck. Lara hopped down next and shut the tailgate. Though her eyes were still guarded, at least her arms were not crossed.

Darien pushed his luck. "So. Lara, huh?"

"Larissa, actually, but Halla likes Lara."

"Well, it looks like you have your hands full." He searched for his next words, knowing that each syllable cost them precious time, yet he couldn't just say goodbye. He rarely interacted with anyone outside his farm, especially no one as attractive or mysterious as Larissa. Besides, Darien still hadn't learned their story. "Perhaps we'll see each other again?"

"And perhaps the Kings and Queens of Old will return. I really should go, but thank you." She tugged at her gloves. "For everything. Halla may be a handful, but she's my world. I owe you, Darien Aagenson."

Darien slid his hands into his pockets. "I hope to collect one day, *Lara*."

Her eyes met his, and Darien wanted to reach out, to prolong this moment somehow. An annoying sensation itched at the back of his mind. Some familiarity called to him, but when Darien reached for it, it slipped through his fingers. In his distraction,

Larissa's gaze shifted and their moment passed. Without looking back, she joined Halla in the cab. He watched the truck pull away. Then they were gone.

Two caws in quick succession broke his reverie. Darien glanced at the raven sitting in the branches above him, cocking its head in his direction. One of its large black eyes bored down on him.

What was that saying about counting the caws of a raven? Had it been a story Aagen told him? Darien shook the thought from his mind. Aagen was always telling one story or another. He tore his eyes away from the bird, walking back to his own truck.

And perhaps the Kings and Queens of Old will return, Larissa had said.

It was a saying that only those outside the Wall would use freely. Such an event—the return to a society before the Empress' reign—was unlikely enough to seem impossible. Maybe Larissa was right. After all, they'd never crossed each other's paths before this, and he'd been doing the supply runs for the past three seasons. Still, he was determined to ask Aagen what he knew about any berry farms close by. Darien mentally kicked himself, wishing he had asked Larissa her last name.

Back in his truck, Darien realized that Larissa's omission of a last name was probably intentional. After all, whoever this family was, they had a secret: a second-born. It was one thing for Darien to claim to be a first-born when no sibling could dispute that claim, and when he had the paperwork to back it up. It was an entirely different thing for two siblings to coexist in the same space. How they'd managed to keep it a secret for this long was astounding.

Darien turned down the road. Would he be wrong to go poking around in search of Larissa? Her tenacity fascinated him, and, if he was being honest, so did her appearance. Light-colored hair was common enough in the south, but pure white was rare, as was her paler skin. It reminded him of the goddess Skaði from Aagen's stories. That eccentricity combined with those honey eyes—Darien could admit it—he wanted to see her again. But was it worth the risk?

Some secrets were best left alone.

He'd long stopped searching for the answers to his own. All Darien could remember of his past was his life on the farm. His first memories began with Aagen, a childless widower who'd found Darien wandering on stubby toddler legs beneath his apple trees. Where Darien had come from was not a topic that Aagen would discuss.

Before Darien could comprehend what was happening, some *thing* dashed out from the trees and into the road. His foot slammed hard on the brake, but the truck, propelled by its own weight, could not stop. He swerved; the figure leapt from the road. The truck continued skidding across the asphalt. Darien felt the truck swing off the side of the road, barreling through the surrounding bushes, shaking Darien like a ragdoll until it slid to a stop in the mud.

When his breathing finally slowed, Darien moved with deliberate caution. He turned his head from side to side, pausing in between. When there was no pain, he stretched out other portions of his body. Aside from some soreness, he was whole. With a grunt he shoved open the door, sucking in a quick breath as his feet hit the ground, then letting out a long whistle.

The truck bore no holes or significant dents, but there was no disguising the surface damage caused by the branches he had barreled through. The dull black paint had never been in pristine condition, but this was just pathetic. Thanking the *Æsir* that the truck had somehow managed to miss every tree in its path, Darien checked the rations sitting in the bed. Relief flooded him to find them undamaged.

A branch snapped.

Darien spun, staring into the trees. The thing that had dashed out in front of the road had been a blur, but he'd assumed it was an animal. It had been small, easily concealable in the surrounding vegetation. Darien picked up a broken branch from the ground.

Another snap, this time behind him. He turned, raising his branch.

A thin young child with tanned skin and hair as black as a moonless night emerged from the thicket. Smaller than even Halla, she couldn't have been older than seven or eight. At her throat, a large ruby pendant pulsed like a second heart.

"Who are you?" Darien asked. Hearing the sharp edge of his own voice, he lowered the branch in his hand. "Are you lost?"

The child shook her head, biting her lip and looking around as if nervous she would be seen. Perhaps she was a runaway, another second-born escaping the Wall. It would be just Darien's luck to come across two in one day. Regarding Darien with wide eyes, she motioned him forward with a delicate hand.

He approached, but cautiously. Darien's innate desire to help was battled by Aagen's stories of the *skogsrå* who lived in the forests and lured men to their deaths. But those were just stories. This child did not have the tail of a cow. He was being ridiculous.

Darien let go of the branch. It was a day for rescuing strays. "What's your name?"

"Anara." There was no fear in her voice.

He crouched down. "Anara, huh? I'm Darien."

The copper in her eyes brightened at the name, but something about her eyes unnerved him. There was no childhood innocence within them, but a depth that only trauma and time could account for. Anara reached out to brush back a curl of Darien's dark hair. At her touch, an electric shock coursed through his body

What?

It was the only thought he could form before all he could feel, all he could think, was a burning sensation running through his body.

The current raced through his veins, not painful, but physically debilitating. Darien tried to move, but his body would not respond. He was frozen in place, crouched low with burning thighs. His eyes darted around his surroundings, expecting an ambush.

When the sensation passed and no sentries appeared, he glared at Anara. She stared back, her eyes brimming with curiosity and...something else. Satisfaction?

Through clenched teeth, he asked, "What did you *do* to me?"

Anara moved closer and cupped her hands around Darien's face, bringing their foreheads together with a light touch that sent another wave of fire through his body. This time, it did hurt. His skin felt hot and cold all at once. Black spots blocked out his vision. Images overlapped in his sight, but he could not make sense of them. The shock coursed through him again.

Giving into the pain, he groaned, closing his eyes.

When Anara spoke, her voice was stronger and more mature, far from that of a child. "I am giving you your life back."

Darien forced his eyes open to see the girl transforming, her limbs elongating until she towered over him in his crouched position. She was now older than Darien, although not by much. That bright ruby pendant hanging just below her sharp collarbones seemed to laugh at Darien's confusion. The gold plating around the gem matched the ring in the woman's nose. She cocked one hip to the side and placed her long-fingered hand upon it.

A terrifying thought pierced the rush of adrenaline clouding Darien's mind. *Shapeshifter.*

Anara smiled, revealing rows of sharpened teeth. "Say thank you."

Stories of Old

Larissa

CHILLY EVENING AIR CREEPED into the cab as the sun set on a long, stressful day. Larissa closed the windows, but wind whistled through cracks at the top. Helga bounced and rattled down the road, shaking Halla against the floorboard where she sat cramped against the seat. Even her small frame was too large to fit comfortably in such a tight space. She shivered, huddling under the jacket Larissa had tossed her way.

Satisfied they were safe, Larissa reached out to touch where Halla's head lay against the ripped seat cushion. "You can get up now."

Halla turned toward Larissa with half-closed eyes. Had she actually slept during the past few hours? Terrified of passing another truck, or worse, Larissa had told Halla to stay hidden. But this road was familiar, as was the forest. They were nearly home.

Halla clambered onto the seat.

With her sister out of danger, Larissa's anxiety finally gave way to the question that had been straining to escape her lips. "How did you get in the truck?"

Halla squeezed her knees against her chest. "Mamma went to join Pappa. She told me to run to the barn, but they were too close. I was afraid they would see me. The truck was right there, and the tailgate was down. I just squeezed in."

Larissa pinched the bridge of her nose; the fear she'd felt upon realizing that Halla was in the truck ran through her again. "Do you know how dangerous that was?"

"It's not like I had a choice," Halla argued.

"Oh yeah? Did you think about letting me know you were in the truck *before* we got to the Wall?"

Halla chewed at her cheek in anxious contemplation, a sign Larissa knew all too well. "I didn't plan to come, Lara, I swear on the Kings and Queens, I didn't. But I thought if I was already in the truck, and if I was quiet, then maybe I wouldn't be seen. And I could see the city."

Larissa groaned. She'd suspected as much.

"Besides, I had Frigg with me." Halla raised her hand, rattling her bracelet in Larissa's face. The amulets for Frigg, goddess of children, and Eir, goddess of protection, clinked together.

Larissa eyed the amulets with distaste but held her tongue. She didn't want to argue about the ludicrous nature of believing in the *Æsir*. If the stories were true, they were dead—long dead. They couldn't save themselves. So, how could they protect Halla?

"Are you mad at me?" Halla asked.

"No. Well, maybe. Mostly annoyed." To be honest, Larissa understood why Halla hadn't revealed herself. In Halla's mind, the gods had placed her in the truck for a reason. In her place, Larissa might've done the same thing. "You've got to be more careful, Halla; you know the law."

"I *was* careful, Lara!" Halla crossed her arms. "You wouldn't worry so much if you believed."

Larissa scoffed. "The *Æsir* have never given me any reason to."

"They've answered my prayers before, you know."

Her voice was so matter-of-fact that Larissa nearly laughed. "Oh really, what did you pray for?"

"An older sister."

"That's not how it works. I came first."

"Well, *duh*." Halla rolled her eyes as if Larissa was the one missing something. Then her face turned wistful. "I wish I could've seen more of the city."

Larissa wrinkled her nose. "The Intake Yard is as far as I ever go, so you've gone just as far as me."

A sly grin crept onto Halla's face. "At least I got to see you with Darien."

"What's that supposed to mean?"

"I have eyes, Lara." Halla poked Larissa's arm. "You *like* him."

Larissa grasped the wheel and took the next turn too fast. Halla's body thumped against the door.

"You did that on purpose!" Halla said, glaring and rubbing her arm.

Larissa evened out the wheels. Ahead, the farmhouse came into view. No Mamma or Pappa outside, but lights burned through the windows. Larissa turned onto the gravel path leading to the house and parked in the usual spot before turning to Halla.

"I," she said, adopting an innocent air, "don't know what you're talking about."

"I know what I saw," Halla insisted.

Larissa snorted. "Yeah, the backside of some crates where I should have left you."

Pappa and Mamma emerged from the house, their feet slamming against the porch steps. Before Halla could move, they'd thrown open her door and drawn her into their arms. Torrents of words and questions crashed over one another. Squished in between her parents, Halla sent a pleading glance in Larissa's direction. "Lara—help—"

Larissa smiled, hopping down from her seat onto the dirt. "Maybe the gods will save you."

Noticing Halla's distress, Pappa withdrew his thick arms. The color returned to his face as he spoke—not to Halla, but to Larissa. "How could you let her go with you?"

"She didn't know, Pappa," Halla piped up, still coddled in Mamma's arms. "I couldn't make it to the barn. Lara didn't know I was there until we reached the Wall."

Their parents stilled; Mamma's arms tightened around Halla. "You went in the city?"

Larissa shrugged, feeling a sudden exhaustion settle on her shoulders. "It wasn't like we had much of a choice. By the time I realized Halla was in the back, I couldn't turn around. They would have followed me." In short words, Larissa recounted her day, smoothing over how Halla had not revealed herself earlier and skimming through the harassment of the sentries. When Larissa mentioned Darien, she paused at the look her parents shared.

"Aagenson?" Pappa asked, his eyes meeting Mamma's. "You are sure he said Darien Aagenson?"

"Yes, I'm sure. Do you know him?"

"I used to know an Aagen, but I thought his wife died during childbirth, along with their child. Finish your story."

Larissa did as he asked. Once she was done, Halla fidgeted under the combined weight of their parents' gazes. Though Larissa had not told them what Halla had said about wanting to see the city, she knew that they knew.

Pappa ran a hand over the back of his neck. "Let's just unload and get inside."

Halla sighed and looked at Larissa, her face full of gratitude. She ran to the back of the truck and waited dutifully as Pappa opened the tailgate and pulled himself up onto the bed. Box by box, he passed down the rations to his family who took them inside to be stored safely. With Halla and Mamma inside, Pappa passed off the last box to Larissa.

"She could've told you she was there earlier," he said with one eyebrow arched higher than the other.

Larissa shifted the box in her hands. "She must've been too scared to think about it."

He humphed, dropping down into the dirt beside his daughter. "Is that the story we're going with?"

"It's the stories that got her into this mess," Larissa muttered.

"What's that supposed to mean?"

Larissa's fingers tightened around the box. The words she'd held back for so long spilled out. "Halla thinks that all of your stories are true, that Frigg and Eir were protecting her today."

"Who says they weren't?"

"I do, because *I* was the one protecting her!" Larissa snapped her mouth shut.

His expression remained unchanged. "Did you ever think," he said, his voice calm, "that maybe the *Æsir* sent you to protect Halla?"

Larissa held her tongue, resisting the urge to shake her head.

"You used to love the story of Aurvandil the Valiant," Pappa continued.

Unwittingly, Larissa's eyes flashed to the constellation above Pappa's head. He was right; it had been one of her favorite stories before the constant fear of Halla's discovery had set in.

Halla. She was an ache in Larissa's chest. Unbearable guilt pressed in on Larissa's heart every time she thought of Halla's desire to see the world, knowing that her own status as first-born stood in her sister's way.

Pappa rubbed the back of his neck. "Larissa, the *Æsir*—"

"I should probably go help Mamma with dinner," Larissa interrupted. She didn't want to talk about the gods any longer. It wouldn't change a thing.

Pappa nodded. "We'll talk when you're ready."

He wasn't one to push, though Larissa wouldn't put it past him to tell Mamma about their conversation. She always knew when Larissa needed to talk.

They went in, leaving their boxes on the floor and joining their family at the table. Mamma and Halla sat with Tucker, an older farm hand, who listened with rapt attention as Halla retold her journey to the Wall.

"You're lucky the old man of the sea was looking after you," Tucker replied when Halla finished. "Old Njörðr is known to be fickle at times, but you must have caught him in a good mood today."

Larissa's chair scraped across the floor. "She's lucky we met another field hand as kind as you, Onkel."

At the endearment, Tucker's eyes crinkled in delight. Although there was no blood relation between them, Larissa had grown up referring to Tucker as her uncle. With no family of his own, he'd embraced his role as "uncle" with full enthusiasm. He had been working on the farm before Pappa had married Mamma. When Larissa came around, he taught her how to protect her hands against thorns and biting insects on the vines. When Halla was born, he took her birth in stride. He didn't care for the Empress' mandates. He'd often been the one to hide Halla in the barn or the woods when the sentries arrived for Inspection Days.

"So she tells me." Tucker's wrinkled eyes crinkled further. "Darien, was it? Halla said you were quite taken with him."

Larissa spun toward Halla who smiled defiantly back. "That is not true!"

"Now, now." Mamma's soft voice was enough to stop Larissa's next words, but they didn't stop her thoughts of payback. One swift kick while Halla was sleeping ought to do it. As Halla smiled in triumph, Larissa pondered her revenge. The rest of their meal passed in a blessed mundane routine.

Mamma rose to her feet, collecting the plates. "A month without sentries will be a blessing."

Halla followed suit, piling up cups and silverware in her hands. "Maybe I should visit the Wall next Produce Day too. Since it worked out so well, you know?"

Four pairs of startled eyes landed on Halla, whose nose turned bright pink. "Too soon?"

Tucker roared. Pappa's laughter was the loudest of all, but Mamma and Larissa shared a look amidst their uncertain chuckles. Halla was joking, but would she always? Would this one escapade give her the confidence to try it again?

Tucker's large boots clomped against the wooden floor. "Today's been much too exciting for these old bones. 'Night all."

A chorus of goodnights followed him as he disappeared down the hall. On other, larger farms, it was normal for the field hands to sleep in the barn, but Tucker was family.

Through the open window situated above the couch, purple rays streaked across the clouds. The nightlife stirred, carrying with it the croak of frogs in nearby streams, the steady hum of insects, and the scurry of the field mice. The symphony of noise soothed away the chaos of the day, easing the tightness that had been in Larissa's chest ever since that morning. She wore her weariness like a heavy winter's blanket. It settled around her, lulling her toward slumber.

"We all should head to bed," Mamma announced.

Halla spun from her place at the sink, her eyes coming alive. "One story! Please, Pappa."

Larissa's sleepiness vanished as alarm shot through her. Surely after today, Pappa would say no. Surely he would see the way these stories only fueled Halla's recklessness.

Instead, he leaned back against his chair and held up a finger. "One story, little one. I'll be there after I help Mamma clean up."

Only Pappa could still get away with calling Halla "little one." She kissed his cheek, springing off to their room to get ready for bed. Larissa finished clearing the table in silence before following

Halla, who had already changed and situated herself on their bed, burying her nose in one of their few books.

It wasn't even a real book. The paper was bound by leather cut by Pappa's hand and words written by Mamma's nimble fingers. After *Ragnarok*, so little had survived. When the Empress took over, the few remaining books were destroyed or restricted to those at the highest levels of society. Like everything else, like rations and electricity, knowledge was regulated.

Larissa changed, then settled into bed beside Halla, peeking at the story she was reading. She recognized it immediately. *Baldr the Beautiful* was written in swirling letters at the top. Her eyes skimmed over the story she knew so well.

Baldr was the most beloved of the *Æsir*, son of the high chief, Óðinn, and the high chiefess, Frigg. When the *mara* sent nightmares of Baldr's death, Frigg used *seidr* to save her son's life. She journeyed across the world, compelling every living being to swear to never harm her son. Once she covered all the lands, convinced that Baldr was invincible, she returned back to the grand halls of the *Æsir*.

Despite all her efforts, Baldr was killed in an accident orchestrated by the trickster god Loki. Frigg had forgotten to request an oath from the lowest plant of all, mistletoe, and it was that plant that Loki had tied onto a spear wielded at Baldr's heart.

Halla shook her head in frustration at that part, as she did every time. "Why would Frigg not remember to make the mistletoe swear the same oath as everyone else?"

"Even the gods make mistakes." Pappa's shadow crossed the threshold. "But remember the lesson this story teaches us. Each winter, we hang mistletoe as a reminder of Frigg's tears that became the berries on the leaves, for mistletoe did not have berries before Baldr's death. We remember how Frigg did not take her vengeance on mistletoe, but showed mercy and compassion as her son would have wanted."

Larissa always thought the moral of the story was a bit different. Frigg overlooked the small plant because she didn't deem it necessary to lower herself to request an oath from it. Frigg's arrogance resulted in her son's downfall. This story was about pride and its consequences, not mercy or compassion.

Pappa settled on the edge of their bed, but when Halla offered him their storybook, he turned it down. "I have a new story to tell tonight."

Even Larissa jolted at this. She'd heard all of Pappa's stories dozens of times. What could he possibly have to tell them that they didn't already know? Halla nearly bounced off the bed in excitement.

Pappa's eyes drifted toward Larissa, then he nodded to himself as though coming to a decision. Larissa had never seen him hesitate to tell a story before.

He cleared his throat. "Let me tell you about the Great *Hrun*."

A Prophecy and a Princess

Larissa

SPEAKING OF THE *HRUN* was forbidden.

It was the story of the Empress' rise to power and the enslavement of the four other kingdoms of Evrópa. Larissa sat up straighter, unable to hide her own interest. Why would Pappa share this now when he never had before?

Pappa placed his hands on his knees, leaning forward toward his daughters. "In the days before the end, mankind dwelled in madness. Then came *Ragnarok* and the defeat of the *Æsir*. When the fires burned out and the waters receded, only the nation of Evrópa remained. A thousand years ago, those descended from the *Æsir* were gifted *galdr*, the power of the gods."

"Pappa," Halla interrupted. "You've told us this story before."

Larissa smirked; she'd been thinking the same thing. Supposedly, after *Ragnarok*, mankind rebuilt with the help of the Norn, who taught them how to awaken the *galdr* within them. Each kingdom possessed its own unique type of *galdr*. Only those of Ancestral Blood could access it, and so they became the first monarchs of the lands. With *galdr* running through their blood, they led unnaturally long lives, ruling for centuries instead of decades.

Larissa knew there was magic in the world, but she doubted man's ability to wield it. If they had, wouldn't the other monarchs have stood a better chance against the Empress?

If Pappa was bothered by the interruption, he didn't show it. Instead he smiled. "Be patient, Halla. I've taught you the history of Rúna, the first queen, and how she helped establish the five kingdoms, but you only know them as they are today. United in captivity under the Empress' authority, but more divided than ever."

Pappa paused, and Larissa's eyes darted toward the open window. She resisted the urge to draw the curtain from unfriendly eyes.

"The first queen of Perle, Rúna, had a daughter, Stjarna. She taught her daughter to respect the Norn and to fear the complacency of the other monarchs. Peace is a fragile thing—hard-fought but easily overcome. The Norn foretold destruction to Rúna. Stjarna carried with her this prophecy of doom; it compelled her to be ever-watchful, even as a new generation of Kings and Queens forgot the warning of the goddesses. Only Queen Stjarna and her husband, with no children to inherit the throne, remained from the old reign. Then the northern King of Diamant passed his title on to his only daughter, the Crown Princess Shiko. She is known today as the Empress."

Larissa knew that her own face mirrored the shock on Halla's. But where Halla's shock mixed with wonder, Larissa instead felt fear. How did Pappa even know the Empress' real name? Before she could ask, Pappa continued on.

"The other monarchs accepted her, of course. They all traveled to Diamant to witness Shiko add her thread to the *Tæpəstrɪs Friðarsamningur*, as all had done before her."

Unlike Larissa, Halla had no qualms about interrupting. "What's that?"

"A grand tapestry that the Norn gifted to the first monarchs. Every monarch since has woven their reign into its pattern. Once crowned, Shiko took her seat at the loom. She drew a dagger and sliced through the tapestry, ripping apart its seams and centuries of history."

Halla gasped. "Why would she do that?"

"To declare war. The Norn themselves had woven the power of the kingdoms into the tapestry. When Shiko destroyed it, she shattered the ties that bound them all together, revealing what lay behind her facade of peace. Shiko possesses the *galdr* of illusion, the ability to make anyone see what she wishes. With it, she'd hidden her armies from the visiting monarchs until they were surrounded. Only through Queen Stjarna's quick thinking was she able to lead the other monarchs to safety, although their guards were slaughtered as they fled.

"The monarchs of Perle, Safír, Smaragd, and Rubin had only one choice: to break their vow of peace and overthrow Queen Shiko, who had declared herself Empress. Having agreed to this plan, the monarchs went their separate ways to return to their lands and prepare for war. Unbeknownst to the King and Queen of Rubin, Shiko had already infiltrated their kingdom, corrupting the lower-ranking members of Ancestral Blood. She convinced them to partake in a dark form of *galdr* that granted them the power they needed to take the throne, but it cost them their humanity.

Rubinian's natural *galdr* is shapeshifting, but those who sided with Shiko lost the ability to control their power. They became monsters, subjected to Shiko's will."

A long howl echoed across their farm lands. Larissa wrapped her arms around her chest, feeling the goosebumps on her skin. As much as she wanted to, it was harder to discredit Pappa's stories in the dark of the night.

"The monarchs of Rubin returned to civil war and fell with their kingdom. Then Shiko turned her gaze to the vast forests of Smaragd. It stood in her way of conquering the southern kingdoms. When her armies arrived, the King and Queen bent to her will, believing that their pacifism was the only way to maintain peace for their people. Shiko agreed to their terms. No harm came to the people, but the King and Queen were executed as a sign. The old ways were dead, just like their rulers. That left only the Kingdoms of Perle and Safír to stand against Shiko."

A sharp pain twisted Larissa's stomach. She'd known all this, or at least bits and pieces from overheard conversations, but Pappa's words painted the Empress' betrayal in stark illustrations. Part of her could not bear to hear the rest of the story, but a deeper part of Larissa that used to love Pappa's stories needed to hear the end of this tale, however fantastical and outlandish it seemed.

Thankfully, Larissa didn't need to say a word, because Halla leaned forward and asked, "Then what happened, Pappa?"

"During this darkest hour, Queen Stjarna sought a way to turn back the tide of Shiko's destruction. She called upon the Norn to guide her, but they declared that the Empress had already won. Relentless, Queen Stjarna pressed the Norn for a shred of hope. Moved to pity, the Norn revealed a possibility. There was only one person who could end the Empress' control of the five kingdoms. Stjarna's daughter, granddaughter of Rúna, the Princess of Perle could save them all."

"But Pappa," exclaimed Halla. "There is no Princess from the Perle Kingdom. Queen Stjarna didn't have any children, you said so yourself!"

There was a long pause as Pappa's eyes seemed to gaze inward.

Finally, he spoke in hushed tones. "No, little one. The Empress has perpetuated this lie to rob the lands of their last hope, but the inception of the lie began with Stjarna herself. When the Princess of Perle was born, the Norn spoke a prophecy over her. They foretold the fall of the kingdoms, claiming that the Perle Princess could one day right all of the wrongs, although it would come at a terrible price. So Stjarna and the King hid their daughter away, pretending to have lost her at birth. But all along, the Princess grew up, hidden from her people."

"Wow," Halla whispered, her eyes as large as their dinner plates.

"With the Norn's prophecy that the Perle Princess might one day dethrone the Empress, Stjarna hid her daughter when Shiko attacked. Even when the last kingdom fell, the Princess was nowhere to be found. She survived, hidden by *galdr*, or time, or perhaps the Norn themselves."

"Shiko crowned herself Grand Empress of Evrópa and decreed that speaking of the Kings and Queens of Old was punishable by death. Fifty years have passed since Shiko's betrayal, since the Great *Hrun*. Those of Ancestral Blood were killed or imprisoned. Kingdoms became commonwealths. Many have forgotten the stories of old, and even fewer know that the Empress lives so long because of her *galdr*. They do not understand, and so they fear what she is capable of. The only hope we have left is in a Princess who vanished more than fifty years ago."

"Do you really think she's still alive, Pappa?" Halla asked. She bolted up in bed, tossing her blanket to the side as though she might leap from the bed and begin searching. Shards of fear pierced Larissa's chest.

Dangerous, she thought, seeing the excitement on Halla's face. *These stories are dangerous.*

Larissa's eyes burrowed into Pappa's bowed head, urging him to look up and see the worry written on her face as she mentally begged him to tell Halla no.

When he did look up, he looked not at his eldest, but at his youngest daughter, weighing his words with care. "Yes, Halla, I do. One day, she will awaken from her slumber. She will set into motion events that I doubt even the Norn could predict. There is one thing we know for sure, though. When she emerges, there will be a price to pay. There always is."

"The prophecy isn't very specific," Halla said, crossing her arms. "Didn't it say *how* the Perle Princess is supposed to defeat the Empress?"

"Why are you telling us this?" Larissa blurted out, if only to distract from Halla's curiosity. "You can't really believe that mankind has the ability to wield the power of the gods?"

"They do." Mamma's soft voice floated in from the doorway. "I've seen it."

Larissa turned to see Mamma leaning against the door frame. She didn't know how long Mamma had been there, listening to Pappa's story, but she seemed less than pleased with how it had ended. Her thin eyebrows were raised in Pappa's direction. "We didn't agree on this story tonight."

"They need to know," Pappa said.

"You've seen magic, Mamma?" Halla squealed. "When? How?"

Mamma walked over to her, running her hand over Halla's hair. "Not magic. *Galdr.* When I was a child, a goddess visited my mother. She had a task for my family. When I turned thirteen, my mother made sure that I knew the task would fall to me." Mamma glanced at Larissa. "We wanted to tell you both at the same time. Halla is nearly thirteen, just as I was. Once she turns thirteen, I'll tell you everything."

"What?" Halla exclaimed, disagreements and protestations flooded from her mouth. But Larissa was watching Mamma who was watching her. Did she mean it? Had she actually seen a goddess?

"Mamma is right," Pappa's voice was firm. "Halla's birthday is in a few weeks. When the season is through and the Inspections slow down, we'll tell you everything."

7

The Encounter

Larissa

A NEW SET OF nightmares arrived the night of Pappa's story. Even as the days passed, the nightmares remained.

As her eyes refused to open, Larissa knew she was dreaming. Pain pressed against her chest and cut off her ability to breathe. *Mara*, Halla would say. *Superstition,* Larissa would retort, but the mental argument did nothing to lessen the paralysis in her limbs. Besides, ever since Pappa's story, Larissa had been less certain of her stance on the gods and magic. Although she clung to the warmth of Halla's unseen body beside her, Larissa slipped back into the darkness.

THERE WERE NO WINDOWS.

The room was well lit with a modern, electric glow that contrasted against the ancient loom sitting in the middle of the room. Larissa tried to examine the rest of the room, but fog obscured the walls, blinding her to what might lay beyond.

A girl appeared at the loom, but her hands and the shuttle rested in her lap. She fiddled with a strand of golden thread hanging from the shuttle as a door opened. An older woman walked in; her hair the color of starlight and her eyes a vivid green. Her gown was elegantly cut and made of the finest material. It dipped low in the back with pearls laced across her bare shoulders.

"Practicing your weaving?" the woman asked.

The girl didn't answer.

The woman sat on the bench. "Do you want to tell me what's on your mind?"

"I want to go outside."

"We could go for a walk in the gardens."

"That's not what I mean, Móðir."

A pause. "I know."

Larissa stood in the corner of the room, watching the girl shake off her mother's hand. She'd had this dream before, but could never remember the ending. Only the fear.

The woman's head turned, her eyes locking on to Larissa's with enough intensity that Larissa stepped back, bumping into the wall. Then the woman stood before her, grasping Larissa's hands in her own. Shocked by their warmth, Larissa yanked her hands back, but the woman was unbothered.

"You have to wake her," the woman said.

"What?" Larissa asked, before reminding herself to not interact with the dream. The more she interacted, the harder it was to wake up. A hot sensation burned at the top of her spine. A warning that initiated the start of each nightmare.

"You have to wake her," the woman repeated, her hands wrapped around Larissa's arms with enough strength to hurt.

"I don't know what you're talking about." She tried to shake free from the woman's grasp, but to no avail.

Blood leaked from the woman's nose, gathering at the corner of her mouth. Her teeth were stained with it. "Then all is lost."

The woman transformed, her eyes blackening until no white remained. A crown of diamonds dripped from her head. A new face snarled, revealing rows of sharpened teeth. The creature lunged, and Larissa was devoured.

ᚾᛁᛗᚵᛋᚾᛁᛗᚵᛋᚾᛁᛗᚵᛋᚾᛁᛗᚵᛋᚾᛁᛗᚵᛋ

LARISSA'S SHOUT WAS SMOTHERED in the cotton pillow.

Shudders cycled through her body, expelling the paralysis that had held her limbs hostage, but the nightmares remained. Over a week had passed since Pappa's story, yet Larissa's dreams were more vivid and memorable than ever. She dreamed about the Perle Princess, or about Rúna. Sometimes her nightmares tortured her with shadowy visions of the Empress. Or at least, Larissa assumed it was the Empress.

It wasn't as if Larissa had ever met these figures or had any idea what they looked like. All images of the Kings and Queens of Old had been wiped from history. She wondered at the green eyes that supposedly belonged to Queen Stjarna in her dream, so similar to Halla's.

Not that she would ever tell Halla, who could speak of nothing else. Every day her sister would ask, "Will you tell us about the goddess you saw?"

And every day, Mamma looked at Pappa and said, "Not yet."

Larissa turned over, squinting against the sunlight. Well after dawn, another late summer day began. Halla hardly slept in when the sun refused to stay in bed, which explained her absence from the room, but not why Larissa had been allowed to remain.

Sure that Pappa had noticed her absence, Larissa raced through her morning routine. Her fingers were still wrapping the band around the base of her braid as she walked into the living room.

"...they'll be here before Halla's birthday at the end of the season," Pappa was saying. At the sight of Larissa, his mouth clamped shut.

Surprise filtered across her parents' faces from where they sat on the couch. They must have thought she was out in the fields already. Larissa had thought the same of Pappa.

Larissa raised an eyebrow, her fingers frozen on her braid. "Who will be here at the end of the season?"

"The sentries, of course," Pappa said, but the lie was evident in his eyes. "They always come to complain about the quotas."

"How are you feeling, *bebe*?" Mamma inserted quickly.

Larissa let her hands fall to her sides. "Fine, why?"

The frown line on Mamma's forehead deepened. "Halla said you wrestled with *mara* again last night."

Now Larissa understood why she had been allowed to sleep in so late. "I'm fine. Halla exaggerates. Speaking of, where is she?"

Noticing her deflection, Pappa raised his eyebrows. "The barn. Halla didn't sleep in like some," Pappa quipped, but his heart wasn't in it. He rose from his seat, replacing his hat on his head. "You should head out, we've got work to do."

It was an obvious tactic to move on from whatever Larissa had just overheard, but it was just as clear that Mamma and Pappa wouldn't share whatever they were hiding until they were ready. As the screen door closed behind her, Pappa's footsteps paused. Faint whispers resumed, but they were far too quiet to be of any use. There had been more of that lately, the whispers and hushed conversations. It had all started after Mamma's claim that she'd seen a goddess.

Shaking her head, Larissa pounded down the porch steps. She would believe that when she saw it.

The screen door creaked as Pappa rejoined her. "Tucker's in the southeast field," he said, not quite meeting Larissa's eyes. "We'll join him."

Larissa didn't speak as they walked through their fields or as Pappa's whistle mimicked the birds of their surrounding forests. She knew it was pointless to push. Pappa would share only when he was ready. They found Tucker bent over the patch of strawberries with several buckets already filled to the brim.

Tucker looked up, a grin spreading across his face. "Wasn't sure if you were working with me today."

Larissa rolled her eyes and knelt on the ground beside him. "Morning, Onkel."

"Someone slept in," Pappa added, picking up the buckets of strawberries. "I'll take these back to the barn, check on Halla, and grab more empties."

Larissa's eyes narrowed as they watched his departure. She wouldn't be surprised if it took Pappa longer than necessary to return. No doubt, he planned on returning to his conversation with Mamma now that there were no more prying ears.

Tucker nudged a bucket toward Larissa. "Get going, lazy-bones. We don't want to be kneeling in the dirt when Sól is high in the sky."

She glanced at the sun. Tucker was right; they only had a few hours before it was truly beating down on them. Tucker and Larissa worked in near silence, their nimble fingers cutting the stems a quarter of an inch above the berry. Only bird calls and Tucker's occasional jokes punctuated their work. Pappa returned, although later than necessary, as Larissa had suspect-ed. He brought some of Mamma's famous jelly sandwiches, prompting a short break. Larissa savored the flavor of tart jelly mixed with sweet cream spread over the homemade dough, licking her fingers once the sandwiches were gone.

"Is Halla coming to help?" she asked.

Pappa shook his head. "She asked if she could spend some time at the creek."

"Again?"

Ever since Pappa's story, Halla had worked through her chores in the barn with a new zeal, often finishing them with time to spare. When she was done, she'd cross over the north-west field farthest from the house and through the field that ran up against a thick line of trees belonging to Barnstokkr Forest. A few miles in, there was a stream that burbled over rocks, forming small waterfalls at certain points. The family would journey there on special days; it was Halla's favorite place to be alone. In the past Larissa had accompanied her, but lately Halla preferred her solitude.

Pappa rose to his feet, brushing the crumbs from his shirt. "Let's get back to it then."

With renewed vigor, hours passed, and the buckets filled up. More rows remained to be harvested, but with Sól's ascension and the rising heat, they would wait for another day. Larissa stood, arching her back and popping her neck. She would be grateful when harvest season was at an end. Though they'd all taken turns transporting their buckets to the barn, several newly filled buckets remained. Tucker and Pappa collected them, heaving them into their arms, but when Larissa reached down to grab her own, Pappa stopped her.

"Go get Halla, would you? She's been gone too long, and we'll need help packaging these up before supper."

Larissa cranked her neck toward the forests. "Sure, Pappa."

Tucker eyed the trees with distaste. "I don't know how you all stand it in there. *Jötnar* live in the woods."

Pappa and Larissa shared a look and smiled. "*Jötnar* live under the mountains," Pappa said, clapping a hand on Tucker's shoulder. "They won't bother us here."

"Those giants live anywhere outside of civilization," Tucker argued.

Pappa shrugged; they'd had this argument too many times. Larissa had made dozens of trips into Barnstokkr Forest and never seen even a trace of the supposed giants. Ignoring the warning in Tucker's eyes, Larissa abandoned the buckets of berries and followed her feet into the shade of the trees.

The woods surrounded her, blocking out the sun and the sounds of the farm. Unlike the open fields, spotted with infrequent bird calls and low hummed insects, the forest was thick with the noise of nature reclaiming its own. Squirrels wriggled up trees, and birds stretched out their blue-colored wings. Every animal added its own notes to the harmony of the forest.

Following the twisting, turning animal trail, Larissa climbed over fallen tree branches and up rocks. The hike was refreshing after spending so long bent over in one position. She reveled in it, taking her time to stretch her legs. The sound of bubbling water greeted her ears long before Larissa saw the creek. She followed the path along the ridge that sat high above the water, keeping an eye out for her sister.

Just as she was approaching the spot that Halla loved, Larissa slowed. Over the sound of the bubbling water, she heard an unfamiliar noise. It took a moment to realize what it was.

Singing.

It began as a low chant, intense and strong, nothing at all like Halla's high-pitched tones. There was a clear invitation in that voice, but the words were strange to Larissa. They were heavily accented and wild, like Pappa's old poetry. Choosing her footing with care to avoid branches or dry leaves, Larissa moved closer. The stream lay just over the ridge and down the steep slope. Larissa hid behind one of the large boulders, but curiosity won out over her anxiety.

Peeking over the rock, she quickly located the source of the singing. A girl, maybe a few years older than Larissa, lounged on a rock in the middle of the stream. What could be seen of her skin was deeply tanned, but her neck and most of her ink-black hair were wrapped in a soft white linen. But it was not the singing girl that caused Larissa's body to stiffen in shock. It was Halla, sitting on the bankside and listening with a rapt expression.

Larissa ducked down before either could notice her presence.

When the song ended, Halla clapped with enthusiasm. "That was beautiful!"

Larissa crawled to the edge of the ridge but kept her body flat against the ground. Her heart thumped painfully into the dirt as she forced herself to remain hidden, even as her mind screamed at her to rush to Halla's side. With measured breaths, she counted until her pulse had slowed. As long as the singing girl didn't see Larissa, she would have no reason to think that Halla was a second-born.

The girl trailed her brown hand over the top of the water. "It's been a while since I've sung about my people."

"Your people?"

"Have you heard of the Rubinians?"

"Oh, I know all about them; Pappa tells me stories all the time."

Larissa ground her molars at Halla's openness, but the singing girl looked pleased.

"Not many are brave enough to tell the stories of old."

"Well my Pappa is!" Pride laced Halla's voice. "He told us all about how the Rubin people betrayed their own rulers and lost their humanity."

The singer's hand clenched into a fist at her side, but her voice remained light. "Not all of them. History records what people want to remember. Rubinians are fluid and aggressive people, true, but also courageous and daring. What the Empress did to them, what they did to themselves, dishonors the Rubinian bloodline."

"What did the Empress do?" Halla whispered, excitement and horror in her voice.

A growl filled the air, and Larissa was shocked to realize it was coming from the girl. "She murdered their souls. Those who joined the Empress are called *draugr* now, as they are no longer human."

"No longer human? Then what are they?"

"Monsters," the singer hissed. "When they corrupted their *galdr*, their skin hardened into obsidian scales. Horns sprouted from their heads, and wings erupted from their backs. Their hands and feet turned into claws that can pierce any metal. They have a barbed tail and tongue that can strip the flesh away from their prey. Though they can still shift as before, they can't hold on to their human forms. Their minds are bent to the will of the Empress. They are more dead than alive."

Halla's brow furrowed. "What do you mean, they corrupted their *galdr*? Doesn't that come from the gods?"

The dark-haired girl waved a hand. "Another story for another day."

Not if I can help it. Larissa's skin itched at the thought of another encounter with this girl. She resisted the desire to slide down the slope and snatch Halla away. As long as Halla wasn't in immediate danger, her status as second-born had to be concealed. Larissa dug her nails into the dirt, forcing herself to remain still.

The singer rose to her feet. Fluid, like the creek that passed by her, she leapt across the rocks until she stood by Halla's side. Jostled by the movement, her black hair escaped the white linen, swinging freely around her face. Sunlight bounced off the gold ring in her nose as she tilted her head down at Halla. "You never asked me about my name."

Halla shrugged. "I figured you'd tell me eventually."

"I'm Anara." The girl shifted her weight between her feet, her eyes never leaving Halla's face. "Does that mean anything to you?"

"Should it?" Confusion colored Halla's tone. Larissa's muscles tightened, ready to spring down the slope.

Anara leaned forward so that her face was on the same level as Halla's. A square-cut ruby pendant fell out from behind her leather jacket, casting a golden shimmer across the stream. "You remind me of someone I'm looking for."

Anara raised her hands, cupping Halla's cheeks in her hands. In swift silence, Larissa rose, still concealing her body behind the rocks. She tensed, waiting to see what Anara would do next, but nothing happened. Halla stirred uncomfortably in Anara's grasp. Seeming perplexed, the young woman cocked her head to the side and dropped her hands.

Bewilderment flickered across Anara's face, and she froze. Her eyes narrowed as she straightened up, turning her body away from Halla. She tilted her head up and closed her eyes, then sniffed.

"Loki's Knot," Anara cursed, turning away from Halla. "I have to go."

"When will I see you again?" But Halla might as well have asked the wind. Anara was already gone, having run off in the opposite direction from Larissa.

Larissa waited a minute, then two, watching for the singer's return. Only when she was certain Anara had truly gone did she rise fully and slide down the slope toward the stream, using the tree roots to slow her descent.

"Lara!" Halla cried. Her voice was joyful even as she cast a quick glance over her shoulder. "What are you doing here?"

"What am *I* doing here?" Larissa echoed, throwing her hands in the air. "Halla, what are *you* doing here? Who was that?"

Halla's eyes fell to her shuffling feet. "Oh, you saw Anara."

"Yes, I saw! Halla what were you thinking? You don't talk to strangers; that's literally life lesson number one!"

"She talked *to* me! I was just sitting by the stream when she showed up days ago—"

"Days ago?" Larissa interrupted, her heart stuttering in her chest. "How many times have you met with her?"

Halla's fingers twisted around the ends of her braids. "Twice. The first time was the day after Produce Day. She likes it when I share Pappa's stories, and she shares stories with me too."

Fear and anger surged up so strongly that for a moment Larissa couldn't even speak. When she did, Larissa's voice shook. "You don't even know who this girl is. You should have come straight home when she showed up—"

"You don't know what it's like being a second-rate second-born, Lara!"

Larissa's jaw gaped open. She would have been less surprised if Halla had slapped her across the face. Even Halla looked shocked at her outburst, but she held her ground regardless. She swallowed. "She said she was a wanderer, just passing through. She sat with me. Talked to me. She treated me like I was a real person."

Halla's words smothered the fire burning in Larissa's chest, dousing her anger in understanding. In a way, it wasn't Halla's fault. Though she was nearly thirteen, she had so little experience with the outside world. She didn't know how to act. Larissa had matured looking after Halla, but Halla's ability to grow had been curbed by the very restrictions set in place to keep her safe.

Larissa reached out, wrapping her sister in her arms and pressing Halla's head against her chest. "Let's go home."

"Before the *Jötnar* get us," Halla offered.

Larissa smirked. "We'd never hear the end of it if Tucker was right."

Before she knew it, they were laughing. They both knew the conversation wasn't over. Larissa would have to tell Pappa and Mamma. The boundaries of Halla's world would collapse even further with strangers moving through their woods. Larissa feared that the tighter they reigned in Halla's protective circle, the more likely it was to shatter. But for right now, she could simply be Halla's sister.

They climbed up the steep slope. Halla slipped, but Larissa knew better than to offer her a hand. It was a matter of pride that Larissa understood all too well. Halla regained her balance, and they continued. At the top, Larissa looked for Anara, but there was no trace of the girl. Larissa could not begrudge Halla's need for companionship; she could only pray it would not have consequences.

Finding an animal trail that ran parallel to their fields, the sisters started down it. The path would take them home without risking exposure. They ambled along in silence, the sound of the rushing stream growing fainter with every footfall. As the trees thinned, Larissa could see the fields of their farm and, off in the distance, the farmhouse. Usually, the sight would have filled her with relief, but Larissa's body went cold instead. Sitting in the usually empty drive was the armored truck of a sentry.

She stopped so suddenly that Halla bumped into her. Before Halla could speak, Larissa wrapped her hands around Halla's mouth and hissed, "Inspection."

The blood drained from Halla's face, but Larissa was already grabbing her hand, dragging her back through the trees. She didn't speak. Her only thought was to get Halla far away from the sentries. Abandoning the path, Larissa ran through the trees, Halla's hand still in hers. They were both panting from exertion by the time they found a large formation of rocks. Larissa collapsed against one, resting aching legs that throbbed with each pump of her heart. Halla flopped down onto the smaller boulder beside her. Only the sounds of the forest accompanied their heavy breathing.

After a moment, Halla pulled herself into an upright position. "What are they doing here? We just had an Inspection."

Larissa shook her head. A fear prickled the back of her mind, but she didn't dare speak it into existence. "I don't know."

"Did they come for me?"

Of course, Halla shared her fear. Larissa grabbed her sister's hand, leaning forward until their foreheads touched. "I wouldn't let them take you, Halla, not ever." Halla relaxed slightly at her words, making Larissa hate what she had to say next even more. "But I have to go."

Halla's grip tightened. Betrayal filled her wide eyes. "You're leaving me?"

Larissa squeezed back, ignoring the pain Halla's nails caused as they dug into her skin. She needed Halla to understand. "It's an Inspection. We don't know how long they've been here. They could be searching for me already. If I don't show up soon, they'll search the woods. You have to stay here, and I have to go. You'll be safe here. I'll come back for you." When Halla didn't respond, Larissa repeated. "I promise; I'll come back."

Fear remained in Halla's eyes, but it was joined by a determination Larissa had never seen before. Halla swallowed and released her grip. Larissa nodded at her, as if to reassure her that it was all going to be okay.

Then a gunshot shattered the silence.

The Edge of Insanity

Darien

EMPTY AIR AND A painful landing awaited Darien should he make one wrong step. Balancing on the tree limb, he felt the world tilt. His eyes snapped away from the ground and up to the apple hanging only a foot in front of him. As long as he was facing forward, his balance would hold. He stepped forward, trusting his feet to find their place, and plucked the honey-tinged fruits before tossing them below. A yelp paused his next drop.

"Hey! Careful, Darien!"

He risked a glance down, peering through branches to see Jon rubbing the top of his head with one hand and holding an apple in the other. He glared up at Darien before tossing the fruit into the overflowing produce bin beside him.

"Try keeping your eyes open, Jon. This is the last tree for the day." Darien plucked another apple, careful to aim through the empty spaces between branches.

Jon mumbled something but caught the apple, tossing it with the others. Darien climbed higher, hearing the moan of the tree limbs that threatened to break under his weight. Being the most limber and slightly built of the field hands, Darien was always chosen for picking duty. It didn't hurt that he had the unnatural agility of a cat. On the few occasions he had slipped, Darien had always caught himself at the last moment. The other field hands refused to go any higher than their ladders could reach, but Darien wasn't one to let something like gravity get in his way.

Darien hugged the trunk on these higher branches. He picked every apple in arm's reach, then stepped out to grab one more. It was an unnecessary risk, but it wasn't in Darien's nature to leave any task unfinished or any question unanswered. Or at least, it hadn't been. But since his encounter with the shapeshifter...

A sight caught his eyes and arrested his thoughts. A young, yellow-haired boy perched out on the edge of the branch, stretching out his arm to claim an apple just out of reach. Letting go of the trunk, Darien stepped toward him, his mouth opened in warning. Too late, Darien registered the sound of the cracking branch.

It snapped, sending Darien and the thief spiraling through the air. Darien shouted, scraping his hands as he caught hold of the lowest branch, his legs dangling like a fish at the end of a hook.

"Darien!" Jon yelled.

Darien grunted, his bare hands burning against the bark. It was a beginner's mistake, a fool's mistake to forget gloves. Hand-over-stinging-hand, Darien worked his way back toward the center until his feet found purchase on the gnarled trunk. Using its grooves, he descended to solid ground and looked around for the boy.

Only Jon stood before him, his eyes scanning Darien's hands. He whistled at the raw damage.

"Where's the boy?" Darien asked, pulling his scraped hands out of Jon's view. No need to make a show of his stupidity.

"What are you talking about?"

"There was a boy on the branch with me. Did you see where he went?"

Jon looked at him strangely. He'd been doing that a lot lately. "I didn't see anybody else up there with you."

Not again, Darien thought. There was no boy lying in the dirt of the orchard. Likely, there had never been a boy in the tree. Only in his mind, just like last time.

Jon hesitated at Darien's silence and laid a hand on the younger man's shoulder. "Let's just call it a day, okay? We've done enough."

"Yeah, sure." Darien shrugged off the hand. "Grab that bin, would you?"

Darien hefted one of the heavy bins, ignoring the sharp pain in his hands, and headed through the orchards toward the storage barn. He could feel Jon's eyes on the back of his head as they walked down the long rows of trees that surrounded the small farmhouse. The deep green of the leaves would change soon to orange and brown as fall came, but it was this vibrant green that Darien loved the best.

He focused on the trees, ignoring the pointed looks that Jon shot his way. Of all the farm hands, Jon was the only one who knew the truth about Darien and his parentage, or lack thereof. If Jon knew that Darien was hallucinating, he would want to help. Darien could trust him with anything, but he wasn't sure what *this* was. Not yet, anyway. It had all started with that dark-haired girl on the side of the road. *Anara.*

Darien's bin of apples thumped on the ground of the barn. "I'll go back for the last bin."

"But your hands," Jon protested.

"No, I'm fine, really." Darien headed back toward the open doors. "Why don't you start sorting?"

Darien fled before Jon could push the matter any further. He needed the solitude of the orchard, the familiar sweet smell of the apples, and the hum of bees to settle his thoughts. His hands shook slightly as he shoved them deep in jean pockets.

Ever since his trip to the Wall, Darien hadn't been himself. Even Aagen had asked about his strange behavior. Darien told him an animal had run him off the road—he had to explain the truck's damage somehow—but he held his tongue about Halla. More importantly, he didn't say a word about Anara.

The truth was, he didn't know how to explain it, not without sounding insane.

Darien could just imagine Aagen's face when he told him. *A girl ran in front of the truck, and when I confronted her she changed into a woman. Oh, and when her hands touched my face, they paralyzed my body and made me black out. Did I mention she was gone when I woke up, and I've been hallucinating ever since?*

If Darien couldn't believe it, how would Aagen? Darien nearly convinced himself it *had* been an animal that ran him off the road and the girl a figment of his subconscious imagination. He would have succeeded, too.

If not for the hallucinations.

Figures from his dreams were walking beside him in real life. Their bodies were blurred as if standing behind rippling water, but they appeared most often when he was alone. They never stayed long. The boy on the tree had been the clearest hallucination yet, which was probably why Darien hadn't realized it at first. It hadn't taken Darien long to guess the hallucinations were connected with the girl he pretended didn't exist.

Two days after the crash, his pretense had crumbled about him. Darien had been out in the orchards trying to ignore the hallucinations that stalked his waking hours by daydreaming about Larissa's golden eyes instead. When he woke, he was not alone.

"Hello, Darien." Anara leaned against one of the trees, smiling as though they were friends.

Darien had leapt to his feet, backing out of reach, her paralytic shock fresh in his mind. She hadn't appeared in child form this time, but rather, closer to his own age. He waited, watching to see if she would shift again, wondering if she was real or just another hallucination. The same ruby pendant, hidden slightly by her leather jacket, winked at him.

"What do you want?"

"Oh, good." Her copper eyes beamed. "We can skip past the part where you pretend you don't remember what happened and get straight to it."

"What did you do to me?"

"I found her, Darien, and I need your help."

Taken aback by the seriousness in Anara's tone, Darien paused. "Explain yourself or get off my land."

Anara covered her eyes, muttering frustrations. "Loki's Knot. You still don't remember. This is more complicated than I was led to believe."

Darien stared in apprehension as the girl rubbed at her temples through her hair, unsure if she was waiting for his response.

She dropped her hands. "I can't make you remember, but I can't give you much more time either. I'll be back soon, so be ready next time. Pack up whatever you need and make your goodbyes. She'll need our help once we find her. I'm sure there are others already on their way."

"Leave?" Darien stared at her, this woman who dared show up in his life and turn it all awry without any explanation. "Look, I don't know who you seem to think I am, but I'm not going anywhere with you. It's time you leave."

She pushed off the tree, her long dark hair swinging behind her. "I can't have you fighting me on this, Darien. I need you to wake up. I'll be back soon."

He opened his mouth to rebuke her claim, but then, from across the orchards, Darien heard Aagen call his name. He'd turned away for a moment, but when he turned back, Anara had disappeared. Darien nearly convinced himself she had been another hallucination.

He'd done his best to go about his day, to forget the urgent look in her eyes. But his dreams grew in intensity and frequency every day since, bleeding into his waking consciousness, invading every moment until he questioned what was real. The boy in the tree was his most recent hallucination, and Darien knew that it would not be his last.

With stinging hands, Darien strolled through the orchards toward the last bin that needed retrieving, replaying Anara's promise in his mind.

I'll be back soon.

Darien had no doubt that she would, but he didn't know what he would do. She didn't seem like a threat, besides the whole paralytic shock incident. He grimaced at the memory. Maybe he wasn't the best judge of character.

The trees shook their baring branches at him as he passed by. Most of the trees in this segment had been stripped by the demands and quotas of the land. Their next delivery was coming up in a few days. Darien was looking forward to seeing Larissa again.

She was the only thought that could banish the anxiety that came with every hallucination. Larissa's fierce, protective spirit came back to Darien as he remembered how she engulfed Halla with enough love and anger to strangle her. Aagen didn't know which farm Larissa might live on, so Darien's only chance at seeing her again was on the road back to the Wall.

"Did you hear what I said?"

Darien spun to find the hazel eyes of the same blond boy that had fallen with him from the tree. Perhaps Halla's age or a bit younger, he held his chin high with adult arrogance. "I said, did you hear me?"

Not real, Darien thought. Before he could decide to speak, another voice answered the first.

"How could I not hear you? You're not exactly quiet."

Another boy, nearly the same build and height as the first, stood behind Darien. Unlike his companion, this boy had wild black hair that he brushed back from vivid blue eyes. There was something familiar about that gesture, but Darien had no time to ponder as the black-haired boy walked straight through Darien as though he had no more substance than smoke. Darien sagged against a nearby tree, surrendering himself to watching the hallucination unfold.

Would he know it when he finally lost his mind, or would he experience a slow, unnoticed descent into madness?

"I was listening to Faðir and Móðir," said the blond boy. "They were talking in the library and didn't hear me. We're going to visit the Kingdom of Perle."

The black-haired boy crossed his arms across his chest, rolling his eyes. "What's so exciting about that? We've visited before."

"This time is different."

"How?"

The blond boy paused before answering, mischief playing around the corners of his green-brown eyes and upturned mouth. "I don't know if I should tell you. After all, it might be a secret for only the Crown Prince to know."

Crown Prince, thought Darien. There hadn't been princes since before the Empress' reign, according to Aagen.

The dark-haired boy snorted. "Sure, which is why you eavesdropped to hear it at all."

Darien smirked as the young boys bickered. Could these boys be more than figments of his shattering sanity? Or were they simply the physical result of listening to Aagen's stories one too many times? The boys were familiar in a way that made Darien's ears tingle. The dark-haired boy stalked away from his companion as recognition blossomed in Darien's mind. He knew this child, but how?

"I don't care about your secret," said the dark-haired boy. Darien could tell he was lying.

"Sure you do." The blond boy jerked his head toward Darien. "So does he. Don't you?"

Darien jolted up from the tree as two pairs of eyes stared at him, waiting for his answer. Waiting for him to engage. Darien hesitated. It was one thing to hear voices in his head, and another thing to answer them.

Frustrated by his silence, the black-haired boy took a step in his direction. “Is he right? Do you want to know the secret?”

The boys’ silence demanded an answer. Darien stood up straight, excitement building in his stomach in defiance against the caution in his mind. He had found the line between rationality and madness. Should he cross this line, he could truly lose his mind.

His mouth turned up at the thought. After all, in all of Aagen’s stories, interesting things hardly ever happened to the sensible.

Darien nodded, letting the two boys grab hold of his injured hands. Surprisingly, not only was their grip solid, but it eased his stinging skin instead of irritating it. They pulled him deeper into the orchards until they came upon one of the largest trees, then let go of Darien’s hands and ran past the tree.

When he slowed down, the blond boy beckoned him. “Well, come on then!”

Darien shook his head, smiling at his foolishness. But even as he raised a prayer for protection, his feet propelled him forward. He passed the tree, and everything changed.

ᚺᛁᛞᛚᛃᚺᛁᛞᛚᛃᚺᛁᛞᛚᛃᚺᛁᛞᛚᛃᚺᛁᛞᛚᛃ

The orchard around Darien disappeared. Tile flooring replaced the soil beneath his feet, and the smell of apples vanished. He stood inside a massive hallway with high ceilings, great tapestries on the walls, and thick rugs on the floors. All along the hall were closed doors with runes etched in their frames. Darien supposed that the Kings and

Queens of Old or the Regents of the Empress would have lived like this.

Crown Prince, *the boy called himself.*

Was this a memory of a time before the Great Hrun? *But if so, whose memory had Darien stumbled into?*

As he raced down the hall, Darien realized several things simultaneously. He was much shorter than before, and he couldn't see the boys running ahead of him. Instead, someone ran by his side. The dark-haired child had disappeared, leaving behind the blond boy, who was now somehow taller than Darien. When he saw Darien watching him, the boy grinned.

His name is Aeron, *a voice in his mind said.*

The name felt right, even if Darien's body did not. Raising his hands to his face even as he continued down the labyrinth of halls, Darien noted how small they had become. His legs were shorter too.

"Slow down," Aeron hissed, yanking Darien's arm. "You don't want them to hear us."

Their feet slowed; Darien passed by a mirror, then nearly tripped as he jerked back to check his reflection. The dark-haired child hadn't disappeared at all. As Darien raised his hand to brush back his hair, the same child in the reflection mirrored his action.

Somehow, Darien was the boy.

The fear of losing himself in whatever irrationality had sucked him into this world pricked part of Darien's mind. But there was another, stronger part that longed to know the end of the story, to learn the secret, even at the risk of his sanity.

As if his borrowed body were responding to this desire, he crept forward after Aeron.

They stopped outside a large door inscribed with more runes. Darien recognized some of them from Aagen's book, the one they hid during every Inspection. Aagen had never shared the meaning of these runes with Darien, but that never stopped him from stealing away during the night to flip through the pages of the book.

Following Aeron's lead, Darien pressed his ear up against the door. Aeron's conspiratorial grin stretched across his whole face, only inches from Darien's own; Darien felt its contagious energy and the subsequent smile that split his own cheeks.

Is this what it's like to have a brother? *Darien wondered.*

He's my best friend. *Darien recognized the voice in his head as belonging to the boy whose body he now inhabited.*

The muffled voice on the other side crystalized into words, spoken by a woman. "I'm surprised Queen Stjarna agreed to our visit."

Told you, *Aeron mouthed. Darien rolled his eyes, pressing his ear closer against the door. Or at least, his body did. He wasn't sure how much of his actions were his own or the boy's.*

A man answered the woman. "It will be good for her daughter to have some friends. We've encouraged this for years."

Daughter? *Darien felt his mouth move to ask the question before he thought it. Aeron nodded, that same mischief shining in his eyes.*

The door opened, sliding away from where it held Darien's weight as he felt his body crash to the carpeted floor. From the muffled thump beside him, it was clear that Aeron had fallen as well. The boys hurriedly rose to their hands and knees as they stared into two bemused faces. The woman's dark lips pulled into a smile, her hazel eyes crinkling at the corners. The man towered over the boys with stern blue eyes set against olive skin. But Darien could swear that a smile hid behind the man's thick, curly beard.

"What do you two think you are doing?"

"We were coming to get a book, right, Darien?" Aeron nudged Darien's side with his elbow, but Darien could only stare.

He called him Darien. *How had Aeron known that was his name? Did he know that Darien was inhabiting this boy's body?*

The towering man turned his gaze to the black-haired boy. "Darien, is this true?"

Darien's mind reeled as he recognized the truth. He knew why the boy had looked so familiar. Whether this was a vision, a dream, or a memory, Darien was the black-haired boy.

9

Over the Edge

Darien

"Wake up, son," said a gruff voice.

Staggeringly cold water splashed against Darien's face. His eyes snapped open. A man towered over him with an empty bucket in his hand, the falling sun at his back outlining his large frame. The falling sun? It had only been noon when Darien followed his hallucinations deeper into the trees. How had he lost so many hours?

A voice echoed in his mind, calling his name. How did his hallucinations know his name? The fuzziness of sleep befuddled Darien's thoughts as he regarded the massive figure standing before him, blinking through the droplets clinging to his eyelashes. "Aagen?"

"Who else?"

Darien shook the water from his hair, then took the hand that his adoptive father offered. With the sun setting behind him, Aagen's red hair appeared to be on fire. It burned and curled at the edges as if alive. Another hallucination.

Sensing his confusion, Aagen gripped his shoulder. "Are you alright, son?"

"I don't know." Darien watched the flames sizzle out, while tendrils of smoke settled into the streaks of gray in Aagen's beard. "What was I just doing?"

"Snoring loud enough to wake the dead in Hel." Aagen snorted. "Jon came in, said you were seeing things. When you didn't come back to the barn, I started to wonder where you'd gotten to." Aagen's eyes never left Darien's. "Is there something you need to tell me?"

Darien shrugged as his brain struggled to catch up. "I don't know. I didn't think I was asleep, but if I was, I had the strangest dream." Darien rubbed the back of his neck. "Aagen, I need to tell you something."

"Don't I know it."

"What do you mean?"

"Something else happened at the Wall, didn't it? Let's go inside and have a chat, you and I."

Walking with a slight limp, Aagen headed toward the house, leaving Darien no choice but to follow. The limp was an old injury—courtesy of a bad fall years before that had never healed properly—but it never slowed Aagen down. Darien rushed to keep up. Once inside, Aagen flicked on one of the lamps seldom used during the summer evenings, closing the door firmly behind him. It bathed the room in a dim yellow as Aagen settled on their old couch with his bad leg straightened out before him. "Alright, son, talk."

Darien could not have stopped the words if he wanted to. He told Aagen the truth about meeting Anara—how he was paralyzed when she touched his skin, how she transformed from girl to woman, and how the hallucinations began shortly after. Darien paced the short length of the room as he described Anara's latest visit and his most recent hallucination.

When he finished, Darien waited for a response. Aagen took his time, twisting a braided section of his long beard between his fingers.

At last, he asked, "You said her name was Anara?"

"Yes."

"And she first appeared to you as a child?"

"Yes."

"But later appeared to you as a woman?"

Darien resisted the urge to roll his eyes. "Yes, Aagen, I've already said this."

"Did she ever take another form?"

Darien scoffed, "No, I would've remembered that."

Aagen stroked his beard. "I didn't think there were any left of the undiluted Ancestral Bloodline. Age manipulation is a complex form of Rubinian *galdr*."

"What's *galdr*?"

Ignoring the question, Aagen leaned forward on the couch, his hands folded under his chin. "These hallucinations, as you call them. What can you recall from them?"

Darien fought the headache forming in his temples. "They feel so vivid when they happen, but afterwards, they're a blur. I can't remember them."

"Or you don't want to."

"What do you mean?"

"In any of these dreams, did anyone seem to recognize you?"

A chill settled on the back of Darien's neck. How did Aagen know that?

Taking his silence as a confirmation, Aagen nodded. "It sounds to me as though these are not hallucinations at all; they are visions of your past. Memories, even. Perhaps there is something that you don't want to remember, and so you war with yourself. The part of you that tries to remember against the part of you that wants to forget."

Darien waited for the loud, horse-like bray that Aagen would expel after a good joke. It did not come. The understanding that his adoptive father was deadly serious settled in his stomach like the flu, threatening to expel itself from Darien's body one way or another.

"You can't be serious." Darien could hear the disbelief in his own voice. "I've lived on your orchard my whole life."

Aagen stomped his good foot against the ground, a sure sign of his growing agitation. "You have lived here only a little more than a year."

The ground seemed to tilt almost as if Darien were back in that tree, his foundation cracking beneath him. "What are you talking about?"

"Look, son." Aagen paused to shift his bad leg out in front of him. When he looked up, there was steel in his eyes. "Darien, for the past year I've treated you like a son. But even before today, we both knew that wasn't true."

Darien ignored the pang in his heart. In Darien's mind, it *was* true. He was Aagen's son in every sense of the word that mattered. He had no memories of the time before he'd been dropped off on Aagen's front porch. He'd been too young. Hadn't he?

Oblivious to Darien's inner turmoil, Aagen continued, "I wish you were my blood. Ever since you've been in my care, you've asked me questions about your origin, but I never knew when was the right time to give you the answers. I suppose that time is now."

Darien didn't respond. After asking for so long, now that Aagen was ready to answer, Darien was afraid. His eyes darted to the floor, tracing the runes that Aagen had carved into the wooden boards. Soothed by their familiar lines, Darien squared his shoulders, forcing himself to look into Aagen's face. "Tell me."

"When the rulers of Safír still belonged to the Royal Blood, I was just a boy working in my father's orchard. I was thirteen when a woman appeared on our porch." Aagen's eyes misted over as though he were lost in that moment. "Even I, the young and naive boy that I was, could feel the *galdr,* the power of the gods, radiating from her. She foretold the fall of Safír, telling us that she would be bringing someone to us. We were to protect this person with our lives. I didn't believe her. I'd only ever known a time of peace; it seemed impossible that our kingdom could fall. My father must have known something because he never hesitated. He swore that he would protect whoever it was she sent to us, but I was surprised when she required the same oath from me.

"I thought it a grand story at the time, and you know how I like stories." Aagen shook his head at his own youthfulness. "Then came the Great *Hrun,* the fall of our King and Queen. You never know fear until you can taste it, Darien, and I knew fear by the taste of copper in my mouth. We expected the woman to return any day, but she did not. The Empress won, my father died in the war, and the Wall was erected. At fifteen, I took over the orchard.

I kept my head down, figuring that whoever the woman meant to send to us had died during the war."

Questions piled on top of one another in his mind, but Darien bit his tongue. As Aagen spoke, images like hallucinations crossed Darien's mind. He could see the woman, but the vision was blurry. When he tried to bring it into focus, the image shattered and disappeared.

"A year ago," Aagen continued, "the woman appeared again, this time with a companion. You."

"You were a tall, lanky boy on the edge of manhood with a glazed look in your eyes. You walked straight to this couch and passed out. She told me your name and that in the morning, you would remember growing up on this farm, and the rest of the field hands would remember it too. I'll admit, I didn't ask questions; I think I momentarily forgot how to speak. I'll never forget what she said to me before she departed. 'Remember your oath, Aagen Oginson. Protect him. Many search for him as we speak. Among them is a friend who will awaken him when he is ready. Until then, he is your responsibility.'

"Then she vanished. I mean, she disappeared from before my eyes like one of the *Æsir*. Freed from my reverie, I carried you to the spare bedroom and stayed awake by your bed, flinching at every noise, convinced that the sentries would come. I didn't know how to explain your presence to the rest of the farm hands; I didn't trust the woman's promise.

"I must have dozed off. I awoke to Jon barging right into your room and waking you. He knew your name, called you lazy, and told you to help him in the orchards. If I was amazed then, I was far more perplexed when you woke up, told him you were on the way, and said good morning to me as if you'd known me all your life. I was overwhelmed with memories that I knew were not my own. I remembered finding you on my doorstep as a young child, raising you as my own, teaching you how to walk out on tree branches, and telling you the stories of the Norn and *Æsir* around bright fires during the dead of winter. I remembered nursing you back to health when you caught the fever as a child. Yet, at the same time, I knew the reality in which you were not a part.

"Two sets of memories occupy my mind. In one, you have always been my son; in the other, you've only just arrived. As the year passed, I chose the memories with you in them. You brought me the joy that fled with my wife's passing. But that resilient voice in my mind persists, reminding me it isn't real. I believe that voice is why the woman chose me. All Safirians hold some portion of Ancestral Blood, but my father and I hold just a bit more, allowing us to sense and resist the *galdr* of our people. It allows me to remember the truth even when no one else can. These two lives have coexisted in my mind for the past year, but I seem to be the only one who recognizes reality. That is, until tonight. You are starting to separate reality from fantasy for yourself now, aren't you?"

Darien stopped pacing, staring at Aagen in horror as he listened to the man he considered to be his father tell him it was all a lie. He wanted to shout, to run through the door and disappear into the orchards, to fall asleep and wake from this awful dream. Yet something inside of Darien confirmed the truth of Aagen's story.

He stepped backward, as if he could escape Aagen's words, and bumped into the wall. He slid down, dropping his throbbing head into stinging hands.

Darien remembered the stories by the fire and the broth Aagen made him when he fell sick. How could this man not be the father Darien thought he was? Yet another set of memories drifted beyond the first. These memories were a vast black sea, empty and tumultuous. They featured a blond boy with a mischievous grin, a towering man with a curling black beard, the sweet croon of a woman's voice, a lock of soft white hair, and a pair of sweet green eyes.

"It's alright to remember, boy," Aagen said. "I knew this day would come."

Aagen waited for his reply, but Darien couldn't find the words to explain what was happening inside of him. Darien *was* remembering something. A strange place, the smell of dirt and the hum of bees. So different from tiled floors and the smell of salt water from his memories. Two boys listening in on their parents' conversation. A revelation. Meeting someone new, who held the hand of a woman with bright green eyes. Halla's eyes behind the crates, terrified to be caught. Larissa stepping in front of her, ready to protect her sister. The car crash. Anara's hands on his face. Again, those green eyes.

"What did she look like?" Darien croaked.

"Who?"

"The woman who brought me to you. What did she look like?"

Aagen smiled as if recalling a fond memory. "She was beautiful, tall, and graceful, but there was also something foreboding about her. I couldn't stare at her face for more than a few seconds. Her hair was the color of starlight, woven and braided. Her eyes were such a bright green, they reminded me of our apples."

The pit in Darien's stomach deepened. He rose to unsteady feet, placing a hand on the wall, breathing hard. He remembered the woman, and she looked just as Aagen said. In his mind, he could see her as she smiled down at him. This memory must have been from his youth because he had to look up to see her face. She was motioning to someone who hid behind her back.

A golden ribbon peeked out from behind the woman's legs. It was attached to a young girl. The Princess of Perle.

Darien's head spun. "Aagen, I have to go."

"Go where? Anara told you to wait, and I'm convinced that the Norn have sent her to be your guide."

"I'm remembering something. I have to find Halla and Larissa."

Aagen growled, stomping his good foot against the wooden floor. "Now isn't exactly the time to be running after a girl you just met, Darien. The girl said to wait; you must wait."

"They're connected to this. I know how it sounds, but I can feel it, Aagen, more strongly than I've felt anything before. I think they're in danger."

Aagen frowned, but leaned forward all the same. "How do you know that?"

"I don't." Darien laughed joylessly. "Obviously, I don't know much of anything if everything you just told me is true. But I can feel this, and it feels real."

Aagen hesitated, but only for a moment. He released his hold on the braid in his beard and clapped his large hands together, rising to his feet. "If the Norn are leading you down this path, then who am I to disagree?"

Unsure whether he was meant to follow as Aagen stomped out of sight, Darien waited. Aagen returned in moments, carrying a large duffel bag that strained against its zipper. "I've had this packed for you ever since your arrival. I knew that the Norn would collect you one day. This bag holds clothes, food, and supplies, but they won't last you longer than a week. The berry farms start several miles to the northeast of our orchard. I'm not sure which of these farms belong to your girls, but you should head in that general direction. It will take you several hours to walk there."

"Walk?" Darien asked. "What about the truck?"

Aagen shook his head. "It gave out this morning. I have it torn apart in the shed right now, but it won't be fixed for hours. Besides, I feel that your journey is just beginning. I don't think it will lead you back here."

Darien glanced up, surprised at the gruffness of Aagen's voice. Aagen's eyes, usually so stern, softened at the corners. He cleared his throat, handing the bag to Darien, who accepted it without a word. All was quiet as the man and boy stared at one another. Darien's heart constricted; even learning that his memories of Aagen were planted in his mind, it did not erase the love he felt for his adoptive father.

"There is something else," Aagen continued. "The woman gave it to my father, who gave it to me to hold onto until I could give it to you. She said I would know when, and if this isn't that time, then let me turn to stone when the sun rises."

Aagen removed something from his pocket and dropped the cold, round object into Darien's outstretched hand. The ring's thick, silver band enclosed a large, square-cut blue sapphire. A silver casing clasped the gemstone at each of the corners. It looked well preserved, but Darien noticed a small scratch in the middle of the gem. When he slipped the ring onto his finger, warmth spread through his body. There was music in his ears and a tug from the ring that urged him to examine it again. What he thought was a scratch was a rune hooked like a shepherd's crook. Sheer power emanated from it.

"It compliments my eyes." It was all Darien could think to say.

Aagen chuckled, nodding in approval before he grew somber again. "The memories may not all have been real, but my love for you is. You are the only son I have. If it's alright, I'd like to give you my blessing before you go."

Darien dipped his head, feeling the lump in his own throat. Aagen placed both hands on Darien's shoulders. "May Óðinn, the great wanderer, guide your steps. May Kári's winds blow you where you must go. May the Norn be kind in their reading. May your journey be fertile, and your labor yield fruit. In times of danger and trouble, may your bonds with others hold tight, Darien Aagenson."

Darien was unsurprised by the wetness he saw in Aagen's eyes and the dampness he felt around his own. Regardless of what Aagen said, they would see each other again. "I'll return, Aagen, and I'll have my own story to share with you."

Aagen smiled, the expression crinkling the corners of his eyes. "I'd like that, son."

The time for further words had passed. Eager to begin his adventure, Darien hefted the bag onto his back, walking out the door of the house that had been his home. It was time to start filling in the gaps of his memory. His *real* memory.

Pointing himself northeast, he set off through the orchards with the setting sun at his back.

10

A Misunderstanding

Larissa

Larissa flattened her body against the dirt, her eyes wildly scanning the forest. Her hands shook upon realizing the gunshot came from the farmhouse. She crawled to Halla, who had fallen to the ground with her hands shielding her ears. Larissa raised her sister from the dirt, wiping the leaves from her hair.

"Halla, listen; listen to me."

But Halla's tear-filled eyes stared through the trees toward their home.

"They're dead, Lara," Halla whimpered. "They're dead because of me, aren't they? Because I went to the Wall."

"You don't know that."

"This is my fault."

Halla's breathing caught in her throat. She hyperventilated, her cries increasing in volume. Scared of discovery, Larissa gripped her shoulders and shook her hard. "Stop it, Halla, they'll hear you. Deep breath. Come on, like that."

Halla whimpered but locked her eyes on her sister's face. Larissa sucked in a breath, motioning for Halla to mimic her as she held her breath. With gentle fingers, Larissa tucked back fallen strands of hair behind Halla's ears, then tugged on the tail of her braid. The movement reminded her of Pappa, which sent a pang of unexpected pain through her heart. She prayed her next words were not a lie.

"This isn't your fault, Halla. No one is dead. The sentries like to show off, that's probably all it was." Then, the hard part. "But I still have to go."

"What?" Halla's voice hitched up an octave. "You can't go now!" She gripped Larissa's shoulders with such desperate strength that Larissa winced. She peeled Halla's hands off, squeezing them to reassure her. She inhaled loudly, nodding for Halla to follow her lead.

"I'll make sure that Pappa and Mamma are alright," Larissa said. "You want that, don't you?"

Halla's chin trembled. "But what if something happens to you?"

The sentry's gun and knife popped into Larissa's mind, but she shoved the image away. "Nothing is going to happen to me, and nothing is going to happen to you, but you need to do exactly as I say. Stay here, Halla. No matter how long it takes or what you hear, you promise me that you'll stay here until I return. If someone else comes to the forest, you go further in and find somewhere better to hide. Do you understand me?"

Halla wiped away the tears puddling at the corner of her eyes and nodded.

"That's better." Larissa held up Halla's wrists; the medallions on Halla's bracelets clinked against one another. "Swear on the Norn that you will not leave this place until you hear my voice. Say it, Halla."

She sniffed, but her small voice was firm. "I swear on the Norn, Lara. I won't leave until you come back."

Relief coursed through Larissa. Halla would never go back on an oath sworn to the goddesses of fate. She tugged on Halla's braid, more gently this time, then rose to her feet. "Good. You keep your promise, Halla, and I'll keep mine."

Before she could reveal her own conflicting emotions, Larissa turned, briskly walking away from Halla and toward the sound of the shot. Once out of Halla's sight, she broke into a run.

Whom had the sentry shot? Pappa? Mamma? Tucker? Why? Was it because Larissa was missing, or had someone seen Halla at the Wall? Larissa's stomach clenched. Had Darien betrayed them?

The sun fell, signaling the evening's rapid approach as the farmhouse came into sight. Two armored trucks sat in the drive, blocking any exit down the dirt path. Larissa ran across the yard, not breaking her stride. If she let herself slow down, who was to say she would not lose her nerve and stop entirely? She bolted up the steps to the porch, flung open the screen door, and ran straight into the barrel of a gun.

Larissa's breath left her in a small gasp as though her body had been entirely robbed of oxygen. Her eyes strained down the loaded barrel resting only inches from her face. The black tunnel threatened to swallow her vision. Would she see the bullet before it killed her? Her heart pounded against her skin as if it might thump right out of her chest and escape her fate.

"Please, stop!" Pappa's voice broke Larissa's fixation of the gun. "This is Larissa; this is my daughter!"

Beyond the barrel stood a sentry dressed in all black, his dark visor pushed back. Behind him, Pappa and Mamma sat on their small couch, frozen in terror. From the way they perched at the edge of the cushions, straining forward, they clearly wanted to stand beside their daughter. Larissa knew they couldn't; if they rose to her aid, it could only make things worse. Broken violet shards scattered across the floor, mixed with soil and flowers. The old TV that hadn't worked in years bore a new hole in the middle of the screen that spiderwebbed into thousands of sharp cracks, clearly the victim of the sentry's bullet.

Pappa leaned forward with one hand in the air, pleading. "Sir, please. You have been asking for her. She was probably wandering in the nearby forests when she heard the gunshot and came running home. Isn't that what you wanted?"

The sentry's eyes did not leave Larissa. He lowered the gun an inch but held it steady. "Where have you been, girl? The Empress' decrees require you to present yourself for all Inspections at a sentry's discretion."

Larissa swallowed, worried that even that small move would provoke a reaction. "I didn't know. I'm sorry. We had an Inspection last week. We've never had two this close together. I was gone from the house before you arrived. I wouldn't have left if I'd known."

"Are you hiding something out there?"

Sweat dripped down Larissa's spine. "No. I just meant that I wasn't here to present myself because I didn't know there was an Inspection today."

"Inspections are random for a reason," the sentry barked. "They often catch people in a lie. So what lie are you telling me? Where were you all day?"

The best lies often contained the truth. "There's a stream running through the forest bordering our field. Some days, after finishing my work, I walk along that stream. I lost track of time."

"Is this not Dal's Berry Farm?"

"Yes, sir, it is."

"Are you not Larissa Daldóttir?"

"Yes, sir, I am."

"And you mean to tell me that you spent the whole afternoon lounging in the woods instead of working in the fields, as is your job?"

Larissa hung her head as if in shame. Her scalp tingled at the exposure to the gun. "Yes, sir."

"Are you aware that your family has been granted specific privileges to work on this farm and live outside the Wall? Only the Empress' generosity provides you with water, electricity, and weekly rations." The sentry's voice was rich with indignation. "This is how you repay her?"

Larissa remained silent, staring at the floor until the cocking of the gun drew her eyes back to the barrel.

"Are you aware," the sentry continued, "that it is within my power to remove you until I am convinced that this farm is working at full productivity?"

Larissa's breath caught in her throat. For the oddest moment, she was not afraid. She was angry.

Who was this man to tear her family apart? Larissa's fury burned, and she was surprised by how badly she wanted to hurt him the way he'd threatened to hurt her family. A scalding sensation rose in her chest as she dared to meet the gaze of the man who held her at gunpoint.

The sentry's eyes narrowed in response. His finger twitched toward the trigger.

"What is going on here?" a harsh voice from behind Larissa demanded.

Larissa's defiance fled, and with it the sudden surge of energy. She swayed on her feet, at once drained and light-headed. Black spots littered her vision. Mamma stared, placing a trembling hand over her mouth as Larissa's legs quaked underneath her. When she turned to see the newcomer, nausea crept up her throat.

A young man, perhaps in his twenties, stood in her peripheral vision, his body taut in perfect posture as he glared down the sentry before him. "I asked you a question, sentry."

Larissa sucked in a deep breath. She didn't know what she'd expected, but certainly not him. The shadow of a neatly trimmed beard clung to his face. His blond hair was shaved close to the scalp on both sides of his head, and thick, wavy strands were braided tightly against his skull. Larissa stepped back, keeping an uneasy distance between both the new arrival and the sentry's gun, which was swiftly lowered under the scrutiny of the young man's pale hazel eyes.

Larissa noticed the emblem stitched on the jacket of the newcomer's chest: three diamonds linked together with a solid line, the Isa rune, drawn down the middle gem. She swallowed the bile that rose at the sight of the Empress' marking.

"*Kafteinn*." The sentry inclined his head in his superior's direction. "This girl is Larissa Daldóttir. She was in the forest all morning, abandoning her work on the farm. I was explaining—"

"Put your weapon away." The *Kafteinn* nudged the broken shards of glass on the floor, his distaste evident in the downturning of his lips. "You've made a mess. Go outside and wait for me."

"Yes, *Kafteinn*." Though the sentry was nearly double the *Kafteinn*'s age, he nodded again, then marched out without another word or a glance at Larissa.

With the sentry gone, only Larissa's breathing and the creak of the couch as Pappa shifted broke the still silence of the room. Mamma's small hand reached out to touch her husband's knee. Larissa knew they were not out of danger.

The *Kafteinn* walked around Larissa, then stopped between her and her parents. Larissa focused on the spot behind his right shoulder, staring at the shards of ceramics and glass on the floor. She knew what "*Kafteinn*" meant. He was a high-ranking official in the Empress' army. He seemed more reasonable than the sentry, but if Halla was discovered, he would be far more dangerous.

"I am *Kafteinn* Calder," he said. His voice was calm, as if he were a friend discussing produce prices or the weather. "I've examined every inch of your allotted land this afternoon, yet you were nowhere to be found. Where were you, Larissa?"

It was an innocent enough question, but Larissa heard the accusation underneath and the way his tongue lingered over her name. The inquisitive look in the *Kafteinn*'s eyes did nothing to assuage Larissa's fears. The answers he sought could lead to her family's destruction. She clenched her teeth at the thought of him roaming their farm, counting the produce instead of admiring the beauty of the vines. Tempering her displeasure, Larissa recounted the same story she'd told the sentry, careful to repeat the exact details.

The *Kafteinn* considered her story, his arms crossed against his chest. "My sentry was not wrong. Your place is on this farm, producing your quota for the city of Safír, but that is a minor infraction. One I can easily overlook given your family's nearly impeccable record. There is something else, however. *Rumors* that require answers."

Larissa suppressed a shudder at the turn in his voice. Something about the way the *Kafteinn* regarded her with genuine interest, the way his voice remained soothingly soft, scared Larissa nearly more than the gun had. Nature taught her that the beautiful animals were the most deadly.

Kafteinn Calder tipped his head to the side as he dropped his arms. With a single step toward Larissa, he caught her glance, forcing her eyes to hold his.

"Are you harboring second-born fugitives on your farm?"

Something snapped in Larissa's brain, a quick switch from fear to anger. She did her best not to think of Halla, to keep her face as expressionless as possible. The *Kafteinn* was guessing, as the sentries always did.

But that did nothing to ease her resentment of these men who came into her home, abusing and manipulating her family for their own agendas. Accusations flooded Larissa's mind, but she held them back. What would they do to Halla if she misspoke now?

"No, sir, we are not," she spoke through gritted teeth.

The *Kafteinn* stepped closer. Too close.

Larissa held her ground, although her mind screamed a warning to step back. Larissa had never met this *Kafteinn* before, but a wave of familiarity washed over her nevertheless. He reminded her of the day she'd slipped from the top of Smarlfoss Falls, submerging herself in its icy waters.

Kafteinn Calder rubbed his jaw, his fingernails scratching the shadow of a beard. "I would like to believe you, Larissa Daldóttir. You seem like a trustworthy young woman. Yet rumors abound."

Larissa remained silent, but her mind whirled. What rumors? What could she say to convince him to leave? She thought of her sister, hiding only a mile away from the farm. *Please, Halla, please stay where you are.*

Calder continued, "We have discovered a rebellious organization beyond the Wall that seeks to smuggle out second-born children. They hide children in barns and cellars. All citizens outside of the Wall have become suspects. You tell me you know nothing about this, yet you have been gone for hours. Supposedly in the woods. Supposedly *alone*."

"But I was," Larissa protested, the confusion in her voice authentic. A rebellion? She'd never heard of anyone helping the second-borns. Could they help Halla if it came to it?

"Perhaps you would be willing to prove your loyalty?"

Larissa's attention shifted back to the *Kafteinn*, thoughts of Halla faded from her mind. Honey laced his voice, dripping into her ears and clouding her thoughts.

"This group is inconsequential," the *Kafteinn* continued. "Nothing more than a small nuisance for the Empress. But she is concerned that their way of thinking will disrupt the peace. We need someone beyond the Wall to check on the other farmers without raising suspicion. To keep an ear to the ground, so to speak. This person would let us know if others became susceptible to this group's dangerous way of thinking. Prove their loyalty to the Empress by finding information on any *sympathizers*."

An informant. They were recruiting her.

A lot of effort over one inconsequential group, Larissa thought bitterly. *Kafteinn* Calder watched her, waiting for an answer as if she could give him any answer but one.

"Whatever the Empress needs." Larissa masked her apprehensions with a false smile. "Please, just let me stay with my family."

"Of course, Larissa. I knew we could rely on you." He flashed her a brief smile then adjusted his sleeves, nodding in Pappa's direction. "The Empress thanks you for your cooperation today. We will return soon. When we do, I hope you have something worth sharing with me, Larissa." His eyes held hers, then narrowed. "There's something familiar about you."

In her mind, Larissa's thoughts stilled, held captive by a foreign compulsion that demanded she reveal her most intimate secrets. There was a voice in her mind, *his* voice, Larissa realized. The *Kafteinn* gazed at her, curiosity warring with confusion as his voice in her mind probed for whatever she was hiding. The pain in Larissa's head increased, along with the sudden impulse to tell him about Halla and the trap door in the barn. She bit her tongue, hard. Why on Evrópa would she want to tell him any of that?

Without warning, he broke her gaze. Like a puppet with cut strings, Larissa slid to the floor.

"I must be mistaking you for someone else." His footsteps thudded against the floor, followed by the slam of the screen door. Then Pappa and Mamma were sitting beside her, their arms wrapped around her. Mamma was saying something as she brushed back

Larissa's hair, but Larissa couldn't understand Mamma's words as she struggled through the wave of guilt that crashed around her.

She'd almost told Calder everything. Why? What could have caused her to even consider that? Mamma's words came back to her, *Not magic. Galdr.*

Truck engines rumbled to life. Larissa hugged her arms around her chest, digging her nails into her skin. If Pappa was right about humans possessing the power of the gods, what else had he been right about?

Mamma's small hands lifted Larissa's face. "Are you alright?"

"I don't know. I thought I was going to tell him everything." She gulped; her words came out as a whisper. "I almost told him about Halla."

Pappa's eyes widened right over the bruise that was forming on his cheek. "You would never do that, and you didn't."

"But I almost did," Larissa insisted. "Pappa, you said that some people have the power of the gods. But those were all royals? And the Empress killed the royals, right?"

If Pappa's eyebrows raised any higher, they would surely disappear into his hair. "I thought you didn't believe the stories."

"I thought I didn't either," Larissa muttered.

"Lara." Mamma broke the following silence. "Where's Halla?"

"We heard the gunshot; I couldn't just stay out there. Halla's safe though. I left her in the woods about a mile in. She swore she would wait for me there until it was safe. I should go get her."

"No, not yet."

Larissa's nails deepened the crescent-shaped dents in her skin. "You think someone is watching the house?"

"If they really think that you are part of some group of people smuggling second-borns, they would wait and see where you run off to once you thought you were safe."

Larissa released her arms. "But we can't leave her out there all night, Pappa. It's going to get dark soon."

"There's no moon tonight," said Mamma, looking at her husband and daughter with meaningful eyes.

Pappa nodded. "Right you are, my dear. We'll have to wait until the darkest part of the night to retrieve Halla. I have faith in her. She'll be alright until then."

"But Pappa," Larissa started, thinking of Halla sitting alone in the woods. She would be waiting for Larissa to come back, wondering why she was taking so long. Her mind would go to the worst places.

"No, Larissa, this is what we must do." Pappa's voice was unusually stern. "Go to your room. We'll wake you when it's dark enough. Your mother and I have much to discuss."

"What about what the *Kafteinn* asked me to do? He won't let us go with another warning if I have nothing to give him when he returns."

"We'll figure it out. Larissa, please, go to your room. Trust us."

"Where's Onkel?" she asked, unwilling to abandon the conversation.

"Another sentry was interrogating him in the barn, I'm sure he'll be in soon."

As if summoned by Pappa's words, Tucker strode in through the door, heading straight for Pappa. "Njörðr's beard, what was a *Kafteinn* doing here?"

"Vern and I will explain later." Pappa rubbed his eyes. "For now, we are all going to our rooms."

Tucker's eyes grew sharp at Pappa's words, as if he understood something that Larissa did not. He nodded to himself as he strode down the hall. "I wouldn't mind a bit of rest."

Larissa hesitated. Mamma laid a hand on her eldest daughter's cheek. "Trust us, Lara."

Against her better judgment, Larissa spun on her heel and went to her room, slamming the door behind her. She needed to be alone anyway. Was that really *galdr* she'd experienced? If so, Calder was more than just a *Kafteinn* under the Empress' command.

Pappa's and Mamma's footsteps sounded in the hall. Then came the creak of their bedroom door shutting. If Halla were here, she would beg Larissa to help her eavesdrop. They would already be sitting in the hallway as quietly as possible with their ears pressed up against the solid wood door. They could never hear anything, but they had fun guessing anyway. Larissa considered it but dismissed the idea.

Without Halla, there was no point.

Larissa's hands shook. If Halla were here, she would pester Larissa endlessly about Calder, but their vacant bed only stirred the unease in Larissa's stomach. Her encounter with Calder had left her weak, her bones aching from the inside out. The shaking in her limbs increased. She fell upon the bed, clenching the blankets but forcing her eyes to remain open. She would rest, but she refused to fall asleep until Halla was safe at home.

What was she going to do? Even if she were to ignore whatever Calder had been able to do, it didn't change what he had asked her to become. A spy, a hunter of the rebellion smuggling out second-borns. How on Evrópa was she supposed to learn any-thing? And if she did, could she bring herself to reveal the rebels to the Empress' *Kafteinn*?

Her mind circled back to Halla. Where were these second-borns being taken? The whole of Evrópa was under the Empress' control. There was no place for the resistance to take them. But if there was, could Halla go too? Larissa groaned, covering her face with her pillow. Halla would never leave her family; even her wanderlust could not separate her from Pappa and Mamma. No, it wasn't an option.

Larissa fought to keep her heavy eyes from sliding shut as she watched the sunlight fade from the window.

ᚾᛁᛉᛚᚠᛋᚾᛁᛉᛚᚠᛋᚾᛁᛉᛚᚠᛋᚾᛁᛉᛚᚠᛋᚾᛁᛉᛚᚠᛋ

"You must find her."

Larissa turned so quickly that her blankets slid to the floor. A woman sat at the end of Larissa's bed. The woman's hair was as bright as starlight and woven with braids that wound around her head and bunched together at the nape of her neck. She wore a long white ceremonial dress embroidered with the many-limbed, long-rooted tree of life. Larissa glanced at it only momentarily before staring into the startling green eyes that had so recently plagued her dreams.

Recognition flared up within her, even though Larissa did not understand how she knew to ask. "Queen Stjarna?"

"You must find her." Stjarna's voice was soft and strong. "She is lost without you."

Anxiety rose in Larissa's stomach; she clenched her fists at her side. "Halla? Did something happen to her? Is she okay?"

"She is not harmed, but something is coming." The Queen paused, a troubled look passing over her face. She raised her hand to her nose and pulled away fingertips splattered with blood. A crimson trail leaked from her nose, thickening. She took what appeared to be a steadying breath and rose to her feet. "Something is coming. Only she can stop it, but you have to find her. You have to wake her."

The former Queen of Perle moved toward Larissa's bedroom door and placed her hand on the handle. Dread smothered the air around them. There was something on the other side of that door—something that should not be let out.

"Don't open that door!" Larissa shouted, gripped with fear.

The woman turned the knob. Beyond it was utter darkness. Within the black, creatures with pure white eyes leered, gnashing their teeth in eager hunger. The woman collapsed to the floor, and the darkness swallowed them both.

Deception

Larissa

A STRONG, GENTLE HAND shook Larissa's shoulder. "Wake up; it's time."

Larissa forced open thick and heavy eyelids to find that the pupilless monsters had disappeared, leaving Pappa and Mamma standing in the dark room. Outside the window was the pure darkness of night. Halla's empty side of the bed lay undisturbed, as if Queen Stjarna had never sat there, as if it had all been nothing but a dream. Larissa blinked hard trying to clear the sleep from her eyes. "Pappa, I saw—"

She cut off, unsure if she wanted to share. Pappa's eyebrows rose in response to her pause before he peered out the window. "You saw what?"

Larissa knew she could never take back the following words. "I dreamed about Queen Stjarna. At least, I think it was her. I don't know how."

"The Norn communicate to us through our dreams." Mamma's hushed voice couldn't conceal the quiver in her words. "What else did you see?"

Larissa gulped. "Monsters. *Mara*, maybe, or something else. I—what are those?"

Pappa shifted the large bags on his shoulders, as if he too had just remembered their existence. "Supplies. Get dressed and meet us out by the truck."

"Supplies?" she asked his retreating back before turning to Mamma. "What does he mean? Halla isn't that far."

"Sit up, Lara." Mamma moved to sit behind Larissa. With practiced fingers, she swept back her daughter's hair and wove the white strands into three braids, then twisted those into one thick braid that hung down Larissa's back. "Your Pappa and I love you and Halla very much. We want what is best for both of our children."

A cold sensation breezed over Larissa's shoulders. "We know that. Mamma, what's going on?"

She finished off the braid, handing Larissa a nearby jacket. It was a thick winter jacket, not suitable for the mildly cool summer nights. Larissa accepted it anyway along with the kiss Mamma planted on her cheek. "Let's go join your Pappa."

She rose, leaving Larissa no choice but to follow. As she walked across the old, creaking floors, familiar sounds that once soothed Larissa now filled her with trepidation. Monsters from her dreams threatened to appear around every corner. She paused at the threshold, the rune for luck catching her eye, and laid her hand on the engraved wood. *I don't know if you're real, but if you are, protect Halla.*

As if in response to her skeptical prayer, the wood burned under her palm. Larissa pulled back, but when she reached to touch it again, the wood was as cool as ever. Had she imagined it, or had the gods heard her?

A muffled thump resounded from outside, causing Larissa to turn. Pappa stood at the back of the truck, having relieved the load from his shoulders, and he wasn't alone. Onkel Tucker stood in the long bed of the truck, rearranging boxes within. He spared her a quick smile but turned back to his work.

Pappa brushed his hands against his jacket. Larissa realized then that neither Pappa nor Mamma were in their nightclothes but fully dressed. So was Tucker. More than fully dressed; they were overly dressed in layers of clothes. It was a cold night, but not so harsh that they needed three jackets. Larissa fidgeted with the jacket still in her hands.

"Are you coming with me to get Halla?"

"No. We'll finish up here while you retrieve your sister."

"Finish what? Pappa, what's going on?"

Pappa met her gaze. "We're leaving."

Larissa's mouth popped open. If they left, they would be hunted.

Pappa plucked the thick winter jacket from her hands, tossing it toward the truck bed where Tucker caught it and stored it. In the dim light of the moonless night, she could only make out what looked like supplies for several weeks. Behind the truck, the farmhouse sat empty and abandoned.

"Where are we going?"

Pappa ran his hand through his thick brown hair. Mamma rubbed his back in small circles. "We can't be here when the *Kafteinn* returns. There's much we need to tell you, but we need to tell both of you. It's only been a year. We thought we would have more time."

More time for what? Pappa wasn't making any sense.

"No matter," Pappa continued. "The Norn have seen fit to determine this timeline, and all we can do is follow it. There are people who can hide us. When you return with Halla, we'll explain everything."

"But Pappa—"

"There are reasons for your dreams, Larissa. Do as I say and save your questions. We need to be gone before the sun rises. I'll tell you both everything you need to know."

"Okay," Larissa agreed after a moment. "We'll be back soon. Then you owe me an explanation."

"You'll get one. Now go."

Larissa didn't need to be told again. She ran across the drive, dirt clouding up where her boots slapped against the ground. She had left these same trees only hours ago, but they felt different now. Their familiarity turned threatening as the lack of light caused Larissa to stumble on roots and rocks. With no moon to see by, Larissa could rely only on memory to get her through the darkness.

Her chest tightened as she worked her way across the uneven ground. Halla was such a tiny thing. She would be defenseless against any animal, let alone the monsters or giants from Pappa's stories. Days ago, Larissa would have shaken off the fear because she knew there were no monsters in the woods. But her nightmare sat with her. She saw pupilless eyes watching her in her peripheral vision, but every time she turned to check, they vanished.

Get a grip.

Minutes passed, but Larissa could not find the rocks where they had taken refuge. Blood thumped in the ears, building up pressure in her throat.

She had no choice but to speak.

"Halla," she whispered, slowing to a jog as she called her sister's name. "Halla, where are you?"

"Over here."

Larissa released her held breath. Halla's voice was only a little to her left.

Thank the gods, she thought before she could catch herself, changing directions and returning to the familiar rock formation. It looked different though. The rocks seemed larger and more formidable while the surrounding trees twisted in unnatural forms, but the biggest difference was its emptiness.

Halla was nowhere to be found.

"Halla?" Larissa called out again, so sure she'd heard her sister's voice.

"Hello."

Larissa turned, finding herself standing face-to-face with her reflection. The woman before her was her exact height and build; her white hair shone even in the muted darkness. Unlike Larissa's hair that was braided back, her reflection's hair was left untouched, hanging down her back and over her shoulders. It blew in the gentle night breeze, as did her dress. It clung to her reflection's upper body and flared out at the waist, its pale pink fabric spilling over the damp forest ground behind her. The most striking difference, however, was the vivid ruby pendant that shone brilliantly just below the pale neck of her reflection.

The reflection spoke again, shocking Larissa with the sound of her own voice. "Do I have your attention?"

Larissa stepped back but hesitated when she noticed a slight change in her reflection. Its eyes were no longer golden, but rather a solid copper brown. "*What* are you?"

Her reflection sniffed. "It *is* you!"

A ripple ran over the reflection's body. As it coursed down the skin, the young woman changed. Her light skin darkened, the pale hair turning to midnight black, and the copper in her eyes became more pronounced. A golden hoop with a ruby jewel pierced her right nostril. Within moments, her reflection had morphed into a different person.

"Sorry for the dramatics," the woman said, her voice shifting, "but I need your undivided attention."

Larissa recognized the voice from the song she'd heard at the stream. "You were meeting with Halla."

The woman's copper eyes brightened. "You don't remember me, but I'm Anara."

Realization dawned in Larissa's mind. "It was you just now calling to me in Halla's voice, wasn't it?"

"It was."

Pappa's words came back to her. *The Rubinian's natural* galdr *is shapeshifting, but those who sided with Shiko lost the ability to control their power. They became monsters.*

It's not possible, Larissa thought. But the proof was before her eyes. This woman was a shifter, which meant she was from Rubin, which meant she worked for the Empress. Larissa edged backward. "Where's Halla?"

"She's safe. I sent her home. Don't be mad at her; she thought I was you. I need to speak with you alone." Anara snapped her fingers. "Larissa, focus. Undivided attention, remember?"

Larissa took another step back. "How do you know my name?"

"I'm here to help you." Anara huffed audibly. "Would you stop trying to move away from me? I'm not blind, you know."

Larissa ran, stumbling over rocks and roots. She could hear Anara behind her, but the shapeshifter was somehow following from up above in the branches. Leaves rustled overhead. Was Anara the monster that Pappa spoke of? Larissa looked up, tripping over a root that sent her plummeting face-first into the hard ground. She spat out soil, pushing to her hands and knees. The woman stood in front of her.

"Larissa, you're hurting yourself over nothing," Anara said. "Just give me a moment." She reached out, her hands cupping Larissa's cheeks, her forehead touching Larissa's, and breathed out one word. "Remember."

The heat Larissa felt from Anara's skin was nothing compared to the shock running through her body, locking her muscles in place. Black dots danced across her vision. In her mind's eye, Anara became a child with a large grin and fanged teeth

Come on, let's go! the child shouted. Then she was swallowed up and replaced by another image.

A man with golden hair and golden eyes that so closely resembled Larissa's own stood at a large, ornately carved desk, studying something with intense focus. When he noticed Larissa, he smiled. He opened his mouth as if to greet her. Then he too was gone, replaced by the woman with starlight hair and bright green eyes.

Something is coming, Queen Stjarna said. The face around those green eyes morphed, surrounded by an array of freckles and accompanied by a small center-set nose as she transformed again into Halla.

Larissa yanked her face out of Anara's hands. "Let me go!"

The shout erupted from within her, tearing through her abdomen and out through her throat. The burning anger was back. Pain coursed through her from her fingertips down to her toes. She had to get back to her family. With tingling fingers, Larissa shoved at Anara, letting her anger burn through. As though thrown by a mighty gust, Anara fell onto her back several feet away, staring in wonder.

"Larissa, did you—"

But Larissa was gone, running back toward the farmhouse. If she could get back, make sure Halla had actually returned home, then Pappa would know what to do. She glanced behind, surprised that she was not being followed. Her fear doubled.

Where was the shifter?

Larissa ran faster, panting harder with every footfall. Exhaustion settled into her bones as the anger fizzled out. She refused to stop even as black dots blurred her vision, turning it gray. But no, those weren't black dots at all. Her foggy mind struggled to make sense of the specks piling on her hair and shoulders. The smell hit the next instant.

Ash.

Ashes to Ashes

Larissa

Larissa coughed, choking on a lungful of soot-filled air. The night sky lightened, but it was too early for morning. Besides, sunbeams did not throw themselves about. They did not crack and pop.

Bursting through the trees, Larissa stopped in her tracks and stared in horror at the flames engulfing the farmhouse. She heard the shattering of windows, the sharp popping of the flames, and the thumping of the porch giving way. Coughs racked her lungs as she stumbled toward the house, searching for any signs of her family. Yet Helga sat idle and empty of life in the driveway only a few hundred feet away from the burning fire.

"Pappa! Mamma!" Larissa circled to the back of the house, her skin singed by the heat of the flames. She didn't care if someone heard her now. "Halla! Onkel!"

Had Calder returned and caught her parents as they prepared to flee? Was it something else entirely? Larissa's dream of the pupilless eyed monsters came back to her again. Pappa's stories of monsters and demons had once seemed laughable, but now they overwhelmed Larissa with fear.

To the right of the house, the small family garden had escaped the fire. But it was trampled as though animals had passed through there. Destroyed vegetables littered the ground, but something else caught Larissa's eye and caused her breath to flee her lungs. A large heap of rags lay on the ground. Only, they weren't rags at all.

Her legs gave out. Then Larissa was crawling toward the mound, hating herself for every inch she covered, knowing she had no choice. She didn't want to know, she couldn't bear to know, but she couldn't stop crawling. In the middle of their destroyed garden, Pappa and Mamma lay side-by-side, crumpled as though discarded without care. Their eyes were open, staring at the sky.

Larissa could not comprehend it. She'd just spoken with them only moments ago. They couldn't be dead. This was the *mara*'s doing. Larissa must be having another nightmare; she would wake up, and Halla would be asleep in their bed.

But one more glance at their faces was all the confirmation Larissa needed. None of her nightmares were so hideous in their details. Incoherent thoughts whipped through her mind as she registered the tears running down her cheeks. She should reach out and close their eyes, give them the proper rites, she should...

She could only stare and fight the nausea in her throat. Nothing she did now could change the fact that her parents were dead, evident through the harsh angles of their limbs and the pallor of their skin. The flames continued to roar and hiss, swallowing up the whole of the house. It would not be long before those flames jumped from the house to the barn to the fields. They would consume everything.

The heat burned the back of Larissa's neck, matching the raw burn in her throat, but she could not move. Words fell from her lips, words of pain and sorrow, of broken promises and threats made to the *Æsir* that had allowed her parents' deaths. Between the sobs and the smoke, her breath came in short, shallow bouts. She dug her hands into the cool soil and screamed.

Convulsions ran through her body, cutting short her screams. The coughing became hyperventilating, and she collapsed into the dirt. In the corner of her eyes, she could see Mamma's small, bare foot; her shoe had come off. The heat of the fire was growing. Survival instincts told her to get up, to move away from the flames.

Why? she thought. The cool soil felt nice pressed against her cheek.

Think of Halla.

Larissa jerked up at the voice, tearing her face from the ground.

But there was no one else around. The command had come from inside her head, Larissa was sure of it. The voice was familiar and strange. It came from within her, and yet she knew it was not her own.

An hour ago this would have frightened her, convinced her that she'd lost her grip on reality. Perhaps the voice was simply her innate inclination to live, or maybe even one of those heartless gods who had allowed this to happen, but she did not care. All she wanted was to be left alone.

Get up, the voice said.

Get out of my head, she told the voice.

Get up, Larissa. Don't disgrace your parents like this.

Larissa dug her hands into the soil, wondering at its dampness. Was it blood?

Are you really going to give up on Halla?

Larissa flinched at the rebuke. *Who are you?*

No answer.

Careful not to look at her parents' bodies, knowing she would never be able to leave them if she did, Larissa stood, scanning the fields nearby.

Halla, focus on Halla. This time her thoughts were truly her own. *It's what Pappa and Mamma would want.*

Her knees ached from where she had fallen, protesting against every step, but the heat lessened as Larissa walked further from the burning house. The weight in her chest, however, remained. She tried calling out Halla's name but fell into another coughing fit. Fighting the fear of what she would find, Larissa forced herself forward.

In the distant fields, she spotted the shadow of a figure. Small, but clearly alive. She faced away from Larissa, the light from the flames dancing off her blonde hair.

"Halla," Larissa croaked.

The voice returned. *Run.*

The pounding in Larissa's ears grew to a roar. Relief at seeing Halla alive soothed the ache in Larissa's knees and muffled the warnings in her mind.

Her pace quickened, but when she drew closer, her stomach fell out of her throat. Halla was not alone. She was sitting, weeping into her hands. Lying on the ground before her was a body, bloodied and torn just like those of their parents. With eyes wide open and unseeing lay Onkel Tucker.

Larissa swallowed back the nausea rising in her throat. She could hear Tucker's laughter at dinner only the night before. She would never hear his deep-throated chuckle again.

The smell of death was so much worse than she ever imagined. She knelt behind her sister and wrapped Halla in her arms, wishing she could erase the images she knew Halla would never forget. Larissa clung to Halla, who shook violently in Larissa's arms, hiding her face in bloodied hands.

Bloodied hands. Larissa frantically searched her sister for the source of the wound. Then, to her horror, she realized it was Tucker's blood coating Halla's fingers. Had Halla tried to stop the bleeding? She wept loudly, and Larissa felt her own tears stream down her face and fall, smoke-colored, into Halla's hair. There was nothing she could say. Had Halla seen their parents? Larissa pleaded silently with the *Æsir* that Halla had not.

"Halla, we have to leave." Larissa didn't know what killed Tucker, but she didn't plan on sticking around to find out. "We have to go. We're not safe."

Halla's whole frame shuddered, but she did not respond. As gently as she could, Larissa grabbed Halla's shoulders to turn her face away from Tucker's body. She brushed back Halla's hair, alarmed at the tufts that fell out in her hands.

Something about Halla's face wasn't right.

Larissa grabbed Halla's chin, lifting her sister's face up to meet her own. Then she gasped. The familiar green in Halla's eyes was gone, replaced by pure colorless white, the pupils and irises erased like those of the monsters from Larissa's dream. Despite her earlier weeping, there were no tears on her face. Instead, Larissa found an upward tilt to the corners of Halla's lips. Lips speckled with blood.

"No." The guttural sound came from Halla's mouth, but it was not her voice. "You are not safe at all."

Larissa never saw the blow that smacked her face with enough force to send her sprawling several yards. She gasped into the dirt, which puffed up to sting her eyes, and moaned at the pain that lanced across her neck from her face. Pulling herself to hands and knees, she looked back to where Halla stood, but it was not Halla.

It had never been Halla.

The child's face listed to one side, smiling at Larissa, a bloodied black claw swinging at her side. Each of her fingers bore talons six inches long. Several of the tips were dripping with fresh blood. Larissa raised a hand to her neck and whimpered, feeling the warm trickle of her own blood.

Not-Halla jerked, its bones and joints seeming to pop out of place. Larissa watched in paralyzed horror as bloodied hair fell from the figure's skull. The creature bent in on itself, its skin darkening and hardening until obsidian-colored scales covered its body, reflecting the fire's light. Over the popping of the flames came the crack of bones. The creature unbent, growing up toward the sky, its clothes fluttering to the ground.

Its naked body was that of an animal, covered in scales, with elongated arms that hung down to its knees. A roar of agony burst from the creature, followed by a ripping noise as horns tore through its skull and circled next to its head. From its back, bat wings burst through its skin, wrenching another screech of pain from the creature. A barbed tail lashed out, snapping in the air like the crack of a whip. Over every other smell—the soil, the fruits, the flames, and even the smoke—came the scent of death and decay.

Larissa gagged against the nausea rising inside her. The transformation had taken only seconds. The creature's stark-white eyes darted open. It advanced toward Larissa, snapping a bone in Tucker's body under its large clawed foot.

She couldn't help it.

Larissa screamed.

A Sword?

Darien

DARIEN'S FEET PROTESTED EVERY step.

Nearly a day had passed since he'd left Aagen's farm. He knew the farmlands were well spaced out—after all, unofficial contact between the farms was not encouraged—but he hadn't realized how *long* his search might take. He'd only passed two other farms so far, and neither of the farmers had daughters. They'd each looked at him strangely when he asked, no doubt believing that Darien worked for the Empress. Just as he left the second farm, an armored sentry truck had made its way up the drive.

Darien only hoped the farmer would not mention him or his strange questions.

Now the sun was setting again as Darien debated whether to keep walking through the short summer night. His body cried for rest, but his mind replayed his conversation with Aagen. He'd always known that Aagen was not his biological father, but to have only spent one year with him was a blow. The further he walked, the more the truth of Aagen's words grew in the pit of Darien's stomach. His childhood memories on the orchard had taken on a blurry and distorted quality. Was this because Aagen had told him the truth, or because of what the shifter had done to him?

If he'd stayed, Anara might have been able to answer that question, but would she have allowed him to find Larissa and Halla? His visions had been unclear, but he'd seen the sisters. Fragments of them, but still. If he found them, maybe they would fill the empty gaps in his memories.

"I'm sure we'll find them," said a reassuring voice.

Darien glanced to his side half-heartedly, already knowing who walked beside him. Maybe finding Larissa and Halla would stop the hallucinations. Until then, they persisted in the form of the black-haired boy from before. As they walked side-by-side through the trees, Darien felt every type of fool for not recognizing his own face at the start. He could have blamed it on the age difference or the fact that he so rarely had the time to stare at his own reflection, but the truth was he'd simply rejected it out of disbelief.

His younger self walked straight through trees as if they were incorporeal as he. Darien envied the boy's feet, certain they did not hurt as his own did. This particular hallucination had come and gone so frequently during the day that Darien no longer questioned his existence, but merely acknowledged his return. In a way, he was grateful for the company. "Thanks, Mini-me."

The boy pointed to his chest. "My name is Darien."

"No, *my* name is Darien. You can be Mini-me, or you can go."

Mini-Darien pouted, kicking a rock—or at least attempting to—as his foot passed through it. "Why are we trying to find these girls anyway?"

Darien hefted himself over a fallen tree. "I've been seeing things—"

"Sounds like a personal problem."

Darien paused at the boy's snicker and raised his eyebrow. Mini-Darien averted his eyes, but the smile remained. Wondering if he'd always been this obnoxious, Darien shook his head and continued. "I don't know if they're memories or visions from the gods, but I saw these sisters. I can't push away the feeling that I need to find them. It's like a stomachache that won't go away."

Mini-Darien nodded, his young eyes serious. "That's how I feel around the Princess. It's like there's a bunch of flying things in my stomach trying to get out."

Darien chuckled. "Are you telling me that you have a crush on some princess?"

"I don't have a crush," he protested, pink splotches rising on his cheeks.

"Sure, kid, and I'm not losing my mind."

Darien paused as the boy's words registered. In his vision, the other boy, Aeron, claimed to be a crown prince. Now this mention of a princess, but the monarchy had been wiped out decades ago. The Empress had seen to that. There was no timeline in which his mini-self should have interacted with any of the royal families.

"Earlier today, you and your friend Aeron—"

"Brother."

Darien stopped. "Brother?"

Mini-Darien mirrored Darien's pause but raised his eyebrows. "Yes, I told you he was my best friend."

"You didn't say he was your brother."

"*Our* brother, actually. I can't believe you forgot him."

"Ouch, kid." Darien drew his hand up to his chest in feigned hurt, though it wasn't entirely an act. He had a brother? The thought stopped him in his tracks.

The image of a smiling boy with dirty blond hair teased the edges of his mind. Some memory was settling into place, but when Darien reached for it, it shattered. Darien huffed as frustration built inside of him. With every answer he unlocked, more questions arose. If he had a brother, what had happened to him?

Panic flared in his stomach as he feared the answer to that question, but it was soon replaced by guilt. What kind of brother was Darien that he could have forgotten Aeron so easily? And worse, to still not remember him?

Mini-Darien rocked on his heels. "Weren't we looking for those girls?"

Darien shook his head, shoving down the emotions. His feelings would have to wait, but that didn't mean he couldn't keep seeking answers. His feet continued down the trail. "You said you and your—our—brother were supposed to meet someone? Aeron thought it was the Princess of Perle, right?"

"Right."

"But that can't be right. There hasn't been royalty since the Empress killed off the old monarchs. That was fifty years ago. How is it possible that Aeron was a Crown Prince or that you—we—would know a princess?"

The boy bounced on his toes, crossing his arms. "I don't remember."

"How can you not remember?" Darien demanded, rounding on the boy.

"You don't remember either!"

Darien ran a hand through his already tousled hair. Was it possible that these hallucinations, these memories, could only reveal what he consciously remembered? Not particularly helpful.

A crackle of leaves caught Darien's ear. He felt eyes watching him. He moved in a slow circle, but no one else was around except for his hallucination. A bird crowed twice; Darien looked up to find a raven perched nearby, its body leaning in his direction. It stared at him through one beady eye. Darien shifted on his feet and considered picking up a rock to toss at the bird.

The raven's wing snapped out as it took flight, circling once in the air before barreling straight at him. Darien threw up his arms to protect his eyes, but instead of sharp talons, he felt a thump on the ground in front of him reverberate through the soles of his feet. Lowering his arms, he found himself face-to-face with Anara, who brushed black strands of hair back from her face.

"Darien, it is you," she said. "Thank the *Æsir*."

"Woah," mini-Darien whispered. "How did she do that?"

Darien side-eyed him. "I was wondering the same thing."

Anara blinked once. "Who are you talking to?"

"Myself, of course." He pointed an accusing finger in her direction. "*You* did this to me, you know? I was mostly sane before you came along."

If Anara felt any remorse, she didn't show it. "We don't have time for this. Larissa and Halla are in danger."

"How do you know about Larissa and Halla?"

"The same way I know you. If you want answers, you'll follow me right now." She captured his wrist in her long-fingered hands.

Darien flinched, expecting the shock, the paralysis, and the onslaught of confusing memories. Instead, he was pulled forward, surprised by the strength in Anara's grasp. A quick glance to his side showed his hallucination had vanished. Then they were running. The bag on Darien's back jostled against his shoulder blades, and his feet cried out, but he couldn't resist the firm pull on his wrist.

"I don't know how much you've remembered, but there must be something there if you've come all this way. Something drew you to Larissa and Halla, right? Dreams?" Anara panted through her words, ignoring the sharp look Darien cast her way. "I've been watching them for days. I spoke with Larissa tonight. She's even more reluctant than you to remember. I was going to go after her, but an overwhelming sense of foreboding stopped me cold. It was as though the Norn had severed my string. Then I smelled you. If my premonition is correct, I won't be able to save her on my own."

"You smelled me?" Darien asked incredulously, huffing as he was pulled along after Anara, who seemed to have boundless reserves of energy. "I realize I've been traveling all day."

"Don't be a *hálfviti*, Darien. Stop here for a moment."

They burst into a small rock-filled clearing. Darien nearly snapped back that he was *not* an idiot, but his mouth hung open at the sight of Anara withdrawing a long object encased in leather. The next moment, she stripped the duffle bag from his back and thrust the object into his hands. "I have a bad feeling you're going to need this. Pull it over your shoulder and strap it around your waist."

Darien eyed it. "Is that a sword?"

"What else would it be?"

"Why *would* it be a sword?" he shot back.

"Darien, something is going to happen if it hasn't happened already; I can feel it. You can feel it. Just put this on."

"You wouldn't happen to have a gun somewhere in those rocks instead?"

Unamused, Anara pressed her lips together. "This is *your* sword, Darien, the sword of your ancestors."

Ancestral Blood, royal blood, and his hallucinations sent a cold wave washing down his spine. He knew that if Aeron had been a prince and his brother, it meant that Darien was...no. He would deal with that later. "Fine, hand it to me."

The sword was heavier than he expected and awkward to hold. With Anara's help, he hurriedly strapped it on around his hips. Still, it felt uncomfortable and foreign at his side. Swallowing his nerves, he posed with one hand on its hilt.

"So, how do I look?"

"Same old Darien," Anara muttered, tightening one of the straps.

He looked away from it, his hands dangling awkwardly at his sides. "What about you?"

Anara's lips pulled back as she moved away from him, revealing sharp pointed canines. "I am my own weapon."

Darien pushed down the instinctual desire to run. "*What* are you?"

"Wait." Anara held up a hand, shushing Darien's questions. He watched as her nose grew, blackening, into the long snout of a wolf. She sniffed once, shaking her head harshly, and the transformation vanished. She spat out a curse. "Loki's Knot! We're too late."

"What do you mean? What did —"

Then Darien smelled it. Burned wood and ash. A faint scream sounded in the distance. Darien ground his teeth in distaste. It was the cry of an animal before slaughter.

The blood drained from Anara's face. "Run, Darien, as fast as you can!"

She dropped to the ground on the paws of a pitch-black wolf, her fur hackling around her neck and ears laying flat. Then Anara was gone, bounding toward the sound of the scream.

"Njörðr's beard!" Darien exclaimed, running after her, knowing he had no chance of keeping up. Through the trees he could see the light burning from a fire, so he ran toward it, his sore feet forgotten. The sword banged against his leg as he ran. Only minutes later he left the trees, emerging into a field. The house before him was engulfed in flames, its roof long gone and the sides of the home collapsing in on one another. The fire reached out with long fingers, stretching and searching for their next victim. Already they lunged across the yard toward the family barn.

A fresh scream drew Darien's attention, reverberating through his skull and grating against it like a hoe scraping against hard rock under the soil. He clapped his hands up against his ears to protect against it. The shriek was cut off by the sharp howl of a wolf.

Only a hundred feet away stood a monster from the old stories, the kind of stories that Aagen would tell in front of the fireplace at night. The creature was bent over something on the ground, but it straightened at the wolf's challenge. At least eight feet tall, the body was humanoid but elongated and distorted, covered entirely with scales as dark as night.

To his surprise, Darien found his hand gripping the hilt of the sword as if by reflex. The weapon no longer felt strange in his hand, but comforting.

The creature bared its teeth and flexed its talons, leaping after the wolf that danced just out of reach. It looked as if the wolf, Anara, was intentionally leading it somewhere.

Darien moved toward her, then stopped. Anara said that *they* needed his help, not her. This had to be their farm. Where were Larissa and Halla?

In the firelight, Darien made out the outline of a limp body lying amongst the bushes where the monster had been standing. The figure's bright white hair was muted by dirt and what Darien feared was blood, but he knew it was her.

Larissa.

Keeping an eye on the beast pursuing Anara, he ran toward Larissa. She was laying face down in the dirt, her hair torn from her braids and sprayed out, covering the side of her face. There were rips in her clothing, but the biggest wound was on her neck, which was coated in blood.

We're too late, he thought.

The depth of his grief surprised even him as sorrow lanced through his chest. He reached out to turn her over, to close her eyes if they were open, to give her some closure in death. But when he touched her, Darien heard a small moan of pain.

"Larissa!" Pure relief colored his voice as his fingers found a pulse on her neck.

Darien cradled her head in his lap. He could see now the wound in her neck was not as severe as he'd feared. It started just behind her ear and wrapped its way onto her face, cutting into her cheek.

It had stopped bleeding, but it would leave a permanent scar. More blossoming bruises covered what skin he could see, but otherwise, she seemed intact. Could she move?

From the field, Darien heard the creature's ear-splitting screech. Larissa would have to move, or Darien would have to move her. They couldn't stay here and wait for the creature to return. He swept strands of hair from her face.

"Larissa, can you hear me? It's Darien. Come on, we need to get you out of here."

She moaned in protest but pushed open her eyelids, her brow lowered over her eyes. "Darien?"

"The one and only." He slid an arm behind her back.

Her golden eyes flooded with tears. Her voice was rough, from emotion or smoke inhalation. "They're all dead."

He paused. "What?"

Her eyes turned to look to his right. Tears streaked her face, forming rivers in the soot and ash on her cheeks. Darien followed her gaze, seeing the body, mutilated and past saving.

Larissa sucked in a harsh breath. "Pappa. Mamma. Onkel Tucker. It killed them all."

"What about Halla? Lara, where is Halla?"

"I don't know. Anara said she sent her back to the house. I thought I found her," she whimpered. "It wasn't her. She's probably dead too."

"Come on, Lara," Darien said, his voice firm yet kind. If there was a chance that Halla was alive, they needed to think fast. He had a feeling Anara could distract that creature for only so long. "Where would Halla go? If she got home and realized there was danger, what would she do?"

Larissa blinked, her eyes staring blindly into Darien's face. Then they sharpened. "There's a trap door in the barn."

"Then we need to look for her there. We can't give up, not if she's alive. Can you stand?"

Darien pulled her to a sitting position, then up to her feet. Anara howled, but differently than before. Less of a challenge, more of a warning. Their reprieve had come to an end. Larissa leaned heavily on him, her breath shallow. Then she screamed.

"No!"

Darien flinched at the word ripped from Larissa's throat. He followed her gaze to the barn, where fire licked up the wooden walls. Larissa took a stumbling step forward, and then another, half-supported by Darien as they raced against the rising flames.

As they drew nearer, Larissa moved with more surety than before, relying less on Darien's help. They were so close now. Smoke billowed from the door.

Another screech caused them both to turn. The monster was back.

"*Draugr*," Larissa whimpered.

The monster, *draugr* as Larissa called it, stood over Tucker's body, screeching as it searched the ground for its missing victim. It sniffed the air, turning its stark white eyes to look in their direction. Anara was gone, perhaps killed by those horrible claws. Though the smoke obscured its face, Darien could swear the monster smiled as its eyes narrowed on its prey.

It never saw the raven that dove through the air, swooping downward with talons extended. Before the creature could react, the raven flew off with one of those pupilless eyes clutched in its talons, cawing in triumph. The *draugr* wailed, one hand covering the hollow and bloody hole in its grotesque face.

Again the raven dove, but the monster was ready this time. The smack of its claw sent the raven's body plummeting to the ground. Darien heard the crack that resounded across the field.

"Anara!" Darien's voice was drowned out by the *draugr*'s roar.

The creature advanced toward the fallen bird. Darien gripped his sword, his head turned in Anara's direction, although his body still supported Larissa. Indecision paralyzed him.

"Go!" Larissa shouted, shoving herself off of Darien's shoulder. "I'll find Halla."

She threw open the doors to the barn, which immediately spewed forth a breath of hot, burning air. Darien could only watch as Larissa threw herself into the dark building, and the smoke swallowed her whole.

The monster cackled at the raven's weak caw. Darien's feet pounded over the soil. The creature lifted the raven by its broken wing. Anara flapped feebly with the other, trying to catch its claws with her sharp beak. Prodding the raven's torn wing with one of his sharp talons, the monster did not see Darien approach. Darien drew the sword and lunged forward with a shout, swinging the weapon overhead in a great arc and bringing it down upon the creature's back.

Pain shot through his arms as the sword clanged against the iron scales on the monster's spine. The blade rebounded, jarring straight out of Darien's hands and flying in the opposite direction. Although the strike left no mark, the creature had felt it. Dropping the raven to the ground with a dull thump, the *draugr* glared at him, licking its lips.

Darien stepped back, his empty hands flailing as they searched in vain for a weapon. "See," he muttered to himself, "this is why I need a gun."

14

Flames of Misery

Larissa

LARISSA LUNGED FORWARD IN the darkness. On her left she could feel the heat of the flames making its way in through the wood. The barn was lined with five stalls on each side. Some were empty, but from some she could hear the grunts and squeals of terrified animals. It was impossible to see anything between the dark and the increasing smoke, but Larissa knew that the trapdoor was in the last stall on the right.

She stumbled forward, pain shooting up the leg she'd landed on wrong when the creature had thrown her. She cried out, tripping over something that darted across her path. The chickens were try-ing to escape. Realizing the smoke was less intense on the ground, Larissa stayed low, crawling the length of the barn through the dirt and hay. All around her, the wooden beams groaned and popped. Every inch of her skin was drenched in sweat.

She was almost there.

The door was already thrown open. Through the haze, Larissa could see the hay that had been swept aside, revealing the uncov-ered trap door. Etched in the hidden wood was the Algiz rune of safety, its three prongs pointing toward the metal handle. Pappa's handiwork.

"Halla!" she shouted.

The rising roar of animals and flames drowned her voice. Larissa pounded on the door twice, their typical code for all clear, before yanking it open.

Halla's smoke-and-tear-stained face greeted her. Blonde hair stuck out at wrong angles. Her bright green eyes were hidden by the shadow of the hole. A long scratch graced her forearm, but Larissa's eyes were captured by the gun pointed at her face.

"Get away from me, *draugr*," Halla hissed.

"Halla, it's me." Larissa pulled her eyes from the barrel. Without waiting for Halla to lower the weapon, Larissa pushed past it and slipped into the hole next to her sister, clinging to her. "It's Lara. *Bebe*, it's me."

The endearment slipped out from relief. Halla resisted for a moment, her body stiff and unresponsive, then collapsed into Larissa's arms. The gun thumped to the dirt floor, and Halla sobbed into her sister's chest, racked with convulsive shaking.

"They're all dead, aren't they?" Halla's voice broke, her sobs transforming into deep-chested coughs as smoke settled into their hole. Sorrow clawed up Larissa's throat, but she could not allow herself to give in.

"We have to go, Halla. We have to go right now." Larissa squeezed her sister, reaching for the gun on the ground. Pappa always kept it concealed behind a false panel in the stall door. Halla must have grabbed it when she hid. What had she seen before she'd found safety?

The pang of grief running through Larissa was swiftly numbed by the moaning of cracking wood. Each breath grew more painful as smoke billowed into their hiding spot. She checked that the weapon was indeed loaded before tucking it into her waistband. She'd never used a gun before, but somehow she knew what to look for.

"The smoke is thinner closer to the ground," she told Halla. "We're going to crawl. Grab my ankle so you don't lose me."

Larissa lifted herself from the hole and immediately gagged on the mouthfuls of smoke. Sweat fell into her eyes. She raised the collar of her soaked shirt to cover the bottom half of her face. She helped Halla out of the hole, doing the same with her shirt. Their beloved barn had become a nightmare of fire and smoke.

Although the flames burned, the smoke made it unbelievably dark. If she had not walked this path a hundred times before, Larissa couldn't have found their way out. They crawled, Larissa in front with Halla's hand on her heel. Minutes passed; still Larissa could not make out the door. The symphony of animals crying out rose around her, but Larissa could not turn aside. She couldn't risk Halla's life for a few chickens.

The heat clung to their skin, burning them. Larissa groaned against the pain, forcing herself to continue. Ahead, she could see the hazy outline of the door.

A tug at her ankle dashed Larissa's relief. Halla pointed to the closest stall door where the family pig squealed frantically as it bashed itself against the wood. Larissa shook her head. There was no time. Above them, the roof wailed. They needed to get out. Now.

Halla let go of Larissa, crawling toward the stall door. The cloth at Larissa's elbows tore as she chased her sister, causing her skin to scrape against the dirt floor. The metal handle on the door had grown hot from the flames, so Halla covered her hands with her long sleeves as she struggled to unlatch the door. It sprang open at last, and the large pig fled through the smoke as a loud crack reverberated through the barn.

Time had run out.

Larissa rose to a crouch, her eyes stinging from the smoke, and squinted in the direction the pig had gone. She snatched Halla's wrist, yanking her to her feet. The walls of the barn shuddered in protest against the flames. They wouldn't last much longer.

There! Larissa ran to the doorway, pulling Halla through the opening and into the cooler night air, not stopping until they collapsed in the dirt several yards away.

On hands and knees, they choked on the smoke in their lungs, peeling their shirts from their faces and heaving ash-filled globs of spit onto the ground. Halla stopped first, rolling over onto her back and closing her eyes against the flames. Larissa watched the flames consume the barn, the roof giving one last moan before snapping and collapsing on itself.

Her blood raced as she checked for Halla's pulse to find it steady. But just above her wrists, Halla's hands were spotted in angry blisters.

"What were you thinking, going back?" Larissa asked. "Look at your hands!"

Halla sat up, favoring her right side and holding her hands out from her as though air itself hurt them. Her bottom lip trembled and, immediately, Larissa regretted her tone. She pulled Halla into her arms, cradling her head. A sob grew at the back of her throat. Larissa wished the tears would fall to soothe her stinging eyes.

"I'm sorry. I'm so sorry. You scared me. I thought I was going to lose you too. I'm so sorry, Halla; I love you."

Halla hiccuped, rising from her sister's lap. Tears flooded her red-rimmed eyes. "Why did you send me home? Why didn't you come with me?"

"*Bebe*, that wasn't—" Larissa protested, her heart screaming out that Anara had been the one to send Halla home, but her words were cut off by the screech shattering the night.

Both girls covered their ears, their heads whipping in the direction of the sound. Darien was backing away from the monster that stretched its wings out as it screamed again in triumph.

Halla whimpered. "*Draugr.*"

But Larissa's eyes were focused on Darien. His name slipped through her lips as she cried out in warning. The *draugr* leapt toward him—

—and a wolf met it in midair, tackling it to the ground. They rolled across the trampled field, each howling in pain and snarling in anger. They leapt at each other, animalistic in their fury, claws and fangs extended. The wolf latched onto its neck with her teeth, drawing dark purplish blood. The *draugr*'s barbed tail stabbed into the wolf's hind leg, and the wolf released her bite, howling as she collapsed.

"Anara!" Darien shouted.

Larissa's eyes widened. The wolf was Anara?

Darien ran through the fields, then reached for something on the ground. He lifted the sword in his hand, charging forward, but had to dodge as the *draugr* tossed wolf-Anara's body. She skidded next to Darien, one of her paws sticking out at an awkward angle. Screeching, the *draugr* pumped its powerful wings and ascended into the smoke and clouds.

Pulling Halla to her feet, Larissa rose from her hiding place. They ran toward Darien, who was kneeling next to an unconscious Anara. The shapeshifter had reverted back to her human form. Halla fell by Anara's side, stunned recognition fluttering across her face.

"Anara?" Halla asked.

"You know her?" Darien asked, surprised.

"Just met," Larissa replied, her eyes searching the clouds. "That thing will be back. Can you carry her?"

"Don't even think about it, Darien Torstenson," Anara muttered. She opened her eyes and, with great effort, pushed herself up onto her elbows. "I'm fine."

But Darien's arms were already under Anara, lifting her to his chest despite her protests.

A flash of darkness broke the dull clouds.

"Incoming!" Larissa shouted.

Plummeting from the sky, the *draugr* landed in front of their group. The force of the impact sent them all to their knees. The smell of death clung to the creature's scales. Swallowing the bile rising in her throat, Larissa reached around her waistband to grab the gun. Two hands on the grip, arms straight, just like she'd been taught, although she could not remember by whom.

She aimed for its chest, but the gun was heavier than she expected. She flinched as she pulled the trigger, and the gun kicked back in her hands before falling from her grip.

The *draugr* screeched as a bullet tore through the membrane of its wing. One of its claws swiped out, reaching for Larissa's leg. In the second before contact, Larissa noticed a shift of color in the bends of its wrists. In between the armored scales were lighter patches of dark gray. Anara had drawn blood from a similar patch on the *draugr*'s neck.

No sooner had this revelation occurred to her than Larissa was jerked upside down by the creature, hoisted by her ankle. She screamed as talons dug into her skin. Out of the corner of her eye, she saw Darien advance on the creature with a sword in his hand.

"The wrists!" she cried out.

The creature turned to face Darien, swinging Larissa with it. A sudden jerk caused Larissa to thump against the ground, gasping for the air that fled her lungs. The creature's shrieks bellowed in Larissa's ears as she fought the claw still holding her ankle captive. She reached for it, only to pull back in horror when she realized the claw was no longer attached to its owner.

The *draugr* screeched, waving its bloody stump of an arm before leaping into the sky, flying unevenly due to the hole in its wing. Larissa tugged at the claw around her ankle, bloodying her fingernails against its death grip.

Then Darien was there. Setting down his sword, he peeled back the amputated claw and tossed it aside.

Anara's eyes glowed like an owl's as a growl escaped her teeth. "Get to the trees!"

On swift feet, Anara led them to the treeline. They ran as the *draugr* swooped down with its remaining claws extended. Anara yanked Halla from its reach with only a second to spare. Then Anara was carrying Halla in her one good arm, her black hair flying in the wind. When the *draugr* dove again, Larissa threw herself to the ground. She rolled away from its outstretched claws, but unbearable pain clenched the muscles in her injured leg. She rose to her feet, took a step, and fell again. Ahead, Anara and Halla had made it to the tree line.

Strong arms hauled Larissa to her feet. "I've got you."

Darien wrapped Larissa's arm around his neck, supporting her with one hand as he gripped his sword with the other. They stumbled toward Anara's encouraging voice. They were nearly to the forest.

The *draugr* dropped from the sky, its legs extended, claws out. They clutched Darien's shoulders and ripped him away before Larissa knew what was happening. With one violent jerk, the monster hurled him across the field. Darien rolled hard several times before stopping, motionless.

"Darien!" Larissa screamed.

"Lara, behind you!" Halla emerged from the trees with wolf-Anara at her side.

Larissa dodged just as the *draugr* dove for another strike. She rolled, with far less grace than she'd hoped, onto something hard and sharp. Beside Halla, the wolf howled, a threat that demanded the *draugr*'s attention. The monster veered toward Anara, pouring its frustrations into a scream that vibrated Larissa's bones. Anara pounced, her extended claws catching on the *draugr*'s already damaged wing and tearing it from the monster's body. The creature's cry of despair mixed with Anara's howl of triumph in a discordant symphony.

"Larissa, get up!" Halla called out.

Attracted by Halla's cry and sensing her defenselessness, the *draugr* pivoted, advancing on the smaller girl. She tried to flee but stumbled over a rock and fell to the ground. She lifted her burned, blistered hands to protect her face.

A fire ignited in Larissa' veins at the sight that nearly blackened her vision. She would not let the monster take Halla too.

Get up.

The voice returned, but Larissa was no longer afraid. She embraced its strength, rising to her feet. She did not feel the pain of her injuries. A different kind of pain replaced it, a scorching kind of pain. Like the fire that consumed the bones of her home, this fire raged just under her skin, ready to consume her.

She lifted the gun, pointing it at the creature, but hesitated. She could hit Halla or Anara.

Dropping the gun, she scooped up Darien's heavy sword and ran toward her sister. Anara was snapping at the *draugr*'s tail, trying to regain its attention, but the monster's focus remained on the weakest of them all. Halla stumbled to her feet. Anara pounced again only for the *draugr* to swat her from the air.

Darien still hadn't moved. There was nowhere for Halla to run.

The creature bent over Halla, its sharp teeth bared in Halla's face. It did not see Larissa coming until a war cry seared through Larissa's throat.

The heat in her bones ripped through her body, racing down her arms and into her hands. Larissa found the light gray patches at the base of the creature's neck, where Anara had already broken through its defenses. Channeling all the fire in her body into the sword, she swung it back, over, and then forward in a high arch.

It came down just as the *draugr* turned its remaining colorless eye to meet Larissa's. The sword finished its downward arc, catching for only a moment on the scales before the blade sliced through skin and muscle. When the sword hit spine, a painful jolt ran up the blade and into Larissa's arms. The *draugr*'s head tilted sickeningly to the side. Both head and detached body crumpled to the ground, the head rolling to a stop at Larissa's feet.

The sword fell from her hands and into the tilled dirt. Larissa could not hold her nausea back any longer. She turned away from the creature's head and, falling to her hands and knees, heaved until her stomach was emptied.

As time passed, Larissa became aware of small hands rubbing her back. Halla.

At least Halla is safe, she reassured herself in between heaves. Larissa continued until only acid and bile remained. When it finally stopped, she spat the taste from her mouth.

All the while, Halla held back the hair that hung around her face. The fire inside Larissa died out, leaving her cold and weak, as if she had stepped out during a winter blizzard. Quiet reigned in the fields without the screeches from the *draugr*, the snapping of burning wood, or the screams of her sister.

Like the feeling of a nightmare she could not escape, Larissa kept waiting for the next attack. She crawled away from the blood of the *draugr* and from her own bile. She could hear Halla following her, asking her questions, but Larissa could not make sense of her words.

She collapsed, rolling to her back and gasping for air. Try as she might, she couldn't catch her breath. The pain in her lungs was worse than when she had been in the barn. Halla's face appeared above her. Those green eyes pinched with worry. Her mouth moved. Larissa could not hear anything, feel anything. Beyond Halla's right ear, Larissa watched the stars wink out of existence.

Then there was sweet nothingness.

Flames of Memory

Larissa

Larissa knew it wasn't real.

Even as Queen Stjarna, draped in a black veil of mourning, took her hand, Larissa knew she was dreaming. Standing on the shoreline, they watched a volley of flaming arrows soar toward the burial boat. The smells of burning oil and wood thickened the air. Queen Stjarna wiped the tears that gathered in her brilliant green eyes.

"Death is a normal part of life, my darling. All we can do is honor those who go before us."

NIⱢᚷNIⱢᚷNIⱢᚷNIⱢᚷNIⱢᚷ

"Lara! Why isn't she waking up?"

"She inhaled a lot of smoke and suffered a tremendous shock."

"I can't believe she killed that thing. I thought we were all dead. I take back every bad thought about that sword."

"She's stronger than she realizes. She'll be alright."

Larissa could hear the voices. She wanted to respond to them, but her tongue felt thick and her head even more so. The cool soil beckoned her back to that peaceful darkness.

Wake up, Larissa.

There was that voice again.

"Who are you?" Larissa reached for the source of the voice, only to be met with silence.

"She doesn't remember us. Did she hit her head?"

At the sound of Halla's frantic voice, Larissa forced her eyes to open. Three faces hung in her view beneath a still-dark sky. Clearly, she'd only been unconscious for a moment, yet her head reeled between dream and reality. Darien and Anara smiled in relief, whereas Halla still stared at her with pinched eyes.

Larissa raised her hand to tug on the burned remnants of Halla's braid. "I remember you just fine. *I'm* fine."

"You've got more than a couple of bumps and bruises," Darien objected.

Larissa could feel them. The burns stung, and the large cut on her face and neck throbbed with pain. Examining Darien, Larissa saw he was no better off. Scrapes and bruises darkened much of his exposed olive skin, and he held his left side to support what were probably cracked ribs.

He'd come for them.

Warmth grew in Larissa's stomach at the thought, comforting and unsettling all at the same time. Darien had helped save Halla twice. Did he know the worth of his actions? Halla was her heart, and by proxy, he had saved it. She could never repay that debt.

Anara coughed, dragging Larissa's attention away from Darien. "We have to go. Someone will have noticed the smoke by now."

"Larissa needs medical attention. She can't go anywhere like this," Darien argued. He gestured to Anara. "Look at us. None of us can."

Anara's left shoulder hung at an unnatural angle. Halla's face and arms bore patches of burned skin, particularly her blistered hands. Larissa's cheek and neck were still covered in blood. Darien's breath hitched with every move.

Anara grimaced at the lot of them and rose to her feet, her left arm swinging loose at her side. With her right hand, she grasped her left wrist, held the arm straight out, and yanked forward until there was a loud and abrupt pop. Anara's head dipped as she hissed through bared teeth.

Darien's eyes narrowed. "I don't think that will work for the rest of us."

Anara exhaled, raising her head. "I'm aware. I'll be back. Wait here."

He flung up his arms, looking around. "Where would we go?"

Anara turned, her body shifting. She landed on four paws and bounded across the field, disappearing back into the trees. Larissa watched her, her own consciousness at war within her.

They're real, she thought. *Pappa's stories are real.* But then her thoughts turned to Pappa and Mamma, and Larissa forced her mind to think of Anara instead. Larissa didn't trust her—*couldn't* trust her. The Rubinian could change her appearance at will, yet Larissa couldn't deny the truth. As assuredly as she owed Darien, Larissa also owed Anara a debt for Halla's life, and she would never be free of her duty until her debts were repaid.

Stifled sobs drew Larissa's attention from the trees. Tears ran unchecked down Halla's cheeks, her freckles shimmering underneath.

Larissa struggled to sit, gasping at the pain every movement caused. Darien supported her from behind, prompting a new wave of gratitude. Larissa reached for her sister. "Halla—"

"I thought you were going to die too," she croaked.

Pappa's and Mamma's faces, twisted in death, flashed before Larissa's eyes. Swallowing the pain, she took her sister's hand in her own. "I'm right here, Halla. I'm not going to die."

"It's my fault."

Larissa brushed back Halla's hair, tucking it behind her ears. "It's not your fault. The *draugr* killed them, not you."

"It killed them because of me!" Halla's voice broke. "I came home, Larissa. *You* told me that it was safe. When I got here, there was a sentry outside the house. She shouted at Mamma and Pappa. I knew I should run and hide, but I was so scared that she would kill them for hiding me. I ran out and told her to take me, to just leave them alone. Then she *sniffed* me, Lara, like a dog! She said she was sent for me.

"Then she turned into that monster. Pappa told me to run. I didn't want to leave them, Lara, but he told me to go. I ran, and I grabbed the gun from the barn, but I was so scared. I could hear the fighting. I could hear the *draugr* screeching and then Mamma screaming."

Darien's eyes filled with sorrow as he stared at Larissa over Halla's head. Larissa knew then that he had hoped the same thing that she had, that Halla hadn't been present for their parents' death. How very wrong they both had been.

Sobs punctuated Halla's words. "It killed Pappa first; I could hear Mamma crying. Then I didn't hear anything anymore. It wasn't until I smelled the smoke that I heard Onkel Tucker crying out, but then he was gone too. And it's because of me. It's because I came home!"

Careful to avoid the burns, Larissa cupped her sister's face in her hands with as much gentleness as she could muster. "Halla, you listen to me. This is not your fault. You did nothing wrong."

"But they're dead, aren't they?"

"Yes." Larissa knew better than to hesitate, to offer that hope.

It seemed impossible that Halla's tears could flow more quickly, and yet they did. "Why did you tell me to come home?"

"That would be my fault."

Anara returned, looking surprisingly healthy. Her arm seemed to be working at full capacity, and even her bruises had lightened. She carried two large bags over her back, dumping one at her own feet and the other next to Darien. "I shifted into looking like Larissa. I sent you home so that I could speak with your sister alone."

"You tricked me?"

Anara rummaged through the bag, a sheet of black hair covering her face. "Yes. It was a mistake."

"A mistake?" Larissa's voice was laced with venom. "Our parents are dead because of you."

"Your parents are dead because of the *draugr*." Anara's words were calm even as her hands paused in their search. "What would have happened if you had gone back with Halla? If I hadn't intervened? Do you think the *draugr* wouldn't have killed you all?"

"You could have warned us!" Larissa clenched her hands. Even in her weakened state, she couldn't help imaging how it would feel to hit Anara, to make her share this pain.

As if sensing her thoughts, Anara stopped searching the bag, meeting Larissa's glare. "You think I knew? If I'd known the *draugr* was here, I never would've sent Halla back!" A growl laced Anara's voice. "If you think I'd ever put you or Halla in danger, you really don't remember anything."

Larissa clenched her fist. "What is that supposed to mean?"

Digging through her bag with savage efficiency, Anara removed a tiny glass bottle filled with dark emerald liquid. She shook it, then unscrewed the lid to reveal a dropper attached to the cap. "We don't have time for this. Someone will see the smoke eventually and come to investigate. Stick out your tongues."

Darien shrugged, and Halla complied. Larissa eyed the mixture. "What is that?"

"It'll take away the pain. Please, Larissa, trust me."

Trust me. Anara had said that to her before. If she'd trusted Anara then, would it have changed anything? If she had believed Pappa's stories, would she still have a father?

She cut off those thoughts. If she let them run their course, they would consume her. Larissa stuck out her tongue. Anara squeezed the dropper over each of their mouths. The drop exploded across Larissa's taste buds, sharp and fresh, causing goosebumps to rise on her skin. In the next moment, she bent over, clutching her stomach at the sudden pain. It felt as if her body were shedding the skin and regrowing a new layer all at once. As suddenly as the pain had appeared, it vanished.

"What was that?" Darien demanded, unraveling from his own hunched position.

"The blisters are gone!" Halla turned over her hands, examining the smooth skin. Hesitantly, Darien stretched his arm over his head and rubbed his once injured side. Larissa probed the gash that stretched across her neck and face. As dried blood flaked to the ground, she could feel the raised scar underneath.

"It's from the forests of the Smaragd commonwealth. In the past, it was extracted from a plant that those of Ancestral Blood could distill into this form." Anara recapped the emerald liquid, ensuring it was well sealed. "This is the last bottle I have. Time to go. Darien, I retrieved your bag from the clearing. Larissa, Halla, I'm sorry; I don't think there is anything salvageable here. We'll find you new clothes somewhere."

Glancing down, Larissa was shocked to find her pale skin peeking through the rips in her clothing. She shivered as the breeze blew over the exposed skin, then crossed her arms over her chest defensively. A thought occurred.

"Helga," Larissa said.

Darien raised an eyebrow. "Anara, does that liquid cause hallucinations? Larissa might be having one."

"Helga's our truck," Halla explained, her voice soft with exhaustion.

"Right," Larissa said. "Pappa and Mamma were stocking it for our family to leave. If it escaped the fire, we can use it. It'll have supplies."

Anara nodded, helping Halla to rise. Larissa stumbled to her feet, caught only by a hand under her arm.

"Whoa there, I've got you." Darien steadied her, then let her go, leaving her skin bereft of the warmth from his hand. Even as her heart and mind numbed themselves against her harsh reality, a twinge of gratitude leaked through. Ignoring Anara's calculating gaze, Larissa led the way across the trampled fields, wrapping an arm around Halla's shoulders. Just short of the drive, they stopped.

The barn and farmhouse burned on, hissing and spitting out embers. Sitting on the drive, Helga had escaped damage, although she was covered in an inch of ash. As she approached, Larissa could see the garden beside the house and the shapes lying within it. She knew the moment Halla saw them too. Her sister's hand flew to her mouth to stifle rising sobs at the sight of Pappa's and Mamma's bodies.

Larissa squeezed Halla's shoulders even as her own face remained dry. "We have to give them a proper burial."

Anara hesitated. "We don't have time. I'm sorry, but—"

"I don't care."

Anara opened her mouth to argue when Darien shook his head at her. She sighed. "Quickly then."

Unwrapping herself from Halla, Larissa propelled herself back toward her parents' bodies. She could not stand to see their open, empty eyes staring at the sky. She leaned down and pressed their eyes closed. They did not look like they were sleeping, as she had so often heard death described. There was too much pain written on their bodies for that to be true, but closing their eyes was a step in the right direction.

"A burning burial?" Darien asked, kneeling beside her.

Larissa nodded, her throat and eyes dry. "It's what they would have wanted."

Halla fell to her knees beside them, weeping as they worked, but Larissa could not weep. Not yet. Halla needed her to be strong; Halla needed her to keep it together. An echo pulsed through the hollow space in her chest with every breath she took, and she realized she couldn't cry even if she felt free to do so. It was as if the fire itself had burned her tears away, leaving her painfully empty.

Darien and Anara scoured the area for dry branches and wood. Making quick work of it, they carried the small bundles back in their arms. Larissa steeled herself to rearrange her parents' bodies so that they were lying side-by-side, with one arm strewn over their chests. Their opposite hands Larissa left by their sides so that she could intertwine their fingers. Darien, Anara, and Halla arranged the wood around the bodies to form two oval shapes, like ships. One for each of them to sail their souls into the afterlife. They tucked the wood in close around their frames and under their sides, but left it open where Pappa's hand covered Mamma's.

They would face the halls of Helheim together.

As she surveyed her work, Larissa's eyes caught a flash of light. Peering at Mamma, Larissa located the shimmer from her closed hand. In the light of the nearby fire, Larissa could just make out the edge of a ring.

Take it.

Larissa recoiled from the voice in her mind. This was too private a moment for her to share.

Take it. She wanted you to have it.

How would you know? she shot back. Whether the voice was her own sanity fragmenting or the gods themselves, she didn't know, and, at that moment, Larissa didn't care.

Swallowing her discomfort, Larissa gently pinched the ring and pulled it from her mother's hand, careful not to touch her skin. The thin golden band bore a single pearl, large and luminescent. It was the pearl that reflected the fire's light.

Why did Mamma have this? Where had she gotten it? Larissa shook her head, pocketing the ring. None of that mattered, not in that moment.

Halla's sobs softened from exhaustion. Darien blinked his eyes rapidly as Anara pulled something from her bag, anointing Pappa's and Mamma's bodies. Larissa walked to the house and yanked off a piece of charred wood from the porch. Dipping it into a nearby flame to reignite it, Larissa walked back to her parents and dropped the wood onto the surrounding piles of sticks. Taking their own scraps of wood, the others followed her example until the fire spread, enveloping Pappa and Mamma within the smoke.

Listening to the crackling flames and Halla's whimpers, Larissa stood apart from the pain she could not feel. Neither the heat of the rising fire nor the sorrow marinating in her own heart could touch her. She only felt the cold.

Sensing Anara's impatience, Larissa found the words she needed. "Hel welcomes all into her halls, but Pappa deserves a place in Valhöll. If there is any justice, Mamma will take her seat at the right hand of the Valkyrie Sigrún. They died warriors' deaths, protecting those they love, never leaving each other, and nothing could be more honorable than that."

Her throat closed again. There was so much more she wanted to say.

Anara laid her hand on Larissa's shoulder. "The sun will rise soon. We need to leave."

"What about Onkel?" Halla croaked through her tears.

Tucker. Larissa's eyes scanned the field, knowing she wouldn't be able to spot Tucker's body from where they sat or how much of his body they could salvage. She could still hear the crack his body had made under the *draugr*'s weight.

Anara's eyes were apologetic, yet unyielding. "There's no time, unless we want to join him in the flames."

Larissa nodded, but Halla remained kneeling in the soil. With firm but gentle hands, Larissa lifted Halla to her feet. For once, Larissa did not know what to say to help her sister. Sometimes nothing could be said. Pressing Halla's head against her shoulder, she guided her away from the pyre.

Halla wobbled, leaning heavily on Larissa. They'd almost made it to the truck when Halla's legs gave out. She collapsed in Larissa's arms, her head lolling to one side.

"Halla!"

Anara's fingers lifted Halla's chin. "She's fine, just passed out. It's probably for the best. Darien, get Halla in the truck; I'll drive."

With gentle hands, Darien lifted Halla from Larissa's arms. He wasn't a large man, but Halla looked so tiny curled up against his chest. He laid her in the passenger seat as Anara adjusted her head and buckled her in. Larissa knew she should be the one taking care of Halla, but she could only watch. Anara spoke to Darien before walking around the front of the car and starting the engine with the keys she found on the dash. Darien closed the passenger door and approached where Larissa stood by the tailgate.

"You ready?"

Nodding, Larissa moved to the back of the truck. As she unlatched the gate, she was struck by the memory of their last encounter. Could it only have been a week ago that they had met at the Wall? Now she was leaving her entire world behind and going with him. How had it come to this?

She lifted herself up to the bed, pushing aside the bags stored there earlier by Pappa and Mamma. They would have water and food, as well as new clothes. The large winter jacket that Pappa had thrown to Tucker was still on top of the boxes. Larissa grabbed it, wrapping it around her body.

Beneath the odor of smoke, it still smelled like home.

Her eyes burned but remained dry as she sat against the side wall of the truck. Latching the gate as he climbed in, Darien sat opposite her. Larissa was hardly aware of his presence as she closed her eyes and breathed in again and again, as if oxygen could erase the horrors of the evening. If only her family had left earlier; if only Anara had never sent Halla home. Larissa could burn in the "if onlys."

Halla said the *draugr* had been sent for her, but why? This was more than just hunting down second-borns.

The idling engine shook Helga's frame. Larissa's fingers ran over the cold grooves in the truck bed. Faithful Helga would get them where they needed to go. But where was that?

The rumble of wheels reverberated under the bed. Larissa stole a glance at Dal's Berry Farm, her sanctuary, her home. The fire from her parents' burial grew. The garden burned and the flames danced as they caught on the bushes of the nearby fields. Would it burn everything? By the time someone came, would nothing but the ashes of her life remain?

The first touches of sunlight chased away the stars. Their family pig squealed as it ran out from the bushes, chasing after the truck, but quickly fell back in the distance, unable to keep pace.

Shivering in the heavy jacket, Larissa sank into numb oblivion.

A Connection

Darien

Darien shielded his eyes against the rising sun. Midmorning air whipped through open slats of the truck bed's walls. He rummaged through his bag. Darien's hands paused in delight as he touched the worn black leather. Aagen had packed Darien's favorite jacket.

Although he winced from the pain caused by pulling his arms through the sleeves, he smiled at the familiar fit of the leather. Whatever Anara gave them had healed most of his damage, but his ribs were sore and protested any abrupt movement. Unfortunately, there were nothing but abrupt movements in the back of the truck as it wound down dirt roads. Darien pulled another shirt from the bag, stuffing it under his jacket to pad his ribs before settling back down and ducking his head from the beams of the sun. As though riding the sun's light, Aagen's words came back to him.

Two horses, Árvakr and Alsviðr, are guided by Svalinn. They pull Sól across the sky, giving light to the world. In the winter, Árvakr and Alsviðr run faster out of fear that the wolves Skoll and Hati will devour them along with the sun.

But the memory was distorted, and another voice that Darien could not remember intertwined with Aagen's. The vision of the man with dark hair and bright eyes flashed in his mind once again.

As she had so often, Larissa caught his gaze, sitting in the same position she had taken hours ago with knees drawn into her chest and head cradled in her crossed arms. She looked as though she were sleeping, but Darien could see the tight strain of her shoulders.

The thick scar left by the *draugr*'s talon was barely visible behind strands of white hair still streaked with blood. Anara's medicine had only healed the wound, not erased it. Darien wasn't sure if he could ever look at it without feeling the heat of the flames and hearing Larissa's cries of anguish when she thought she'd lost Halla. It wasn't fair that she would have such a constant reminder of all she had survived and all she had lost.

Darien hissed as the truck struck another pothole. Larissa rolled with it, absorbing the impact, hardly shifting from her spot. Either she had incredible self-control, or she was lost in the darkness of grief. The fire in Larissa's eyes when she'd saved Halla had been extinguished, and Darien didn't know how long it would take to rekindle. He just wanted to be there when it did.

"You're staring." Those golden eyes bore into his own, glazed over and unfocused. Her stare was better than her silence.

"How are you?" Darien clenched his jaw, cursing his own stupidity. "I meant, obviously, you're not great. Do you need anything?"

Boxes of water, food, and supplies surrounded them. They were both splattered with blood, and their clothes were a mess. Surely, there was something he could offer, something he could do to help. Something to take away his uselessness as Larissa stared through him. Darien waited, wondering if he should repeat his question. When she spoke, her words were mumbled under a sigh.

"How did we end up here?"

"If you mean how did our existence in this world come to be," Darien answered, his mind grasping at the first thing he could think of, "my father, Aagen, said mankind was formed from ash trees. If you're asking how I ended up in this truck, I decided to rescue a girl who didn't want my help, crashed my truck, was paralyzed by a little girl who turned out not to be a little girl, and followed my hallucinations to your farm where I was attacked by a monster."

Larissa's brows pinched together. "Do you know you're babbling?"

"I do."

Larissa nodded, but already her eyes were glossing over. He had to keep her talking, anything to keep her from falling into despondency once again. "How do you know Anara?"

"I don't. Not really. Halla befriended her a couple days ago, but she showed up again last night." Larissa paused. "She looked like me."

Darien nodded. "She was a child when I first met her."

"She's a shifter, a Rubinian."

Darien nearly pointed out the obvious but stopped at Larissa's tone. They both knew Anara was a shapeshifter, but the look on Larissa's face revealed her unspoken fears. If Anara was from

Rubin, the land that most fully supported the Empress, why was she helping them?

"We can trust her." To his surprise, Darien believed his words the moment he spoke them. "We wouldn't have survived the *draugr* without her."

Larissa looked away. "Not all of us did."

Darien didn't know what to say. *I'm sorry for your loss?* What good would those empty words do? Instead he reached out, his fingers brushing the top of her hand. "You saved Halla. That's what your parents would have wanted."

Larissa swallowed, her hand tightening into a fist, but the expression in her eyes was dead. "I should have listened. I think Pappa knew something was coming. He kept telling us stories about the Empress and the *draugr*, but I didn't think they were real. We were going to leave the farm; he said there were people who could help us. I should have listened to him."

"You couldn't have known—"

"Yes, I could have," she snapped, withdrawing her hand from his. Tears spilled over her cheeks, but she made no move to wipe them. "I just had to listen."

Helga's motor whined underneath them. Darien thought of Larissa's parents and of the body he had found in the field. There hadn't been time to bury the field hand. He didn't even remember what Halla had called him. Would his soul ever find rest? Darien sent up a prayer that the Norn would guide his soul.

"The Norn don't always reveal our fate," Darien murmured. It was something Aagen often said to him.

Larissa sniffed, rubbing her hands against her eyes. "I didn't believe in the Norn, or any of the gods, not really, but now…"

Larissa let the sentence hang in the air. Darien knew what she meant. He'd always believed in an abstract sort of way, but his understanding of the world had expanded in just one night. If the *draugr* were roaming Evrópa, were the gods doing the same?

Larissa shook her head. "Either way, I'm not holding my breath for their help."

A shiver ran over Larissa's body, drawing Darien's eyes and mind back to the present. He scooted toward a box where a blanket lay on top. Careful of the truck's bouncing, he moved to sit next to Larissa and wrapped the blanket around her, tucking it behind her shoulders. Darien's fingers paused when a lock of white hair brushed against his bruised knuckles.

"Why did you come for us, Darien?" Larissa asked.

Startled, he snatched his hands back. But if Larissa noticed the way his hands had lingered, she didn't show it. "Anara told me you needed help."

"There aren't any farms close enough for you to arrive in time, which means you were already on your way. Why?"

Darien settled next to her, extending his legs alongside her own. How could he say this without sounding crazy? "Anara found me the day I met you and Halla. She touched my face, and it felt like..." He paused, trying to think of the right way to say it.

"Like a shock from a cut wire?"

Surprise filled his face. "How did you know that?"

"Finish your story."

He considered pushing her for the answer, but her tears had finally dried. His story, at the very least, could offer a distraction from her grief. "Ever since then, I've been seeing things. I thought they were hallucinations, but Aagen said they might be memories."

"Your father?"

"Not technically."

Larissa stared in silence.

Darien picked at the frayed edge of his jacket. "Aagen found me abandoned in his orchard when I was a toddler, and I've pretended to be his son ever since. Or at least, that's what I thought. Turns out everything about my childhood was a lie." Darien cracked his knuckles one finger at a time. "I have memories of growing up in that orchard, learning how to cultivate the land. In my mind, I have lived with him for most of my life. Aagen says I have only been with him for a little over a year."

The surprise on Larissa's face matched Darien's own initial shock. She shook her head. "But you have memories of growing up there."

"Aagen thinks they are false memories, planted there by whoever brought me to him. I've had enough visions, or memories, that I'm inclined to believe him."

Darien stopped, hesitant to share about his supposed royal birth. He still didn't understand that one himself. Besides, he didn't want Larissa thinking he was trying to impress her.

"Why would someone bring you to him?" Larissa asked. "Who *could* do that?"

Darien shrugged, instantly regretting the decision as his ribs protested. "Aagen said the woman who brought me first appeared to him before the Empress took over, then again a year ago when she brought me to him. He never got her name. He said she had hair the color of starlight and eyes as green as our apples."

Larissa's fingers knotted together in her lap. "That's not possible."

"Tell me about it, but these dreams and visions drove me to your farm." Darien paused, but he knew he had to be honest. "I saw you and Halla in my dreams. I don't know how, I just knew that I needed to find you. I wasn't far from your farm when Anara found me, and, well, you know what happened next."

Larissa nodded, staring blankly ahead. Darien brushed back the loose curls from his eyes, wishing she would say something. Did she think he was insane now? It was probably a good thing he hadn't mentioned the prince thing. He leaned back, at a loss for words for once in his life.

"Thank you," Larissa said.

When Darien glanced over, Larissa was staring at him. To his surprise, the hint of a smile grew beneath those golden eyes. "For what?"

"Following whatever instinct led you to our farm. We would have died if you and Anara hadn't come when you did. You've saved Halla twice."

"You're the one who rescued Halla from the barn," Darien said. "You ran into those flames without a moment's hesitation. You're either exceptionally brave or stupid."

"Maybe a little of both," she muttered, her slight smile sliding from her face before Darien had the chance to appreciate it. "I've seen her too. The woman Aagen said he met."

"You have? Where?"

"In my dreams." She looked up, grimacing as she rolled her eyes. "I know, it sounds stupid."

"No, it doesn't," Darien hurried to say, turning his body to face her. Their knees touched. "After everything we've been through, it doesn't sound stupid at all. Obviously there's more happening than we know. When did you start dreaming about her?"

"After Produce Day, my Pappa told us the story about the Kings and Queens of Old. He said the royals were descended from an Ancestral Bloodline that could practice the power of the gods. He called it *galdr*. When the Empress took over, she killed them all except for some Princess from Perle. Supposedly, the Norn prophesied to the Perle Queen that her daughter could overthrow the Empress. That woman you're describing sounds like Queen Stjarna. At least, that's how I've been imagining her in my dreams."

Darien didn't know what to say. Not only because he wasn't sure where this was going, but because Larissa had never said so much to him at one time before, and she clearly wasn't finished.

"What if Queen Stjarna is the one who brought you to Aagen? What if she also hid her daughter at the same time she was hiding you?" Larissa's voice grew more agitated. "It sounds impossible, but what if I was dreaming of the past?"

"Aagen said that this woman brought me to him only a year ago," Darien said. "Even if the Princess did survive, Queen Stjarna's body was burned inside the palace when the Empress took over decades ago."

Larissa shrugged, her eyes cloudy as she gnawed at her lip.

Darien searched Larissa's face. "There's something you're not saying."

"It's just...Queen Stjarna's eyes. They remind me of Halla's."

The implication sunk in. "You think Halla is the lost Perle Princess? The one that has been missing for over fifty years? You do realize that sounds a bit—"

"Insane?" Larissa threw up her hands. "I know. Their eyes aren't exactly the same, but they're similar. And when that *draugr* saw Halla, it said that she was the one they'd been looking for, remember? Pappa told us that those of Ancestral Blood lived longer than everyone else because of the magic in their veins. Someone who had lived sixty years would still be relatively young, right? We don't know how young the Princess was when she vanished. We don't know how old she would look today."

Darien had to admit that, despite Larissa's assumptions about Ancestral Blood, it was a convincing argument. "You think Halla's been alive for over fifty years? Wouldn't she know who she is?"

"You didn't know you were anyone else."

"Point taken."

Larissa rubbed her eyes so fiercely that Darien worried she might gouge them out. "I don't understand why I keep seeing Queen Stjarna in my dreams if I'm not supposed to do something about it. She keeps telling me that I need to wake someone up, but what does that even mean?"

"Wait," Darien chased after a memory that lay at the tip of his tongue. "Anara visited me before at the orchard. She said I needed to wake up. What if 'waking up' just means remembering who I was before I was brought to Aagen?"

"So you think the Perle Princess doesn't remember who she is either?"

"She might not. She might be like me, believing whatever false memories have been given to her."

"But if that's the case, why were you chosen, Darien?"

He paused. "What do you mean?"

"Someone thought you were special enough to hide. If we're right, the same people who hid the Perle Princess hid you too." Larissa shifted, unable to meet his eyes. "So my question is, who are you?"

It was the question Darien had been hoping to avoid. "I don't know."

"Do you remember anything about your past yet?"

"A little. I've been distracted, what with battling a monster from Hel and all."

"Technically, the *draugr* came from Rubin, not Hel."

Darien paused, trying to determine if she was being sarcastic on purpose.

"Why don't you try now?" Larissa asked.

For the first time since Aagen had given it to him, Darien looked at the ring on his hand. He rubbed his thumb over the large square-cut sapphire. Ever since he had put it on, it had been pulling on his mind, as if it could help him unlock the secrets of his memories. Yet for all his love of stories, he'd put it off. He'd been rushing to save Larissa, he told himself, but maybe that was an excuse. Maybe he was worried that learning about his past would erase what he remembered about Aagen.

"Please, Darien." The intensity in Larissa's voice was enough to shake Darien from his thoughts. "Your memories might tell us if Halla is actually the lost Princess. I need to know what I'm protecting her from. She's all I have left."

Darien couldn't have refused her if he wanted to. Truth be told, he wanted to know. He needed to know. He fiddled with the ring on his finger, its deep blue stone glinting in the sunbeams. Larissa leaned toward him and reached out a hand to cover one of his own, her golden eyes holding his, as clear and bright as the sun itself. An electric current ran over her fingers, shocking Darien's skin.

Then everything changed.

Revelations

Darien

Sand shifted beneath Darien's feet as he stood on the shore. On the horizon, the sun sank past the rippling waves. He was no longer in the back of the bouncing blue pickup truck. In the distance loomed the silhouette of a large palace built into the cliffs.

Darien still wore the same ripped and bloodied clothes as before, but his body was free from the pain. He glanced to his right to share his confusion with Larissa.

She had vanished. Only the crash of the waves accompanied him.

A young man approached from farther down the beach. Darien stared. It was one thing to hallucinate himself as a child; it was another thing entirely to see himself as he was. For the other young man was Darien himself, exactly his height and build. His hair was a bit longer than Darien's, and his clothing was far different, but his face could have been a mirror. Other-Darien wore a dark blue suit with silver buttons running down the front. On the right breast pocket was a square cut symbol of a hooked rune embroidered across the fabric. A sword hung at other-Darien's hip. His dark curly hair wafted in the sea breeze.

This was not a hallucination, but a memory. Darien could taste the salty air and feel the suffocating tightness of that jacket.

Other-Darien did not appear to notice him. He paced across the sand, oblivious or uncaring to Darien's presence, as he kicked up sand on his pants. Every so often, he would pause and glance at a watch on his wrist only to resume his pacing a moment later.

"What in the name of Óðinn's right eye are you doing out here, Darien?"

Both Dariens' heads turned at the sound of the newcomer.

The stubborn little boy from before was older, taller, and broader at his shoulders. The blond in his hair had darkened, but it was Aeron. He was dressed similarly to his brother, if not with more refinement. His suit was cut to the exact shape of his shoulders and chest. The rune of Safír was etched onto his breast pocket, but his buttons were golden.

The brothers clasped hands and greeted each other in obvious comradery. Jealousy and sorrow battled within Darien at the sight.

"Óðinn would understand," other-Darien said, grinning. "I was claustrophobic waiting for them inside. They should have been back by now."

Aeron ruffled his younger brother's curls. "You worry like old Grímnir frets over his ravens. They'll be fine, but I won't be if you make me greet these guests all by myself."

Other-Darien struggled to tame his hair. "As heir to the throne, that particular honor belongs to you, allowing me to worry in peace."

Heir to the throne, *thought Darien. The words summoned other memories of his father and mother, the King and Queen of Safír. They taught their sons the importance of their Ancestral Bloodline.*

It would be Aeron's duty, as heir to the throne, to uphold the peace. That made Darien—

"Why Prince Darien," Aeron placed a hand on his chest and leaned back as though stunned, his voice serious and lofty, although the edge of his mouth twitched. "Do you mean you won't be the first to greet the lovely Perle Princess upon her arrival? Whatever will she do without her escort?"

Other-Darien paused in flattening his hair. "You really don't mind if I escort her this evening? When we were kids—"

"That's all in the past." Aeron turned from his brother with an easy stride, but Darien saw the flash of jealousy in Aeron's eyes. "As first-born, it is my duty to marry within our kingdom to keep our galdr strong. Even as a second-born, you should not let your emotions run away with you. She's not a Safirian; there's no future there."

"I don't know what you mean."

"Darien, I'm serious." Aeron turned back, laying a hand on his brother's shoulder. "People have noticed. They're all wondering who she is, this daughter of Perlian aristocrats who shows up to every gathering alone and has claimed the heart of a Safirian Prince. It makes people curious. It could be dangerous if anyone realized who she is. For her sake and yours, you should distance yourself."

Other-Darien stiffened. "I'm well-aware of the danger, Aeron."

"I say this because I care about you—both of you. I don't want to see either of you hurt. It's better to accept the reality of the situation now."

"Your Majesties!"

The brothers turned to face the arriving guard, who looked as though he had been running. The holster that carried the gun on his hip was unclasped. Both Aeron and other-Darien touched the hilts of their swords, their nearly identical sapphire rings glinting against the steel. Gray fog crept over the sand, rising up around their knees.

"What is it?" Aeron barked. "What happened?"

"A messenger just arrived with word from your parents," the guard said, one hand on his chest as he caught his breath. "Queen Shiko attacked the other monarchs at the coronation. Your parents escaped. They are strategizing with the other monarchs and will return shortly. Prince Aeron, they have instructed that you ready our soldiers for their arrival. We already turned away the citizens for tonight's celebration, but there is one guest who will not leave. She claims to be an aristocrat from Perle and demands to speak with Prince Darien."

The other-Darien's face drained of color. His voice echoed in Darien's ears. "I'll see to her."

Then the gray fog rose to consume them all.

Darien stood in the nothingness, his mind swirling with questions. The ring on his finger warmed. Etched into its surface was the same hooked rune he had seen on Aeron's and other-Darien's jackets. The name of the rune came back to him. Laguz. The Safirian rune.

As he let his eyes focus on the rune, color bled into the gray fog around him. Memories from a thousand different moments played out around him. Darien's fingers twitched at his sides. If he could just reach out and grab one, he knew he would be flung into the moment. But which one to choose?

It all depended on what he needed to know.

Who was he? Aeron had made the answer to that question clear. He was Prince Darien of Safir, or at least, he had been. Those events, the fall of the kingdoms, had happened decades ago. How could Darien have been part of them? Those of Ancestral Blood aged slowly because of their inherent galdr, *but Darien knew his body. He had not lived for half a century,* galdr *or no* galdr.

Where had he been for all of those years? Why could he not remember the past decades, even as other memories returned?

Desperate for answers, any answers, Darien flung out his hand into the moving array of images, clasping onto the nearest one.

A voice called out from the mist. "Son, with our nation on the brink of war, it is time you start taking your responsibilities seriously."

The gray fog faded to reveal other-Dairen standing at the foot of a long table strewn with maps and books. At the head of the table, a larger man leaned forward, bracing his hands against the wood. His eyes were hard and glossed over, his mouth set in an unyielding line as he glared at his son.

Other-Darien met his father's glare with one of his own. "I do take my responsibilities seriously."

"With Aeron heading to Smaragd, I can't have you running off to Perle. We need you here."

"Lovisa needs me."

The name clicked. The warmth in his stomach and the rush in his veins told Darien two things. One, that Lovisa was the Princess of Perle. Two, that he had loved her.

But the warmth of her name was doused by the way Darien's father, his real father, ground his teeth at his son's answer. "Our nation is more important than your infatuation, Darien."

Other-Darien clenched his hands and worked his jaw before replying. "Queen Stjarna believes that hiding Lovisa, Anara, and I is the best option until we learn how to defeat Shiko. Aeron should have come with us, not gone off to Smaragd on his own."

"And that's what you want? To hide?"

As if in response to Darien's discomfort, the scene before him was already fading. The gray fog returned, blurring out his father's anger. Unbidden, Aagen's understanding gaze and his blessing played in Darien's mind in stark contrast to his father's disappointed frustration. Pushing aside the unsettling thoughts, Darien's mind returned to the bright spot of the memory that warmed his very core.

Lovisa.

Surrounded again by the fog, Darien wrestled with his thoughts. The yearning he felt for Lovisa was palpable, burning in his hands and aching in the back of his throat. Yet his mind strayed to Larissa's golden eyes. Focusing on the rune of his ring, Darien called back the dizzying array of memories that swirled around him. As if reading his mind, the images all featured one person.

Lovisa.

Darien reached for another image and stepped out of the fog onto a lakeshore. The full moon threw its light on the cresting of the waves. The other-Darien was there too, pacing again. He'd abandoned his dress clothes for dark pants and a black leather jacket, clearly assisting him in going unnoticed in the shadows of the night.

"Darien," said a soft feminine voice.

It came from behind him, but before Darien could turn to look, the girl ran past so quickly that all he caught was a blur of starlight white hair. She threw herself into the arms of other-Darien, whose feet sank into the sand as he steadied them both.

Darien's heart knew her before his mind could catch up.

Princess Lovisa of Perle.

Darien's heart thumped erratically against his ribs. Other-Darien cupped the back of the Princess' head, his fingers absent-mindedly playing with the loose hair as he released her from the embrace. Darien couldn't help but wonder if it was as soft as Larissa's.

"It's okay, I've got you," other-Darien said. His voice took on a bitter twist. "Rubin betrayed us."

"Did you hear?" Lovisa whispered, burying her head in other-Darien's chest. "Shiko executed the royal family of Smaragd, even after they surrendered."

Other-Darien's fingers stilled. "I heard."

"Do you think Kiah could have survived?"

"I don't know."

The memories of this moment came back more strongly than any of the previous. Darien remembered thinking that Kiah, Princess of Smaragd, had most likely been killed along with her unborn child, but not having the heart to tell Lovisa. As if drawn into other-Darien's mind and emotions, he moved closer.

"Have you heard anything from Aeron?" Lovisa asked.

Aeron had gone to give aid to the Smaragd kingdom. That was before they had realized Smaragd had no desire to fight. Aeron had departed for a lost cause. Weeks had passed with no word from Aeron or his men. Upon hearing the news, his father's dark moods had only grown worse.

Other-Darien cleared his throat. "No."

The girl lifted her head, but Darien could only see the back of her hair, laced with braids. "Anara is stuck in the middle of Rubin's civil war, Aeron is missing, and Smaragd has fallen. I catch my mother staring at me all the time. My father worries about our people. Shiko hasn't even reached our borders, and I feel like we've already lost."

"This isn't like you. Look at me. What's going on?"

Darien still couldn't make out Lovisa's face. Her shoulders bunched up tightly against her neck. There was something familiar about that posture.

"Will you leave me too?" she whispered.

"No." Other-Darien's hands grasped hers. "No, I swear on the Norn, I will never leave you."

"Don't swear when you might not have a choice." She paused, then flung herself into her next words. "My mother is planning something, Dar. She won't talk about it, but I don't know if we'll have a choice in what happens next."

"Nothing can separate us."

The fog returned, covering the sand. Darien was losing his grasp on the memory. He was so close; he needed to know. He sprang forward, meaning only to face the Princess himself, to remember her face, but found himself standing exactly where other-Darien had stood. He had taken over his counterpart's body; he knew it by the feel of Lovisa's soft hands in his.

The faint scent of cherries washed over him, stirring the blood in his veins. He looked into the Princess' face, struck dumb by its familiarity, by the small nose set just beneath a pair of bright eyes, as golden as the blazing sun.

ᚺᛁᛞᚱᛊᚺᛁᛞᚱᛊᚺᛁᛞᚱᛊᚺᛁᛞᚱᛊᚺᛁᛞᚱᛊ

"Darien, are you alright?"

Awake from his vision, Darien stared into the same golden eyes as before, now filled with confusion and fear. Why was he lying in the bed of the truck? Who was he? Field hand or prince? The two sets of memories, of separate lives, battled in his brain for dominance. In the end, the facade was swept aside by truth.

He remembered the promise he had made to Lovisa. The promise he had broken.

"Darien?"

It was *her* voice. How could he have forgotten her voice?

Without thinking, he raised his hand, cupping Larissa's—*Lovisa's*—uninjured cheek, wanting nothing more than to draw her into an embrace, to apologize for leaving her. The shock on her face stopped him; he forced himself to pull back even as the truth plunged like a knife into his chest.

She didn't remember him.

A ripple of pain shot through him. He still cupped her face in his hand. Encouraged that she wasn't pulling away, he cleared his throat. "I know you."

She shifted. "Well, I should hope so after what we just went through."

"No, I *know* you."

Her eyes narrowed. "You've been sleeping for hours, Darien. Did you remember something? Was it Queen Stjarna? Was she the one who took you to Aagen's house?" She clenched his hands more tightly, her voice rising with desperate hope. "Is Halla the Princess?"

Darien shook his head, his voice a whisper. "Lovisa, it's you."

Larissa's eyes darkened. "What did you call me?"

"Lovisa, you're the Perle Princess."

Part Two
Svikari

"A MAN LEFT TO his own devices
Without protection or shelter
Will wither like a vine
Left to burn in the sun."

-Urðr, *Book of the Past*

Rejection

Larissa

LARISSA JERKED BACK, SHAKING off Darien's hand and ignoring the hurt that flashed in his eyes. "I'm not the Princess."

Darien swayed with the truck bed as Helga bounced out of a particularly large pothole. Larissa scooted away, suddenly desperate to put space between them. The new look in Darien's eyes was too intense, too focused. He'd seen something, that much was true. What was worse, the voice inside of Larissa told her to listen.

"I don't know what's happened since, how we got here, or why we lost our memories, but it's true. Fifty years ago, before the Empress took over, I was a Prince of the Safír kingdom. That's how we met."

"You're a Prince?" Skepticism laced her question.

"Yes."

"I'm a Princess?"

"Yes."

"From fifty years ago?"

Darien caught her tone that time. "Lovisa, I'm telling the truth."

"That's not my name," she shot back. Standing on wobbling feet, she pounded her fist against the metal top of the truck cab. Larissa didn't know why, but the name twisted her guts as guilt settled in her intestines.

Tires squealed. The truck stuttered to a halt, flinging Larissa back, landing her in Darien's lap. Heat flushed to her face as they attempted to untangle their limbs; Darien's murmured apologies caressed her ears. They had only just detached when the back tailgate opened, revealing Anara and Halla standing side by side.

Anara raised an eyebrow. "What's going on?"

"It's not exactly a smooth ride back here," Larissa retorted, scooting further from Darien's lap.

Anara hopped into the truck bed, hoisting Halla up after her, then placed a hand on her hip. She turned her sharp eyes back to Larissa. "Why'd you want me to stop?"

"Darien's lost his mind."

Anara turned questioning eyes toward Darien, but he was already staring at her. His mouth had dropped as his eyes re-focused. Recognition dawned; he leapt to his feet, throwing his arms around Anara with a smile so wide it stretched across his face. Larissa's breath caught at the sight.

"Guess I owe you my thanks after all," Darien said.

Confusion vanished from Anara's face, and Larissa tasted jealousy on her tongue from the look of understanding they shared. "Darien! You remember me?"

"Mostly." He held a hand to his temple. "I'm still trying to piece it together, but I do. I remember you, Anara. How did this happen?"

"I only know bits and pieces myself. I tried to wake you."

"In the woods." Darien nodded. "That shock when you touched my face. I started to remember things after that, but they came slowly."

Anara's mouth twitched at the corner. "Tell me about it. I thought it would be instant, that you would just remember. I've searched for you both for years."

Darien's grin turned sheepish. "It's a good thing I'm worth the wait."

Anara rolled her eyes, though she playfully landed a fist against Darien's shoulder, but Larissa's mind was stuck on two words.

You both, Anara had said. Larissa clenched her hands at her side to stop them from shaking. "What on Evrópa are you talking about?"

The smile fell from Anara's face. "You still don't remember, do you?"

"What doesn't she remember?" Halla asked, sitting next to her sister's feet.

"There's nothing to remember." Larissa could hear the panic in her own voice. What they were saying wasn't true; it couldn't be. She had no blank spots in her memory like Darien. She was the daughter of Dal and Vern, sister to Halla.

But a voice in her mind, the same voice as before, spoke. *Be still and listen.*

Pressure on her fingers brought Larissa back into the moment as she found Halla's hands gripping her own. If she was the Princess, it would mean that her parents had not been her parents. It would mean that Halla was not her sister.

Larissa could not stand the three faces staring at her, expecting something from her. She rose to her feet. Thoughts of escape were dashed by the clinking sound of the pearl ring rolling across the bed of the truck. Anara snatched it up before it could disappear behind the boxes.

"Larissa, where did you get this?" Anara spoke slowly, examining the ring.

"Why?"

Halla gasped. "That was Mamma's!"

Larissa shook her head. "I've never seen it before today. Why do you keep looking at it like that, Anara?"

Anara rubbed one finger over the surface of the pearl, then held the ring out to Larissa. "This is no ordinary gem. Look at it, closely."

Go on, the voice whispered.

Reluctantly, Larissa leaned in, noting the slight imperfection in the pearl itself. "It's scratched, so what?"

Anara shook her head. "Not scratched, etched. It's a rune."

The minuscule lines formed an elongated X enclosed by vertical lines. Larissa found herself unable to look away, her eyes transfixed by the rune. In the pearl's reflection, she thought she could see a pair of green eyes.

She shook her head, forcing herself to look away. "Why does it matter?"

"In Pappa's stories, stones and runes have magic," Halla answered. "Remember, Lara?"

"*Galdr*," Anara corrected, "but otherwise, you're right."

Darien peeked over Anara's shoulder, "I wouldn't exactly call a pearl a stone."

"The translations have been garbled over the years," Anara explained. "People found it more pleasing to say 'stones and runes' when, in fact, the original word simply meant 'gems.' Those of Ancestral Blood could access their *galdr* without the use of these gems, of course, but gems made them more powerful. Each of the royal families and even their aristocrats had specific gems and runes associated with their bloodline. This is the Dagaz rune. It is a rune of awakening and awareness. This is the rune of Perle."

Anara held out the ring once more to Larissa. A ruby pendant flickered out from beneath her clothing as she leaned forward. Larissa kept her arms crossed pointedly against her chest. "Why would Mamma have this? We've lived in Safír all our lives, just like our ancestors."

"She kept it for you."

Larissa's head swung back toward Halla. "What?"

Halla's eyes had changed. An agelessness shone through their green brilliance. It was more than just the trauma of what she had gone through, but before Larissa could comment, Halla blinked. Her eyes looked as they always had. Had Larissa imagined it?

Halla plucked the ring from Anara's hand. "Mamma's story about the goddess who visited our farm. She told it to me."

"No, she didn't," Larissa argued, but Halla wasn't focused on her. Her eyes looked inward at some memory Larissa couldn't see.

"It was before you came to us," Halla whispered, almost trancelike as she stared at the ring. "Mamma said the goddess made her promise to hide someone, and she gave us the ring to give to that person. Mamma told me that she'd been waiting her whole life, but the goddess never returned, so I would carry on her promise when I got older. That night I prayed to the *Æsir* for a sister to help me when the time came. The next morning, you were there."

Larissa felt Darien's eyes on her. Anara could only stare at Halla, as though her words were unlocking some secret in Anara's mind.

Halla paused, her voice colored in confusion. "But Lara, that doesn't make sense. You've always been with me. Haven't you?"

Larissa snatched the ring out of Halla's hands, shoving it deep into her pocket. If only she could dispose of these questions as easily. "Always, Halla. You're remembering wrong."

"It's possible you're both remembering what someone wants you to remember, just like me and Aagen." Darien's voice quickened. "My father said he lived with two memories, so maybe Halla has too and just didn't remember them before. Think about it. I was the Prince of Safír, and I was hidden with Aagen. You're the Princess of Perle, and you were hidden with Halla."

Halla's eyes widened. "You're the Perle Princess, Lara?"

"No, I'm not," Larissa snapped.

Anara laid a hand on Darien's forearm. "Give her time. *Draugr* don't act on their own; we're most likely being followed already. We need to find somewhere safe, and the roadside won't cut it."

Panic flared inside Larissa. "Where can we go? Why should we even travel with you? You're a shifter from Rubin. You belong to the same family of the monsters that killed my parents. How do we know you're not taking us straight to the Empress?"

"How about because I nearly died saving your life, and to do so I had to attack my own kind?" Anara spoke through gritted canine teeth, her slitted eyes glowing yellow. With visible restraint, Anara shook off the transformations. "I nearly died protecting you, and I would do it again. Besides, if I were a *draugr*, I would've lost hold of my human shape by now. You're going to have to trust me. For Halla's sake, at least."

"Where are you taking us?"

"To Perle."

Larissa's stomach dropped. "I'm not the Princess, Anara."

"We aren't going there because of you. I'd rather stay away from Perle as a whole; Shiko's sentries are everywhere there, but I have contacts with people inside the Walls who can show us the way to the Viðnám."

"Viðnám?" three voices asked in unison.

"The resistance group against Shiko. They'll protect you."

Larissa huffed. "If I agree that I'm this Princess?"

"They'll protect you even if you say that you're not. They'll protect Halla, too."

It was exactly the right thing to say, and Larissa knew that Anara knew it. "Fine."

Larissa dropped back to the bed of the truck, pulling Halla down beside her and making it clear that she would ride with her sister from here on out. Darien could ride in the cab with Anara. She did not miss the look of hurt that crossed both their faces, but she chose to ignore it.

How could they not see that they were wrong? She was no Princess. They were only causing unnecessary pain with their false hopes. She did not watch them walk away but heard the shutting of truck doors and felt the vibrations as Helga roared to life, pulling back onto the road.

"Lara, are you mad at me?" Halla asked.

Larissa glanced at her sister, remembering the day she had been born. Remembering that small, warm bundle of a new baby sister. How Halla had grasped her finger. Darien and Anara were wrong, they had to be. "Of course not. Here, sit in front of me, your hair is a mess."

Halla obliged. Larissa pulled out the hair bands that had long ago failed at their jobs. Quick searching revealed a hairbrush in a nearby bag. There were flowers painted on the back of the wood, and Larissa knew it was Mamma's. She blinked away the tears in her eyes as she worked through Halla's tangled strands, using water from bottles to loosen the dirt and dried blood. Rinse, brush, repeat. The rhythmic process allowed Larissa's mind to wander.

What if they were right?

It was a preposterous idea, but still. What if this was not her Mamma's brush at all? It just belonged to some woman who had taken her in? She remembered baking in the kitchen with Mamma when Halla had accidentally upset the bag of flour, which had covered them all in white powder. How could that not be real when she could still feel the way the flour tickled her nose and made her sneeze?

And what about Halla? If Larissa was not truly the first-born of Dal and Vern, had she displaced Halla? Forced her into hiding as a second-born, when all along she should have had the freedoms that Larissa had stolen? Had the *draugr* been searching for her and not for Halla? Had it smelled Larissa on her? Were Halla's parents dead simply because of Larissa's existence?

"Lara," Halla asked, "are you sure you're not mad at me?"

"I already told you no."

"Then could you stop taking it out on my head?"

Halla's hands clasped around her head to protect the roots of her hair from Larissa's furious yanking. Larissa dropped the weaponized brush. "Sorry, Halla, let me just finish braiding this back." Fighting the wind breezing through the slated walls, Larissa wove a passable braid and tied it off. "There, much better."

Halla shifted to face Larissa and pulled the braid over her shoulder, twirling the ends of it. She chewed the inside of her cheek, a habit Larissa had noticed only recently.

"What is it?" Larissa prompted.

"What do you mean?"

"You're biting your cheek, Halla. Out with it."

"Lara, what if you *are* the Princess?"

Larissa sighed. She supposed it was her fault for asking in the first place. "Halla, I'm not the Princess."

"How do you know?"

"I just do, Halla."

"But what about the ring and what Mamma told me?"

"You didn't even remember that until a couple of minutes ago."

"That doesn't make it any less true," she protested.

"Enough, Halla, please."

Only the loud growl of Helga's engine broke the silence. Larissa felt Halla's eyes on her but stared into her lap; she could not stand to look into Halla's green eyes that so frequently reminded her of her visions. What would Halla say if she knew Larissa had been having dreams? Most likely, it would just reinforce the whole "Princess" notion. Larissa rubbed her temples. What was she going to do?

"I'll still love you, you know."

Larissa yanked her head up, meeting Halla's eyes. Her sister had been watching her the whole time. "What?"

Halla scooted closer, leaning into Larissa's side and laying her head on Larissa's shoulder. Still fiddling with the braid, she spoke.

"Even if you are the Princess, even if someone planted false memories in my mind, even if you've only been my sister for a year, I'll still love you."

Larissa blinked, trying to quell the tears. She pulled Halla closer, burying her face in her sister's hair, not minding the smell of dirt and smoke. "I'll always love you too, little one."

For the first time, Halla did not object to the phrase, and Larissa knew they were both thinking about Pappa.

"Mamma wanted you to have the ring, Lara. I know you don't believe in Pappa's stories, but he would want you to have it too."

Larissa swallowed hard before pulling the ring from her pocket. She'd told Darien that she believed in the Norn, but she also meant what she said. Larissa wasn't waiting on the goddesses of fate for help. She could only help herself.

Princess or not, Halla was right. Mamma had died with this ring in her hand. If Halla said she kept it for her, then Larissa would be dishonoring her memory by ignoring it. She held out the ring so that they both could examine it. Larissa turned it in her fingers, running them over the thin gold band and the large pearl. She brought it closer to her face, turning it to catch sunlight on the edges of the rune. What had Anara called it? The Dagaz rune?

A high peal of laughter tickled in Larissa's ears.

"Did you hear that?" she asked.

"Hear what?" Halla was still looking at the ring.

"Laughter, I think."

Halla turned her gaze away from the ring and back to Larissa. "I didn't hear anything. Maybe you're remembering something?"

Larissa groaned. "Halla, not this again."

"Would it be so bad being a Princess? Plus, didn't Darien say he was a Prince?" Halla asked knowingly. "He's pretty handsome, don't you think? Don't the Prince and the Princess always end up happily married?"

"Halla!" Larissa exclaimed, suddenly embarrassed.

Halla tilted her head back and smirked. It was the same smirk that Larissa had known all their lives, but it vanished as quickly as it had appeared. Halla's somber eyes seemed to hold the weight of the world. "Lara, I think it would be wonderful to learn you were the lost Princess."

Larissa chose her next words carefully. "If I really am her—and I'm not saying that I am—but if I am, then the *draugr* was coming after me. Our parents are dead because of me."

Halla leaned her head back on her sister's shoulder. "Maybe you are the Princess, and maybe the *draugr* did come for you, but that wouldn't make it your fault. It wouldn't change a thing. Pappa and Mamma loved you."

"Don't you see, Halla? If I really am the Princess, then they didn't choose to love me. They could have been forced into loving me because of the memories that someone or some *thing* planted in their mind!" She broke off, choking on the words.

"Someone may have planted memories in my mind too, but I still love you, and so would they."

It isn't that simple, Larissa thought. She turned her face away from Halla, looking again at the ring in her lap. Halla wouldn't have said anything if Larissa had left it back at the farm. So much pain over such a tiny thing.

"You should wear it," Halla said.

"Why?"

"It might help you remember. Come on, Lara. If I'm wrong, you have nothing to lose."

Larissa looked down into Halla's wide and hopeful eyes. *If you're right, I have everything to lose. It's all just a story to you, isn't it? Another one of Pappa's grand stories.*

But if this was one way to keep Pappa's memory alive, who was Larissa to not even try? She would put on the ring, and nothing would happen. Halla would be satisfied that they had tried, and then they could move on.

Put it on.

Larissa stiffened at the return of the voice in her mind. Holding her breath, she slid the ring onto her right hand's ring finger. She and Halla stared at it, then at each other. Larissa released her breath, resisting the urge to laugh. Was she actually disappointed?

"See, Halla? It's just a ring."

She raised her hand to show it to Halla, but Halla was gone.

THE BRANCHES OF THE tree touched the sky, blocking out half of the sun. No matter how far back she tilted her head, Larissa could not see the top of the tree. She knew without needing to be told that this was Yggdrasil, *the tree of life from Pappa's stories.*

Peals of giggles drew Larissa's attention back to the base of the tree, where a small child walked along the edges of a wide stone well, teetering every few feet. Her brilliant red hair floated and twirled around her face in the still air. Her skin was nearly translucent; it glowed. Power, like heat, radiated from the child.

Kings and Queens! *Larissa's mouth went dry, and sweat gathered on her palms.* She's a goddess.

At the base of the well, two figures lay with hands clasped together. She recognized her own white hair splayed across the grass. She was stepping closer, her eyes on the boy with black hair, when she realized the laughter had stopped.

The child-goddess stood still on the edge of the well, but she stared straight at Larissa. Her head cocked to the side like a bird's as a smile grew across her face.

Her voice was like the tinkling of rain. "Do you believe in us now?"

Larissa's hands shook as she grasped the ring, but no matter how she pulled, it remained on her finger. Likewise, her feet were cemented to the ground, refusing to budge at her command.

The child-goddess leapt from the well, her feet floating over the grass. "It's time to wake up, Princess."

She reached out, her small hands cupping Larissa's cheeks just as Anara's had. A shock, more painful than before, coursed through her. The child-goddess breathed into her face. "Remember."

Behind the girl, the waters of the well rose to the brim and whirled in a dizzying performance of light and images. Larissa caught Halla's face reflected on the waters before it was replaced with her own, but a net of pearls pulled her hair away from her face. Then the waters trembled and Larissa saw a woman in black towering over a man kneeling before her. She drove the sword toward his chest, and dyed the waters red. More images replaced the others, swirling faster and faster, but held in the goddess' grasp, Larissa could not look away.

"Release her, Verðandi," a deep voice ordered.

The girl pouted but let her hands fall to her sides. Larissa's lungs hurt; she couldn't breathe. She stumbled forward. Her waist hit the stones of the well and her body tumbled forward, pitching her face first into the waters. Panic had only a moment to set in before the waters swallowed her whole, blinding her in their swirls of light and drowning her in dreams.

19

On the Run

Darien

"You've been quiet."

Darien glanced over at Anara, shaken that only yesterday he had no memory of her whatsoever. "Trying to sort through my thoughts. There's a lot to go through when a lifetime's worth of memories comes back at once."

"I don't know if I would call it a lifetime. You were barely seventeen when you went missing." Anara smirked at his unamused expression. "You used to enjoy humor, Darien."

"Let me know when you start being funny."

She rolled her eyes. "Do you remember everything now?"

"Hardly." He pushed his hand through his hair, scratching the back of his head as he stared out the front window. "It's like every memory from both lives make up this giant ball of string. Every time I try to focus on one memory, it pulls four other strings with it that seem completely unrelated. Why is it that I can remember my father's face, but not his name? Why is it that I can't remember my mother's face, but I can still feel the touch of Lovisa's hand in mine on the night of the Jóltide Festival?"

Anara chuckled. "You never were any good at hiding your feelings for Lovisa, not even as a child."

"I better start learning then," he grumbled. "It's clear she doesn't remember me. I don't want to push my feelings onto her when she's still struggling to remember who she is."

Anara grew serious. "You're right, and I'm sorry, Darien. I understand the pain you're feeling right now, but give her time. She'll come around just like you did."

"Why can't you help her remember like you did for me?"

Exasperation dripped from Anara's tone. "I did, Darien. It didn't work for her. I don't know why."

"How do you not know?"

"I wasn't given all the answers. I've been searching for you both for half a century; I'd almost given up on finding you. I swear I've searched Safír dozens of times. You and Lovisa were never there."

"Then what made you come back?"

Anara smirked. "Would you believe me if I told you the Norn sent me a dream?"

"I do, although"—Darien rubbed the back of his neck—"if I didn't know it was possible, I wouldn't believe it."

"Which part?"

"*Half* a century? You still look the same from my memories. Okay, maybe a little older than you were back then, but certainly not over fifty."

"The more we use our *galdr*, the more it slows the growth and decay of our bodies. After the Great *Hrun*, I lived in exile and used my *galdr* every day. There were weeks on end when I lived solely as a raven just to survive. *Galdr* affected me significantly, as it has affected you."

"What do you mean?" Darien lowered the visor, quickly opening it to check his cracked and foggy reflection. Apart from his shorter hair, he looked the same as he had that night on the beach with Lovisa. "Still just as handsome."

Anara flipped the visor up. "That's the thing. You look *just* the same. Queen Stjarna planned to hide all four of us, but I don't know how she hid you and Lovisa like this. She was powerful, yes, but so powerful that you both disappeared for fifty years? Whose *galdr* was fueling that? I've hardly aged, but you both look as though you *never* aged. Even extensive use of *galdr* couldn't have frozen you in time like this."

"Four of us," Darien repeated, his mind buzzing, his thoughts on the blond-haired boy from his memories. "Anara, do you have any leads on where Aeron might be? Could he have been placed with another family like Lovisa and I were? Is that why we're going to Perle?"

She hesitated. "What do you remember about Aeron?"

The ring on Darien's finger burned against his skin, calling to him. "What do you mean?"

She kept her eyes firmly on the road. "If you don't remember, it's not my place to tell you."

He would have argued, but his mind was already reaching back, picking up and discarding memories until he found the one he was looking for.

ᚾᛁᛉᚱᛋ ᚾᛁᛉᚱᛋ ᚾᛁᛉᚱᛋ ᚾᛁᛉᚱᛋ ᚾᛁᛉᚱᛋ

HE WAS STANDING IN the palace. Word had come that Shiko was marching on Smaragd. Aeron wanted to send help; he wanted to go himself, but their parents had not yet returned from Shiko's corona-tion and attempted coup. Darien begged his brother to wait for their parents' return. The people of Smaragd had no armies, leaving them entirely defenseless. Even if Aeron had brought the entire Safirian force, he would have faced unbeatable odds.

But Aeron wouldn't listen. It was an opportunity from the gods, he said, an opportunity to prove his valor. Aeron couldn't pass it up. In the moment before his departure, Darien had argued with him.

"Your pride will kill you, Aeron."

Aeron scoffed, adjusting the ceremonial sword at his hip and the gun on his other. "We can't all hide in someone else's skirt."

Darien's hand slashed through the air. "Don't do this, brother. You'll never make it back."

Aeron took his men and departed. When their parents returned, Darien's father assembled more men to reinforce Aeron's forces, say-ing that his eldest son had done the right thing. But before their soldiers could depart, a messenger came with the news of the battle. There was only one survivor.

And it wasn't Aeron.

ᚾᛁᛉᛏᛋᚾᛁᛉᛏᛋᚾᛁᛉᛏᛋᚾᛁᛉᛏᛋᚾᛁᛉᛏᛋ

PAIN LANCED THROUGH DARIEN'S chest. He gasped, worried that his heart might tear its way out of the ribcage enclosing it. Tears welled up in his eyes. Of everything he had forgotten, how could he have forgotten this?

"Aeron's dead." It wasn't a question.

Anara reached out, touching his arm in shared sorrow. "I'm so sorry, Darien."

The truck wound its way past another bend, down another dirt road, and toward the falling sun. Night would be coming upon them quickly, but Darien was already overcome by darkness. Aeron's death unlocked a slew of memories that hurled themselves at Darien with increased ferocity, as if in vengeance for Darien's forgetting his brother at all. He bent his head, enduring the turmoil that racked through his mind. If Anara noticed Darien's tears, she never mentioned them.

"Torsten," she said.

"What?"

"Your father's name is Torsten, King Torsten of Safír."

Like a key, the name clicked in Darien's brain, unlocking new memories and numbing his pain. "Thank you."

They traveled the road in silence as Darien worked through his memories. Although his heart lingered on Aeron, his mind tugged in another direction. "Anara?"

"Yes?"

"I get that someone must have given Dal and Vern a new name for Lovisa to help hide her, but who could have done that? Why not change my name as well?"

"Why indeed? The Norn have the power, but they haven't been seen since *Ragnorak*."

"You really think the goddesses of fate are involved?"

"They sent me the dream that helped me find you; why not this? Something is stirring. Even the animals I sheltered with felt it. Worship of the gods has only increased since Shiko's reign. You'll see what I mean when we get inside Lystheim."

Anara tilted her head toward the open window, breathing deeply through her nose. Darien was reminded abruptly of a dog, but decided to keep that resemblance to himself. Anara cracked her knuckles. "We won't reach the Klarälven River before nightfall. We'll have to stop here tonight and continue on tomorrow."

Anara pulled off the road, urging the clanking trunk over the underbrush. When she could go no further, Anara parked the truck in a shaded area. It would be easy for any passing driver to miss the truck hidden in the shadows, not that they had seen another driver for hours. Most vehicles granted to farmers were expected to stay within a certain range of the farm. Farmers received a gas quota during each visit to the Wall, mainly enough to get them home and back to the Wall for their next drop.

Darien mentally thanked whatever forethought caused Dal to save up enough gas over time to fill the tank. They were more likely to run into a sentry patrol than anything else, but had so far managed to avoid them as well. Darien attributed that more to Anara's skill than to luck. The Norn weren't that kind.

Darien hopped down from the truck and made his way to the back, his legs cramping up after sitting for so long. Upon opening the tailgate, he was surprised to find Larissa fast asleep in her sister's lap. Halla held a finger to her lips, but Larissa was already stirring. The next moment, she jerked upright, her eyes wide with fear.

Halla tugged on her sleeve. "You okay, Lara?"

Larissa's eyes roved over her sister in confusion before finding Darien. She stilled and drew in a shaky breath, nodding to Halla and laying a hand on her sister's arm. Even though he knew she was Lovisa, Darien could see parts of her that belonged solely to Larissa. There was an innate distrust in her eyes that Lovisa had never possessed, but also a newfound fierce spirit. She was two people: the Princess and the farm girl.

Her smile was strained. "Just a bad dream, Halla."

"*Mara?*"

Larissa hesitated. "Maybe."

Halla's eyes widened. "Did you see—"

"Why are we stopping?" Larissa asked, turning to Darien, her eyes capturing his.

The sound of her voice was all it took for Darien's emotions, so fresh and compounded by the memory of Aeron's death, to explode anew. He longed to hold her as he had before, but the wariness hovering in those golden eyes stopped him. She didn't remember, didn't seem to want to remember, and he didn't know what he could do to change that.

Beside him, Anara scoffed. He hadn't heard her approach. Apparently, she could walk as silently as a wolf even in human form. She spared Darien a glance of exasperation before turning to face the girls. "We've been driving for hours. We haven't eaten. Some of us haven't slept in days. We need to rest."

"I thought you were worried about someone following us," Larissa argued.

"I am, but it won't do us any good to be caught dead on our feet. We'll rest for a few hours then move on. Besides, we're near the Klarälven River. If there is a *draugr* on our tail, it won't come near the waters."

"Why not?" Halla asked, her interest piqued.

"It's pure, and they're not. Besides, it'll cover our scent."

"Our scent?"

Anara wrinkled her nose in response. "It's pretty strong."

She hoisted herself up into the bed of the truck, inching her way around Larissa and Halla to rummage through the boxes. Finding four identical bags, Anara tossed one to Halla, who just managed to catch it.

She clutched the bag against her stomach. "What's this?"

Another bag flew out. Darien caught it with the tips of his fingers.

Anara lifted the last two bags. "Your parents thought of nearly everything. We'll be quite comfortable unless it rains."

Anara dropped the third bag into Larissa's lap. Her hands gripped it by reflex, but Darien was alarmed to see that her eyes had glazed over. From the look on her face, Anara noticed Larissa's distraction as well. Halla was already opening her bag. It contained two blankets but no tent. Opening his own bag, Darien found the same.

"Come on." Anara hopped down from the tailgate. "Sól's going to sleep, and so should we."

They walked a bit further into the woods before the sun sank down over the horizon, stealing the day's light. In the dimness, Darien unrolled his blankets then turned to help Halla with hers.

"Here, kiddo, this one goes on the bottom." He pulled out the coarser fabric, rubbing his thumb over it. "You can tell because it's thicker than the top blanket."

"Thanks." She wasn't looking at the blanket, though; she was staring at him.

"What?" Darien asked.

"You're really one of the Princes from Safír?"

"Yeah, I guess so."

"It doesn't surprise me."

Darien cocked his head to the side. "No? It sure surprised me."

Halla shrugged. "You were too handsome to be a farmer. The princes in Pappa's stories are always the handsome ones."

Darien laughed. Behind Halla, Larissa shook her head, but Darien could've sworn she smiled. Her eyes rose to meet his, and for just a moment, they shared their amusement. Then Larissa's eyes clouded over, and she looked away. Darien's tongue worked against his teeth, but there was nothing he could think to say. He didn't know how to break through the wall she'd erected around herself. As everyone collapsed upon their blankets, the darkness of the night settled around them, making it nearly impossible to see each other.

"We won't stay long," Anara whispered. "I'll take first watch. Darien, I'll wake you soon. With any luck, that beast of a truck will get us to the Klarälven River by early morning."

"Hey," Halla's indignant voice sounded to Darien's left. "Helga's doing the best she can."

Darien stifled a laugh.

"With any luck, *Helga* will get us to the Klarälven River by early morning," Anara corrected. "There's a bridge that marks the boundary lines between the Safir and Perle commonwealths. Once we cross it, we'll be in Perlian territory."

Near Halla, Larissa's blankets rustled. "If the *draugr* doesn't find us first, you mean?"

"Precisely." Anara answered. "Sleep tight."

20

Hall of Memories

Larissa

LARISSA SHOULD HAVE TAKEN the first watch.

Exhaustion curled up in her bones, yet she fought the heaviness behind her eyes. If she slept, she risked falling into dreams. The young goddess' glowing face appeared every time she closed her eyes. Larissa swore she could still feel the child's hands on her face. Her cheeks tingled from the memory.

At some point after falling asleep, Halla curled up against Larissa's chest. Her back warmed Larissa's front, lulling her into a peace she hadn't felt since waking up in the back of the truck. Larissa's breathing softened to match Halla's deep sleepy sighs. The ring on her hand grew warm, and her eyes slid shut.

ᚾᛁᚼᛏᚴᛋᚾᛁᚼᛏᚴᛋᚾᛁᚼᛏᚴᛋᚾᛁᚼᛏᚴᛋᚾᛁᚼᛏᚴᛋ

THE LONG HALLWAY STRETCHED into infinity with doors on either side. The floor under Larissa's feet was tiled black and white like a chessboard, and gold veins ran the length of the hall. Each door was shut tight, etched with the same rune that matched her ring. Larissa turned to see if the hallway extended just as far in the other direction. She half-expected to find the goddess, but someone else waited for her this time.

Queen Stjarna blocked her path, wearing the same clothes from Larissa's dreams but no longer bleeding from the nose and mouth. Her eyes were just as green and bright as always, but Larissa could make out a subtle difference in their shape compared to Halla's. It had been a fool's hope to think they were the same.

"Where am I?"

Queen Stjarna placed her hand on the closest doorknob. "Are you ready to remember?"

Larissa fidgeted with the ring on her finger. Halla wanted her to try. Pappa and Mamma would want her to try. Larissa nodded at Queen Stjarna and turned the knob.

Together, they stepped into darkness that soon lessened into a gray haze. Smoke arranged itself into shapes that then drew color into existence. Larissa stood alone in a courtyard; Queen Stjarna had disappeared. Grass, flowers, bushes, and trees filled the expansive grounds. They had clearly been well-cared for; every plant was intentionally nurtured and cultivated. The smell of damp soil reminded Larissa of the berry farm, but something else tugged at her memory. Cherry blossoms.

Then came a shout, one of joy and excitement. A young, barefooted girl burst through the bushes. From her size, Larissa guessed she was around Halla's age. Her white hair looked as though it had been carefully styled and pulled away from the girl's face at one point in time, but it had fallen out during the child's play. She stopped running and laughed to herself, looking back into the bushes where she had run from. Her golden eyes sparkled with mirth.

The resemblance was undeniable.

Larissa had no pictures of herself when she was younger, nothing to prove her hypothesis except for the innate ability to recognize oneself. This child was her.

All at once, younger-Larissa stopped laughing. Larissa thought that perhaps the girl had noticed her, but no. She was looking past Larissa into the bushes from where she had emerged, listening intently.

A low growl, the rumble of a vibrating chest, shook the leaves. A wolf pup exploded through the underbrush. Its body, though small, was outstretched with its claws extended toward younger-Larissa.

Larissa rushed to the child, knowing she was too late, already imagining those claws slicing through the girl's skin and splattering blood onto the ground. But there was no blood. No collision.

Younger-Larissa smiled as she raised one hand, a ring sparkling from her thumb. Just before the wolf pounced on her, it collided into an invisible barrier and was tossed back by its own momentum. Landing on its feet, the creature raised its muzzle to the sky, releasing a long and joyful howl. The fur on the wolf's back ruffled until a small, brown-skinned girl with black hair dressed in sweatpants and a loose shirt took its place.

"Anara, you kept your clothes on!"

Larissa noted the other girl's copper eyes and mischievous grin. Her cheeks were rounder and her hair was not quite as long, but it was Anara. There was no doubt.

Larissa shook her head. They'd known each other?

Anara bared her teeth, still in canine form, in the resemblance of a smile and touched the ruby at her throat. "Amma taught me. She said I was getting too old to be shifting without keeping my clothes. It was either this or I wasn't allowed to shift outside my room anymore."

"That does seem like it would be a problem." Younger-Larissa nodded with false severity. "You couldn't reach me, so I declare myself the winner."

"How'd you stop me anyhow?"

"Móðir has been working with me on our galdr *too. She says it's all about being able to feel the energy around me." The girl's face was serious, her voice was lofty, and her nose pointed in the air. Then, she laughed and shrugged. "To be honest, I'm not really sure how I did that. I just reached out, and it worked."*

"Your galdr *is so strange." Anara sat on the ground, crossing her legs.*

Younger-Larissa mirrored Anara's posture. "My galdr *is strange? You can literally change everything about you."*

Anara grinned wildly. "I figured out how to do something really cool. Want to see?"

"Yeah!"

Anara inhaled and exhaled, closing her eyes. When she opened them, they were no longer copper but bright green. Starting at the roots, her black hair lightened until it was nearly silver.

"Anara, that's amazing! You look like Móðir. I thought you couldn't do a human transformation yet."

Anara shuddered, the transformation fading from her. "I still can't, not really. I've only mastered the raven and wolf forms. It's harder to shift to humans. Amma says that's because the Norn never intended our galdr *to be used for deception."*

"Think about how cool that could be though. You could look however you want. You could have purple hair and orange eyes!" The girls'

laughter faded into a sigh. "I wish I could do that. No one would even know it was me walking right out the palace walls."

Anara leaned back on her hands, tilting her head back. "I think it's beautiful here."

"Not when it's the only place you've ever known."

The familiarity of her words slammed into Larissa. It was something Halla would say.

"Oh come on, you don't want to sit out here moping all day." Anara stood up. "The Safirian royal family will be arriving any minute."

"What?" Younger-Larissa rose to her feet, brushing herself off. "Darien and Aeron are coming today? How long have you known about this?"

Anara looked up at the sky as though pondering the question. "I could have sworn I mentioned it."

Huffing, younger-Larissa raced off toward where they had come from, with Anara fast on her heels. Larissa tried to follow but found herself back in the tiled hallway. The smells of the garden still lingered in her nose, even as she touched cold and solid walls. She was surrounded by doors once more.

Just a dream. Larissa breathed deeply to steady herself, doubting her thoughts even as she had them. Her dreams had never felt quite this real. But if they weren't dreams, that would mean Darien was right.

These were memories. Her memories.

More voices came from the door to her left, but Larissa's hand hesitated on the doorknob. Even if these were her memories, all they had proven was that Larissa had known Anara as a child. They proved nothing about her being a Princess. Not really. Pappa said that even some outside of the royal families could use galdr. *It was possible she was the daughter of an aristocrat or even an abnormality.*

The voices beyond the doors grew louder, piquing Larissa's curiosity. She cracked open the one next to her and slid through the gap. Confusion halted her in her steps.

The door she had opened stood before her once again, closed shut. The only difference was the small girl crouched low with her ear pressed against the door. Larissa recognized herself in the figure more readily this time, although she looked even younger than before. She was tiny, and there was no ring on her thumb.

The sound of voices came again, and Larissa dropped next to her younger self, mimicking her posture. On the other side of the door, she could hear a man's voice.

"I understand your fears, Stjarna, but we cannot keep her locked up inside this palace for the rest of her life."

"I never said her whole life, Mikkel, just until she is old enough to protect herself."

A pause.

"This is because of the oath your mother made you take, isn't it?"

"She was wise, Mikkel. She may not have been the best mother, but she learned many things on her travels. She warned me that the peace was coming to an end. I keep having these dreams about Lovisa—"

Larissa gasped audibly.

"Shhhh," said the child. "I'm trying to listen."

Larissa stared golden eye to golden eye with her younger self. The little Princess was missing one of her front baby teeth. Larissa waved her hand in front of the girl's face. "Can you see me?"

"Duh. Now shhh. *" Lovisa rolled her eyes, pressing her ear back against the door.*

"*I have sent messages to the royal families of Rubin and Safír,*" *the man said. "We trust them, Stjarna; they have been our friends for over a century. She needs to be able to socialize with other children.*"

As the Queen acquiesced, Lovisa rose from her crouched position. "Móðir ended up letting me meet them."

"Meet who?"

"Princess Anara from Rubin came first. Then Darien and Aeron, Princes of the Safír Kingdom."

Princes. *So Darien had been telling the truth about who he was. And Anara was a Princess? Larissa would never have guessed that one. She looked into her familiar younger face, wishing she could deny the similarities. "What happened to you? To us?*"

Instead of answering, Lovisa skipped down the hallway.

Larissa rose to her feet, compelled to follow her. "Hey, wait."

Lovisa was surprisingly quick as she passed through a doorway. Larissa darted after her, only for her world to tilt and swirl.

The door led to a grand sitting room with a set of large swinging doors left open to the balcony beyond. The moon, which looked double its usual size, could be seen through the open doors, and its light reflected off a frozen lake below.

Jóltide, *the voice in her mind informed Larissa,* when we celebrate the turning of the wheel and the renewal of the year. *Laughter and revelry came from below the balcony, but Larissa focused on the four occupants of the room. She recognized Anara on the couch closest to her immediately, but her eyes lingered on the handsome boy beside her.*

Darien was dressed formally in a sharp navy suit with silver buttons and a large rune sewn onto the shoulder. Even as he pulled at his tie and ruffled his curly hair, making it more wild than before,

Darien looked, well, princely. He twisted the ring on his finger, his gaze locked onto someone else.

Larissa forced her eyes to follow that gaze, finding herself, or more accurately, Princess Lovisa.

The young woman leaned against the balcony, looking down at the people below, but turned, as if sensing Darien's eyes. Though she looked to be the same age as Larissa, Lovisa appeared different in every other aspect. The Princess oozed regality with white hair that cascaded down her back in loose waves. A small band of pearls set in a golden net pulled the hair away from her face. The gold in her eyes was accentuated by the pale gilded edges of her gown that hung off her shoulders. Dozens of pearls dripped like waterfalls down her bare back.

When she moved, the gown came to life. Runes sewn into the fabric a thousand times over glowed with a strange power.

"You look stunning, Princess."

It was not Darien who spoke, but another young man whom Larissa was sure she'd never seen before. He sat next to Darien on the couch, dressed in a crisp black suit, lined with brilliant gold accents that complemented Darien's silver. His hazel eyes drank in Lovisa's presence. Short strands of his dirty blond hair were braided back above clean-shaven cheeks, but there was something odd about his face.

As hard as Larissa tried to make out the boy's features, it was like looking through a fogged-up window. Besides his eyes, the face was distorted. Even so, Larissa could not deny its familiarity. Only, it wasn't a pleasant familiarity. His very presence struck a discordant note in her mind.

He tapped his fingers in an idle rhythm against the arm of the couch. On his right hand, he wore a ring with a large blue stone in the middle. Similar to Darien's, except that his band was golden instead of silver.

Princess Lovisa's gaze flickered. "Thank you, Aeron."

Darien's brother, *the voice reminded Larissa.*

Darien leaned forward, relaxing his hands on his lap. "He's right, Lovisa. Truly stunning."

Larissa didn't miss the look between them. Neither, apparently, did Anara, who rolled her eyes. "Freyja help you both."

Larissa blushed right along with Lovisa at Anara's call upon the goddess of love. Darien took it in stride. "Anara, you're as beautiful as your tongue is wicked."

She smirked. "Then I must dazzle you all."

Anara was indeed beautiful, dressed in vivid red fabric that clung to her torso and arms, the edges laced in bright, silvery gems. Her dress fell in three layers around her legs, held together by a sash and embroidered with petals and runes that Larissa had never seen before. The sash wrapped around Anara's waist and fell over her left shoulder. Dangling red and silvery gems sat atop her forehead, matching the jewelry at her ears and throat. The bangles on her arms clicked together when she moved.

None of the jewelry shined as bright as the ruby at her throat. Her copper eyes contrasted against the dark kohl outline as she smiled at Darien's compliment. Her teeth were needle sharp.

"Always practicing, aren't you?" Lovisa asked, a smile on her lips.

When Lovisa turned back to the balcony, Larissa joined her.

Together, they surveyed the groups of people in the courtyard below, waiting for their turn to enter the palace. The guests were so small;

Larissa guessed she was several stories high. Naked cherry blossom trees filled the courtyard, and their fallen petals lay strewn across the ground. Even the lake's icy surface glowed white and pink. Peace stole over Larissa, but she sensed impatience from the Princess beside her.

"Princess Shiko's coronation is in a few weeks." Lovisa said, turning to face the others. "I wonder what she'll add to the Tæpəstrıs Friðarsamningur."

Darien leaned back, crossing one of his ankles over the other knee and weaving his hands into his hair at the back of his head. "Don't look at me. Of the four of us, I'm the only one who will never have to worry about that."

"I assume I'll do what my ancestors have done," Anara shrugged. "By the time we are crowned, we usually find our animal form. We sew in the image of our shape as a signature of our reign. Right now, I like the raven, but I haven't rejected the wolf. What about you, Aeron?"

"A decree," he said firmly. "Promising a grand future for Safír; one built on prosperity. A land that outshines all that the Safirian Kings and Queens of the past have done before me."

Darien chuckled. "Come on, Aeron, think big. You wouldn't want us to think you lacked confidence."

Aeron smirked. "I know it will only be possible with you by my side, little *brother."*

Darien ignored him. "What about you Lovisa? What will you add on your coronation day?"

There it was, *thought Larissa,* the truth in absolute terms.

A pit of guilt ripened in her stomach, blossoming into bewilderment. How had she gone from palace to farm? Why had the consequences of her past been laid at the feet of her family, her Pappa, Mamma, and Halla? Or could she even still call them family?

Beside her, the Princess seemed to share in Larissa's unease. Lovisa's shoulders tightened as she paced. "I have no idea what to add. How could I? My people don't even know I exist. What could I possibly have to offer them? Nothing."

"Lovisa, that's not true," Anara admonished, not unkindly. "They may not know who you really are, but you know them. I've seen you interact with them."

"Right," Aeron added. "Who cares if they think you're just the ward of the King and Queen? They'll know who you are soon enough."

"What Aeron means," Darien interrupted, "is that they care for you now. How much more will they care for you when they learn you are their Princess?"

The toll of a bell echoed through the room. Exhaling, Lovisa released the stress from her shoulders. "That's our cue. Prince Darien, would you escort me?"

Darien rose without hesitation, failing to hide the grin on his face or to notice how Aeron's lips tightened. Lovisa must have noticed it, for she added, "Prince Aeron, you know that it is expected of you to escort someone of your same rank."

Anara rose from the couch, sauntering over to Aeron and looping her arm through his. "Come on, Aeron, I don't bite."

Aeron chuckled, unable to hold a straight face when Anara flashed her teeth. "I know you better than that, Anara. I still have the marks from when we were children."

Anara's reply was lost as Aeron escorted her from the room. Darien gestured to Lovisa, but the Princess stood in the center of the room, her fingers fidgeting with the fabric of her gown.

"Darien, wait. I want to talk to you."

Larissa stepped back, willing herself to blend into the shadows. With Anara and Aeron gone, the atmosphere had changed from playful to private. The roaring fire now crackled intimately, and Larissa felt like an intruder in her own memory.

Darien dropped his arm, looking over his shoulder once. Was he checking to see if Aeron was still there?

"What is it?" he asked.

"My sixteenth birthday is only a week after Princess Shiko's coronation."

"We've been friends since you were six, Lov. I know when your birthday is."

"My parents are going to announce my heritage to the Perle Kingdom on my birthday."

Darien exclaimed, "That's great! You can finally address your people like you've always wanted to. Why aren't you happy?"

She stared back over the balcony where the Perlians gathered below for the Jóltide Festival. "I'm scared, Darien. I've been dreaming of this day for my whole life, but what if I mess up?"

"Look at me." Darien's hand grasped hers. "You'll be amazing."

She shook her head. "You don't know that."

"Yes, I do."

He grasped her chin, tilting her face up to meet his. A small reluctant smile broke across her lips. Only the crackle of the fireplace and the murmur of voices below broke the silence. Heat rushed toward Larissa's face—or was it rushing toward Lovisa's face? She was having a hard time separating herself from her past. She could feel Darien's hand in her own. But no, he was holding Lovisa's hand, wasn't he?

Darien closed the distance between them and whispered, "Lovisa, I've wanted to tell you—"

Lovisa leaned in when he paused, her eyes wide as though she did not want to miss a moment. "Tell me what?"

Darien's other hand cupped Lovisa's face. He took a steadying breath. "I think you're more beautiful than the morning and stronger than the seas. When you take your place as Princess, your kingdom will be better for it. And I ..."

"Yes?" she breathed out.

"If you'll let me, I'll be by your side through it all. Neither the Æsir nor the Jötnar could ever come between us." He leaned in, lowering his face to meet her rising lips Lovisa's eyes slid shut.

"Lovisa, Darien, are you coming?" Anara called.

The intimacy of the moment vanished as their bodies froze, their lips only inches from meeting. Darien released a low chuckle and muttered, "Perfect timing." In a louder voice, he called, "Coming!"

But neither of them moved until Darien tilted up his chin and brushed his lips across Lovisa's forehead. "Next time, Princess."

Larissa felt the flush that burned in Lovisa's cheeks. Darien straightened his shoulders and offered his arm, the perfect picture of propriety. "Ready, Lov?"

She placed her hand on his, slightly entwining their fingers. "I'm ready, Dar."

His eyes softened, and he led her from the room.

Released from the memory, Larissa looked away. The room faded from her view, but Darien's phantom touch remained.

She found herself in the same hallway as before, with doors on either side. Voices called to her from behind each one, beckoning for her to listen and learn.

What was the point? She had already determined what it was that Halla had asked her to learn. She had once been the Princess of Perle. It left a bitter taste in her mouth, although she could not say why. These memories were laced with guilt—a guilt that rose within her, a guilt she did not want to release.

She could leave this place. She could return to reality and refuse to remember any more. But then she would have to face Halla. Of course, Halla would love to hear that Larissa was the Princess, but she wouldn't think of the cost. How would the Empress punish Halla if she learned that Larissa was actually Lovisa? It would be better for Larissa to forget all of this, to pretend she didn't remember. Then Halla might actually stay safe.

Larissa grasped the ring, knowing that if she removed it, she would wake up.

Then stopped. Safe? The draugr *had already proven that to be impossible. Even if they joined the resistance, there was no promise of protection there. Would they demand that Larissa accept her past as Princess? Would they throw them out if she did not? Anara had said otherwise, but there was no guarantee.*

Larissa's ignorance had already been Pappa's and Mamma's downfall. No, if she was going to protect Halla, she would have to know the truth, or at least enough of it. She shoved the ring back, feeling the frustration pouring through her. Beneath her, the ground quivered and shook.

Were there earthquakes in memories?

Larissa's fingers drifted across the wooden doors, dipping in and out of the carved runes. She was searching for something, even if she did not know what it was. Finally, there was one door. It stood slightly ajar, and it squeaked open at Larissa's barest touch. Through the doorway, she thought she could hear the quiet sound of crying.

Stepping into the room, Larissa immediately recognized it from her dreams. A loom sat in the center of the large, windowless room, but it held no tapestry this time. There was, however, a fireplace and a small sitting area where the Princess sat huddled against the couch. Rather than her finery, she wore simple pants and a shirt with long sleeves she used to wipe at her cheeks. Without her royal regalia, Larissa was struck by the similarities in their appearance. It was like looking into a mirror.

When the door creaked open again, Lovisa sniffed and looked up. Her hands fell to her lap and, for the first time, Larissa noticed that she was holding three letters. The ink was smeared, bleeding through the paper.

Stjarna rushed across the floor, skirts rustling, as she sat next to her daughter. "Lovisa, what is it?"

The Princess handed over the letters. "Your plan won't work, Móðir. Rubin is overcome with insurgents. Anara writes that she'll come when her parents have regained control of her kingdom, but she says to not wait for her."

"What of the other two letters?"

"They're both from Darien. The first says that he must wait for Aeron's return before he can come. The second—" she stopped as another tear escaped out the corner of her eye. "He says that only one of Aeron's men returned from the last battle. Smaragd has fallen. Aeron is dead."

Lovisa collapsed into her mother's lap. Stjarna brushed back the hair from her face as emotions chased themselves in the Queen's eyes. There was anger and sadness, but most of all, there was fear.

Stjarna raised her daughter's face, one hand cupped under her chin. "We'll mourn all of our losses one day, and we'll honor them. If anything, this proves that we have run out of time. Your father and I had hoped that we could turn back the tide so that this did not all fall on you, but the Norn were right. Of course they were."

"Me? What are you talking about?"

The ground shook again, and Larissa nearly fell from the force of the tremor. Neither the Queen nor the Princess acknowledged it.

"Lovisa, there is so much that I should have told you. Your grandmother Rúna had a vision—"

"That the peace would end. I know, Móðir. That's why you've kept me hidden all my life."

"There's more to it than that. She had a vision that our bloodline would be involved not only in the destruction of the old regime, but in the creation of a new one. I hoped that responsibility would fall to me, but I always knew that it would have to be you. After Shiko's coronation, your father and I stopped in the Smaragd forests before coming home."

Another rumble. The tile beneath Larissa's feet shattered. The cracks grew in width, running the length of the floor and up the walls, separating Larissa from Stjarna and Lovisa. What was happening? Was the memory broken?

"Myrkviðr Forest?" The Princess' voice faded in Larissa's ears.

The tile in front of Larissa fell, revealing a bottomless pit below. Another tile followed suit, and another. The abyss crept toward her feet. Larissa could not hear Stjarna's reply over the crumbling of the floor and the roar of the growing earthquake in her ears.

Heart pounding, Larissa fled back into the hallway, slamming the door behind her. A crack splintered the door right up the middle then leapt from the door to the stone wall, traveling up toward the ceiling of the hallway. The world shook with renewed fury. Larissa watched in horror as the crack raced along the ceiling, branching off at every new door to splinter the wood beneath it. The entire palace was coming apart.

"Kings and Queens!" Larissa exclaimed, one hand on the wall to steady herself. She gripped the ring, but it was stuck as though burned into her skin.

"Why are you running?"

Queen Stjarna stood in front of her, oblivious to ground shaking beneath their feet and the cracks that spiraled down the hall as chunks of ceiling fell to the ground.

"What's happening?" Larissa shouted over the roar in her ears.

"This place holds your past, Lovisa, and it's being destroyed."

"Who's destroying it?"

"You are."

"What?" Larissa ducked as another piece of stone fell beside her. "I'm not doing this."

"You are by rejecting your past."

"I haven't! I can admit it. I was the Perle Princess."

Stjarna shook her head as, for the first time, she too was shaken by the quake. The Queen placed a hand against the wall to steady herself. "It is not that you were the Princess, Lovisa, it is that you are. Understanding that makes all the difference. If you cannot accept *your role in the past, then you will never accept your role in what is to come."*

"How am I supposed to do that?"

Queen Stjarna gestured to another door, the only door that remained whole and unbroken. The Dagaz rune, etched into the center of the wood, seemed to burn. Larissa yanked the handle, but the door would not budge.

She groaned in frustration. "It's locked."

"It will be until you accept who you are."

"This is ridiculous!" she shouted over the next quake that rolled through the corridor. "I've already told you that I accept who I was, but that's not me anymore. I'm Larissa, daughter of Dal and Vern, sister to Halla; I can't just forget all of that either."

Queen Stjarna raised a delicate eyebrow in response.

"Oh, forget this!" Larissa snatched her hand away from the door and took a step back, raising her leg and kicking at it with all her might. The door shuddered but remained closed. She tried again.

"That won't work."

Stjarna walked toward her, and Larissa noted the thin blood trailing from her nose just as it had done so many times before in her nightmares. Another shift of the ground caused Larissa to fall forward into the Queen's arms.

The blood was flowing more heavily now. Larissa stared in morbid fascination. "Why does this keep happening to you?"

Stjarna touched her nose, then stared at the blood on her finger as though unsurprised by its presence. "I gave up everything so that you could live. I don't regret any of it."

The rumble reached its crescendo as a final loud crack reverberated through the tile, shattering the ground into hundreds of pieces. The floor beneath them gave way. Then Queen Stjarna was gone, and Larissa was falling, falling, falling into the blackness.

Resistance

Larissa

"Larissa, wake up."

Even after opening her eyes, the darkness remained. A fine layer of dew had settled over her entire body. In the dim light of the rising sun, Larissa could make out the curious expectancy written across Halla's face. "What's going on?"

"You were dreaming."

Larissa sat up, aware that Darien and Anara were listening. "People tend to do that when they sleep. Is it my turn to stay awake?"

"No," Anara answered. "We let you sleep; you seemed to need it."

"You kept saying Lovisa," Halla added. "Were you remembering?"

Larissa rose to her feet, rolling up her damp blankets.

Halla tugged on her arm. "Are you the Princess or what?"

"Not right now, Halla. We have to go." In truth, Larissa wasn't sure what they needed to do, only that she wasn't ready for this conversation. She'd taken a few steps when Halla raced in front of her, blocking her path.

"You can't just avoid the question, Lara."

"Watch me." She sidestepped Halla, strolling back toward the truck. Larissa tossed her bundle of blankets into Helga's bed, only for Halla to follow and do the same. Anara and Darien had followed, but they kept their distance, something Larissa was grateful for.

"Lara—"

"Let it go, Halla."

She stomped her foot on the ground. "What is your problem? Would it really be so bad if you were the Princess?"

"Yes, it would!" Larissa snapped, wrapping her arms around her chest not only to block out the morning chill, but to shield herself from the consequences of her revelations. "Don't you get it? I won't be your sister anymore! I'll be the reason our parents are dead, but I can't even say that. They'd be *your* parents, not mine. Is that what you want?"

Halla stood on her tiptoes trying to see eye-to-eye with her sister, her face flushed. "You can be the Princess and my sister."

"No, I can't."

"Why not, Lara?"

Larissa flung her arms out. "You want the truth so badly, Halla, but the truth means I'm not *Lara*. It means I'm Lovisa, but I don't know who that is either. It's like a past life." Her voice broke. "So if I'm not Larissa or Lovisa, then who am I?"

Halla shrugged. "You can be both. Being Lovisa doesn't mean you can't be my sister."

Larissa groaned, holding her head in her hands. "Kings and Queens, Halla, you don't get it. I *stole* your birthright. I'm the reason you're considered a second-born. I'm the one who caused you to live in fear of your own existence!"

Silence reigned in the forest. Darien and Anara stood as still as statues watching the sisters. Larissa leaned against the tailgate and closed her eyes against their scrutiny.

Halla's small footsteps crunched over the gravel. Larissa felt Halla hoist herself up onto the tailgate and rest her head against Larissa's shoulder. "Lara, Lovisa, I don't care what your name is, and I don't care about being first- or second-born. I asked the *Æsir* for you. I love you, and you remembering any of this is a good thing. Remember what Pappa told us? The Princess can help restore peace to our nation. You can do that."

"No, I can't." Larissa's words were ragged, as though she had been running a long time. She hopped down from the tailgate. "I *was* her, Halla, but I'm not her anymore. People change. I might have been Lovisa at some point, but I can't help anyone. I can't even keep you safe."

Halla huffed and jumped down, reaching out to grab her sister. "You're being stupid, Lara, come on—"

The moment before Halla's hand made contact with Larissa, it flung back as though hitting and rebounding off an invisible barrier. The momentum caused Halla to step back. Her foot twisted on a rock, and Halla fell hard on her rump.

Before Larissa could react, Darien was there, pulling Halla to her feet as Anara stood between them. Larissa stared in horror at her shaking hand outstretched toward Halla. A golden aura emanated from Larissa's fingers, and the pearl on her ring shone even brighter.

"You need to calm down," Anara ordered. "You too, Halla. Stop pushing her."

Larissa lowered her hand. "Did I do that?"

The answer was as clear as the glow that crackled between her fingers.

Halla pulled away from Darien and brushed the damp leaves from her clothes. "It's fine. I'm fine."

Anara stared at the glow, an odd sort of triumph mixing with sadness in her eyes. "It's your *galdr*. You might think you're not the Princess anymore, Lovisa, but the longer you continue to deny yourself, the more unpredictable your *galdr* will become."

"My name is Larissa." Static crackled in the air as she spoke.

Anara's voice fell flat. "Fine, *Larissa*."

Adrenaline coursed through her, pulsating with every breath. Larissa shoved her hands into her pockets to hide the glow. When her fingers finally stopped shaking, she dared to look at her sister. "Halla, I'm so sorry."

"I'm fine." She threw out her arms as if to emphasize her point, and Larissa nearly smiled.

Anara reached out a cautious hand and sighed when her hand rested on Larissa's shoulder without meeting a barrier. "We really should get back on the road." She held up her hand when Halla opened her mouth. "No more, Halla. We'll get to the river, and then we'll talk. Darien, you're riding with me."

Larissa sighed with relief at the reprieve in her interrogation, even though she knew it would resume soon.

Darien nodded at Anara but offered his hand to Halla. "Want some help, kiddo?"

She beamed at him, taking his hand with an air of regality. "Yes, Your Highness."

Darien winced. "You don't need to call me that."

"What about Your Majesty?"

"No, not that one either."

Using Darien's hand, Halla boosted herself into Helga's bed. "Why thank you, Your Princeliness."

Anara snorted. "I like that one."

Darien pushed his hand through his hair, and for a moment, Larissa saw him as he was during the Jóltide Festival. Her heart felt that familiar flutter from her dreams, the heat of the burning fireplace, and the warmth of his lips pressed against her forehead. She looked down just as he turned to her, but she was certain he could see the blush in her cheeks.

"Want some help?"

Larissa looked up to see his offered hand. She nearly reached for him but pulled back, fearing what memories his touch might awaken. She lifted herself up into the bed. "I'm good, thanks."

"Freyja help you both," Anara muttered. "Let's go, Darien."

She grabbed the collar of his jacket, practically dragging him back toward the cab of the truck. Helga's engine roared to life as Halla and Larissa settled themselves between the crates, wrapping a blanket around their legs. Larissa laid her head against the truck bed's side and closed her eyes to stem off Halla's questions. By the time Helga reached the main road, the morning sun had peeked over the horizon. Despite the warmth, Larissa couldn't shake the cold feeling in her gut and the memory of the blood on Queen Stjarna's face.

22

Ghosts of the Past

Darien

HELGA RATTLED OVER THE bridge, shaking Darien like a dog in the passenger seat. He could only imagine how much worse it must be for Larissa and Halla in the back. Surely they'd all be black and blue by the time they reached Perle.

Anara's hand relaxed out the open window, catching beams of sunlight between her fingertips. Sól climbed a steady pace up the sky, infusing warmth into the late morning. Under the bridge, Darien caught sight of the rushing waters.

"This river marks the boundary lines between Safír and Perle," Anara explained. "The shore we just left is still Safír; that shore up there is Perle. We'll drive a couple miles down the the river and then stop to eat and bathe."

"Bathe?" Darien asked.

Anara wrinkled her nose. "Let's just say I'm done riding with any of you until I can breathe fresh air again."

Looking down at himself, Darien noted the ash and blood still clinging to his clothes. Now that Anara had mentioned it, there was a general smell rising from his jacket. It occurred to him then that Anara had rolled down her window the moment they'd gotten in the truck hours ago. Darien leaned further away from Anara, but the movement only emphasized how gritty his clothes felt chafing against his skin.

As promised, Anara pulled the truck off the road a few miles past the bridge and parked behind a clump of trees. Darien followed her toward the back of the truck where Larissa and Halla waited on the tailgate. Halla scratched at her clothes, while Larissa stood stiff in her own.

"The riverbank is just through those trees," Anara said, taking her bag from the bed. "Grab a change of clothes."

"Oh, thank the gods!" Halla cried. She reached past Larissa, scrambling to grab a bag and rush after Anara.

With Halla's sudden absence, Darien wasn't sure where to look. Larissa was searching through the supplies for her own bag. Darien could see where Anara had tossed his own, right beside Larissa. She crouched down as her shifting jacket revealed the gun tucked into her waistband. Darien had nearly forgotten it, but its presence reminded him of the burning barn and Larissa's screams of terror.

Shaking off the thoughts, he leaned in; his fingertips grabbed his bag at the same time they brushed Larissa's calf. She recoiled from his touch, backing further into the truck bed.

"Sorry," he muttered, snatching his hand and bag out of the truck.

Larissa shook her head. "No, it's fine."

Darien's fingers tapped against his leg as he tried not to let his mind slip back into his memory of the Jóltide Festival or to think of how soft Lovisa's hair had been tickling the tips of his fingers. Would she ever allow herself to remember? Or was it better if she forced herself to forget? Then she would never remember how he had left her after swearing he wouldn't.

Larissa hopped down, slamming the tailgate behind her, but her eyes refused to meet his. "We should catch up with the others."

He nodded, cursing his tongue for its silence.

The trees disappeared a little farther in, and the dirt turned to pebbles beneath their feet at the shore of the Klarälven River. Water flowed downstream, not hurriedly or sluggishly, but at its own intentional pace. A couple hundred yards down, it bubbled over and passed through a collection of large boulders and rocks.

Anara and Halla were pulling clothing from their bags. Darien breathed in the air. It was not the salty smell he associated with home, but it was familiar all the same.

"I remember this," he said. "We used to come here as children."

"It's where I learned to swim," Larissa murmured.

Darien stared at her, but Larissa had already dropped her glare to the ground, an angry red flush contrasting with the harsh white scar on her cheek.

Halla clapped her hands together. "Lara, you're remembering more!"

She kicked at a pebble, nonresponsive.

Anara looped her arm through Halla's, who had opened her mouth again but shut it at Anara's touch. "Let's head over to those boulders for a little bit of privacy. If you want to sit with me in that truck again, you better get yourself cleaned up, Darien. Not even your good looks can mask your smell."

Anara led the girls away far beyond the shelter of the boulders. Darien worked to stifle the hope still burning within him. Larissa would remember or she wouldn't. There was nothing he could do. At least, that was what he kept telling himself.

He walked to the water's edge. Anara had been right about the smell. He dropped his bag, careful to hold his breath, and stripped off his bloodstained clothes. His body was smeared with a mixture of dirt, blood, and ash. A bruise that covered the entire left side of his chest and ribs was beginning to fade from blue to yellow. The scratches along his arms had scabbed over, some of them already shiny from new skin. Mentally, he thanked whatever it was that Anara had given him to heal the wounds.

He toed the water with his bare foot, then yanked it from the icy current, debating his actions. Was it really necessary to jump all the way in? He sniffed himself again. The answer was an undeniable yes. Though the sun was still high in the sky, Darien would rather be long done in the river before the sun started its downward descent.

A loud splash and then a sharp squeal echoed over the water, followed by high peals of laughter. Darien grinned, wondering if it had been Larissa or Anara who had thrown Halla in. If she could bear the cold, so could he. He sucked in a breath, then leapt into the water.

It was worse than he thought. Gritting his teeth to keep them from chattering, Darien scrubbed at his body furiously, rubbing off the layers of dirt and blood. Without mercy, he ducked his head under the water, scratching his fingers through his hair and feeling flakes of blood dissolve. After several dunks, with his toes going numb, he decided it would have to be good enough.

He dried himself off and, grabbing a new set of clothes from his bag, moved back into the cover of the woods to change. He could still hear the voices of the others coming from downstream. Darien sat on the rocky beach, letting the fading sun dry his hair and pulling down the sleeves of the jacket to his fingertips. He twisted the ring on his hand, feeling the cold stone underneath his fingertips.

Let me show you how it's done, brother.

Darien did not flinch at the voice in his mind; he welcomed it like the sun on his face. It was not a hallucination, as those had stopped ever since he had remembered who he was. No, this was just a memory, and yet it played out before his eyes like pictures on the page of a book.

ᚾᛁᛣᛦᛋᚾᛁᛣᛦᛋᚾᛁᛣᛦᛋᚾᛁᛣᛦᛋᚾᛁᛣᛦᛋ

Four children stood on the riverside. Aeron, the oldest and tallest, bounced a pebble in his hand. Lovisa was still searching for her own on the ground. Mini-Darien offered her the one in his own hand, while Anara watched from the sidelines.

"Alright, form up," Anara ordered in a lazy tone.

Aeron toed the water. "Let me show you how it's done, brother."

With a flick, Aeron's pebble flew over the surface of the water, bouncing four times and sinking on its fifth.

Darien went next, his stone sinking on the third skip.

Then Lovisa moved into place. A yellow glow hummed around her finger tips, encasing the smooth white pebble. When she sent it flying, it skipped nine times across the water.

Anara laughed. "A clear winner, again."

"Only because she used her galdr,*" Aeron protested.*

Lovisa snorted. "I could beat you without galdr *and my hands tied behind my back."*

Darien gathered more stones and handed one to Lovisa. His eyes held a challenge. "Best two out of three!"

ᚾᛁ�ᚱᛋᚾᛁᛗᚱᛋᚾᛁᛗᚱᛋᚾᛁᛗᚱᛋᚾᛁᛗᚱᛋ

AERON'S LAUGHTER RIPPLED ACROSS Darien's mind as the children slipped from his vision. The shoreline was the same, but Darien knew that even if all of his memories returned, he never would be. Not without Aeron. His hands clenched into fists as his eyes burned behind his closed eyelids.

I'll find out who killed you, Aeron, he thought. *I'll make Shiko pay; I promise you that.*

"You alright? Your face looks weird."

Darien opened his eyes to find Anara standing over him, blocking the sun. He cleared his throat, forcing his hands to relax. "I happen to like my face, thanks. You shouldn't sneak up on people like that. What if I hadn't realized it was you?"

Anara shrugged, but Darien caught the glimpse of a smile as she sat next to him on the rocky bank. "Like you could take me. Larissa and Halla are finishing up; they needed a minute alone."

The silence lengthened. Darien sighed. "I was remembering Aeron."

She looked around. "He loved it here; we all did."

"I'm going to get justice for what happened to him."

Anara nudged his shoulder. "I'll help you."

Darien nudged her back, more grateful than he could put into words. Pulling at the cuffs of his sleeves, he noticed a faint scar on his wrist. With Aagen, he had always assumed the bite mark had come from some small animal when he was a child. Now, he wasn't so sure. "Anara?"

"Hmm?"

"I remembered something interesting. Something about someone taking a game too seriously." He raised the wrist at her. "You wouldn't happen to remember how I got this scar, would you?

Anara's eyes were wide and innocent, too innocent. "I'm sure I wouldn't know."

"I'm pretty sure—"

"Here they come." Anara stood, brushing the dirt from her pants.

Larissa and Halla walked back toward them, stopping every few feet to pick up pebbles. The sisters examined each one, then discarded it for another. Eventually, they settled on one before joining Darien and Anara. Halla's small fingers curled around the smooth pale stone in her hand.

"What's that, kiddo?" Darien gestured at the rock.

Halla shared a look with Larissa. There was a long silence. "It's a family thing."

"We'll need to get back on the road soon," Anara offered the awkward silence. "We should eat first, though. Halla, will you help me get something out of the truck?"

Darien watched the small girl trail after Anara, her hand still clutched around the stone. He didn't even notice Larissa's approach until she spoke.

"It reminds her of our parents."

"The rock?"

She nodded; her voice tightened. "When Pappa would do the produce runs, he would stop by the seashore and bring her back a pebble. Every time. He called it her own little piece of the outside world."

He thought again of Aeron. "I'm sorry for your loss."

Larissa shrugged, but tears gathered in her eyes. "If I'm really Lovisa, do I have the right to call it my loss?"

"They were still your parents, just like Aagen is mine. The Norn placed us with them for a reason."

"The *Norn*." Derision coated Larissa's voice. "If the Norn are so wise and powerful, why did they let this happen?"

Darien was saved from answering by the return of Anara and Halla. They'd brought back a small box filled with an assortment of canned and fresh produce that they quickly portioned out. When they all sat down and began to eat, Larissa and Halla both looked at the berries in their laps in silence. It was all too easy to guess who they were thinking about.

Setting down the food, Larissa turned toward Anara. "I need to know more about the Viðnám and how they can protect Halla."

"I'll tell you in the truck; you can ride with me."

"I'm not getting back in the truck until you answer my questions."

Anara pinched the bridge of her nose, then exhaled through gritted teeth. "At least your stubbornness is intact. Fine, but eat while I talk." When she spoke, it wasn't to Larissa, but to Darien. "First thing, Darien, your father is alive."

23

A House Divided

Darien

WHEN DARIEN HAD BEEN a child, he'd fallen from a tree. The breathlessness he'd experienced then was the same he felt now. The very air he tried to breathe felt thin. When he had remembered Aeron's demise, he'd shared the same grief over his parents. He had been so sure of their deaths. Darien stared at Anara, an opened can of peaches forgotten in his clenched hand.

"My family is dead. I remember it."

In the corner of his vision, Larissa flinched, as though she felt his loss personally.

Anara shook her head. "When Shiko gained control of the five kingdoms, she spread word that all the previous royal families had been killed, but that wasn't true. You, your father, Lov—sorry, Larissa, and myself are the only survivors I know about.

"To prevent further rebellion, Shiko proclaimed the death of the royal families, all the while chasing whispers of the lost Perle Princess. She conducted raids throughout all the commonwealths, but Perle suffered the greatest." Anara took a deep breath, steeling herself. "Their population was halved in a matter of months as a warning to the rest of the commonwealths."

Darien set down the can, feeling the food he'd eaten threaten to come back up. Halved? What kind of monster could destroy a people group so severely? Larissa looked ill as well, tucking her chin into her chest and staring at hands that knotted themselves against each other in her lap.

"Kings and Queens," she murmured.

"Thousands of citizens were imprisoned or killed," Anara continued. "Perle became the example to keep the other commonwealths in line. When the order came about banning second-borns, most people complied, fearing that Shiko would turn her wrath on them if they did not. But some rebelled. King Torsten, Darien's father, created a resistance for those who fled Shiko's lands. At first, it was merely a hiding place. Over the years, it has grown as more refugees seek to escape every new restriction and cruelty that Shiko puts in place. It became known as the Viðnám."

Darien's mind swam with the new information but continued to circle back to one idea. "He's really alive?"

"He was the last time I saw him, but that was years ago, and the members of Viðnám lead dangerous lives. I haven't traveled with them in nearly three decades."

"Why'd you leave?" Halla asked.

Anara's lips tightened. "Ever since the Great *Hrun,* our primary objective at Viðnám had been to locate Prince Darien and Princess Lovisa, although they only knew her as the lost Princess of Perle. Very few knew her name. Lovisa's story became legend. Even though the Norn's prophecy surrounding her was vague, people believed that if we found her, the gods would use her to make everything right."

Darien glanced at Larissa, who set down her food, a green tinge coloring her otherwise pale cheeks.

Anara continued, "Several decades ago, the people of the Viðnám lost hope. They believed the rumors that you had never existed or, if you had, that you had died in the war. The search ended, and the searchers took on new responsibilities. When Torsten agreed to this, I left."

Darien leaned back on his hands, doing his best to appear unbothered while he worked through the emotions. His father was alive. He had stopped looking for Darien, his own son. Had he bent to the will of Viðnám, or had he truly given up hope on ever finding him? Darien clenched his jaw. Would his father have stopped the search if it had been Aeron? His hands dug into the forest floor as Darien forced his focus back to what Anara was saying.

"—I've been on my own since then, but I never doubted that you were alive. Now that I've found you, our best protection lies with the Viðnám."

"They're in Perle?" Confusion saturated Halla's voice.

"Not exactly. The Viðnám was always mobile, never in the same place and never all together, but we always left at least one person in each city to tell any refugees where they could go to find safety. Our informants typically set up shop within the Walls as physicians—"

"Perle has a Wall too?" Halla interrupted.

All eyes turned toward her. Darien often forgot how little Halla knew of the world outside her farm.

"Every commonwealth's city is enclosed by a Wall. Only the farmlands are allowed to exist outside of it," Anara explained. "The Empress claims the Walls protect the cities, but it imprisons them. That's why our spies reside within the Wall. There's always someone trying to get out. If we can get within Lystheim—that's the city of Perle, Halla—then we can find my informant and find the Viðnám."

"Why didn't we just go within the Wall at Safír?" Darien asked. "It would have been faster."

"And possibly crawling with *draugr* searching for your scent." Anara paused, meeting each of their gazes, even Halla's. "Perle will have its own dangers, but hopefully, they will not be searching for you here as they would have in Safír."

Larissa's eyes darted to Halla. "You promised us safety, but you don't seem to completely trust them—so how can we?"

"My issues with the Viðnám won't affect you. You're not Rubinian," she muttered. "Halla will be safe; the protection of children is honored there."

"I'm not a child." Halla interrupted, glaring at Anara and Larissa.

"Halla—"

"I stopped being a child the moment I burned my parents' bodies."

There was a collective pause.

Darien could see Larissa battling her next words. "You're right, Halla," she finally said. "You're not a child, but you're still my sister. If I put you in this danger, then I need to see you out of it. We'll go to the Viðnám, but Anara, I can't help them. I'm not *her* anymore."

"You're wrong, Larissa. Whatever you decide to call yourself, whoever you choose to be, there's so much your presence alone could do. You're a different person now—we all are—but you're not free from your past. The Ancestral Blood still resides within you as strong as ever. You felt the *galdr* earlier. You know it's true."

Larissa bristled. "I couldn't control what happened. I don't even know *how* it happened. How am I supposed to help anyone if I can't even control myself?"

"*Galdr* comes from a place of understanding and self-reflection. When you didn't know your past, your *galdr* remained dormant inside of you. Now that you are fighting those memories, the *galdr* is also fighting to be released. You're at war with yourself, and unless you find a way to make peace, you'll only destroy yourself. You can't push away who you are forever."

Larissa said nothing, but Darien could see the tightening of her shoulders and the way she ducked her chin to one side. For all their childhood, Lovisa had been so open to others, desperate in revealing her heart. So often alone, she had longed for companionship. This Larissa, who stood to the side and avoided others, left jagged, glassy shards in his chest that hurt with every breath. He had seen stubbornness from Lovisa as a child but never to this degree. Larissa was terrified of remembering, that much was clear, but what was it that had her so resistant to the truth? What had happened to her that she so desperately did not want to remember?

He could not stand to watch it.

"What about me?" Darien asked. "I've remembered so much, not everything, but enough. Why hasn't my *galdr* returned?"

Gratitude swept across Larissa's features as Anara's attention diverted to Darien.

"It has," Anara said shortly, as though she knew what Darien was doing.

"What?"

"Just because you haven't used it doesn't mean that it's not there. I've felt it grow inside you since we left the farm."

"You can feel it?"

"Once you've fully recovered your memories, you'll be able to sense *galdr* in those around you, though my sense will always be stronger. Consider it an animal instinct. Meditative techniques will help you regain your memories and your *galdr*. Now that you've rested, you'll need to practice. We won't be able to enter Perle until you regain control, Darien."

"Why me?"

"Your *galdr* is one of persuasion. You can influence the minds of others, though some have been taught to resist the influence of Safirian royalty. We're entering Perle tomorrow, so you'll need to influence the sentries to get us through the Wall unnoticed."

Darien leaned forward. "Tomorrow?"

"We can't linger in one spot for too long. A *draugr* might avoid the river, but whoever sent it will not."

"Calder," Larissa said.

All eyes turned toward Larissa, but this time she met their gazes head on. For just a small moment, Darien could see the Lovisa he had known.

"Before the *draugr* attacked, a *Kafteinn* named Calder came to our house during an Inspection. He threatened to take me away unless I promised to spy on the Viðnám. He kept calling them a small group of runaways. I didn't realize the connection until now."

"Did you tell him anything about them?" Anara's voice was sharp.

"I didn't know anything about them," Larissa protested. "We were going to leave that night after I retrieved Halla. Now I wonder if Pappa knew about the Viðnám all this time. I overheard him telling Mamma that someone was coming after the season had finished. He said it was the sentries, but I think it might have been the Viðnám."

"Calder." Darien tasted the name on his tongue. "I've never heard of him before, in either set of my memories. Anara?"

Anara shook her head. "Not the name, no, but there are stories of a *Kafteinn* under Shiko's command, known as her War Dog. He's been searching for the Viðnám since its inception. He has killed or captured countless refugees seeking asylum. He nearly discovered me a number of times. I've never seen him face to face, and no one knows his name, but I don't believe in coincidences. If a *Kafteinn* came to your home, I'm betting it was him. We need to find the Viðnám before he finds us."

Darien felt her gaze, as hot as the sun. Though his stomach tightened in displeasure, he agreed. "Alright. Just tell me what to do."

Anara's eyes darted to the shoreline. She rose, offering a hand to Halla. "We're too exposed here. Any sentries traveling between Safír and Perle will use that bridge. We need to get closer to the city, then make camp in the cover of the forest. Back to the truck, everyone."

"That truck has less cushion than—" Darien's groan was stopped short by Larissa's sharp look. "I mean, it's a very nice truck."

"*She*," Halla interjected. "Her name is Helga."

Darien raised his hands in surrender. "*She*'s a very nice truck, kiddo."

Satisfied, Halla followed Anara back through the trees. Darien chuckled at her retreating back. He grabbed his own bag from the ground but stopped when he saw Larissa's eyes locked on the river.

"You okay?"

Larissa acknowledged him with a slight glance before returning her gaze to the river. "Do you know the saying about the Norn?"

"There's a lot of sayings about the Norn."

"'Fear not death for the hour of your doom is set—'"

"'—and none may escape it.'" Darien finished, shifting on his feet. "Yeah, it's in the old stories of the heroic Volsungs. Why?"

For a moment, Darien wondered if Larissa would answer at all. Finally, she said, "I dreamed about the Norn. If they're truly turning this wheel, I don't know how much of a difference any of us can make. Even if I am the Princess."

Darien shoved his hands into his pockets. "The stories also tell us it's better to fight and fail than to live without hope. You could be that hope for so many people, Lara."

Her eyes slid closed. "No, I can't."

Larissa's feet slapped against the rocks as she disappeared into the trees, heading back toward Helga. Darien cast one last look at the river, half expecting to see the ghost of his brother standing on the shore. But there was only the rushing water.

Empathy

Darien

HOURS LATER, THEY MADE camp several miles south, only a dozen or so miles away from the Wall surrounding Lystheim, the main city of Perle. Anara led them to a small clearing just large enough for them to roll out their blankets around another small stockpile of food. Larissa and Halla sat together atop a blanket, their eyes glued on Anara and Darien as they discussed what was coming next.

Anara's plan was simple, or so she'd claimed while explaining it on their drive. Produce Day was tomorrow. They would drive up to the Wall with a delivery. They would convince the sentry to allow them entry past the Intake Yard, and from there Anara would guide them to the contact. Of course, the entire plan relied on Darien's ability to persuade the sentry by accessing the *galdr* he hadn't remembered he'd possessed until only a few hours ago.

Which led to his current predicament.

"Darien," Anara snapped her fingers, jolting Darien from his thoughts.

He cleared his throat. "I'm sorry, what did you say?"

To his surprise, Anara turned away from him. "Halla, would you mind if Darien practiced with you? It won't hurt, I promise."

Halla bobbed her head, moving to stand.

"No." Larissa had put a restraining hand on Halla. "No offense to Darien, but he doesn't know what he's doing; there's no way I'm letting him practice on Halla. Why can't he practice on you?"

"Because I have to guide him, and I can't do both."

"Fine." Larissa rose to her feet only to settle herself in front of Darien. "He can practice on me."

"Are you sure?" Darien asked.

She nodded, but her eyes held a challenge. "You say you knew me."

He swallowed dry air, his heart thumping at her sudden closeness. "I did."

He had known her, the little girl who had yearned so longingly for companionship that she had given her heart away to her very first friend. And he felt that he knew her now, the girl who would go to Hel and back for the sake of her sister. He had loved the first girl and admired the second.

Finally, she said, "If you really knew me, and you are who you say you are, then maybe you can help me remember."

Anara placed herself beside them both, creating the three points of a triangle. "Start by obtaining eye contact."

Darien stared into those golden eyes that were trying so hard to appear unafraid. His gaze strayed to the thick cut on her right cheek that stretched behind her ear. It had scabbed over, but in some places the shiny scar beneath peeked through. Behind Larissa, Halla inched towards them, fascination written on her face.

Darien forced his eyes to return to Larissa's gaze. "Anara, are you sure this is a good idea?"

"Yes, now be quiet. To access your *galdr*, you must first connect with the individual you're trying to influence. This connection comes from empathy and understanding. You can persuade someone without eye contact, but it's much easier this way. Next, you reach into their own thoughts to understand their feelings. Once you've made that connection, bend their thoughts to match yours."

"As long as it's simple," Darien muttered dryly.

"Just focus on gaining that connection first."

Larissa's face had cleared of emotion as Anara had spoken, but now her eyes betrayed apprehension and...something else. Curiosity? It was a ledge that Darien could grab on to, something he could relate to. He focused on his own feelings of confusion when the hallucinations had begun, how he had sought after answers, and how Larissa must have felt the same uncertainty as the pieces of her life were stripped away.

An overwhelming fountain of emotions poured into Darien. Larissa's emotions latched onto him like a string between their two minds, taut and liable to snap. He tried to prod them gently but feared he would lose them if he didn't hold tight. He pushed forward with his own mind. Doubt clouded Larissa's thoughts, but beyond that, he could feel something deeper, something stronger that left a bitter taste in his mouth. He recognized it instantly. Guilt, the kind of guilt that kept a person up at night. Forgoing caution, he dove in, inching his way past the confusion and anger, reaching for the source of the guilt. What did Larissa not want to remember? In his mind's eye, he saw a door.

He reached for the handle to open it.

"Enough."

Someone shook his shoulder. Darien blinked, looking into Anara's face, then past her. Larissa's eyes were closed, her dark lashes contrasting against her paled cheeks. Halla was supporting her from the side. Darien felt the similar sickness as before but knew this guilt was all his own. "What did I do?"

Anara's eyes were kind as she removed her hands from his shoulder. "You found the connection, but you went past it. Your influence allows you access to a person's thoughts and feelings, but you should never push too far. You risk exploiting who they are and the places they keep private. Knowing your boundaries is a key tenet of your *galdr*. I didn't know you would regain the ability to do so much so soon, or I would have warned you."

"Larissa, I'm sorry." The apology sounded weak to Darien's own ears.

But Larissa only pushed herself off of Halla's shoulder, the color returning to her face. To Darien's surprise, her eyes held not anger but understanding. "You doubted."

"What?"

"I could feel your thoughts too. I didn't realize you felt that way. You seemed to accept it all so easily, our past." She paused at her own admission then turned to Anara. "How is it that I know what he was feeling?"

"The connection goes both ways when both parties possess *galdr*. Darien's *galdr* is powerful, but it also makes him vulnerable if his opponent is mentally stronger than him. "She turned to Darien. "Relearning the nuances of your *galdr* will take years. Let's try again."

Darien glanced at Larissa. "Are you okay?"

"I'm fine." She resettled, facing him. "We need to get to the *Viðnám* and find safety, right? If this is how we get there, then we can't waste time."

"Alright then." Anara put a hand on Darien's shoulder. "This time, once you make the connection, stop digging. Focus instead on presenting a new thought for Larissa to follow. Something simple and noninvasive. Try making her yawn."

Larissa was so close, Darien could see his reflection in her eyes. He resisted the urge to tuck back a strand of hair that hung in her face. Picking up on the same feelings of fear and doubt as before, he held them loosely, careful not to follow them too deeply. A memory rose unbidden: two children sitting on the riverbank, telling stories by firelight. His fingers itched to grab the memory, but he let it slide past unhindered. He narrowed his eyes, maintaining the contact but blocking out everything else to focus on Larissa's thoughts and feelings.

You're tired, he thought. *You feel like yawning.*

Darien's eyes widened as Larissa yawned in response. As if unaware that she had done so, she sat still, waiting for his command.

A smug smile tugged at Anara's lips, but no, Darien could not let his mind wander; his connection with Larissa was waning. All at once, his head felt light and off-balance. He should probably stop, but he wanted to try something first.

Focus, he thought.

Instead of forcing Larissa to remember, he shaped his own thoughts, revealing the acceptance and peace he had come to feel over his own past. He fed those feelings to Larissa. Not as a command, but as a suggestion. If he could help her in this way, he had to at least try and show her what acceptance could feel like. Her shoulders, always so tight and pulled up around her neck, loosened and lowered if only an inch. It would have to be enough.

Without warning, the connection snapped. Trees spun around Darien in a nauseating dance. Anara held a bottle filled with water to his lips. He took it from her, draining it. "What happened?"

"That was the strangest thing I have ever experienced." Larissa rubbed her temples, but she didn't appear to be in pain. "Is there any way to guard against it?"

"There is, but that is a lesson for another night." Anara was smiling. "Well done, Darien."

"Did I do it wrong? I feel awful."

"An unfortunate side effect of working with *galdr*. The power of the gods comes with a price. Every time you use it, it feeds off your own strength and energy. It's why we practice to build up our endurance."

"You can practice on me, too," Halla offered.

"No one else is practicing anything tonight," Anara said. "We're all exhausted, and the sun is nearly down. We'll only have a few hours of rest before we must leave."

"What if someone comes for us when we're asleep?"

"Don't worry, Halla, I'll stay up."

"We can watch in shifts," Darien suggested.

"No. I appreciate that, but you all look dead on your feet. I'm used to less sleep."

Weariness killed any further protests. Exhaustion nestled into Darien's bones, leaving them brittle and tender with every move- ment. He could tell the others felt similarly by the way Larissa lowered herself onto her blankets, taking care not to move too quickly. She lay down on her side, removing the gun from her waistband and setting it next to her blankets.

Yawning, Halla dragged her blankets closer to her sister before settling down. By the time the sun had truly set, they were settled. Anara propped herself up against a nearby tree, her yellow eyes glowing in the dark.

Although the girls nodded off immediately, Darien remained awake. His body cried out for sleep, but his mind thrummed with renewed energy. The *galdr* had awakened his old self more than his memories ever could. Images flooded his vision: hours spent training with Aeron, learning not only how to control their *galdr*, but when it was to be used and how it should never be abused.

Darien could only dwell on thoughts of Aeron for so long without wanting to put his fist through a tree. Not knowing how his brother died ate at Darien's soul. He tossed to his side, gazing at Larissa's sleeping form only a few feet away. Her long white braid lay coiled on the ground. His racing mind slowed at the sight as he pondered what he had felt in her mind. What lay behind that door he had seen? Why was she overwhelmed with guilt? Would she ever remember him?

He chastised himself for his own self-absorption. Larissa's feelings for him were the least of their concerns.

Darien turned onto his back, staring up through the tree limbs that twisted and curved into one another. The night sky was alive. In the middle of Darien's vision, twin stars reflected their brilliance off one another. The sight triggered another memory, a story he had once been taught about the stars. His eyelids sagged.

Then Halla whispered, "Lara. Lara?"

A muffled grunt.

"Lara, are you awake?"

There came the rustling of blankets followed by Larissa's sleep-heavy voice. "I am now. You okay?"

"I can't sleep."

"What can I do?"

"Tell me a story?"

"You know more of Pappa's stories than I do. What one do you want to hear?"

"Tell me something I haven't heard before. Come on, Lara, I'm sure you heard different stories when you were the Princess. You have to remember *something*."

For a long time, there was silence. Darien forced himself to stay still, his eyes closed, in case Larissa turned and saw that he was still awake. Finally, he heard her say, "Okay, I remember one, but you have to close your eyes and try to sleep."

"Okay."

"Halla."

"Yeah?"

"Your eyes."

"Oh, right."

Darien grinned. He could picture Halla now, her eyes closed, but every so often opening to peek at Larissa. He could hear more movement. Was Larissa brushing back Halla's hair to soothe her? Even as a child, Lovisa had always been jealous of Darien and Aeron's relationship. She had always wanted a sibling.

Perhaps the Norn had given her one after all.

"There once was a lovely giantess named Skaði, born to the *Jötnar*..." Larissa's soft voice pulled Darien into a trance.

Her words painted images on the back of his eyelids—giants, gods and goddesses, tricksters that could shapeshift, a maiden hidden in a walnut, a fiery death, and an unusual marriage. All the while, Darien's heart raced because he *knew* the story, and he knew who had told it to her.

Larissa's voice was no more than a whisper as she finished her tale. "That is why, every winter, when the twin stars shine brightest in the sky, we remember how Skaði's loyalty and bravery put an end to further death and destruction."

Halla's yawn floated across the wind. "I like that story. Who told it to you?"

"A friend, I think. Try to get some sleep now."

"We should all get some rest," Anara added from her watch point. It seemed they all had been listening.

Larissa's heavy breathing followed Halla's quiet snores. Unable to resist, Darien rolled over to see Halla wrapped in Larissa's arms, the two of them fast asleep. The warm feeling that started in his stomach reached his face as his lips broke into an unhindered smile. Larissa said she didn't remember him, but he knew the truth behind her words even if she did not.

They'd been only children when he told her that story, but some part of her remembered.

With the grin still on his face, he finally slept.

No Right Choice

Larissa

FOUR CHILDREN RACED ALONG the lakeside. Two boys battled with wooden swords, their faces covered in sloppy warpaint and the wild abandon of childhood joy. Two small girls, one with dark hair and another with light, called out to the boys, who paused in their game. Yet none of the children spared Larissa a glance from where she watched in the shadows.

We were always together, *the voice in Larissa's mind reminded her.*

But if that were true, why had they been separated?

Like rain on a windshield, the images ran and blurred before her. Then Larissa was back on her farm; flames raged around her more fiercely than they had before. Pappa and Mamma cried out to her, begging her to save Halla before the draugr *killed them both. Then Halla stood before her, weeping over their parents' bodies as the* draugr *advanced on her from behind. Larissa leaped between them, catching the* draugr's *claw across her face. Blood dripped from the wound. Larissa looked up from the ground to see it was not the* drau-

gr, but Kafteinn *Calder standing over her, holding a bloodied knife in his hand. His pale hazel eyes sickened her with their familiarity.*

Let me show you how it's done, he said, bending down. The knife pierced Larissa's skin, and she screamed. Calder's hand covered her mouth, silencing her pain.

ᚾᛁᛞᛗᚠᛋᚾᛁᛞᛗᚠᛋᚾᛁᛞᛗᚠᛋᚾᛁᛞᛗᚠᛋᚾᛁᛞᛗᚠᛋ

LARISSA'S EYES SNAPPED OPEN; there was nothing to see in the darkness. Her screams stilled at the back of her throat. It had all been a dream, except for the hand still covering her mouth.

"Larissa, stop, it's me," a voice whispered fiercely.

She paused mid-thrash, her gaze locking on dark hair falling over sea blue eyes.

"I'm going to lift my hand," Darien whispered. "Don't scream, they'll hear you."

When she nodded, Darien removed his hand, but only to brush back the hair that had covered her face and the tears she hadn't noticed slipping from the corners of her eyes. She was suddenly aware of his nearness, of the way his body lay pressed up next to hers. He was as taut as a bowstring. His words registered in her mind. *They'll hear you.*

Her body tensed, relaxing only slightly when confirming Halla's slumbering presence next to them.

"Anara smelled people approaching." Darien spoke hushed words into Larissa's ears, and she told herself she only shivered from the cold. It was then she noticed Anara's absence. "She woke me and went to find out who they are. We need to wake Halla, in case—"

Larissa's next shiver truly came from her fear.

The sounds of approaching footsteps and male voices reached her ears. Off in the distance, beams of light flashed through the dark night. Larissa started to rise, but Darien's hand wrapped around her elbow, gently yet firmly holding her in place with his finger over his mouth. Noting the distance of these newcomers, Larissa understood why. Whoever was out there hadn't noticed them. Yet.

Mimicking Darien's strategy, Larissa reached out a hand over Halla's mouth. The girl stirred instantly, then calmed when she saw Larissa's face. A finger over her mouth and the distant voices were enough to silence Halla's questions.

Leaves rustled in the woods near them, followed by the snapping of branches as bodies broke through them.

"Found 'em!"

Other voices rose, cursing and grunting. A woman shouted, "Run, Juni!"

Larissa nearly yelped, having bit her tongue at the sudden shout, but the voices came from some distance away. They were not yet discovered.

"Oh no, you don't!" A curse, followed by a moan.

"Got 'em, Fenris."

"Well done, boys. Three more to add to the auction tomorrow."

Auction? Larissa's breath froze in her throat. Darien's anxious glance revealed he had made the same connection. These men could only be *thræll*, slavers who traded in human flesh. Given special privileges to roam the lands in between the cities, never bound by the Wall, the *thræll* hunted men, women, and children—particularly second-borns.

Larissa's hand slipped into the blankets, fingers curling around the grip of her gun.

From the sound of the scuffle, the *thræll's* victims were putting up quite the fight. Beside Larissa, Darien's fingers twitched, his body leaning toward the commotion. He wanted to help. Larissa could feel his indecision radiating off of him.

He's always been this way, the voice in her mind spoke.

But they didn't know how many were out there. They didn't know where Anara was. Larissa couldn't let the *thræll* see Halla.

She did the only thing she could think of and linked her fingers through Darien's, pulling him back toward her. At her touch, Darien stilled. Like a man waking from a dream, he looked down at their entwined hands and then up at Larissa. She shook her head, her gaze motioning him toward Halla, willing him to understand. She couldn't risk Halla, not even for those voices that cried out against their captors.

Darien breathed deep, the cost of his restraint evident in the clench of his jaw. But with a look at Halla, he nodded, letting his thumb rub absent-mindedly over the back of Larissa's hand. It was Larissa's turn to still, letting the movement wreak havoc with her heart. She told herself it didn't mean anything. Then something caught her attention, banishing the conflict within herself.

The *thræll's* voices, raised in triumph, were growing louder and closer by the second.

Darien released Larissa's hand and rose into a low crouch, readying himself for the fight. Larissa drew the gun, pushing Halla behind her back. The lights danced closer and closer. Where was Anara?

A howl filled the night air. The lights paused in their advance. The voices of the *thræll* quieted.

"One of yours, eh Fenris?" a voice jabbed, uncomfortably close to their clearing.

Before the slaver could answer, Anara's disembodied snarl rose above the wind. Even knowing that Anara was on their side, the sound set Larissa's teeth on edge. The enormous wolf materialized before them, pacing the bushes and trees that separated the *thræll* from the clearing. Her snarls raised into vicious barks that warned the slavers against advancing any further.

Somewhere in the dark, a man chuckled. "Not one of mine. A she-wolf protecting her cubs."

"Should we kill it?"

"No," the man answered with a growl of his own. "We've hunted worthier prey tonight."

Anara's snarls heightened, daring the *thræll* to test that hypothesis. Then they were leaving, walking around the clearing and dragging their prey behind them. Larissa tried to close her heart to the victims' whimpers and muffled pleas, but she would never forget the guilt of knowing she had done nothing to help them.

Once the *thræll* were finally out of earshot, Larissa flung her arms around Halla, clutching her sister tight to her chest. Halla's own heart beat like a hummingbird's, revealing the fear she never would have admitted.

Anara materialized out of the shadows, shaking off her transformation. "We need to leave."

Darien bounced on his heels, fuming. "Kings and Queens, Anara, what was that?"

Anara paused at the venom in Darien's voice "What?"

"Why didn't we *help* them?" Darien's voice shook. "We could've saved them!"

Anara's eyes tightened as she set her mouth in a hard line. "You don't know what you're talking about."

"We defeated a *draugr*, what're a few *thræll*?"

"You mean a few dozen *thræll*? Who have reinforcements down the river?" She snapped. "We nearly died with the *draugr*; we got lucky. Use your brain, Darien. What would have happened if we lost? Best case scenario, we're all sold into slavery. Worst case, they realize who Lovisa is and hand her over to the Empress."

Larissa was too shaken to correct Anara's slip. Darien shook his head, defiance rolling over him. "We could've done something."

"We could've, but we might not have won. Blame me if you must Darien, but you're alive and free because I make the decisions no one else wants to."

Darien's jaw, like his hands, clenched. Larissa agreed with Anara. It had come down to the strangers' safety or Halla's. Larissa would choose Halla every time, regardless of the guilt that ate away at her soul.

Anara turned away from Darien. "Pack up everything as quickly as you can. We need to get out of here."

26

Out of the Fire

Larissa

Larissa gripped the safety handle above her head as Anara navigated the truck out of a particularly deep hole in the road. Darien had been unwilling to meet Anara's eyes after packing up the camp, so he had opted to ride in the truck bed without saying a word. Halla had insisted that Larissa take the seat in the cab where it was more comfortable, though *comfortable* was a relative term.

The darkness of the morning had been stripped away by the sun, yet Anara had not said much in the hours that passed. After being tossed about like a marble in a jar, Larissa would be happy to never ride in Helga again. These roads were never intended for their use; that much was clear. They were meant only for the use of the Empress' armored vehicles that could maneuver the neglected asphalt.

As sore as she felt, Larissa patted the seat cushion almost reassuringly as if to make up for her negative thoughts. After all, it wasn't Helga's fault the roads were so bad. She had gotten them this far.

As the road leveled out, Larissa let her right hand drift out the open window, catching the breeze across her fingers. She tried not to hear the voices in her mind crying out for help, tried not to think about the way Darien's fingers had felt interlaced with hers. It was easier this way, focusing on the way her fingers danced in the wind instead of how close they had been to being caught. Or the stupidity of what they were about to attempt.

"You're mad at me too, huh?"

Larissa jumped at Anara's voice. "No, I agreed with your decision."

"Because of Halla?"

"Yes," she said simply, hoping Anara couldn't hear the way guilt tightened her throat.

"How are your memories coming?"

Larissa shrugged, shoving down the image of the locked door in her mind. "It's harder for me to remember than it is for Darien."

"I wonder why," Anara muttered, her voice so soft Larissa almost missed the sarcasm.

Almost.

"You think I'm intentionally suppressing my memories?"

"Honestly, yes." Anara stretched her neck. Larissa flinched at the cracks that reverberated through the other girl's body. "You've never been a coward. You were nearly fearless when we were children, so determined to get out of your palace and see the world. This version of you that hides from the truth, I don't know who she is."

The pain came out of nowhere, sparking in her heart and followed by the swift flood of sorrow. Larissa hadn't expected such a strong emotional response to Anara's words, and she hated herself when tears sprang to the back of her eyes. She batted them away and clenched her jaw. Why on Evrópa should she care what Anara thought of her?

But she did.

In her mind's eye, she saw the two little girls playing on the side of the lake.

"Oh, *víti*." Anara stared at her, ignoring the road. "I'm sorry. I didn't mean it the way it sounds. You were my best friend, and I can see parts of you. Like how much you hate that we left those people with the *thræll*, even if you won't admit it. Or your love for Halla. But the rest of you is hidden underneath the fear and doubt. You're not yourself, but that doesn't mean that you're not the person I loved."

Larissa couldn't meet her gaze. "That was confusing, but I appreciate it anyway." A moment passed. "I remember you."

"You do?" Anara asked, caution laced with hope.

"Not everything, but I remember you were my first real friend."

"You were mine. You weren't intimidated by my royalty or *galdr*."

Larissa snorted in quite an un-princess-like kind of way. "If I remember correctly, you weren't as powerful back then."

"If you remember anything at all, I'm glad."

They quieted, but the tension evaporated. Finally, Larissa whispered, so softly she wondered if Anara would be able to hear her, "You're right. I don't want to remember everything, but I do want to remember some parts. Like you."

The corner of Anara's mouth twitched up. "Darien's another one of those parts, I'm sure."

"What?"

"I've seen the way you two look at each other." Anara stuck out her tongue in mock disgust. "It's almost as sappy as before. Worse, actually, with the whole tragic I-forgot-you-existed element."

Again came that rush of unfamiliar emotions—the heat that started in her stomach, crawled up her throat, and rested in her cheeks. Larissa crossed her arms over her chest, propping her knees against the dash. "I don't know what you're talking about."

"Yes, you do." Anara's eyes were filled with mirth. "But I'll pretend you don't if that makes it easier."

Larissa snorted, refusing to acknowledge this line of conversation any further. Anara could make all the insinuations she wanted, but they didn't mean a thing. Larissa's only focus was on finding safety for Halla with the Viðnám. Darien didn't look at her in any specific way, and she certainly wasn't looking at him any certain way either.

Shifting in her seat, she withdrew the gun from her waistline and rubbed her thumb over its bumpy grip.

Anara eyed the motion. "You're gonna shoot me 'cause I called you out on your crush?"

Larissa rolled her eyes as she checked how many bullets remained. She hoped three would be enough for what came next.

"Better keep that hidden once we reach Perle," Anara added.

"I know."

"We'll be there soon."

Larissa nodded, her tongue suddenly dry. Today was Produce Day, the perfect cover to enter the city alongside hundreds of trucks passing through the gates. Larissa had volunteered to drive Helga in, but Anara objected. What if the sentries had already been alerted to what happened in Safír? What if they'd been told to keep any eye out for her? Besides, there wasn't nearly enough produce in the truck bed to convince the sentries they were there for a drop-off.

It would have to be Darien, and he would have to use his *galdr* to persuade the sentries that everything was in order.

Larissa grabbed the useless papers, still sitting on the dash, that confirmed her credentials as Larissa Daldóttir, the first-born and only daughter of Dal. The words leapt from the page, accusing Larissa of her lies. She had stolen Halla's birthright; that was as clear as the writing on the page. Everything she did now was for Halla's sake. She would get Halla to the Viðnám, where her birth status would be inconsequential, where neither the *thræll* nor the Empress' sentires could ever find her. She owed Dal and Vern that much. Larissa crumpled the pages in her hands before unceremoniously dumping them on the floor mats.

Her stomach turned at the thought of what awaited them within the Walls, her mind already imagining a hundred different ways it could go wrong. At least if she were the one driving, she could react to whatever happened, but hiding in the truck bed with Halla, Larissa would have to put her full trust in Darien's abilities.

"It's a calculated risk," Anara said.

Larissa sighed in exasperation. "I didn't realize your *galdr* helped you read minds."

Anara smiled. "I don't need *galdr* to know what you're thinking."

Larissa bit her tongue before she could start arguing with Anara about their plan. They'd made their decision. She had to think about something else, anything else. She asked the first question that came to mind. "What are the different forms of *galdr*?"

Anara's brows pinched together. "You don't remember?" She sighed when Larissa shook her head. "You've already seen the Rubinians' and Safirians' *galdr* first hand. My people are shifters. Safirians can manipulate a person's thoughts and feelings, often without them knowing it."

The back of Larissa's neck tingled. She had been aware of Darien's intrusion in her mind the night before, but to think that someone else might have been capable of doing it without her knowledge was unsettling. A thought occurred, and she wondered how she had not seen it before.

"Do you think someone of Safirian blood erased Darien's and my memories and replaced them with false ones?"

Anara scowled. "I've thought of it, but it wouldn't make sense. The most powerful Safirian alive is King Torsten. He thinks you're both dead. Even if he wanted to, he wouldn't be strong enough to do it."

Larissa shook her head. "Then who?"

"Possibly the gods themselves."

Larissa scoffed. "Why would they care about us?"

"Someone cared enough to hide you." Anara sniffed the air before taking the left at the fork in the road. "Diamantians are illusionists. It's part of how Shiko gained the upper hand at her coronation."

"How is that any different than what Darien can do?"

"Darien's *galdr* allows him to influence someone's actions. Diamantians can make you believe you're seeing, hearing, smelling, and touching things that don't exist without you being aware that you were being manipulated at all. The most powerful wielders, like Shiko, can create entire worlds of illusions." Anara's voice hardened. "On my worst days, I wondered if I'd been captured by Shiko and imprisoned inside one of her illusions, condemned to seek you and Darien for the rest of my life. Always alone, always moving, always fearful."

The hair on Larissa's arms stood up. "How do you know that you're not?"

Anara flashed a quick grin, but shadows lingered in her eyes. She'd hinted with the slavers at the hard decisions she'd made to survive. What had Anara endured in the past fifty years?

"Halla," Anara answered. "Much too creative for Shiko's taste."

Larissa chuckled. "She's probably talking Darien's ear off about the *Æsir*, *Vanir*, and *Jötnar*. Those stories mean everything to her. Probably even more so now."

"That's how she sees you, Lara. A princess from the storybooks."

Larissa groaned, covering her face with her hands. "Thanks for making it worse."

"Do you still see them as stories?"

Larissa dropped her hands. "No. I can't anymore."

"What changed?"

The face of the red-headed goddess swam in her mind. "The Norn came to me in a dream."

One of Anara's eyebrows raised as she cocked her head. "Apparently they enjoy doing that."

Larissa's hands grappled with one another until her knuckles turned white. "I don't understand. If they're real, then where are they? Why aren't they killing the Empress themselves instead of sending us dreams? What happened to the rest of the *Æsir*?"

"I don't know, Lara, but if the Norn are calling to us, we'd better listen."

Larissa quieted, her fingers absent-mindedly caressing the gun in her lap. "What about the Smaragd commonwealth? You hardly mention them."

"That's because they're private people. If the old stories like to exaggerate how the blood of Rubinians burns like the volcanoes off our shores, then the Smaragdians run as smooth as a stilled lake."

"You don't exactly make that sound like a good thing."

Anara snorted in derision. "That's because it isn't. Their self-righteous pacifism allowed Shiko to advance her empire into the southern commonwealths without so much as a fight."

"Aeron," Larissa mumbled.

Helga swerved as Anara's hands slid from the wheel. "You remember Aeron?"

Larissa bit her cheek, wishing she'd kept her mouth shut. "Only a little. Enough to remember that he died trying to protect Smaragd from Shiko."

A growl emanated from between Anara's clenched teeth. "The royal family was weak, and their surrender made his death worthless."

Larissa wasn't sure what to say to that.

Anara released a heavy breath. "To answer your question, however, they practice healing *galdr*. Like I said, they're private people."

"And Perlian *galdr*?"

Anara scrunched her nose. "I've always said your *galdr* is the strangest of all."

"I remember you saying that."

"You do? Well, I stand by it. Your *galdr* allows you to manipulate energy."

"What does that even mean?"

"Don't ask me; that's how you explained it, but I never understood. Shifting is a clear and defined art, but what you do…" She shrugged. "Your mother told you energy is in everything. Your family has always been able to sense that energy more acutely than others. Once you latch onto it, you can manipulate it, move it, wield it, or even harden it like a barrier—like you did with Halla earlier."

"But I didn't know I was doing it."

Helga slowed without warning. For a moment, Larissa feared the old truck was giving out on them until she realized Anara was pulling over to the side of the road. She turned her entire body to face Larissa, who squirmed under Anara's intense stare.

"I want to try something before we get to Perle," Anara said. "Will you trust me?"

"What do you have in mind?"

Anara lifted her eyes, muttering, "Loki's Knot, your distrust will be the death of us all."

Larissa followed Anara to the back where Darien had already popped open the tailgate and waited with Halla, looking at Anara for answers for their sudden stop. From the frown on his face, he was clearly still angry about the night before.

Larissa did her best not to stare. She'd told him she didn't remember him, but with each passing minute, she was remembering more. Not only that, but she was *feeling* more, and every feeling added a tangled layer of confusion she didn't have time to unravel.

The touch of Darien's hands last night resurfaced in her mind as it drew out a memory of him holding her in his arms on a shoreline in Perle. It had been nighttime then; they weren't meant to be sneaking around outside. It wasn't safe, but she had to see him. The moonbeams danced off the water and settled on Darien's hair. His arms had surrounded her in warmth and safety. It would be easy to lean into that memory, but before she could, rationality returned.

She chided herself. She wasn't that person anymore, and, regardless of what Darien said, neither was he. She wouldn't hold him to any kind of obligation he felt toward Lovisa, no matter what feelings the memories stirred. But every time she looked at him, she could not shake the gut-wrenching longing in her stomach.

If Darien noticed Larissa's disquiet, he didn't acknowledge it. He turned to Anara. "Are we close?"

"Yes, Lystheim is only a few miles away. Darien will drive from here. First, we need to move the fruit crates on top of the other supplies. If a sentry looks back here, it needs to look authentic. Darien, it will be up to you to persuade the sentry at the gate. We also need to create space for Larissa and Halla to hide between the boxes."

Halla crossed her arms behind her head as a smug grin spread across her face. "Don't worry. I've got practice sneaking into the Wall. Just leave it to me."

Darien leaned back on his hands, looking up at her. "If I remember correctly, didn't some strong, handsome guy have to save you?"

The tip of Halla's freckled nose turned pink. "I would've been fine."

"Sure, kiddo."

"Alright, both of you, get to work."

Darien and Halla obeyed Anara's order, continuing their discussion over the necessity of Darien's heroics. As they worked, Anara turned to Larissa. "I want you to try to access your *galdr*."

Larissa's heart sputtered like Helga's engine on a good day. "I can't."

"Nothing big, I promise. If you're able to start controlling small amounts, that should stop you from accidentally releasing it. We can't have you doing that in the city. It could get us killed."

Larissa gulped, recalling how she had lashed out at Halla without even a forethought. "Okay, but something small."

"Can I see your gun?"

"Why?"

"Because your *galdr* might work better with an object you've already connected with. You've barely stopped touching it since we left this morning. Come on, Larissa, haven't I earned your trust by now?"

It was a fair question. Larissa handed the gun to Anara, who laid the weapon in the dirt. "Alright, focus on the gun. Try to sense the energy that surrounds it. Bring it to you without touching it."

Larissa pursed her lips, trying hard to take Anara's words to heart while they fell empty in her ears. She focused on the gun, trying to imagine it moving, coming toward her. She fixated on the bumpy texture of the grip in her hands.

Nothing.

"This isn't working."

"Stop giving up," Anara snapped. "Take a breath; look at your ring. Focus on the Dagaz rune, the movement of the lines.

These stones and runes are intimately connected to your Ancestral Bloodline and are meant to help you access your *galdr*."

Feeling exceptionally ridiculous, Larissa raised the hand with the ring in front of her. Truth be told, she had avoided acknowledging it for fear that she would be sucked back into another whirlwind of memories, but she had been unable to take it off either.

Looking at it, she felt that familiar pull, like a hook around her gut, dragging her into the past. The rune etched onto the pearl was more distinct than ever, its lines darkening and stretching before her. A spark of vitality came from the ring, pulsating.

Anara noticed the shift. "Good. Keep that focus, and try again."

Keeping her hand raised, Larissa's eyes drifted from the ring to the gun. Immediately, the intense pull vanished. The gun was a dead, lifeless thing. She scoffed at her own failure before realizing her audience had grown to include Halla and Darien.

"I told you it wasn't working," she muttered, snatching up the gun and returning it to the waistband of her pants. She ignored the disappointment on Darien's face, knowing it was reflected all around.

She had told them she was not that person anymore; they were the ones who wanted to keep pushing. Their disappointment was their own fault.

But, for the first time, she wished she was the Princess they so clearly missed.

Her cheeks burned as she met Halla's eyes. "Can I talk to you? Alone."

Halla's eyebrows pinched together, but she hopped down the tailgate and followed Larissa only a few yards away from the others.

Before Larissa could speak, Halla said, "You just have to keep trying. I'm sure you'll get it."

"Look, Halla, you need to promise me something."

"What?"

"If everything goes wrong in there, you run. Even if the rest of us are trapped."

Halla blanched. "What? I couldn't leave you."

"Yes, you could." Larissa's voice was firm. "No heroics, Halla. I'm only going through with this to get you to safety. Promise me you'll run."

"Lara, that's not fair. You keep treating me like a child."

Larissa set her jaw. "Promise me, or I won't go any further."

Halla crossed her arms and set her own jaw, mimicking Larissa's posture.

Stubborn silence between sisters trickled by. Anara and Darien's low murmurs floated across the breeze.

Larissa released her pent-up breath and arms at the same time. Softening her voice, she tried another tactic. "I can't go in there thinking I'm leading you into danger. I can't undo what happened to Pappa and Mamma, but I can protect you. I won't be able to focus on anything unless I have your word you won't do anything stupid."

Halla's arms relaxed to her sides. "I won't do anything reckless, but that's all I can promise."

Larissa rolled her shoulders in surrender. If worse came to worst, she would force Halla to safety. She tugged her sister's braid, pushing aside her sense of foreboding, but she couldn't shake the rising anxiety at what they sought to do.

Only idiots would sneak into the Wall.

"You ready, kiddo?" Darien called from where he stood in the truck bed. Halla nodded, walking back and accepting his hand to join him.

He had arranged the boxes in such a way that they formed a hollow hiding place that Halla squeezed herself into. There was just enough room left for Larissa. Shaking her head, Larissa followed suit, hoisting herself up into the truck bed and nestling herself beside her sister.

"We'll see you on the inside," Anara called before walking away.

Helga's engines whined and sputtered as Darien pushed the last box toward the opening of their hiding place. His brilliant blue eyes were the last thing Larissa saw before the box shut out the sun.

27

Return of the Stowaway

Darien

THEIR GAS INDICATOR WAS undeniably low. Darien would see if they could get more while in Perle. He ran his hand down the steering wheel, taking comfort in its rough grip.

It's just like any other Produce Day.

From the passenger seat, Anara offered directions. "Turn right here." "Right again." "Left and then straight to the Wall."

At the last set of instructions, Anara shifted. Her skin quivered and darkened as feathers sprouted from her pores. The next moment, a raven with sharp, beady eyes gazed in Darien's direction. Anara blinked once, as though offering encouragement, then flapped her wings, taking flight through the window. She would be scouting from above and watching for complications.

In the distance, the trees thinned and a line of trucks waited to enter the gates of Lystheim. All too soon, the Wall loomed before them. Darien took his spot in the queue. His first impression was one of déjà vu; it was so much like the Wall back in Safír, except fewer sentries walked the top of the Wall and manned the entrance. That was most likely a byproduct of the reduced population.

Anara claimed the Empress had halved the people of Perle in her great purge while searching for Lovisa.

Darien's hands squeezed around the steering wheel. The Empress had already taken Aeron; he wouldn't let her take Larissa too.

The line moved along both agonizingly slowly and far too quickly for Darien's liking. The familiar trickle of sweat gathered in his hairline and ran down his spine. He recognized Anara, perched on the wall, scanning the trucks as they entered the city. Outside the gates of the Wall, a statue had been erected of an aging goddess carrying a small ashen box in one hand and a loose blindfold in the other. On a plaque beneath the statue, Darien could just make out the words: "The Knowing One."

Vör, the goddess of wisdom.

The statue's eyes locked onto Helga, as if it knew the secret cargo carried in the bed of the truck. A small smile played on Vör's wrinkled lips. Whether that boded well for Darien's chances, he couldn't say.

Only one truck remained in front of them. Their window of escape had passed; either Darien's *galdr* would work, or they would be running for their lives. The statue no longer seemed to be smiling. A black-garbed sentry motioned him forward.

As per protocol, the sentry stood at the gate, a handgun on one side of his waist and a large hunting knife on the other. He held out a hand. "Paperwork."

Darien bent over the passenger seat, his hands reaching for Larissa's crumpled identification papers on the floor. He wished for a moment he had his own, but he'd left them behind with Aagen. Besides, if all went well, it wouldn't matter what he held in his hands. He smoothed them out over the dash before handing them off to the sentry. "Must have sat on them at some point."

The sentry huffed in frustration as his eyes scanned the papers. Annoyance colored his voice as he threw the papers back at Darien. "What game are you playing, *slápr*?"

In his anger, the sentry's eyes met Darien's gaze. It was the opening Darien needed. The guard was frustrated, hot, and annoyed—all emotions that Darien could grasp with ease. He slipped into the man's mind, careful to hold on to the edges and cautious to not dive too deep.

"No game." Darien's calm words contrasted the sharp thump of his heart. "My papers are in order; send me through the gate."

For just a moment, the sentry stared, his eyebrows pulled together in anger, then all expression fled his face. The sentry nodded, his blank eyes unfocused as he waved Darien through. "Follow the previous truck into the unloading area. Once you're finished, you may collect your family's rations."

Darien nodded, worried that anything he might say would prolong the conversation or break their connection. Releasing his pent-up breath, he passed through the gates. In the rearview, the sentry shook his head before harassing the occupants of the next truck. Darien had succeeded at the first stage, but the next would be far more difficult.

He parked at the Intake docks, leaving the key in and the engine running. Like in the Safír commonwealth, the loading bay was a large dirt yard filled with trucks, sentries, and confusion. Unlike Safír, slaves with clinking metal restraints outnumbered the day laborers, running from truck to truck. Beyond the loading area was another smaller wall and gate that led into the industrial section of the city. Just beyond it, Darien could see the tops of buildings rising from the city within.

He jumped from the truck and meandered toward the back. He needed to grab the attention of a single sentry without alerting the rest. He took his time unlocking the tailgate and popping it open, allowing the full squeal of hinges to grate against his nerves. A flurry of feathers crossed his vision as Anara glided into the back of the truck, landing on the crates that hid Larissa and Halla.

She cawed loudly enough that several farm hands nearby looked, probably wondering why Darien didn't shoo the creature, but the sentries continued to ignore him. Darien stepped away from the truck, then stretched and yawned—once, twice. Nearby the sentries stood talking; perhaps they were truly as incompetent as Anara had suggested. But the third yawn got a response.

"Move it along, *slápr.*"

Turning toward the high voice, Darien was surprised to find himself facing a boy dressed in sentry's armor. He had to be even younger than Darien. The boy was gangly, his armor hanging on his slim frame, and acne broke out across his too-large nose. Where was the Empress recruiting such young sentries?

He noticed Darien staring and placed his hand on the gun at his side. "Did you hear me, or do I need to *make* you hear me?"

Embarrassment, pride, arrogance. Darien latched onto the emotions, entering the boy's mind before he could notice the lack of produce in the back of the truck.

"Be quiet," he said. But further words died in his throat. The boy's eyes were not glazed over but wide with fear. Although he could not speak, he was aware of Darien's intrusion in his mind; worse, he seemed to be fighting back.

Like a hammer in his mind, pain pulsated through Darien's brain as the boy revolted against Darien's presence. He could feel the boy's fear like it was his own. It soured in his mouth, but fear was an emotion he knew all too well.

With a not-so-gentle mental push, Darien regained control, and the boy's face went mercifully slack. In his peripheral vision, Darien saw Anara hop onto the truck's slatted sides; she would alert him if anyone was coming, but he had to move quickly.

Careful to keep his gaze steady, Darien lowered his voice, appealing to the boy as if he would a friend. "We need your help. Lead us out of the loading zone, take us into the city, and hide us somewhere the other sentries won't look."

He nodded in response, as though he'd chosen to take Darien's side instead of being persuaded into it. "I'll tell the sentries I've confiscated this vehicle. They won't bother us if they think I'm taking you prisoner."

Distrust flooded Darien, but no, his *galdr* was holding.

Anara croaked in the back of her throat. Someone was coming.

"Fine," Darien said, "but I'm sitting up front with you."

A harsh caw from Anara signaled that their time was running out. Darien thrust out his hands, exposing his wrists to the sentry's restraints. Just as the metal snapped, another sentry appeared.

"What's going on here?"

The young sentry grabbed Darien by the crook of his arm. "This one gave me an attitude. I'm confiscating his truck and taking him to confinement. He can think through his actions there for a few days."

"Teach that worthless *slápr* a lesson." The other sentry slammed the tailgate; the lock clicked.

Darien allowed the younger sentry to drag him toward the passenger seat and shove him inside the cab. As the sentry walked around the front of the truck, Darien watched, careful to catch if his *galdr* should slip from the young sentry's mind. To Darien's relief, the boy entered the driver seat with the same blank look in his eyes as before. Pulling out of the loading dock, he drove further in toward the city gates where another pair of sentries, upon recognizing the driver, waved Helga through.

Black spots colored Darien's vision as weariness sat heavy behind his eyes. His connection to the young sentry's mind wavered, but Darien held tight. He could not risk letting go now. Even so, his head dropped lower, his chin nearly touching his chest.

A dark blur crossed his sight as a raven flew in from the open window. In the next moment, Anara sat on the bench tightly squished in between the sentry and Darien. Still held under Darien's *galdr*, the boy did not so much as flinch at Anara's arrival.

Darien's vision wavered. "Anara, I can't—"

His connection to the sentry snapped. Through his darkened vision, Darien couldn't see the boy's reaction, but he heard his words. "How in Hel—"

A soft thump was followed by the swerve of Helga's tires. Then, just as abruptly, Helga straightened out. Darien forced his eyes to open, blinking until his vision cleared. The sentry lay slumped against the door while Anara, half in his lap, directed the truck down a side alley.

"Don't forget to breathe, Darien; I can't have you passing out on me."

"Who? Me?" But his words were weaker than his bravado as his *galdr* took its toll.

Into the Pan

Larissa

IN THE DIM LIGHT filtering in between the boxes, Larissa met Halla's eyes. It was, ironically, the fear in Halla's eyes that calmed Larissa's thumping heart. She scooted toward her sister, laying a hand on her arm and pressing Halla's head onto her shoulder. They sat that way in silence as minutes passed. They'd heard Darien's voice and what Larissa assumed was the sentry's voice a while ago, but they hadn't been able to make out more than muffled voices since.

Larissa waited, her fingers tapping against her lap. Halla stiffened against her side. The pressure of the gun was digging into the small of Larissa's back, but rather than regretting the pain, she took comfort in its presence. Already, she was prepared to pull it from her waistband at the first sign of trouble.

She wouldn't let anyone take Halla.

Still, the waiting ate at her. When Helga slowed to a stop, Larissa's intestines spasmed in her stomach. She could have dealt with discovery, would have fought her way out, but the uncertainty constricted her heart with fear. The pressure on her chest combined with the thick air suffocated her. It was like her very skin was stretching to bursting point. She needed out. Larissa imagined shoving past the boxes, gulping in fresh air, but then Halla would be revealed.

So she sat, drowning in her silence.

A thump of feet hit the truck bed, shifting one of the boxes. Larissa and Halla flinched from the sudden light peeking into their hiding place.

Anara peered in. "Ready to get out of there?"

"You have no idea." Halla grabbed Anara's hand, pushing out of the enclosed space. "That was worse than the first time. I forgot how claustrophobic it gets in there."

Larissa accepted Anara's hand next, blinking at her surroundings. They were in a deep alleyway between two tall, degrading buildings. The paint, whatever color it had once been, had long ago been stripped away by age and abuse, leaving an odd grayish color mixed with dirt and water stains. Parts of it were crumbling. Someone had drawn three intersecting triangles on the wall to Larissa's right. Trash and other indescribable matter littered the street, smelling worse than it looked.

At the end of the alleyway, Larissa made out a road, likely the one they had come down. They had found their way inside of Lystheim, the heart of Perle, but she felt no relief. A countdown ticked within her mind, marking the moments before they were discovered. With the city crawling with sentries, it was only a matter of time. That time would be cut even shorter if Calder or the *draugrs* had followed them to Perle.

Pappa's words came back to her. *Get in, get out, and get home.*

Larissa swallowed against the memory; there was no going home.

A quick glance at Helga's cab revealed an unconscious sentry, but Larissa's gaze settled on Darien. He leaned heavily against the dash, pinching the bridge of his nose between two fingers.

Without thought, she walked toward him, laying her hand on his shoulder. "You okay?"

He tilted his head toward her, his hair tickling the back of her hand. A smile played on his mouth even as his eyes remained closed. "I'm alright, Lov."

Larissa froze. She recognized the endearment. Darien had called her that sometimes, in a different world, a different life. If Darien realized what he'd said, he showed no sign of it as he returned his head to his hands. Larissa withdrew her hand, crossing her arms against her chest. Turning, she found herself face to face with Anara.

"Will he be okay?" Larissa asked.

"Just fine," Anara said. "*Galdr* takes its toll, and he hasn't used it like this in some time." Bending down, she slipped a small bottle from a side compartment in her boot. It was the same green mixture she'd used to heal their injuries on the farm. She handed it to Darien. "Don't drink it. I've hardly got any left, but take a couple sniffs. It'll help."

He accepted the bottle, inhaling deeply.

Anara moved around to the driver's side. "Larissa, Halla, help me with him."

She yanked open the door, catching the unconscious sentry's body before it could hit the ground. Larissa rushed forward to grab the sentry's feet. Together, the two girls carried the sentry to the truck's bed, where Halla waited with wide eyes.

"What do I do?" she asked.

"Find some rope and something to gag him with." Anara grunted as she lowered the boy to the ground.

"We're going to leave him here?" Larissa asked as Halla searched the truck bed.

Anara cast her a hard look. "That's the only option, unless you want to kill him."

Halla stopped searching. She looked between Larissa and Anara, her hands clasped around a coil of rope.

Larissa's palm found the grip of the gun under her shirt. Anara watched, clearly leaving the choice up to Larissa. It was the smart decision. If they left the sentry here, even bound and gagged, it would only be a matter of time before he was able to call for help or get free. It was the same logic that Larissa had used to refuse helping the runaways in the forest.

"We can't," she said. "It's not right."

To Larissa's surprise, Anara smiled. "I knew Lovisa was still in there."

"Still where?" Darien asked. The color had returned to his cheeks, but he was frowning at the sentry on the ground. "What are we going to do with him?"

"Bind him," Anara answered, plucking the bottle from Darien's hands and returning it to her boot. "Just make it tight and pray to the gods it holds him until we return."

They made quick work of it. Darien surprised them all with his knotting abilities, a skill he had gained in his recent life as a farm hand. They used one of Pappa's shirts to gag the boy then hid him in the same nook that had recently housed Larissa and Halla. Once they'd reorganized the boxes, the boy had completely vanished. There was nothing else they could do but pray.

Anara was the last to jump down from the truck bed, and when she did, she carried four knee-length jackets with wide hoods. She handed one to each of them and pulled the hood around her face.

"The citizens won't be looking for new faces," Anara explained, "but these should help hide you regardless."

Their biggest problem was finding a way to hide Darien's sword, which was much more noticeable than the gun Larissa slipped in her waistband.

In the end, they strapped it to his back and gave him one of Dal's jackets that was just big enough to hide the bulk of his weapon. It also made the sword nearly impossible to access. If all went according to plan, he would not need it. Larissa touched her gun and readjusted the jacket, praying that she would not need it either.

"I'll lead the way from above." Anara said. Shifting into a raven, she took to the sky and perched on a swaying cable that hung across the mouth of the alley. She cawed, indicating their path was clear.

Larissa swallowed, and yet, she could not ease the dryness in her throat. She knelt next to Halla and adjusted her hood. "Remember your promise."

Halla's freckles popped against her pale cheeks. "I remember, Lara."

"Ready?" Darien asked.

Larissa nodded. Some small part of her was ready to see the city that had supposedly once been her home. They reached the mouth of the alley, and Larissa took in her first impression of Lystheim.

War had come to the city. Evidently, it had never left.

Narrow streets ran jagged lanes between decrepit buildings, a combination of old and new, but all falling into ruin. On every street, half-destroyed buildings sat next to residentials repaired with patchwork and prayers. Smashed up against one another and stacked on top, the buildings allowed room only for the roads snaking between them and up toward the center of the city.

Drying clothes hung out of windows and on cables running overhead between the buildings. According to Anara, only a quarter of those cables worked to provide electricity to the citizens. The rest had shorted out years ago, left to fade and crack in the sun. The smell Larissa associated with the alley was not much better in the streets.

A surprising amount of foot traffic occupied the pavement in front of them, though Larissa attributed it more to the lack of overall space than the actual number of people. She cast one last look at Helga at the far end of the alley. Unease made her skin itch. They would come back for Helga if they could. If they made it back.

If they made it out.

Another caw cut off Larissa's doubts as Anara swayed on a dead cable hanging above them. She stretched her wings, then glided to the next cable, indicating the path they should take.

"It's so big." Halla's hushed tone betrayed her awe.

Halla was finally getting her wish to see the city, but all Larissa could see was devastation, made worse by a pesky overlay in her memories that told her this was not the Perle kingdom she remembered. The look of distaste on Darien's face told Larissa he felt the same.

"It's so..." He hesitated. "Different."

It's broken, Larissa thought, but she kept that to herself. She adjusted her hood, tugging it particularly hard on the right side to cover her scar. "Come on. Anara said we'll find the physician's shop in the central market."

They clumped together as they walked, keeping to the side of the road as they followed Anara through the streets that wound deeper into the city. It wasn't long before they were huffing in exertion. All of the roads were built at an incline, running toward the center. Far off in the distance, Larissa occasionally caught glimpses of the top of the Second Wall that separated the common people from the Court of the Aristocracy. Whenever the wall came into sight, Larissa would pull her hood forward and resist the urge to walk in the opposite direction. As time passed, Larissa wondered if Anara knew the way; they seemed to wander the streets without direction, at times doubling back or making sharp turns.

Larissa's fear ebbed into a dull worry upon realizing the other citizens traveled without a look in their direction. They walked with purpose in mind. They didn't stop to say hello or ask questions. Keeping their heads down, they spoke in low tones and only to those who accompanied them.

Halla crept next to Larissa, her fingers brushing the back of Larissa's hand. A young woman disappeared down an alleyway after catching Larissa's eye. Halla edged closer to her sister.

"What's wrong with them?"

"I don't know," Larissa answered, but in her heart, she did.

"They weren't always like this," Darien whispered. "The people of Perle were more reserved, yes, but they were also kind and welcoming. These people are broken."

My people.

Larissa jerked away, but she could not escape the voice inside her mind. She finally recognized it as belonging to Princess Lovisa.

Her past had been calling out to her this whole time, only now bitterness bled from the mental intrusion.

Larissa looked in dismay at the city around her, seeing the brokenness Darien had so aptly described. Lovisa's sorrow welled up, mixing in with Larissa's fear. The swirling emotions left her feeling distinctly sick.

Halla paused mid-stride. "Do you hear that?"

Larissa started to shake her head, then stopped. She *did* hear it. The sound grew louder with every step they took. It was the low rumble of voices that accompanied a crowd of people. The three looked at one another in relief; surely, they had found the market square. They hurried in that direction, turning down the next road.

A large crowd had gathered in front of them. They hurried forward but Larissa slowed as a loud squawk rang out from behind them. Anara drifted to a lower cable, rustling her wings and shifting her feet. Larissa stopped, "Guys, I don't think—"

But when she looked, Halla and Darien were already at the back of the crowd, their eyes focused on whatever was ahead of them. In her hurry, Halla's hood had fallen back, revealing her bright yellow hair.

Larissa shook her head and cursed. "Kings and Queens!"

She ran after them, hearing the flap of Anara's wings following close behind her. She skidded to a stop, nearly toppling into Halla and the man in front of her, who shot them both an angry glance. She muttered an apology, but the man paid her no heed, his attention already diverted to something else.

Larissa yanked Halla's hood back up, concealing her young features. They stood in the middle of the large, open courtyard.

Around them, the crowd grew. More people came in behind them, enmeshing them in the gathering mob. Many hid behind hoods of their own, but others stood with heads uncovered, their clothes dripping with wealth and prestige. All faced the wide, raised platform before them. The stage was too packed with people for Larissa to see what was being sold.

Darien's mouth was set in a grim, hard line. Larissa was about to ask him what was bothering him when she heard it. More specifically, heard *her*.

On the stage, a small girl was shoved forward. Above the clanking of metal that encircled the girl's neck, wrists, and ankles, Larissa heard her cry out. Larissa recognized that voice in an instant and, from the sound of Halla's gasp, so did she.

It was one of the runaways from the forest.

Deceit & Belief

Larissa

"Lara." The fear in Halla's voice was palpable.

Larissa squeezed her hand, cutting off Halla's words. Darien's hands fell on her and Halla's shoulders, pulling them away from the scene, but then the crowd quieted. Larissa stilled, not daring to draw attention to herself.

A robust man with a sharp chin and graying hair stepped forward. On his left bicep, a white band striped with black strained against the width of his arm. It marked him as a *thræll*, a slave trader authorized by the Empress herself.

"We've got ten up for auction today, folks. Seven are of the normal variety, unable to pay their debts, but three attempted to *leave* our fair city."

At those words, three of the captives were shoved forward. A short woman and a tall boy, most likely her son, stood erect; the woman raised her chin at the crowd, accusing them with unflinching eyes. A smaller, dark-haired girl stood huddled apart from them. She was the one who'd cried out. The one Larissa had left behind in the forest. Acid surged in her stomach.

"Let's start the bidding," the *thræll* said.

Disgust fermented in Larissa's mouth as the citizens called out numbers. These were their neighbors. How could they treat each other like this?

Burning fire raced along her veins, just as it had when she'd fought the *draugr*. Larissa realized then what it had always been: her *galdr*. Her fingertips tingled, almost painfully so. She glared at the *thræll* who stood center stage, feeling the heat rising inside of her.

This was wrong. Larissa had been wrong to let it happen. They had to do something. *She* had to do something. She took a step forward.

A hand grabbed her wrist, stopping her mid-step. Darien's eyes were gentle, but his fingers locked around her wrist were firm. He shook his head, even as his own body leaned toward the stage. With enormous effort, he tore them both away from the spectacle.

"There's nothing we can do," he whispered into her ear.

"This is wrong," she said, but in her heart Larissa knew he was right. Halla stood behind them, her face paling as the proceedings continued.

Like a match dropped into a bucket of water, the anger inside Larissa sizzled out. They could not publicize their presence, especially not with Halla. She looked too young. Sentries, if not the slavers, would demand proof of her status as first-born. Technically, the sentries could make that demand of any of them. Though Larissa had such papers, she'd left them in the truck as they were useless outside the Safír commonwealth. Any one of them could be seized at any moment. Larissa slumped against Darien in defeat.

"Come on." The reassurance in Darien's voice could not soothe the regret that poisoned Larissa's stomach. He tugged her away from the stage.

"Sold to the gentleman in the glasses!" the *thræll* announced. "You may retrieve your merchandise behind the stage once you have paid in full."

Larissa stood rooted, unable to look away as the mother and son who had tried to escape their prison were sold to a man near the front of the crowd. She noted his graying hair and half-moon spectacles before he was swallowed by the crowd. Only the little girl remained on stage.

My people, Lovisa's voice wept in Larissa's mind. She clenched her teeth, closing her heart against it. Allowing Darien to lead her, they cut through the crowd, keeping Halla tucked firmly between them. They traveled far enough that the sounds of the auction buzzed uncomfortably in their ears, but not so loud as to make out the bidding prices.

Ducking into an alleyway, Larissa slumped onto a broken wooden crate, pushing back her hood and inhaling muck-filled breaths. Halla sat beside her, leaning a trembling head on Larissa's shoulder. Even Darien looked shaken as he stood at the mouth of the alley, checking to make sure no one had followed.

A blur of feathers consumed Larissa's vision as Anara glided down. She shifted in midair then stood before them with arms crossed over her chest. "I tried to warn you."

"I didn't hear you," Halla whispered.

"It's not your fault, kiddo." Darien rocked back on his heels, shoving his hands into his pockets. "I didn't hear her either."

Anara leaned against the wall. "The deeper we go, the more dangerous this becomes. Between the *thræll* and the sentries performing random identification checks—"

"Identification checks?" Darien shot Anara a glance. "We haven't seen any sentries."

"That's because I've been guiding you away from them as best as I could." Exhaustion laced Anara's words. "Unfortunately, that took you closer to the *thræll*."

Darien narrowed his eyes in her direction. "Anara, are you alright?"

"Never better," Anara quipped, but her words didn't erase the deep pockets under her eyes or the way her shoulders slumped forward. Larissa couldn't remember when Anara had last slept. Had it been before the *draugr* attack?

Darien only stared, one eyebrow raised.

"*Galdr* feeds off our energy," Anara said. "I'm just tired."

"We can rest for a moment," Darien offered.

"No, we're too close to stop now. You've been quiet, Larissa. Are you alright?"

My people, Lovisa's voice repeated, directing her anger at Larissa.

There's nothing I can do, she argued. But shame rose up within her regardless.

Larissa rose from the crate, dragging Halla up with her. "Let's find this physician and get out of here."

Anara stared at her a moment more as if she could see the internal struggle in Larissa's mind. She sighed. "You're only making this harder. Follow me."

With their hoods concealing them once again, they wound their way around the auction, although Larissa swore she could still hear the bidding. Even through the haze in her mind, recognition of these roads returned unbidden. She remembered these streets, the Jóltide Festivals, the cherry blossom trees, and the market square decorated with golden streamers. The memories left her with a confusing double vision and a headache.

Yet there were marked differences as well. Even before the Empress, every kingdom had a patron god; that had not changed in either of Larissa's memories, but she didn't remember it quite like this. Statues of Vör, the goddess of wisdom, were plentiful around the city, but there were many other relics and paintings as well. Runes for safety and luck were painted on walls, even etched into doors. Charms jangled on the wrists of people passing by. It was the same sound that the medallions around Halla's wrist made.

The streets grew more crowded as they entered a large open square. Shops lined the four walls of the market. In the middle of the square, stalls had been hurriedly thrown together on plywood, held together by strings as shop owners called out products ranging from food to clothing to amulets they swore could bring back the dead. Everywhere that Larissa turned, she noted the presence of the gods. A small icon here, an amulet there. One man had shaved his head and tattooed it entirely with runes. A large metal symbol made up of three intersecting triangles and attached to a thick chain sat just below the man's collarbone.

Leaning toward Anara, Darien let out a low whistle. "You weren't exaggerating about the worship of the gods increasing."

Anara nodded. "We all believe in something."

Larissa's dream of the red-headed child-goddess flashed before her eyes. The gods, or what remained of them, existed. But that didn't explain where they were. The people of Perle were crying out; why did the gods not answer back?

"I get that, but—" Darien eyed a shop owner as he passed off a bottle of sludgy liquid to an ill-looking woman. "I don't believe *that* has any healing capabilities whatsoever."

Anara's eyes darted to and from the bottle. "You don't want to know what's in there."

Halla tugged on Anara's jacket. "Why? What's in there?"

Although the market held a more joyous atmosphere than the auction block, there was still a glaring absence of children. Subconsciously, Larissa reached for Halla's hand.

"No," Anara snapped. "That will just draw attention. Let her be."

Larissa snatched her hand back. "Where are all the children?"

"Children's identifications are checked more frequently than adults'. Most parents keep their children indoors, even if they are first-born. It's less hassle."

Anara strode into the square, leaving the others little choice but to follow. The smell of food wafted across the air, and Larissa's stomach rumbled. Hours had passed since their canned meal in the forest. They passed by a shop that advertised meat pies. The scent was enough to cause Larissa's mouth to water, though she did her best to hide her hunger.

As they walked, Larissa was grateful for the crowd that surged around them. Many of them walked with their hoods or collars up and their heads down, allowing their group to blend in without too much effort. People came for a specific purpose, an intentional shop, and then they were on their way. Few stayed to browse or mingle with the crowd. Anara was one of those few. She scanned the stalls and shops with a curious gaze, but Larissa could see that her eyes were sharp.

Anara stopped in front of a shop built into the actual perimeter of the market square. It was one of the few shops without customers. The door was made of wood instead of glass and lacked any identifying name. The Ehwaz rune with its pointed edges was etched in the wood and promised protection.

Pushing the door open, Anara stepped inside. Apart from a counter and a large bookshelf behind it, the shop was empty of any other furniture. Bottles of various liquids and books covered in a fine layer of dust sat at odds on the bookshelf. On the counter, a small statue of Eir, the goddess of mercy, smiled at the man who stood in front of the bookshelf, writing in his ledger. At the sound of customers, he held up one finger and finished his writing before looking up at them over his half-moon glasses.

"How can I help you?"

Anara settled her elbows on the counter. "I'm looking for the extract from the dwarf cornel blossom."

"We don't sell that here."

"Are you sure? We can pay any price." Anara's voice oozed confidence.

The old man pushed up the glasses that slid to the tip of his nose. "I told you—"

His eyes drifted from Anara, freezing on Larissa. Though wrinkled around the corners, his eyes were a bright, undiluted blue that pierced straight through her. Larissa looked away, turning to examine the stain on the wall to her left, anything to break his stare. He felt oddly familiar.

The old man cleared his throat, his eyes returning to Anara. "That is an extremely rare extract. I'm afraid I don't have any here."

"Will you be getting any in soon?"

What on Evrópa was Anara talking about? Larissa eyed Darien. He shrugged and shook his head in similar confusion.

The old shop-owner cleared his throat. "Actually, a shipment is coming in tonight at sunset. Unfortunately, I won't be able to pick up any until tomorrow. You could go directly to the seller. I could provide you with directions to the warehouse."

"Perfect."

He ripped a sheet of paper from the book in front of him, scribbling the directions. Larissa shared a glance with Darien. The man held out the paper, but not to Anara. He offered it to Larissa. She hesitated, then stepped forward, intending to snatch the paper and step back, but when she grabbed it, he held the other end tightly between his fingers.

"Do I know you?" he asked.

Larissa yanked the paper from his grasp. "No, I don't think so."

His eyes skimmed thoughtfully over her before passing over Halla and Darien, then back to Anara. Could he feel the tension in the air? Larissa's hand inched back toward the gun at the small of her back. She would not kill him, but she would knock him out if she had to.

Smiling, he returned behind his counter. "An old man's mistake. My apologies."

Larissa hesitated, her fingers itching to grip her gun. Anara drew a handful of folded paper bills from her pocket, setting it on the counter. "For your trouble."

Before they could leave, the noise outside the shop shifted. What once had been the murmur of the market transformed into the rush of frantic, fleeing feet accompanied by demanding shouts.

"Identification papers! Up against the wall, papers out."

Darien pressed his face against one of the windows. "Sentries. A whole squad of them."

Without thinking, Larissa grabbed Halla, pushing her behind her back and searching for another exit that did not exist. There was nowhere for them to go.

They were trapped.

30

Unexpected Company

Larissa

"I TAKE IT YOU don't have identification papers."

Larissa spun toward the old man, careful to keep Halla between herself and the wall. She had nearly forgotten him, focused entirely on the squad of sentries growing ever closer by the minute. He pushed up the half-crescent glasses, triggering Larissa's recognition.

"I do know you," she spat. "You were buying slaves at the auction."

From the corner of her eye, Larissa noticed Darien's hands close into fists. Anara shifted on her feet.

The old man stood unruffled at the accusation. "They've found better homes with me than they would have at the hands of anyone else."

"You can't just buy people."

"You most certainly can in Perle. That's why you're hiding the child behind you. A second-born, right?"

Larissa drew her gun, though she didn't point it at him. Not yet, at least. "You won't touch her."

Her quick movement caused her hood to slip back, revealing more of her face and hair. The man's eyes hardened behind the glasses, but he wasn't looking at the gun. He was staring at Larissa, at the scar that stretched behind her ear. There was something in his gaze that Larissa had not expected—not fear or even anger, but curiosity. Raising his hands, he stepped toward the bookcase.

"There's no need for that. I've already decided to help."

Grabbing the side of the bookshelf, he heaved. It moaned then creaked as it swung out on rusted hinges, revealing a passageway cut into the wall.

Larissa looked at Anara and Darien. Her own concerns were mirrored across their faces. What if it was a trap? Just a cellar with no way out? What if he was simply containing them to turn them over to the sentries?

As if reading her thoughts, Darien asked, "What choice do we have?"

Pounding came from the shop next door. There was no choice at all. Larissa shoved the gun into her waistband. Grabbing Halla's hand, she ran into the dark passageway. Anara's footsteps sounded behind her. Just as Darien entered the tunnel, the old man returned the bookcase to its proper place, plunging them into total darkness. Through the wooden bookshelf came the muffled noise of the shop door bursting open.

"Identification papers," came the impatient voice of a sentry.

"I have them right here," the old man said.

"Was there anyone with you in your shop today?"

Larissa covered her mouth, her own breath harsh in her ears.

"I had four guests a little bit ago, but they passed on before your arrival. I also purchased two slaves at auction today, but I have sent them on an errand to the Wall."

"Your papers are in order, but I do not see the slave licenses."

"As I said, I received them today. The auction said they would be sending along the licenses soon."

The sentry harrumphed. "By imperial mandate, you are required to come forward with any information regarding second-born citizens or runaway slaves."

"Yes, yes, I am quite aware of the mandate. May I go back to mixing my medicines, or is there perhaps something I could sell you since you have scared off all of my business for the day?"

The front door slammed in response. Only the soft padding of the man's shoes against the tiled floor remained. His footsteps approached the bookshelf, then came the sound of glass being moved and books shuffled about. When he spoke, it was low and muffled, as though he had pressed his face up against the wood. "They're still in the market square. Continue down the tunnel. It will exit out onto another street."

In the darkness, all Larissa could feel was Halla's hand in hers. All she could hear was the harsh, anxious breathing of the others until Anara whispered.

"Our only option is forward. Go slowly and quietly; this tunnel passes between other shops."

"How do you know that?" Darien asked.

"I can hear them."

Larissa couldn't, but she trusted Anara's heightened senses. She reached out her open hand to find the wall but scraped her knuckles against stone. She pulled back, cradling her throbbing hand. "Kings and Queens!"

"That's not very Princess-like," Halla whispered.

Anara chuckled low in the back of her throat. "Actually, it's extremely Princess-like, although it used to be more my thing than Lovisa's."

Larissa tried again, more cautiously, and felt the cold of the wall seep into her palm. "Maybe we should focus on getting out of here instead of whether I meet Princess criteria."

She edged forward. With the wall to guide her, hesitance turned to confidence with every step. Soon she heard voices outside the walls from shops or homes. Just as the voices faded, Larissa's foot jammed into a barrier in front of her.

"*Viti!*" she hissed.

"I'm going to vote a 'no' on the whole Princess-criteria debate."

"Shut up, Darien."

"At least you found the way out," Halla offered.

Larissa glared in her sister's direction, then felt in the darkness for the door handle. In that instant, she was reminded of the locked door from her memories. Shaking aside the thought, she pushed against the wood. It opened a crack, allowing dim light to stream in. Not direct sunlight, but still too bright against the pitch black of the tunnel.

She blinked against it, forcing her eyes to remain open and alert. Based on the smell and the copious amounts of trash piled against the door, the hidden passageway had opened into a shaded alleyway. Larissa slipped through the opening, careful of her footing, followed by the others, who blinked just like she did as they adjusted to the shaded light.

Larissa turned on Anara. "What was all that about in there? Why were you asking about a dwarf comet?"

"Dwarf cornel," she corrected, leaning heavily against the wall behind her. "The nectar that I used to heal you before is extracted from the fruit of that flower."

"You said it was exceptionally rare; why would it be here? What happened to asking about the Viðnám?"

"She was," Darien said slowly, as though choosing his words. "It's a code, right? There's no shipment of dwarf cornel fruit."

"None whatsoever. However, there will be someone at that warehouse tonight who can get us out of here and take us to the Viðnám."

Larissa closed her eyes. This whole day had been more complicated than she'd hoped. She reached in her pocket for the instructions and handed the slip to Anara. "You'll understand that better than me."

With apparent effort, Anara shoved off the alley wall. Only then did Larissa realize she had been leaning there for support. She considered reiterating Darien's earlier offer of rest but changed her mind. The sooner they got out of there, the better. Glancing at the directions, Anara moved toward the mouth of the alleyway. Larissa made to follow then stopped at the tug on her sleeve.

"You weren't really going to shoot him, were you?" Halla's brow furrowed.

"Who?"

"The store owner."

"Of course not." Not if she didn't have to anyway.

Halla's raised eyebrow questioned Larissa's truthfulness.

"Halla, you know me better than that. I was just scaring him, you know, a little bit."

She rolled her eyes but let go of Larissa's arm. With Anara leading and Darien at the rear, the group emerged from the alley. Hoods drawn, they passed briskly from shadow to shadow, following Anara as she glanced at the slip of paper in her hands at every street crossing. How she understood it, Larissa would never know. Most of the streets were missing sign posts, and the ones that did exist were unreadable.

As they made their way back toward the Wall, the crumbling, decrepit buildings intermixed with newer warehouses built for storage. No doubt they had been strategically placed away from the people who desperately needed the food and closest to the loading bays and sentries' outposts.

Within reach of the destination, Larissa noted the alarming lack of people on the streets. If a sentry spotted them, they'd stand out.

Darien must have been thinking similarly. "Anara, is there a curfew we should be aware of?"

Anara's response was labored with harsh pants. "People are expected to be in their homes long before sunset. We need to get to the warehouse before then."

"Are you alright?" Larissa asked in alarm.

"Just drained. I'm fine."

"Do you—"

"I'm fine; we're nearly there."

"How do you know which one—"

"I know." Anara bit out the words.

Darien shot Larissa a glance. She shrugged then jogged after Anara. What could they do?

The warehouse loomed in their vision long before they found the correct street to turn on. It was a massive building with metal rolling doors lined up on the sides of it. Heavily armored trucks sat empty in the neighboring dirt lot. It had the look of a place recently deserted, but one that could become heavily active at the turn of a switch.

Anara released a sigh of relief when they arrived. She did not hesitate, plunging straight ahead and opening the entry door, which obeyed without resistance. The others followed, with Darien closing the door behind them.

Though not as pitch black as the tunnel had been, a shaded darkness encompassed them. Speckles of dirt in the air caught the fading light from skylights scattered across the high ceilings. The cavernous space hosted an array of vehicles and stood at least two stories tall, based on the railings and walkways that ran along the upper walls. Over a dozen doors along the walls led deeper into the warehouse. Boxes sat stacked in uneven groupings around the room.

It smelled like a combination of soil, gas, and produce. Larissa sighed. It smelled like home.

Walking to the far side of the room, Anara lowered herself to the ground and closed her eyes. "Now, we wait."

Halla sat beside Anara, mimicking her posture, but like Larissa, Darien remained standing. Was adrenaline pumping through his body too? Larissa rocked on her feet, trying to shake the tension from her shoulders. Every passing second ticked closer to their inevitable discovery.

"How long are we waiting here?" she asked. "I feel exposed."

Anara glanced at Larissa through squinted eyelids. "The physician said sunset. We'll wait until then."

"This doesn't feel right," Darien said.

Anara closed her eyes. "We don't have a lot of options. If they're not here by sundown, we'll leave and find the Viðnám another way. For now, we wait, and I rest."

Darien looked torn, pacing for a moment more before taking his own spot on the ground next to Anara and Halla. Larissa remained upright, at times walking around the perimeter of the room or simply rocking in place. An odd mixture of exhaustion and exhilaration tore at her body. She wanted to tell Anara what she had felt at the slave auction, the way the *galdr* had built up inside of her, but whenever she tried to grasp that feeling again, she came up empty. It was as if the power had never existed at all.

The sound of a slamming door boomed through the room.

Halla jumped. "What was that?"

Anara tilted her head in the direction of the sound; her ear elongated and grew fur as she inhaled deeply through a long snout. After several tense seconds, she snorted, shaking off the transformation and leaping to her feet. "Stay here. If I'm not back in five minutes, get out of Perle."

"Wait, where are you going?"

But Anara had already dashed across the empty space and darted through one of the doors that led deeper into the building.

Halla rose, folding her arms around her stomach. "Where is she going?"

Darien reached out before Larissa could. "It's okay, kiddo. She probably just went to see if someone from the Viðnám finally arrived. Come on, let's find a better place to wait."

He led her to the side of the room where the boxes were stacked more closely together. There was a small gap between them and the wall. It was an ideal hiding place. Halla squeezed in immediately. Larissa reached out to touch Darien's arm and spoke softly enough that Halla could not hear. "Thanks for reassuring her."

Darien swallowed, and Larissa saw his eyes flit down to where her hand still rested on his arm.

"Of course," he murmured, his voice rough with emotion.

She knew she should let go, but a memory was surfacing in her mind. There was a boy and girl standing beside the shoreline under a full moon. As the image crystallized in her mind, Larissa felt the warmth of Darien's arms around her, but she knew it wasn't real. She let her hand drop before the memory could return in full.

"Should we go after Anara?" she asked him.

"She told us to wait."

"That doesn't mean we have to listen."

Running a hand through his hair, Darien shook his head. "What about Halla?"

Gratitude surged through Larissa, knowing that Darien understood how she felt. She feared for Anara, but she couldn't lead Halla into danger or leave her alone. It didn't matter if Halla didn't think she was a kid anymore; she was Larissa's responsibility. If anyone was going to check on Anara, it would have to be Darien.

"Go," Larissa said. "We'll wait here for both of you."

Darien's eyes held her own, and within them she saw a battle of emotions she wished she didn't recognize. Darien reached up, tucking back a strand of hair that had fallen from Larissa's braids. His fingers brushed against her healing scar, and she resisted the overwhelming urge to lean into his touch, to find strength and comfort in his presence.

He dipped his forehead, nearly touching her own. "Be safe, Lara. For me."

When he pulled away, confusion and regret flooded through Larissa. Even as she tried to push away the emotions, her heart ached for his return.

Leftover emotions, Larissa's brain chided her heart. *From a different time with a different person.*

But Larissa wasn't sure she believed herself anymore.

31

Familiar Faces

Larissa

LARISSA SQUEEZED HERSELF IN between the boxes, settling next to her sister.

"I saw that." Halla's knowing smirk stretched across her cheeks.

"You don't know what you're talking about."

Her smile widened. "I knew I was right about you two."

Larissa said nothing, knowing it would only provoke her sister further. Instead, she leaned her head back against the wall and willed her heartbeat to slow.

But as seconds slid into minutes, Halla's mirth drained from her expression. She pulled her knees into her chest as the silence of the warehouse deepened. Larissa's fingers tapped impatiently against her thighs. She closed her eyes and counted the passage of time. They could only wait so much longer for Darien and Anara to return. Larissa calculated the closest escape route, her mind forming the prayers for protection her lips could not utter.

"Do you think I'm brave, Lara?"

Larissa opened her eyes, turning to her sister. "What?"

"I don't think I'm very brave."

"What are you talking about?"

"The Norn come to me in my dreams. They help me remember my life before you were my sister." Halla's tiny voice was muffled as she spoke into her knees. "Even before you, I've always wanted to leave the farm, but when the *draugr* came, I ran. I've been afraid ever since."

Larissa rubbed Halla's back, shaking her head at her sister's words. "Halla, look at me. You're one of the bravest people I know in either set of my memories. Being afraid doesn't mean you're not brave. It means you're maturing and gaining wisdom. Well, a little bit of wisdom." Larissa emphasized how much wisdom by pinching her fingers together and showing Halla the small space in between them. "You can still be a total *hálfviti* sometimes."

Halla jammed her elbow into Larissa's side, but it was so half-hearted that Larissa knew Halla didn't mean it.

"Are you afraid to remember your past?" Halla asked.

"Is now really the best time—"

Larissa cut off at the expression on Halla's face. The way Halla chewed on the inside of her cheek revealed the depth of her fear. If Larissa could distract from that fear, she owed it to Halla, no matter how awkward the conversation.

"In my memories, there's a hallway full of doors," Larissa whispered. "There's a door I can't open. I don't know what's behind it, but it makes me feel sick on the inside, like there's something wrong on the other side. I'm afraid if I open it, I won't like what I discover, and I won't be able to lock it back up again."

Halla scooted closer to lean her head against Larissa's shoulder. "Are you scared of disappointing me?"

"I don't know. Maybe."

"Do you think you did something wrong?"

Larissa cracked her knuckles. Halla could be disturbingly insightful at times.

The long creak of a door saved Larissa from answering. Both sisters' heads snapped toward the sound. Larissa raised a finger to her mouth and placed a hand on Halla's bouncing knee. She strained her ears, fighting the urge to peek over the boxes. Then came heavy boots falling against the concrete floor.

The footfalls were unhurried, seeming to walk from one end of the room to another as though their owner was searching for something. It was not Anara or Darien; they would have announced themselves. Could it be one of the Viðnám? Should she reveal herself to them?

"It's okay, you're safe. You can come out."

Larissa's shoulders fell in relief at the sound of Darien's voice. She rose to stand, ready to berate him for not announcing himself, but Halla yanked her down hard. Wide-eyed, Halla shook her head so frantically that Larissa hesitated.

"Where are you?" the voice asked.

Larissa heard it that time. The voice was a close match, but it was not the same. It was not Darien at all.

Larissa sank lower, her back against the wall. She covered Halla's hand on her arm with her own to let her know that she understood. They were both thinking the same thing—*draugr*—but even knowing the voice wasn't Darien's, its familiarity grated against Larissa's nerves.

"Larissa, I know you don't trust me, but you can," the voice continued. "The people you're with have been lying to you since your parents' death. They're leading you into a trap."

Like honey, the words dripped into Larissa's ears, blocking out Halla's distraught whispers. A voice wriggled into her mind. *Believe me,* it purred. *Trust me.*

"Larissa, please, trust me."

She could not resist the pull. Her body spasmed in rebellion, but it was no match for the voice in her mind. Larissa stood, nearly tumbling as her mind and body fought against each other, and revealed herself to the owner of the compelling voice.

It was not Darien, or even a *draugr* that looked like him.

It was *Kafteinn* Calder.

The shock at his presence was enough to shake Larissa from whatever had prompted her to stand in the first place. She had not seen him since the house inspection. Anara's words echoed in her mind: *There are stories of one of the* Kafteinn *under Shiko's command. He has been searching for the Viðnám since its inception.*

The Empress' War Dog had found his prey.

Her mind cleared. Larissa snatched up her gun, pointing it directly at Calder's chest with her finger resting on the trigger. He raised his hands in a show of surrender, and a strand of blond hair fell forward into his eyes. The movement triggered a memory, but Larissa shied away from it. There was something painful about that memory, something she didn't want to remember. Calder's face was tranquil as he regarded the gun pointed at his chest.

"How did you find me?" Larissa asked.

"I've been looking for you ever since you left the farm. You should come with me."

"So you can turn me over to the Empress?" Larissa's hands tightened around the gun's grip. "I don't think so."

Calder lowered his hands, shaking his head with true distress in his eyes. "Larissa, I don't know what you've been told, but you're in danger."

"From you," she snapped.

"No, I want to help."

His hazel eyes locked onto her own, and, for the slightest moment, Larissa felt compelled to believe him. She could not look away. Still, a buzzing in her mind prompted her.

"Why?" she asked. "You work for the Empress, *Kafteinn*."

"Call me Calder."

His voice was smooth, kind, and soft as he stalked toward her. Held captive by his eyes, Larissa's body refused to move.

"Larissa, there are things you don't understand," Calder said. "The Empress is not after you; she's after the Viðnám. *They* sent the *draugr* to your home that night. They must have learned that I was asking you for information about them. The Viðnám is the reason why your parents are dead."

Larissa's grip on the gun loosened. That voice in her mind that she associated with Lovisa was shouting, urging Larissa to hold on, to fight. But Larissa couldn't remember what she was supposed to be fighting. If what Calder was saying was true, how could she trust Anara and the Viðnám? Was Darien in on it too? Her head felt as heavy as her hands; the gun slid an inch lower in the air.

"That's right, put down the gun. I'm not here to hurt you." Another step closer. Calder's gaze captivated her entire focus, enticing her to obey. It was as though someone pumped fog into her brain, clouding everything. He moved closer, reaching to grab the gun. "I want to help you."

"Liar!" Halla jumped onto one of the boxes behind them, holding no weapon but the tiny hands she clenched into fists. "The Empress sent that *draugr* because Larissa is the Princess and the rightful ruler of Perle!"

"The Perle Princess?" Calder sneered, his eyes never leaving Larissa's. "Is that what they've told you? That you're this long-lost Princess who can lead their rebellion? They're playing you, Larissa. There never was a Princess. It was always just a story."

"Just a story," she repeated.

It was what she'd often told Halla after Pappa's stories about the *Æsir*. This was just a story too—a story she had taken too seriously, a story she allowed to warp her brain.

"They will use you to further their agenda," Calder said, "and they won't care if you get killed along the way. Think of your sister. She won't be safe with the Viðnám. I'm sure they've promised to protect her, but they're trying to start a war. How can they keep her safe in a war?"

"Don't listen to him, Lara! He's *influencing* you!"

Halla's voice was muffled, as though she was shouting through water. The words sank away before Larissa could process them. Calder was right. If Larissa went to the Viðnám, she would be leading Halla straight into a war zone. How could she protect her there?

"If you come with me, I can promise you protection. You'll both be safe. Isn't that what your parents would have wanted?"

Calder's voice turned forceful. There was no other way of thinking besides his own. Larissa could see that now. He reached out, his hand wrapping around Larissa's wrist. He lowered her arm until the gun pointed at the ground. Firm pressure on her tendons loosened her grip, and the gun clattered to the floor.

"There you go, Lovisa," Calder whispered.

"Lara, what are you doing?" Halla shouted, leaping from the box and sweeping up the gun before Calder could reach it.

Calder pivoted with surprising speed, yanking the gun from Halla's hands. He brought the weapon down hard across her face, sending her sprawling into the boxes that collapsed around her.

Whether it was the break in eye connection or the sight of Halla's unconscious body, the pressure in Larissa's mind lessened, allowing her to think clearly.

He'd called her *Lovisa*.

Larissa snapped awake. As though someone had thrown her face first into the Klarälven River, realization washed over her in waves. She'd felt this way once before, when Darien had practiced his *galdr*. It was the same persuasion, the same manipulation of the mind inherited only by those of the Safirian Ancestral Bloodline.

Larissa drew back her arm, knowing she had only this moment of clarity. Calder turned to face her at the exact moment she threw her punch. Her knuckles slammed into his jawline with a satisfying crunch.

Calder stumbled backward, stunned as the gun flew out of his hand and slid across the ground. He raised a hand to touch his lip where it had split on impact; a gold and sapphire ring winked at her from his fingers. Larissa cradled her throbbing hand, delighted that his pain had to be worse than her own. But as Calder pulled his red-tinged fingers away, Larissa wavered on wobbly legs at the onslaught of a new memory.

She remembered a little blond boy falling into the Klarälven River and splitting his lip on the side of their boat. Aeron had smiled at Lovisa, even with the blood still on his chin, as if to reassure her. *It's not that bad,* Aeron had said. *Don't worry, Princess.*

There was a reason his voice sounded so similar to Darien's, a reason he looked so familiar as he glared at her with those unflinching hazel eyes. Her memory clicked into place. The name slipped from her tongue in confused disbelief.

"Aeron?"

Behind the anger in Calder's eyes, Larissa could have sworn she saw a hint of satisfaction.

"Miss me, Princess?"

32

Blood Beckons Blood

Darien

THE WAREHOUSE WAS A maze.

Every door led to another that opened into hallways and closets. If Darien didn't find Anara soon, he would have to return to Larissa and Halla empty-handed. An itch of unease had been crawling over his skin ever since he left them. Darien opened the next door, determined it would be the last one before he turned back.

Immediately pinching his nose, he choked on the sudden and intense stink of death. Darien had come across a dead deer once on the outskirts of the orchard. The creature had been ravaged by scavengers and filled with maggots. Yet the smell of that animal was like a bouquet compared to what assaulted Darien's nose now. His eyes burned from the sheer weight behind the familiar smell. Only last time, the smell had been mixed with ash and smoke.

Stripping off his jacket, Darien swung his gear around so that his sword rested at his hip. He kept his hand on the hilt as he stepped into a room lit by the sporadic light of the failing sun.

Darien squinted against the dimness. A few yards in front of him, crumpled against the wall, lay a dark shape too small to be a *draugr*. He crept closer, his hand tightening around the hilt. The fan of white hair speckled with blood stopped him cold.

"Larissa?"

In three strides, he crossed the room, falling to her side and rolling her over to face him. Larissa's head flopped unrestrained. Why was she there? Where was Halla? But these questions buzzed unanswered in the back of his mind, overwhelmed by the sheer amount of blood covering her skin. Gagging on the smell of decay, Darien placed a hand at her throat and one at her wrist.

She had no pulse.

"Larissa, wake up," Darien whispered. "Come on."

Cradling her head in his lap, he prayed to the *Æsir*, to the Kings and Queens of the past, to anyone who would listen, that Anara would appear with her healing nectar. His breath constricted in his throat; they were alone. He brushed back the hair from Larissa's face, smearing blood that leaked from a wound on her forehead. His fingers paused on the smooth, unblemished skin of her right cheek where her scar should have been.

A guttural growl came from behind at the same moment Larissa opened her eyes. They were entirely white, and when she smiled, her teeth were pointed like needles.

Draugr.

Darien felt the impact before he saw it coming. Not from the creature as he expected, but from his side as something shoved him away from the *draugr*. He rolled across the floor, raising himself to his hands and knees, then realized what had hit him. Or rather, who.

A massive wolf crouched in front of him with giant paws extended forward and ears flattened low. Wolf-Anara's jaw hung open, a growl emanating between bared teeth. In front of them, the *draugr* stood mid-transformation, its scaled talons extending as it snarled with Larissa's face. Anara leapt at the same time the *draugr* finished its transformation. They tumbled to the ground in a flash of claws and teeth.

Darien unsheathed his sword, rushing toward them, but he couldn't get closer without being crushed by the *draugr's* flailing wings. Then the *draugr* was underneath as Anara snapped at its throat, aiming for the unarmored skin at its neck.

The *draugr* twisted, rolling on top, and raked its talons across the wolf's stomach, slashing through fur and skin. Anara's howl of agony formed a discordant harmony with the draugr's screech of victory.

Darien lunged forward, taking advantage of the *draugr's* distraction, and swung. With a thunk, a wing fell from its body, splattering Darien and Anara with dark purple blood that felt hot on Darien's skin. The creature roared, arching its bleeding back. Darien raised his weapon, bracing himself for an attack.

But the attack never came. With one last roar, the *draugr* fled through the open door. Even knowing it could be a trick, Darien couldn't wait. Sheathing his sword, he raced to Anara, who had lost control over her transformation.

Her body lay at an odd angle, her bloodied hands splayed against her stomach. A gaping wound stretched under her hands. Muscles heaved underneath the jagged cut, pushing blood through the wound with Anara's every breath. The muscles themselves, although not severed, had been damaged. Darien found the jacket he'd flung aside earlier. Snatching it, he balled it up and pressed it against her wound.

She groaned.

"Anara, you're alive!" Darien said, hope surging through his body.

Sweat gathered at Anara's temples. She panted from the pain. "Not for long. Darien, the nectar, in my boot."

He reached down and unzipped the boot, pulling it from her leg. The side pocket sewn into it was meant to cushion the bottle and protect it, but the fight with the *draugr* had been too much. The glass was cracked, and nectar seeped into the fabric of the boot itself. Only a few drops remained. Darien cradled the bottle in his hands, tilting it to keep any more from escaping.

"Anara, do I use it all? Is this enough? Anara!"

Her eyes closed, and her brown skin turned a nasty gray color. Her breaths were quiet now—too quiet. Darien uncovered the wound, removing the jacket already soaked by blood.

Please let this work, he prayed to the gods, tilting back Anara's head and placing the vial at her lips. Three drops slid onto her tongue. The vial was nearly empty. Instinctively, he scattered the remaining droplets across the wound.

For a moment, nothing happened. Anara's breathing quieted, then stopped.

Darien held his breath.

Anara gasped, her eyes flinging open, pure agony written across her face as she clawed at her stomach with wolven nails. Lunging forward, Darien clasped her hands together to prevent her from worsening the wound. Even in her weakened state, Anara was strong. Darien bared down as she growled and thrashed.

Then, just as swiftly as the outburst had started, it stopped.

Anara went limp in Darien's hands. Her eyes rolled back. What had once been a gaping wound was now a tightened line that extended the full length of her abdomen. The majority of the wound had sealed, but the entire area was raised, red, and irritated. Darien could almost feel the heat rising from it. The wound wouldn't kill her, but the infection might.

"Darien?" Anara whispered, her voice weak.

"Anara! Oh, thank the gods."

"What happened?"

"There was a *draugr*. The nectar's gone; there were only a few drops left, and I don't think it was enough."

Wincing, Anara forced herself up onto her elbows. She looked down at her waist. Her eyes met Darien's. "I've had worse."

He shook his head, but his lips twitched into a smile at her deadpan expression. "Can you walk? The *draugr* will be back."

With apparent effort, Anara nodded. "Where are Larissa and Halla?"

"I left them in the main room. The old man must have betrayed us to the Empire."

"I was so sure of him. I could've sworn he was—nevermind." Her dark eyes clouded with pain. She extended her hand. "Help me."

Even with Darien's help, it took Anara far too long to rise to her feet. Darien's eyes darted to the open door, worried when the *draugr* would make its next appearance. Anara shrugged off her jacket, and although she did not complain, Darien could see how every movement cost her. Clenching her jaw and panting under her breath, Anara folded the jacket long-ways in half before tying it around her stomach to support the wound.

"Thank you for what you did," she said.

"I was so stupid. I thought that thing was Larissa. It could have killed me before I realized what was happening."

"It's one of their tricks, pretending to be someone you love."

Heat rose to Darien's face, but what was the point of denying it in front of Anara? He watched as she took a step forward on her own, grimacing at the pain. "I could carry you if that's easier?"

Anara's hiss was answer enough.

"Can I at least offer you my shoulder?"

She hesitated, then acquiesced with a sharp nod. "We have to get back to the others. I doubt that *thing* is here alone."

Without further discussion, they made their way back through the maze. When Darien hesitated at a crossroads, Anara would sniff then offer directions with a quiet voice. Four intersections later, Anara's body stiffened against Darien.

She gasped. "It can't be! Hurry!"

They rushed down the hall and passed through the final door, returning to the large space they'd left behind. When they entered, Darien hardly felt Anara's weight on his shoulder or heard the growl reverberating through her chest. He couldn't make sense of the sight before him.

Halla lay crumpled on the ground. Larissa was supporting her right hand with the other and staring in horror at the man in front of her. As for that man, even with the difference caused by time, Darien would recognize his brother anywhere.

Darien moved toward him. "Aeron?"

The blond-haired man sneered. "The name is Calder to you. *Kafteinn* Calder."

Larissa shook her head, worrying Darien with how she swayed. "It's him, Darien. He used *galdr* to persuade me." She sank to the ground, then looked up as though uncertain how she'd gotten there.

"Careful," Calder smirked. "*Galdr* has strong side effects when you're not used to it."

It was him. Darien's brother. *Aeron*. Relief, confusion, and anger fought for dominance in Darien's stomach until he thought he might throw them all up just to be rid of them. Anara laid a hand on Darien's shoulder, the other still holding her stomach, as she snarled from the back of her throat.

Calder spared her a lazy glance. "Anara, is that you? Looking a bit worse for wear, darling."

She stiffened. "You look pretty good for a dead man."

"I've been searching for you for a long time. Always one step ahead of me. You never knew it was I who hunted you though, did you?"

Anara's face paled, whether from his words or from her own pain, Darien wasn't sure. He clenched his sword, the anger taking predominance over his joy at seeing his brother alive. "What are you playing at? Where have you been?"

Calder spun on Darien. Only then did Darien see the anger building in his brother's eyes. "Where have *I* been? Where have *you* been?"

"You were dead, Aeron! They told us you died!"

"Couldn't be bothered to confirm it though, could you?" Just as suddenly as the anger had come, it was gone. His face was wiped smooth, as though every emotion had been extinguished, leaving behind only the shell of a man. From his waist, Calder unsheathed a long sword of his own. The sapphire ring glinted on his right hand. "As I said, I am *Kafteinn* Calder now. I order you all to surrender in the name of the Grand Empress of Evrópa."

Darien sucked in a breath but didn't lower his sword. His brother was alive. The thought played over and over again in his mind, but Darien forced himself to push it aside. Aeron wouldn't persuade Larissa against her will. Aeron wouldn't draw his weapon on his brother. No, Aeron wouldn't sneer at him like this, as if he took pleasure from Darien's internal struggle.

This was not his brother. What had he called himself? Calder? That was the only way that Darien could think of him, and *Calder* was in his way.

Behind him, Halla lay motionless beside the pile of fallen boxes. Larissa still sat on the ground with her head hung in her hands, incapacitated by whatever Calder had done while inside her mind. That invasion into Larissa's privacy, more than anything else, made Darien's blood burn. Calder would pay.

At Darien's side, Anara's body quivered. He could sense her *galdr* building for transformation. They would have to act in sync.

"Get them out of here," Darien said under his breath.

She nodded, moving in step with Calder as they circled one another like three points of a triangle. Someone would strike. The only question was who would strike first.

Darien sensed the surge of *galdr* from Anara; she spun away from them toward Larissa and Halla.

Calder charged.

33

Separated

Larissa

Her head was too heavy.

She couldn't move, couldn't look up to understand the clash of steel ringing in her ears. As if she could clear the fog from her mind, she shook her head, instantly regretting the wave of dizziness that accompanied it. What was happening to her? Darien's persuasion hadn't crippled her like this.

Darien. Lovisa's voice cut through the din, giving Larissa the strength to look up. Darien collided against Calder—but no, it wasn't Calder. *Aeron* attacked Darien. Aeron was *alive.*

And he was trying to kill them.

"Larissa, focus."

She tilted her head toward the echo of the voice. Anara's face swam in and out of her vision. Larissa's thick tongue stumbled over her words. "What did he do to me?"

Anara grimaced. "You're experiencing the aftereffects of forced persuasion; it'll fade, but we need to get out of here."

Anara pulled Larissa to her feet, propping her against the boxes and moving to do the same for Halla. In the center of the room,

Darien and Aeron fought. They lunged forward and darted away from one another, their swings and clashes looking like a dance, as if they'd done this a hundred times before.

They have, Lovisa's voice reminded her. *They were evenly matched before.*

But fifty years had passed, and while Darien's skill had lain dormant, Aeron had clearly been practicing. He swung and blocked with ease, while Darien grew more desperate and lethargic with each passing moment.

Anara returned with Halla leaning heavily on her shoulder. A large bump was forming in Halla's hairline where Aeron had hit her with the gun.

"She's awake but unsteady," Anara said. "What happened?"

At the sight of Halla's pale cheeks, Larissa pushed herself up, ignoring the wave of dizziness. "Aeron happened."

"Help me with her."

Larissa threw Halla's other arm over her shoulders. "What about Darien?"

"One problem at a time." But Anara's glance in Darien's direction betrayed her anxiety.

"I'll take Halla," Larissa said. "Can't you help Darien?"

Anara glanced down. "I—"

A shriek ripped through the warehouse, reverberating off the cement walls. The echoing sound shattered Larissa's ears, tearing into her brain. Involuntarily, she flung her hands up to shield her ears from the pain, as did Anara. Halla slipped from their grasp, slumping back to the floor.

Anara clutched at her stomach; her eyes were pitch black, and ripples of fur and feather appeared on her skin only to disappear. It was almost as though Anara was losing control of her *galdr*. Larissa stepped back, placing herself in between Anara and Halla.

Darien and Aeron stopped, covering their own ears, but Aeron smiled through it so fiercely that it looked more like a grimace than a grin.

From the railings above, a *draugr* flung itself down, landing between the brothers and Larissa's group. It rose lopsided due to its missing wing. Although bloodied and wounded, the hatred in its eyes made up for any perceived physical weakness.

"Kill them all except Princess Lovisa," Aeron shouted. "The Empress wants her alive!"

Bellowing, Darien threw himself back at his brother. Larissa could not follow their fight any further. Her vision was swallowed up by the massive creature in front of her, its whip-like tail searching for a victim. She reached for her hip only to find air where her gun used to rest.

"Kings and Queens," she hissed.

It was gone, wherever Aeron had thrown it. She looked around for a weapon, anything, trying to see past her tilting vision. The *draugr* leapt forward. She raised her hands, reaching for the hot *galdr* she prayed was inside of her, but came up cold. There was nothing there.

Anara leapt past her, meeting the *draugr* in wolf form, her open jaws wrapping around the creature's neck. Larissa stumbled against the next onslaught of vertigo but forced herself to remain upright.

The scrape of steel drew Larissa's attention as Aeron yanked the sword from Darien's grasp. The *draugr* roared in delight, catching hold of Anara and throwing her through the air. Larissa flinched at the crunch of Anara's body as it collided with the wall. Across the room, holding his sword to Darien's throat, Aeron laughed at the sight of Anara's crumpled form.

Like a match in the darkness, Aeron's laughter sparked the rage in Larissa's mind. Aeron, who had never enjoyed someone else's pain, laughed as Anara struggled to rise to her feet, as he threatened his own brother with death. This man was not the boy she remembered.

Let us help you.

The voice in Larissa's mind was not Lovisa's, and it sent a swooping sensation through her body. Larissa knew without a doubt it belonged to the child-goddess from her dreams, the youngest of the Norn.

There was no time for doubt or questioning. She opened her mind to the goddesses' presence. A surge of white-hot energy tore through Larissa's body. She doubted whether she could survive the building heat, but as it surged again, she no longer cared. Larissa raised her hands, the pearl ring glowing on her finger. Queen Stjarna had once told Lovisa that their *galdr* was energy, and that energy was meant to *burn*. Everything around Larissa slowed as the *draugr*'s talons plunged toward Anara's chest and a bead of blood appeared at Darien's throat.

The fire inside erupted, blazing up her spine, and then she was screaming words she would never remember. She threw out her hands, and hot-white crackling energy like lightning burst through her fingers, scorching on its way out. With immense effort, Larissa guided it, pushing a wave of her *galdr* to wash over the *draugr* and Calder. It threw them into a large pile of crates that splintered under their weight, burying them in debris and dust.

Larissa was not done, and neither was the child-goddess who urged Larissa on, directing her to reach out her hands toward the second floor railing. *Galdr* scorched through her as an electric golden hue surrounded her fingernails, crackling with unrestrained energy. Clenching her hands, she ripped the balcony from its supports, collapsing it on top of the rubble and burying Calder and the *draugr*.

Chunks of concrete rattled against the splintered floor. Darien stared at Larissa, his eyes wide and amazed. He reached down and retrieved his sword before the rubble could bury it entirely. Then the ground tilted, her legs wobbled, and she crashed to her knees, cracking them hard against the stone.

In the back of her mind, she knew she had never controlled her *galdr* like this, even as Lovisa. Bracing her hands against the cold floor, Larissa shivered, her body bereft of any warmth. Just as swiftly as the energy had consumed her, it abandoned her. Along with the goddesses.

"Lara!"

A hand under her chin brought her face up so that she could look into those wide blue eyes she had so often tried to ignore. "Darien."

"I've got you." His body shielded her from the debris that still fell from the second floor. When it had finally stopped, Darien asked, "How did you do that?"

Though she searched for it, Larissa could not find the child-goddess' voice anywhere within her mind. Larissa gulped and shook her head. "I don't know. Are they dead?"

The wreckage around them shifted as the ground shook. Darien grabbed her arms. "I don't think we're that lucky."

Clinging to him, Larissa rose to her feet. Halla stirred feebly behind them as Anara stumbled forward. Darien reached for her before she collapsed.

Larissa moved toward them. "I'll help Anara if you carry Halla." She slipped under Anara's arm, a more difficult feat than she imagined with the way Anara clutched at her stomach. Pain clouded the Rubinian's eyes, but there was also joy when she looked at Larissa. "I knew you could do it."

It wasn't all me, Larissa wanted to say, but now wasn't the time. "Let's get you out of here."

Larissa leaned down, flinching against the flash of sunlight in her eyes. Peeking out from underneath a pile of boxes was the barrel of her gun. Snatching it up, she shoved it into her waistband. Darien carried Halla in his arms, but his eyes locked on the pile of debris in the middle of the room. Pain, anger, and longing chased each other across Darien's face as he looked down on his brother. Darien's eyes hardened. He set his jaw, turning toward the entry door.

Larissa followed with Anara leaning heavily on her shoulder, unable to go faster than a brisk walk. Only once they were back outside did Larissa realize how she had been choking on the smell of the *draugr*. She sucked in greedy breaths of the clean evening air. Dusk covered the streets; shadows beckoned. Darien looked to Anara.

"Get back to the truck," Anara said. "Someone will have heard that."

But someone already had.

The sound of dozens of booted feet announced the sentries closing in on their location. Then came an all-too-familiar screech and the cracking of concrete from within the warehouse. Soon the *draugr* would free itself, and possibly Aeron too. Larissa's eyes fell to Anara's trembling form. Halla's eyes blinked sleepily as her head lay cradled against Darien's neck. What could they do?

A lone sentry appeared at the mouth of the street. "You there, stop!"

"Split up," Anara ordered. "Meet at the truck!"

Supporting Anara, Larissa ran down the street to her left. With one last glance, she watched helplessly as Darien, still carrying Halla, took the street to their right. There was no time to wait and see which pair the sentry would follow. They could only run, so run they did.

Running down streets and alleyways was agonizing, with Anara growing heavier on Larissa's shoulder every second. Larissa forced them both forward when Anara's feet faltered and slowed. They had to push through the pain. They could not stop, never knowing if the sentry was right behind them. Anara murmured directions, but her voice grew weaker at every turn.

"Which way, Anara?" Larissa asked again when she could not hear the other girl.

"Right." The word was less than a whisper. "Down to the right."

"Hang on, we're almost there."

Larissa reached for her *galdr*, something to sustain her, but nothing remained to latch onto.

As she dragged Anara down the alleyway, Larissa spotted Helga in her glorious rusted blue. For once, something had gone right. She nearly ran the whole length of the grime-coated path, then stopped. Dread coursed through her. The boxes in the trunk had been moved, revealing an empty hole between them. The sentry was gone.

Her eyes darted around, but no sentries rushed out from the shadows to ambush her. Had the other sentry only just managed to free himself? Was he even now bringing back reinforcements? Larissa froze, unsure of what to do. Should she take Helga, or would that attract too much attention? Could they even make it out on foot? Anara leaned heavily on her shoulders.

"Anara, what do we do?" she asked.

"Start the truck."

"But the sentries—"

"Larissa, I—"

Anara slumped forward, her dead weight propelling them both to the ground.

"Anara!"

Brushing aside Anara's hair, Larissa reached for her neck and located her weak pulse. The ruby pendant at Anara's throat looked oddly dulled, the rune within it darkening. But Larissa's eyes could not linger long. They were drawn to the dark maroon jacket tied around Anara's waist. Only then did Larissa remember that the jacket should have been brown.

Her fingers frantically undid the knot at Anara's waist as Larissa tried to ignore the warm wetness of the blood coating her fingers. The wound was worse than she had imagined. Blood pooled in the large gash. It was as if her stomach had been sewn back together only to be ripped open again. Larissa gagged at the pulsing muscle underneath and replaced the jacket, pressing down hard on the wound.

She stared down the alleyway, indecision tearing at her mind. There were bandages in the truck. If Larissa stopped applying pressure, Anara would bleed out, but if she did not seal the wound,

Anara would bleed out all the same. So focused on the warm blood gathering beneath her hands, Larissa registered the footsteps behind her a second too late.

A hand, so large it nearly covered her entire face, pressed a sharp smelling cloth over her nose and mouth. There was no escaping it. She could not breathe, and when she tried, the harsh scent of the cloth burned her throat. Stinging spice filled her nostrils and lungs.

Larissa reached behind her, dragging her nails down the arm of her assailant. A man grunted in pain, but the pressure against her face only increased. More footsteps approached as Larissa sank into the shadows.

Part Three
Muna

"*In the days long forgotten*
  Giants, older than the gods,
  Roamed the world.
  They hid under mountains
  Waiting for a weary traveler."

-Urðr, *Book of the Past*

34

Blinded by Loss

Larissa

LARISSA'S BODY ACHED AGAINST the rough vibrations of the truck bed. Heat radiated from her body, baking in what she could only assume was the midday sun.

The blindfold around her eyes prevented her from confirming her suspicions.

Her stiff hands reached for the cloth only to scream against the pain in her bound and blood-crusted wrists. *Blood. Anara!*

Larissa kicked her legs, attempting to swing herself up into a sitting position, only to find them bound as well.

"She's awake!" Something pounded on the cab of the truck. "Stop fidgeting."

Larissa froze. "Where are you taking me?"

"Quiet."

"What about my friend? Where is she?"

"The bleeding girl? She's here too." The man scoffed. "We should've left her; she's half-dead anyway."

Larissa's head turned as if she'd forgotten her eyes could not see. "Can I check on her?"

"I said be quiet." His tone allowed no argument.

Larissa clenched her jaw, the burning around her wrists intensified as she strained against the binding. No matter how she tried, the restraints were too tight. Besides, there was no way of knowing how many sentries guarded her. There was nothing she could do except wait.

Impatience rose within her like a scream building in her throat. Larissa wanted to lash out against whoever had taken her and check on Anara, but the fight and fury had drained from her body. The *galdr* she felt before was long gone, leaving her an empty, useless vessel once again. At least Darien and Halla were not with them. Larissa prayed to the *Æsir* that they would make it out of Perle and find their way to safety; they could not help her now.

No one could.

Larissa and Anara were on their own. If she was honest, Larissa expected to meet the Grand Empress long before ever seeing Halla again.

Tears gathered in her eyes, and Larissa found herself grateful for the blindfold that covered them. She would not show weakness to these men. She would gather her strength, then free them both. Until then, she could only wait.

And wait.

Minutes dragged into hours as the ridges of the truck bed dug into Larissa's side. Occasionally, she could hear the rustle of her captor as he tried to make himself more comfortable and his curses when he failed.

When she stretched out her legs, her bare feet touched another body. Though there was no verbal response, Larissa was certain it was Anara. If she kept very still, Larissa could feel the rise and fall of Anara's breaths. As time passed, Larissa stretched out again and again to check on her, reassured by the faint movements as she counted the girl's shallow breaths.

Once or twice, she struggled to find that reassurance, and Larissa's desperation nearly suffocated her until she could find the pattern again. Thoughts of Darien and Halla threatened to consume her. Were they alive? Captured? Dead? When she could stand it no longer, Larissa reached out, matching her breathing to Anara's own rhythm. They were alive. As long as they held breath, they had a chance.

The sharp squeal of tires was like music to Larissa's ears. She knew that squeal. They were riding in Helga. Of course they were. Faithful Helga had made it out with them, wherever they were heading. The movement beneath her stopped.

"About time," the man muttered.

Heavy footsteps circled the truck, followed by the high-pitched screech of the tailgate's lock.

"They're still following us," another voice called out. "Let's get them out of here."

Larissa's mind struggled to understand. Who would follow sentries?

The man beside Larissa spat. "Halvor better be ready to explain why we risked so much for these two."

She couldn't help herself. "Who's Halvor?"

"None of your business," the man snarled.

Large hands grasped Larissa's arms, yanking her off her feet. She thrashed, her legs searching for a target. "Let me go!"

"Would you rather fall off this truck and break your neck?"

"Maybe," she snapped.

The hands lowered her until her feet touched the bed. She shuffled one foot at a time, convinced the edge could not be that far. At the prod from behind, she took another step. Her foot fell through the air just as the hand caught a fistful of her jacket.

"Next time, I'll let you fall," he hissed in her ear.

"Enough, Jari," the other voice ordered. "Lower her down."

The man swooped her into his arms only to drop her into thin air. She stifled a gasp as she fell into another set of arms. But these hands were gentle as they righted her feet on the ground and led her to sit on the grass a few feet away from the heavy exhaust.

"I'm going to remove your blindfold, but if you try to run, I'll put it back on. Do you understand?"

Larissa flinched against the sudden onslaught of light, blinking as the sunbeams filtered through the trees. Helga idled off to her left; there was no road in sight. On her right, a wall of rocks stretched indefinitely in either direction. She tilted her head back. Unable to find the top of the cliffs, she was forced to look away before vertigo could set in.

The two men lowered Anara, laying her to rest beside Larissa. Anara's shirt was shorn just above her stomach. Dried blood crusted the jagged edges of the fabric. Tight bandages wrapped her entire abdomen, but the deep red stain revealed the shape of the wound beneath them.

A shadow fell over Larissa, blocking out the sun. Her mouth fell open at the sight of the man before her. How had she not noticed his size?

He towered over them, seeming as broad as he was tall. As though sensing his own physical presence, he curved his shoulders inward, not that it would fool anyone. He would have to cut off his own legs to make a difference. Surely if the giants from Pappa's stories had ever existed, a descendent of the *Jötnar* stood before Larissa today.

She forced her mouth shut. He watched her, a curious expression on his face. Five shallow scratches ran down his forearm right where Larissa knew she had clawed at her attacker.

She'd never stood a chance.

The giant-like man crouched down beside her. "My name is Haki."

Larissa held her tongue, silent even as Haki waited with surprisingly kind and inquisitive eyes. She'd never seen anything but superiority and contempt in the face of a sentry before. While this man wore their clothes and their weapons, he looked nothing like them. His gaze drifted to Anara.

"What happened to your friend?" he asked Larissa.

She bristled. "Like you don't know."

The other man, the one called Jari, walked into view. Like Haki, his size was intimidating, though he was slightly thinner. No wonder he'd been able to lift her like a rag doll.

Larissa's eyes darted between the two men. "You're twins."

Jari snorted. "Oh really, we never would've known."

An armored sentry truck skidded to a stop next to Helga, silencing Larissa's retort. The three-diamond crest was painted on the sides. Just the sight of it was enough for Larissa's pulse to quicken. A man dressed in black gear emerged, his face hidden by the door as he struggled with the captive still inside. With a final heave, the sentry wrenched his blindfolded victim from the vehicle, and Larissa's hope shattered.

Darien.

"Careful," the sentry barked to Jari, shoving Darien down beside Larissa. "This one's got an attitude."

Still blinded, Darien swung upward with bound hands. "Untie me, and say that to my face."

On the opposite side of the truck, another door opened, but the driver was hidden from view. Larissa scooted toward Darien, who pulled against his restraints. Like her, he was barefoot, most likely a tactic to keep them both from running.

"Darien."

He stilled, his head turning toward the sound of her voice. "Lara?"

"Yes, and Anara. I thought you and Halla had escaped."

Darien's face paled. "I'm so sorry, Lara."

Fear pinched the back of her neck. "Where's Halla?"

"She woke up as we were running. We got separated. I was attacked; I told Halla to run, but a group of *thræll* came out of nowhere. I tried to follow her, but they knocked me out. When I came to, I was alone. Lara, I'm so sorry. Larissa?"

His words crashed over her. After everything she'd done, none of it mattered.

Halla was gone.

Descent into the Dark

Larissa

Ragged breaths echoed in Larissa's ears. She squeezed her eyes shut, hardly feeling the burn of the restraints against her wrists.

Thræll. Halla was with the *thræll*.

Larissa trembled as fear and rage battled for dominance inside her. Darien's apologies buzzed in her ears. How could this happen? She'd left home, followed Anara, risked going to Perle, all for Halla. Through the darkness of her grief, a spark of *galdr* grew until it burned Larissa from the inside out. She didn't know how long she could keep hold of it. She ducked her head, looking for her ring, knowing she could draw strength enough from it to escape. Perhaps she could even call on the child-goddess to empower her as she had before. Then Larissa would go after Halla herself.

But the ring was gone.

Even as she turned her hands over as best as she could in their restraints, she knew it was no use. The ring, like Halla, was gone. A quick glance confirmed Darien's fingers were similarly bare.

"Looking for this?" A man bent down, opening his closed fist and revealing her ring.

The buzzing in Larissa's ears silenced. Her eyes followed his hand to his arms, up into the face of a man with familiar half-moon glasses.

"You?"

"Me." The old shopkeeper removed his glasses, tucking them into the front of his shirt. Without them he stood taller and looked younger, stronger. With swift fingers he removed Darien's blindfold. Darien blinked against the fading sunlight before focusing on the man before them. His eyes widened in recognition. Behind the shopkeeper, the sentry that had shoved Darien to the ground hopped into the armored truck that roared to life at the turn of the key. Then the truck and the sentry were gone, leaving only the six of them with Helga.

The old man gestured to Anara. "Your friend would've died without us. We lost one of our own removing you from Lystheim, and you carried stolen ancestral rings. You owe us an explanation. Who are you?"

The warning on Darien's face was unnecessary. Larissa refused to answer.

"If you remember," the old man prodded, "you came to me for help."

"Yeah, you've been a great help." Darien's voice dripped with sarcasm.

"We don't have time for this, Halvor," warned Jari. "Why not leave them here and go before the Empress' War Dog catches up?"

The old man, Halvor, ignored the twin, still speaking to Darien. "You don't want the Viðnám as your enemy."

"The Viðnám?" Darien scoffed, jerking his chin at the symbol etched onto the giant-man's jacket. "We're not idiots; we know what that symbol means. You're sentries and pawns of the Empress."

"That's only partially true." The other twin, Haki, crossed his arms over his broad chest. "We are sentries, technically, but we certainly don't work for the Empress. We help the Viðnám."

"If that's true, then why are we being held captive?" Darien demanded. "We came to you in good faith."

Halvor stilled. "Good faith? My men showed up at the warehouse, but you weren't alone. The Empress' War Dog and the demon creature entered behind you. Yet you left, unhindered. What else could you be but spies working for the Empress, trying to reveal the Viðnám's presence within Perle?"

War Dog. Larissa knew he meant Aeron. No, not Aeron. Calder.

"Unhindered?" Darien spat. "We barely made it out with our lives!"

"If you're not spies, then how did you escape both the *Kafteinn* and the *draugr*?"

"We *survived*," Darien snarled. "Or did you not just say that our friend would have died without you? Do you think they would've nearly killed us if we were on the same side?"

"I'm not asking you why you survived; I'm asking you *how*." He turned his attention from Darien to Larissa, twirling the ring before her eyes. "Do you know what this is?"

Larissa held his gaze, willing herself to not look at the ring, no matter how she longed to lunge forward and snatch it from the man's hand. She didn't care if he was a sentry or from the Viðnám.

Anara had almost been killed, Darien had been forced to attack his own brother, Halla was gone, and they had done nothing to stop it. They could not be trusted. Larissa tilted her chin up, narrowing her eyes at his challenge, letting him see her defiance seething over.

To her sweeping surprise, Halvor blinked and muttered. "Kings and Queens."

The twins shuffled and shared a glance. "What is it?"

"I knew a woman once who had your steel," Halvor spoke to himself as much as he spoke to Larissa. "Her child was just like her."

The shopkeeper's sharp gaze ricocheted from Darien to Larissa to Anara and back to Larissa again. Understanding dawned in his eyes even as his face paled. His soft voice returned in full force. "Óðinn's right eye, it *is* them. Release them!"

"What?" Jari asked, disagreement evident in his voice.

"Do as I say," Halvor thundered. "He has the face of King Torsten. That is Princess Anara. And this girl is, without a doubt, the daughter of Queen Stjarna. She did it. After all these years, she found the lost Perle Princess."

Larissa's heart plummeted. What had she done?

Haki raced forward, quick to remove the restraints from Larissa's wrists. She avoided the undisguised hope written in the giant twin's eyes. Only when he moved on to free Darien did she dare to look up again.

Larissa flexed her fingers to encourage blood flow, noticing how Jari's face tightened at the sight. He gripped his knife, though his feet stayed rooted to the ground. Unlike his brother, Jari's eyes held no hope, only hatred.

Darien rubbed his wrists. "You knew my father?"

"I *know* your father," Halvor corrected, pulling Darien's ring from his pocket and dropping it in his hands. "You don't recognize me, little Prince?"

Confusion clouded Darien's face, then gave way to recognition. "You were the son of my father's advisor, but you were younger than I was the last time I saw you."

"Precisely why, when I saw you three in my shop, I thought I'd finally gone mad. You all look the exact same as you did fifty years ago. I knew that *galdr* could have that effect, of course, but seeing it with my own eyes...I thought it was some trick of the Empress to reveal my ties to the Viðnám. When my men gave me your rings, I couldn't believe it was true." He presented Larissa her ring. "Princess, it is a miracle to see you again."

Larissa snatched the ring from his palm, her *galdr* itching to be released. "The four of us."

"Excuse me?"

"There were four of us in your shop. My sister." She choked on the word. "My sister, Halla; we have to go back."

His brows lowered. "There was a fourth, hiding behind you. But how can that be? You were an only child."

"Not anymore." Larissa rose to her feet, standing eye level with the man before her. "My sister is in there, in the hands of the *thræll,* and it's your fault. We have to go back."

"I'm sorry, Princess, but—"

"My name is Larissa, and you will take me back."

"And then what?" Jari sneered. "You think you can just walk back into the city you left in an uproar, demand your sister back, and be on your merry way? You nearly died the last time. Would have, too, if not for us. Who do you think fended off the sentries and got you out of Lystheim?"

She pivoted, advancing on the twin although her face only reached his massive chest. The air crackled around her. "My sister would be here if not for you."

"If not for us—"

"That's enough, Jari," Halvor said. The twin quieted; Halvor's word was law, it appeared.

A wailing shriek, though faded and distant, sent a spark of fear racing through Larissa's veins. She knew that shriek and, by the look on Darien's face, he knew it too. He reached for his sword, only to find it gone. Larissa's hand found nothing but air tucked into her waistband.

"Give them back their weapons and shoes," Havlor said, answering their unspoken questions, "but we don't have time or resources to fight. No doubt the demon creature is accompanied by more than just the War Dog this time. We must escape into the tunnels."

"What about my sister?" Larissa asked.

"You can't save your sister if you're dead, Princess."

Darien's hand touched her arm, grounding her in their reality. As much as she wanted to wait for Calder, to demand he take her to Halla, Larissa knew they were outmatched. Her *galdr* sizzled to a dying flame. "What about Anara?"

Haki was already carrying her in his massive arms like a priceless doll.

Jari's arms were crossed again. "If we're gone for much longer, they'll notice our absence."

"Consider your undercover assignments terminated." Halvor's voice was firm and final. "Jari, take the truck and lead them away from here."

"I don't know how far I can go. What little gas we were able to add before we left the city is nearly gone."

"Go to the northern entrance then. If the truck can make it, add it to our inventory."

Jari nodded, his lips set in a firm line. He clasped Haki's arm. "Be safe, brother."

"May the Norn guide you," Haki responded.

Larissa watched as Jari drove Helga out of sight. Dal and Vern. The farm. Halla. Now Helga. Just one more piece of her stripped away. She shook Darien's hand off her arm, fearful she might crumble beneath his touch.

"Now what?" she asked, already missing Darien's support.

Halvor's hands ran along the edge of the looming rock wall until they caught in a large crack. Planting both hands on the stone, he heaved. The wall moved in stubborn inches until the crack became a crevice just large enough to squeeze through.

Only darkness greeted them. Larissa's throat closed up at the thought of so much rock pressing down on her. What madness was this? They would be buried beneath the mountain.

Halvor motioned toward the darkness. "Now, we descend."

36

Homecoming

Darien

DESCEND WAS TOO LIGHT a word, Darien decided. It did not aptly describe their plummet down into what felt like the core of the earth, perhaps even into Hel itself.

The floor beneath them dropped at a steady decline that only worsened as they carried on. Multiple times, he'd held onto a ledge to drop down onto a landing below with nothing but Halvor's word that solid ground lay beneath them. With only one flashlight between them, there was hardly enough light to see more than a few feet ahead. The sword at Darien's hip made maneuvering the path even more difficult. Still, he was grateful for its return, even if it did bang awkwardly against his leg. As they continued down a new path, Darien knew he could never escape the tunnels without Halvor.

The air thickened, and sweat gathered at his neck. Every so often, his eyes caught on the enormous human being in front of him whenever the flashlight's illumination was blocked by the man's impressive bulk. Halvor called him Haki, and he had to walk at a constant crouch to avoid banging his head against the ceiling.

The giant cradled Anara in his arms as though she were no heavier than a blanket and navigated the tricky terrain without breaking a sweat. Anara stirred occasionally, but she fell back into her medicated sleep with only a small moan each time.

Larissa followed in silence. Darien reached out once to stop her from falling after a particularly rocky patch. She thanked him but moved away with a swiftness that left him hollowed. Not that he blamed her.

His mind returned to Halla, playing the scenario over and over again. If only she hadn't woken up. If only she hadn't offered to run on her own. If only he hadn't been attacked. If only the group of *thræll* hadn't been there. If only the Viðnám had known he was their ally, they could have helped him rescue Halla. The "if onlys" did him no good. He was on his way to the Viðnám while Halla was held in the hands of the *thræll*.

The harsh sound of Larissa's breathing intensified, drawing Darien's attention back to the present. More than exertion, the sounds she made were painful. Only then did he realize Larissa had stopped following, her hands pressed up against the rock wall as if to keep from collapsing.

"Lara, you okay?"

Silence, except for her ragged breaths. Halvor's flashlight bounced down the tunnel, away from them.

"Do you need to rest?" He reached out in the dark, his fingers brushing the hair on her shoulder.

"I can't do this."

"Do what?"

Leave Halla? Join the Viðnám? Forgive him? Really, her options were endless.

"I can't...breathe..."

Fear rushed over him. "Are you hurt?"

"No," she gasped. "I don't think so. The stone. It's too much. We'll die underneath all this stone."

It hit him. "Larissa, you're having a panic attack; take deep breaths."

"I don't...get...panic attacks."

"If you don't stop hyperventilating, you're going to pass out. Come on, slow breaths, in and out."

"Darien." Dry sobs heaved from Larissa's throat. "We left Halla."

She stumbled forward, crying softly into Darien's chest, struggling to breathe between the tears and his bloodstained clothes. Her body tensed as she held her breath, trying to regain control, only to make the crying worse as she gulped in air for her begging lungs. Darien wrapped his arms around her, knowing they could not shield her from her pain. They clung to each other, sharing their sorrows and regrets.

"We're going to get her back," Darien said.

When she pulled away, he let her go. "How?"

Her absence hurt worse than any of his wounds.

"Larissa, I know you don't want to be, but you're the Princess. We're heading for the Viðnám. Anara said the people believe in you. They need you."

"I'm not her anymore, Darien," she argued, exhaustion lacing her words. "I wouldn't know how to be her again."

"Look at how Halvor and Haki responded to you. They need you. And if they need you that badly," he pressed, "they might be willing to do whatever you need them to do."

"You think I could demand that they rescue Halla?"

"I don't know if I would use the word 'demand,' but I think they'd do anything to have the Perle Princess back."

Larissa stilled, the cogs of her mind moving behind her eyes.

Darien knew it wasn't what she wanted, even if he didn't understand. The Lovisa of his childhood was terrified her people would reject her, but only because of how badly she craved their acceptance. She'd wanted nothing more than to be their Princess. But Larissa was not Lovisa. She had changed, clearly, and Darien couldn't say if that was a bad thing.

She was more reluctant to take authority, but she was brave and loyal enough to run into a burning barn, to fight off a *draugr*, and to enter the dark and unknown. Yes, she was different, but he only loved her more for it.

Love. The word stuck in his throat. He'd always known it, even before, but they didn't have time for that kind of thinking now, not en route to the Viðnám, not with Halla in the hands of *þræll*. But if they were to get Halla back, maybe...

He buried the thought where he stood in the mountain. Larissa needed him; that was enough.

"You two alright?" Halvor asked, returning with Haki and the flashlight.

"We're fine," Darien answered when Larissa remained silent.

If Halvor noticed the red around Larissa's eyes and nose, he didn't mention it. This time Darien and Larissa followed as Halvor led them again.

"The road gets easier from here." Halvor's voice echoed off rock walls. "Not all of our tunnels are as rough as this one. It wouldn't be wise to make it too difficult for our own people to get out."

"Is the Viðnám underground?" Darien asked.

"Kings and Queens, no, that would be highly impractical. We're currently traveling under the Nordryggen Mountains—"

"How is that possible?" Darien interrupted. "They're impassable even during the summer."

"Yes, and for that reason we were unaware for some time that in the middle of those mountains is a vast valley. It's surrounded on all sides and all but impenetrable. The Viðnám made that valley its home twenty-eight years ago."

"Anara said the Viðnám was constantly on the move when she was with them."

A shadow fell over Halvor's face. "Those were deadly times. Right after the Great *Hrun*, we were nomadic, never in one place for long. The Empress' men picked us off one by one. We split into smaller groups to avoid detection. For decades we lived in the shadows, always running and always hiding. The people lost hope in ever finding the Perle Princess. Then word came that Princess Anara left us. She was one of our most valiant fighters and figureheads. We thought it was the end of the Viðnám."

"What changed?"

"Our people fled to these mountains. We knew it was only a matter of time before the Empress sent her men to find us. Our backs would be up against the wall, literally, but we were out of options. If we were to make a last stand, we would make it together. Then the *Jötnar* found us."

Darien snickered but stopped at the look on Halvor's face. "I'm sorry, but the *Jötnar*? Giants who live in the mountains and eat unfortunate wanderers? *Those Jötnar*?"

Halvor's eyes crinkled in amusement. "The very same. Although, I wouldn't mention the 'giant' misconception to them; it's quite offensive."

"You can't be serious?"

"He is." Haki grinned back at them. "They're not that big, not really."

Darien eyed him. "Well considering you're half-giant, forgive me if I don't take your word for it."

"You'll see them for yourself soon enough," Halvor continued. "They've been living in these mountains since *Ragnarok*."

"That's not possible. The Royals would've known."

"The *Jötnar*'s secrecy lies in their *galdr*, I've been told. They taught us the secrets of the tunnels that lead in and out of their valley. It drives the Empress mad. She knows we're somewhere in these mountains, but her men can't find us. She's lost many in the attempt. Ever since we reduced our presence in the commonwealth, she's stopped sending her men. She seems content in waiting for us to die in these mountains."

"What are you waiting for?" Larissa asked.

Halvor stopped dead, causing Darien to bump into him. Even in the dim light, Halvor's raised eyebrows were apparent.

"Isn't that obvious? We've been waiting for you."

Darien tensed, waiting for Larissa's argument, her denial. But to his surprise, she did not object. She lifted her chin, but only asked, "Are we almost there?"

"Nearly—" Halvor's words were cut off by Haki's roar of surprise.

Anara fell from his arms as he reeled back. Darien drew his sword, ready to defend them from whatever was attacking, when he noticed that Anara landed on her hands and feet. Except they weren't hands at all, but rather sharp claws coated in blood. Thick scratches ran down Haki's left forearm. Now he had a matching set.

One of his large hands covered the scratches, but blood was already rising to the surface. As Anara stumbled to her feet, her dazed eyes narrowed on Haki's sentry uniform. Sheathing his sword, Darien ran to place himself between them.

"Anara, stop—he's not an enemy!"

Her head whipped toward him, and she cut off mid-growl. Yellowed eyes jumped from Darien to Haki to Larissa to Halvor. The fangs in her mouth contorted her words. "You're the old man from the shop."

"Yes. I would say I'm surprised you didn't recognize me, but it has been a few decades. We saw each other in passing before you left. Perhaps my name will remind you. You might know me better as Halvor."

Anara sniffed the air, her fangs retracting. "You got old."

"Not all of us can be blessed with eternal youth," he said lightly.

Anara relaxed, her claws reshaping into hands. She pressed them to her stomach, wincing as she leaned against the tunnel wall. Her eyes tracked Haki's movements as he pulled bandages from his belt. "You're a sentry."

"Haki's on our side," Darien interjected. "He got us out of Lystheim. They're taking us to the Viðnám."

"Not quite the welcome party I expected," Anara muttered, but her eyes were unfocused as they searched the black tunnel behind them. "Where's Halla?"

Larissa's hands clenched into fists, but Darien knew she would not cry, not again. He answered for her. "She was taken by the *thræll*."

Anara's shoulders drooped. "Larissa, I'm—"

Larissa held up her hand, turning away from them. Anara met Darien's gaze. There were questions in her eyes, too many that could not be answered at that moment. Breathing deeply, Anara steadied herself, facing Haki. "I'm sorry I attacked you."

Haki shrugged, tying off the bandages around his arm. "It's just a scratch; I'll be fine."

"With Princess Anara awake, this makes things much easier." Halvor said.

Anara winced at the title. "Just Anara is fine."

"Haki," Halvor continued, "go straight to King Torsten and tell him that I'm coming with guests. Only tell him that I must see him in the throne room immediately and privately. Bring us three hooded cloaks. We will take the back tunnels, but if anyone sees us, they must think that I have brought new runaways. The King must be the first to know of Their Highnesses' return."

Haki nodded; in only a few long strides, he disappeared into the darkness.

Anara turned to Halvor. "Won't he get lost?"

Halvor chuckled. "Hardly. He knows these tunnels better than myself."

"Ow." Anara slid to the floor, glaring at the offending bandages wrapped around her waist, betrayal in her eyes. "Didn't the nectar take care of this?"

Darien knelt beside her. "It would have if you hadn't shifted again to fight off the *draugr*."

"Oh, yes," Halvor said, clearing his throat. "It would be best if you kept that under control while with the Viðnám."

There was a beat before Larissa understood his meaning. "Excuse me?"

"Public perception of Rubinians has only gone down since Anara left. It's no secret they sided with the Empress early on in this war. Our people don't trust those with your type of *galdr*."

Darien bristled. "That's ridiculous. If it weren't for Anara, we'd be dead."

Halvor lifted his hands in surrender. "I'm not saying it's fair, it's just how it is. The people will learn to trust Anara, but that will be harder if they fear that she is a *draugr*."

Larissa plopped down beside Anara. "I see why you left."

"It's fine," Anara said. "This prejudice was here before, and I didn't expect it to be gone. Besides, I've used too much of my *galdr* recently, and I'm exhausted. That last bit of partial shifting was all I had left." She touched the stone beneath her. "Where are we anyway?"

"The Nordryggen Mountains. Under them anyway."

"The Viðnám rejected using these mountains before. They were impassable."

Darien shrugged. "*Jötnar*, apparently."

"Loki's Knot," she murmured. "He actually found them."

"What do you mean?"

"In the weeks before I left, Torsten brought up the mountains again. He was obsessed with the thought of the *Jötnar*. We've all heard the stories. I thought they were long dead, but Torsten thought differently. He told me that King Mikkel, Lovisa's father, told him about their presence in these mountains."

All questioning eyes turned to Larissa who threw her hands in the air. "What do you want me to say? I told you, I don't remember."

Halvor's eyes widened. "You don't remember—"

Darien cut him off. "How did King Mikkel know about the *Jötnar*?"

Anara cringed as she pressed two fingers against her bandages. "Queen Stjarna spoke of them. That's all Torsten would tell me."

Halvor scratched at the stubble on his cheeks, his mind clearly on what Larissa had said. "I never knew he was searching for them."

"Yeah, well, there's a lot Torsten doesn't share with others." Anara pulled at her shirt, trying to cover the wound. "Don't take it personally."

Halvor grunted, turning to Larissa. "When you say you don't remember—"

His voice died at the sound of footsteps.

Haki returned, his face flushed from running. Three long, heavy-looking cloaks hung from his arm. Halvor tossed one to each of them.

"Never mind, you'll share your story soon enough," Halvor said. "Put these on. Do not draw attention to yourselves. It's imperative the King sees you first."

Darien clasped the cloak tight across his chest and pulled up the wide hood. If he was going to ask, he had to do it now. "Halvor, how is my father?"

Halvor hesitated. Darien's mind replayed the image of his father's disappointed scowl when Darien had chosen to rejoin Lovisa in Perle instead of remaining in Safír. Their last conversation had been one spoken in anger and accusations.

"He's a changed man," Halvor finally said. "The death of your mother and brother combined with your disappearance broke him for a while. He's different than you remember him to be, but he will be happy to see you alive." He looked at each of them. "All of you."

Darien's eyes skitted to Anara, who gave a small, nearly imperceptible nod. So the Viðnám didn't know that Aeron was not only alive but also the Empress' War Dog. Torsten didn't know that his eldest son was alive.

And a traitor.

Darien swallowed the bitterness that exploded across his tongue, knowing he would have to tell him. Larissa watched him, her soft red cloak contrasting vividly with her white hair. His hands reached out, pulling the hood down and tucking her hair behind her ears, careful to not let his hands linger. "Your hair is too noticeable."

Halvor offered his hand to Anara. "Are we ready?"

"I could carry you again if you'd like," Haki offered.

Anara rose to her feet. "I can walk on my own, thanks."

Haki shrugged, his large shoulders straining against the black gear. "Let me know if you change your mind. I'm told all the young ladies enjoy being held in my arms."

"Haki, she is a Princess!" Halvor hissed, his tone appalled.

Anara laughed, the sound clear and loud. "It's about time the Viðnám found more amusing people to join the cause. I should go away more often."

Though Halvor shook his head, Anara followed Haki down the tunnel, clearly unoffended by his words. After a few minutes, the light in the tunnel changed. With every footstep, the darkness faded, replaced by a growing light. The air was also thinning out; what had once felt stifling was now almost refreshing.

They found themselves at a large opening in the rock. The light of the falling sun was intense after so long in the dark. Darien found himself grateful for the hood that shaded his eyes. They stood on a ledge overlooking the vast valley below. Sprawling across the fields was an immense city.

They'd found the Viðnám.

37

The Viðnám

Darien

SURROUNDED ON ALL SIDES by towering cliffs, the valley ran on for miles past what Darien's eyes could see. The city below was just that: a city. It was no settlement roughly thrown together in disorganized chaos as he'd expected. From above, he could see the planning of each street, the placement of houses, and even the open market squares. The Viðnám had created its own nation in the heart of the mountains.

Anara took in the view with a long whistle. "It's grown."

Darian shook his head. "Bit of an understatement, don't you think?"

"The people are ready for rebellion." Halvor's wrinkled mouth turned up at the sight. "We just needed the return of our royalty. Of our Princess."

Darien tensed, again waiting for Larissa's rebuttal. None came. She was looking out at the valley, and although there was a pale hue to her face, her eyes were set in determination. A wind picked up along the crest of the ridge, throwing back the hoods of their

cloaks, but Larissa never turned from the city. Darien fixed his own hood and then pulled up Larissa's as well.

"Lara, you okay?"

Her skin had taken on a gray tinge, but she nodded anyway and tore her eyes from the sight of the city.

"We'll travel along the upper trail," Halvor said, leading the group along the ledge that ran close to the cliff wall. "Our guards patrol the tunnels. The entrances and exits are watched at all times. This path will take us around the city."

The narrow path was made smooth with concrete, winding its way along the surrounding cliff walls and giving Darien the perfect vantage point into the valley. The Viðnám was thriving. As the sun sank lower, street lights flickered on, lighting the paved roads.

He turned to Halvor in wonder. "How did you build all of this in so little time?"

"We didn't. Although we've expanded the city, the *Jötnar* were thriving long before our arrival. Unlike the common-wealths under Shiko's control, this valley is developing at a steady pace instead of regressing."

"Do you live here or in Perle?"

"Primarily in Perle, smuggling out whoever and whatever I can. Jari and Haki handle the runaways once I get them past the Wall. It's dangerous to be gone for so long without my absence being noted in town."

"Yet you're here with us now," Anara said, the question evident in her statement.

Halvor's gaze fell on Larissa. "Things have changed."

Larissa stiffened. "Do you make it a habit of buying slaves?"

His graying eyebrows pinched together. "They were foolish. I tried to help them, but they thought they could make it out on their own. If they were to disappear now, people would talk. I've told them about the Viðnám and, once they fade from public memory as slaves do, I will transfer them here. Until then, they'll be safe minding my shop. Ah! Turn here."

Halvor stopped, flicking his flashlight toward another tunnel. Unlike the last, this tunnel was lit by the steady pattern of electric wall lights decorated in the glowing runes of the gods. Two guards stood at the mouth of the tunnel, alert at the sound of footsteps. They relaxed upon recognizing Halvor, although their eyes drifted back to the three hooded figures. Darien tugged at his cloak, concealing his face from their curious eyes.

Halvor stepped forward. "King Torsten is expecting us."

The guards parted, allowing the group to pass by. Before long, a large, ornately carved wooden door appeared at the end of the hall. Runes decorated the door frame, runes that Darien could not remember from either of his lifetimes. He would have asked about them if not for the unease gnawing at his stomach.

His hands clenched at his sides. His father stood on the other side of that door. *A changed man*, Halvor called him. The man who stopped searching for his son. The man who believed he was the only living survivor of the Safirian royal line. Again, Darien thought of the last words they'd spoken to each other. Would his father even receive him? What would Darien say about Aeron?

No, not Aeron, Darien reminded himself. *Calder. Aeron is dead.*

Before Darien could sort his thoughts, they stood before the door. Anara's light touch on his arm drew him from the storm in his mind. Though her smile was reassuring, it could not touch the pit that deepened in his stomach.

The doors opened. Darien followed the others into a grand room that seemed old enough to have been carved into the mountain before *Ragnarok*. Electric lights drilled into stone walls evidenced a modern attempt to remodel the chamber. A large chandelier hung from the high ceiling, illuminating the empty throne set against the far back wall. Thick carpets were spread across the tiled floor, welcoming Darien's aching feet. Wide and spacious, the room housed various tables, some bearing books piled in leaning towers while others sat bare. On one table, giant maps were strewn on top of one another. A man pored through these, occasionally making notes to himself. He appeared oblivious to the intrusion, but Darien's eyes fixated on his father.

Beneath the gold and sapphire studded crown, the man's black curly hair was gray at his temples. Streaks of white ran through his beard. Though his eyes were decorated with wrinkles, they were just as blue and sharp as they'd been the day he'd caught Darien and Aeron listening at the library door.

King Torsten glanced up, his eyes brightening when they landed on Halvor. He scanned over Darien but, unable to see past the large hood, quickly returned his attention to Halvor. Torsten replaced the map, striding forward. "It's been too long since your last visit, my friend. I could use your advice." He nodded to Haki. "Ah, hello again Haki."

The giant bowed low. Beside Haki, Darien's foot tapped against the cushioned floor with barely concealed impatience. He nearly ripped the hood from his face, desperate to see his father's reaction.

Would he be overjoyed by Darien's reappearance or disappointed that the Norn had returned the wrong son?

Kings and Queens, Darien would have to tell his father about Calder.

"I see you've rescued more recruits from the commonwealths," Torsten continued, "but why all the secrecy in bringing them before me? I dismissed all of my advisors as you requested. We were working on a solution to the crop problem, and—"

Unable to wait any longer, Darien threw back his hood and stepped forward. Remembering his childhood training, he bowed low and presented himself to the King. After the appropriate amount of time, he risked raising his head to meet his father's gaze. Darien's stomach turned at the look on his face.

There was no delight; rather, King Torsten had turned a sickly color. "*Draugr.*"

The words struck Darien like a blow. "No, Faðir, it's me. It's Darien."

"That's not possible." Storm clouds gathered on Torsten's face as he turned to Halvor and demanded, "Explain yourself."

"It's him, sire, I swear it on Forseti."

The King held himself back, but his eyes devoured Darien, scanning every inch of his son's face. Almost against his will, he stepped forward, his hand outstretched. When his palm landed on Darien's shoulder, the King exhaled in wonder. He fell forward, wrapping Darien in his arms in an embrace tight enough to be painful. "It's really you."

Unable to speak, Darien returned the embrace, fighting the burning behind his eyes. Perhaps his father had forgiven him after all.

King Torsten pulled back, though his hands remained firmly on Darien's shoulders, as if afraid that Darien might disappear should he let go. "Are you really alive?"

"Yes, Faðir." Darien's tongue finally loosened. "I've come back."

Torsten laughed in amazement. "Your mother, Great Wanderer guide her soul, would be happy to know that one of her sons found his way home."

The smile on Darien's face cracked. *I have to tell him about Aeron.*

"Where have you been?" Torsten asked.

"Safír. Working on an orchard outside the Wall."

Torsten shook his head, confusion bleeding into his joy. "How is that possible? It's been fifty years."

Darien ran a hand through his hair. "It's a long story, and I'll need help explaining it."

"Help from who?" King Torsten then seemed to notice Larissa and Anara who, still hidden by their hoods, stood behind Darien. "I apologize. I've forgotten myself. Darien, introduce me to your companions. Or have they returned from the dead like you?"

"Not precisely, Torsten." Anara pulled back her hood. "They'd have to kill me first."

"Anara?" Shock, confusion, and understanding chased one another across Torsten's stricken face. "*You* found him. You never stopped looking then, but who—"

The words died in his throat. Unnoticed in the commotion, Larissa had removed her hood. Even with the scar that marred her cheek, Larissa had never looked more like the Lovisa Darien had known. There was a righteous anger in her eyes that Darien knew stemmed from her loss of Halla.

Standing in blunt bewilderment, Torsten's hands fell from Darien. The King and the Princess stood locked in a silent battle that neither were able to break. Darien moved beside her, ignoring the way his father's eyes narrowed at the movement, ignoring the unease that crept back into his stomach.

"Faðir, let me reintroduce you to Lovisa, Crown Princess of Perle."

38

A Choice

Larissa

Darien has his father's eyes, Lovisa whispered in Larissa's mind.

Larissa ignored it. She couldn't worry about the past, not with Halla's life dependent on her next actions. She would do whatever it took to find her. Be whoever she needed to be.

"It appears you have quite the story to tell," Torsten said, "and I must hear it, all of it. But there is someone else who should hear it as well." King Torsten turned to the twin who still bore the crest of the Empress. "Haki, send a guard to find the Speaker. She must join us. Then you may return to the barracks. Eat, rest, but speak of this to no one."

Haki nodded, but as he left, Larissa found herself oddly disappointed by his absence. King Torsten gestured to a table, pulling out a chair.

"We should sit."

Larissa chewed her tongue. She didn't have time for the manners and niceties of the King. She wanted to start planning how they were going to rescue Halla. A light grasp on her arm stopped her from speaking.

Patience, Anara's fingers urged.

Larissa released her breath, accepting the chair the King pulled out for her. Darien pulled out a chair for Anara, who wore a strange smirk around her lips that evolved into a painful grimace as she sat. Darien took the seat to his father's left. Was that habit from when Aeron always took the right? Halvor sat on the King's right, leaving an empty seat between them. Like a thorn, its emptiness stabbed at Larissa's consciousness.

Someone would have to tell Torsten about Aeron.

"Your Majesty," Larissa started.

The doors opened. All around her, those at the table rose to their feet. Larissa was the last to follow suit, not out of disrespect, but because her mind blanked at the new arrival.

This woman was beautiful, but in such a way that it hurt Larissa's brain to stare at her. No one could be that perfect, but somehow this woman was. Her skin was dark, the darkest Larissa had ever seen, yet it radiated light. Her close-cut hair curled around a perfectly shaped head. Even the harsh electric light shimmered on her cheekbones. As she strode toward them, she towered over the men in the room. She was taller than even Haki, yet she walked with grace contradictory to her height.

The woman's amber eyes rested on the table but gave nothing away. They bore neither curiosity nor surprise, but an empty serenity.

King Torsten pulled out the empty seat beside him. "Welcome, Speaker."

"I wondered about the commotion I've been feeling." Her gaze floated toward Larissa. "Your lost Princess has returned."

Her voice was like velvet in Larissa's ears, but the recognition struck her to the core. She knew she should wait to speak, but any thought of formalities was pushed aside. "How do you know who I am?"

"I knew your mother," the woman said. "A long time ago by your standards. Where have you been?"

Dumbstruck. There was no other word to describe the muteness that kept Larissa from speaking. Taking advantage of Larissa's silence, King Torsten said, "I'm surprised Haki found you so quickly."

The woman waved a manicured hand. "I was already on my way. I could sense them coming. Couldn't you?"

Torsten raised an eyebrow at the taunt. "We have much to discuss. I haven't yet heard the story myself."

Over tight dark pants, a long ivory coat fluttered behind the Speaker as she lowered herself at the King's side. She faced Anara, and bemusement colored the Speaker's expression. "You're a Shifter."

Anara stiffened. "I am."

"At least some of your kind remain with their souls intact."

From the look on his face, Darien felt just as baffled as Larissa.

King Torsten cleared his throat. "This is Speaker Skaði of the *Jötnar* people."

"Skaði?" Darien asked. "As in the daughter of the giant Thjazi?"

Larissa resisted the urge to sink in her chair. Darien must have been awake when Larissa had told that story to Halla after all. Did he remember that he'd told her that same story by the same river a lifetime ago? Larissa pushed away the thoughts; she had to focus.

"No known relation," Skaði answered, unperturbed by Darien's interruption. "I took on her name when I became Speaker of my people in the hopes that I would lead them with the same loyalty that the original Skaði showed her father."

"But you are really a *Jötunn*?" Anara asked.

"Yes."

"You're not quite what I expected."

Skaði pursed her lips. "Ah, the *giant* thing."

"She is the reason the Viðnám has survived as long as it has," King Torsten interjected. "She offered us sanctuary when we had nowhere else to go. Speaker Skaði, this is Princess Anara of Rubin, my son, Prince Darien of Safír, and as you already mentioned, Princess Lovisa of Perle. But enough of these introductions. Anara, you left us twenty-eight years ago. What has happened since?"

"Has it really been twenty-eight years?" Anara asked, directing the question at herself. "I'll spare you the details and skip to what you want to know. You may remember, when I left, it was because of your decision, Torsten. You called off the search for Darien and Lovisa."

Torsten's brows tightened, his eyes darting to his son before turning his glare on Anara. "Our people were dying. We didn't have the resources."

"When I left," Anara continued, "my search wasn't easy. I could find no sign of them, not even a whisper. About a month ago, I was sheltering with a wolf pack when the Norn sent me a vision. In my dream, I stood before *Yggdrasil*, its branches blocking out the sky.

On the well before the tree, a child with flaming hair etched runes into the stone. She called herself Verðandi."

"You dreamed of the Norn?" Speaker Skaði asked.

"She was as real to me then as you are to me now." Anara leaned back in her seat. "She took my hand, and her touch paralyzed me, but in that moment I saw Darien and Larissa lying in the grass. I ran to them, but they disappeared. The girl told me to follow the salt and sea if I wanted to wake them.

"I traveled south toward Safír the next day. I'd searched the commonwealth before, but when I arrived, I sensed volumes of *galdr* that told me I was on the right trail. It was Produce Day, and I followed a scent toward the Wall, but the sheer number of bodies mixed up the scent of *galdr*. By the time I picked up the scent again, it had passed out of the city. I followed it and found Darien. When I revealed myself, I never imagined he wouldn't remember who I was or who he was."

King Torsten leaned forward, glancing toward his son. "What do you mean, he didn't remember?"

"Look at them, Torsten." A challenge entered Anara's voice. "They look the exact same as they did fifty years ago. They haven't been in hiding, they've been stuck in time, shielded by *galdr* we can't comprehend. Something or someone buried their true memories and planted false ones to protect them."

"She actually did it," Skaði murmured, a look of incredulity in her widening eyes.

"Who did what?" Irritation seeped through Torsten's voice.

"One story at a time. Princess Anara, please continue."

"Anara is fine. When I realized that Darien didn't know me, I remembered how the girl in my dream held my face to show me

Darien and Lovisa. I tried to do the same with Darien. A shock ran through my body and into his. I'd never felt this *galdr* before. The gods were working through me. Then Darien fled. After all those years, I found him only to lose him again."

"You didn't, though," Darien interjected. Words flowed from his mouth as he picked up the story, filling in the details from his own perspective. When he shared Aagen's story of the woman who brought Darien to Aagen's home a year ago, Halvor scratched his beard.

"Your description sounds like Queen Stjarna," he said.

"It's not possible," Torsten interjected. "She died the same night you both disappeared."

He looked briefly at Larissa as though apologetic for his words, but she felt only a dull ache. How could she grieve someone she hardly remembered?

"Aagen?" Halvor asked, still scratching. "The name is familiar, but I can't place it."

"He's a good man. A good father." Darien murmured. An uncomfortable silence spanned the space between father and son.

Anara shifted in her seat. "Darien wasn't the only one at the Wall that day. After he fled, I picked up Lovisa's scent. It took me to the outskirts of the Safirian farmlands, where I found a young girl. Lovisa's smell was on her, but she looked nothing like Lovisa. Only her eyes reminded me of Stjarna. I wondered if whoever had hidden Lovisa and Darien had changed Lovisa's appearance too, but when I tried to wake her, there was no shock. No recognition. I returned to Darien, convinced he could help me find Lovisa. By the time we'd returned, we were too late."

Anara's voice grew detached as she ran through the *draugr*'s attack, but Larissa's skin turned cold. She could hear the monster's screech in her ears, feel the heat of the fire burning her skin, and see Halla's freckles smeared with ash and blood. Larissa curled her fingers, allowing her nails to dig into the skin.

Get it together, Larissa ordered herself.

King Torsten's skeptical voice broke through her panic. His hard eyes questioned her. "*You* killed the *draugr*?"

Larissa fought the urge to cross her arms, thinking of how Halla would tell her it wasn't the princess-thing to do. "I had help."

Torsten slid his gaze to Halvor. "I can't imagine Princess Lovisa killing off a *draugr*."

Larissa swallowed. "You'll find, your majesty, I'm not the Princess you think I am. I go by Larissa now."

Ignoring Torsten's look of surprise, Anara summarized the rest of their travels, from burning Larissa's parents to fighting off Kafteinn Calder and the *draugr*, although she managed to omit the truth about Aeron's identity. Darien willed his face to go blank, apart from the tight, unyielding line of his mouth that he could not relax. It wasn't time to mention Calder, not yet. When Anara finished, her voice was hoarse and scratchy. Silence settled in the absence of her story.

King Torsten pressed the pads of his fingers under his chin. He had closed his eyes some time ago as he listened to their tale. As he opened them, his brows lowered in bewilderment. "If I didn't know your integrity," he said at last, "I wouldn't believe it."

"I may be able to offer some illumination." Speaker Skaði commanded their attention. "Before the Great *Hrun*, Queen Stjarna suffered from visions. She traveled the nations searching for an interpreter. Perhaps guided by the Norn, she found us. Her dreams were plagued by *Yggdrasil*, but the tree was on fire. We couldn't decipher its meaning anymore than she could, but we told her of those who could." Skaði's voice died off.

"Well, out with it," Torsten demanded.

But Skaði's eyes remained fixated on Larissa. "First, I must determine who sits before us. Are you truly Princess Lovisa of Perle?"

"I've already told you my story." Irritation crept into Larissa's voice. Didn't they understand every minute they wasted kept them from rescuing Halla? "I was her before."

"You were, but not are?"

Larissa stiffened. "I don't have to justify myself to you. I just want to know how we're going to rescue Halla."

"Halla?" Torsten asked.

"Yes, Halla, my sister; the one Anara told you was taken by *thræll*."

"Oh yes." He leaned away from the table. "Your *adoptive* sister. Halvor, you have experience with the slave industry. What are the possibilities?"

Although his head was turned respectfully toward the king, Halvor held Larissa's stare. "If they keep to their pattern, she will be sold within the next few weeks. Likely to one of the aristocratic families—they prefer young girls."

Larissa's intestines twisted when Halvor hesitated. "And if they *don't* keep to their pattern, Halvor? Tell me."

Halvor sighed. "Young girls often bypass the auction blocks in the cities. The *thræll* seem to be particularly fond of them. I've heard they collect the young girls from all four commonwealths to take directly to Diamant. Rumor says the Empress will pay highly for them."

Larissa gripped the edge of the table, fighting the way the room spun. "We need to leave as soon as possible, before they take her out of the city."

Torsten pressed his fingers together once more. "What are the risks?"

"A stealth mission to retrieve Halla from one of the aristocratic families would result in covers blown and lives lost." Halvor's sympathetic look did nothing to ease Larissa's panic as he continued, "That's if she is sold at a normal auction block and not held for later transfer, which would be infinitely more difficult."

King Torsten shook his head. "A high price to pay for one child."

"Faðir," Darien protested. "Halla is more than just a child, and Larissa is asking you to do this for her."

"Yes, but what is *Larissa* willing to give?" King Torsten mulled over the name.

Larissa leaned forward, her ring smacking against the table. "Anything."

"There is another option, my lord," Halvor said.

"Yes?"

"Advance on the city. With the Princess' return, we can inspire the people to take back their commonwealth. Kings and Queens know at least a third of our forces are refugees from Perle. Give them a chance to reclaim their homes and rescue Halla in the process."

"There is more to lose with that plan," King Torsten pointed out.

"And more to gain. This is what we've been waiting for. As we speak, the Empress is devising a way to force us out of hiding. We should make our move before she can make hers."

Larissa forced herself to remain still, even as her body screamed at her to flee. She'd never intended to start a war, but if that was what it took to get Halla back, then a war it would be.

Torsten stirred from thought. "The Viðnám is growing complacent in its fear. I'm grateful for the safety we found within these mountains, but our people are losing perspective. This valley is not sustainable. Even now we are a drain on the *Jötnar* resources, as Speaker Skaði reminded me only last week. Every day, we smuggle more people from the commonwealths; we grow in number and yet not in strength. My people need a spark, something that will make them fight for their homes, their families, their land. Halvor is correct."

Larissa held her breath. Was Torsten agreeing to the plan?

He shifted his hard eyes toward her, and for a moment, they look nothing like Darien's. "You could be the hope they need. The return of their lost Princess. If you were to lead the way—metaphorically speaking, of course—you could turn the tide."

"No pressure," Anara muttered.

Larissa ignored the churning in her stomach. "If I agree to be *her*, will you save Halla?"

"I give you my word."

"A moment, King Torsten." Speaker Skaði held one delicate finger in the air. "Do not put your faith in the seed sown in the field before it takes root. We have yet to determine if this is indeed the Princess you speak of."

"What are you talking about?" Darien snapped, his tone as sharp as Larissa had ever heard it. "Look at her; if you met Queen Stjarna like you say, then you should be able to see the resemblance. Even if you can't, my father recognized her, and Anara and I vouch for her. What more do you want?"

"Peace, Prince. I'm not arguing she was the Princess once, but it is as she herself said, she *was* the Princess." Skaði cocked her head to the side, her peering eyes dissecting Larissa where she sat. "King Torsten, correct me if I am wrong, but you require the current Princess of Perle. You don't want to present a false figurehead to your people only to have her crumble before them."

Torsten tapped his fingers. "The Speaker has a point. You claim to be the lost Princess, and yet you won't even say her name. So, *Larissa*, are you or are you not the Crown Princess of Perle?"

Just say yes, Lovisa urged her.

Just say yes, and they'll rescue Halla, her own mind cried.

"Yes," she blurted. "I'm Lovisa."

But the slump in Darien's shoulders and the droop of Anara's head only mirrored the disappointment in Torsten's face at Larissa's unconvincing declaration.

The Speaker shook her head. "There is a block in your mind—one of your own making. You refuse to accept your past, you dismiss who you are, and because of that you are unable to remember. Our own history is hard, but if we ignore the past, we destroy our future."

"Then how do I break this block?" *How do I save Halla?*

The Speaker reached across the table, taking Larissa's hand in her own and turning the pearl ring on her finger until the rune caught the light. "Use the runes of the gods to open your mind.

It might take time, but only once you remember can you be the Princess the Viðnám needs you to be."

King Torsten rose to his feet. "Unfortunately, time is not something we have an abundance of. I can see you all drooping from exhaustion. You three will be shown to your rooms. Rest and think things through."

He pulled out Larissa's chair, his hand guiding her to her feet. Calluses decorated his palms, scratching against the calluses on her own hands. "I'll need your answer by dawn. If you're still the Princess I once knew, the Princess with the supposed power to end the Empress' reign, I will make the announcement of your arrival to the entire Viðnám. We will march on Perle, take back the commonwealth, and rescue your sister."

"That's not much time to break the block in her mind," Anara said. "What if she can't do it?" Anara rose, ignoring Darien's offered hand. "Will you leave Halla to her fate? Like you abandoned your own son?"

The muscles in Torsten's forearms spasmed, but his words were deadly soft. "If Princess Lovisa is truly gone, the Norn have already sealed all of our fates." He turned toward his son. "Darien, stay behind. We should talk."

Larissa felt Darien's eyes dart in her direction. He set his jaw. "I have to help Larissa."

Torsten's eyes tightened. "I see. Then I'll see you all tomorrow."

Larissa didn't miss the resentment residing beneath the king's expression, and from the look on Darien's face, neither did he.

Revival

Larissa

THE ROOM WAS SPACIOUS and luxurious, fit for royalty. The numerous lights hanging from the walls illuminated every inch of the wall carved into the mountain. The stone floor was covered with rugs to battle the cold. In the center of the room sat a vast bed, and off to the side Larissa saw a door leading to the bathroom. Through the crack, Larissa caught sight of a large tub she was itching to step into.

Literally. Her skin itched from the dirt and blood that flaked to the floor even as she stood still in the middle of the room. More than anything, she wanted to slide into that bath, but she would have to wait. She could not escape Lovisa's voice in her mind, urging her to return to her memories and unlock the block in her mind.

The discomfort in her side drew her attention. Larissa yanked the gun from her waistband, laying it on the bedside table.

Anara and Darien walked in behind her instead of retreating to their own rooms. Taking one look at the bed, Anara collapsed upon it, not minding her own filth and blood-stained clothes.

Darien slumped against the door, the deep nod of his head revealing his exhaustion as dark strands covered his eyes. Larissa told herself it was Lovisa's thoughts, not her own, that urged her to reach out and brush back his rumpled hair. Forcing herself to walk away, Larissa paced the length of the room, her feet relentless as they trampled the plush carpets.

Anara's half-closed eyes trailed Larissa. "What are you going to do?"

"I don't know."

"How do you plan to break the block in your mind?"

"I'm not sure."

"Do you have any kind of plan?"

"Not really."

Anara rolled her eyes. "Great."

Larissa stepped toward the bed. "What do I do, Anara? You told me I didn't have to be her!"

"You don't have to, but then you won't get Halla back. Sometimes you have to make the hard decisions, Princess."

Larissa stepped back, surprised at the bite in Anara's words. "I told you, I'm not—"

"—that person anymore, yeah, I heard you the first hundred times." Anara swung her legs over the bed then winced, glaring at Larissa. "It was fine at first, fair even, but now you're intentionally blocking your past. For what? Because you're scared? You want to know what you should do? Do what *Halla* asked you to do."

Anara's words fell like physical blows on Larissa's heart. "What's that supposed to mean?"

"Halla believes in you. I believe in you. Darien believes in you." Anara threw up her arms. "Hel, even King Torsten wants to believe in you! The only one of us who doesn't believe in you is *you*."

Larissa stepped back from Anara's accusing finger. "I—"

But Anara wasn't done. "You can't keep running from your past forever. This is it, Princess, you've hit the wall where you either decide to throw it away forever or face whatever it is that you're hiding from."

Darien dropped his head in his hands. "Anara, maybe just back off."

"No, Darien. I've given her time, you've given her time. Now it's time for tough love. Larissa, what you did at the warehouse, taking down the *draugr* and Aeron—"

"Calder," Darien hissed.

Anara paused a beat. "Fine, Calder. A farmer's daughter couldn't do that. Princess Lovisa couldn't have done it either. Not even at the peak of her power. You've changed, but you're stronger than before. So use that strength instead of hiding from it. Don't force yourself to be who you were; accept who you have become and use your power to rescue Halla."

Larissa slid down the wall, plopping beside Darien and burying her face in her hands. She didn't bother mentioning the child-goddess who had somehow amplified her *galdr*. Anara was right. There was nowhere left for Larissa to run. No excuses. Still.

"I can't lead the Viðnám. I'm only seventeen."

Darien raised his head. "Technically, if we count all the years that we were gone, you're really like sixty-seven."

The two girls met his words with scathing glares.

"Not that you look it," he hurried to add, his hands in the air. "You look good, I mean you look seventeen, not that Anara doesn't look good, and she really is sixty-sev—You know what, I'm going to stop talking now."

Anara snorted. "Good decision. Look, Larissa, no one is asking you to lead the Viðnám; they just need a figurehead, someone to inspire the people to follow King Torsten in the resistance."

"It feels dishonest."

"Don't you want the Empress gone so that Halla can live a life without fear?"

"Well, yeah."

"That's all the Viðnám want, too: a life without fear. You can relate to the people more now than you ever could before. If you just remember who you were and who you are now, you might find that you actually want to be that inspiration."

One last fear nagged at Larissa. "I don't know how."

Holding her arms against her stomach, Anara joined them on the ground. She grabbed Larissa's hand, twisting the ring on her finger. "You do what the Speaker said. Use the rune of your people to pull you back into your memories."

Anara and Darien leaned toward her. Their two faces, so honest, so eager, so covered in dirt and blood, invited Larissa to trust them.

Weeks ago, she'd been content with her life. Her biggest complaints had been Pappa's stories and Halla's limitless belief in the gods. But it had all been a story of someone else's making.

This was her chance to take authorship of her own story.

"I'll try." Her eyes strayed to Darien. "Will you help me?"

"Always." He moved toward her, his eyes never leaving her own. Larissa was grateful he understood what she needed. She didn't fight him when she felt his persuasion sink into her thoughts.

"It's time to remember, Lara."

Leaning into the compulsion in his voice, Larissa looked at the rune etched into the pearl. It shone brilliantly, pulsing with her own heartbeat. Larissa felt as though she were hanging from a cliff, her fingertips digging into the earth until they bled.

Remember me, Lovisa urged.

Larissa let go.

ᚾᛁᛉᚱᛋᚾᛁᛉᚱᛋᚾᛁᛉᚱᛋᚾᛁᛉᚱᛋᚾᛁᛉᚱᛋ

"You came back," Lovisa said.

Larissa touched a hand to her face, feeling the rough edges of her scar. It was the most blatant difference between her and Lovisa. The girl stood in front of her, surrounded by the ruined remains of the hallway, uneven tiles and cracked walls running infinitely in either direction. She wore the same gown from the Jóltide Festival. An array of simple braids pulled back her hair, and light from the unseen moon glowed on her smooth cheeks.

"Are we ready?" Lovisa asked.

Only one door remained intact within the destroyed hallway. Swallowing her fear, Larissa tested the handle, unsurprised to find it locked.

She resisted the urge to kick at the door again. "Why won't it open?"

"Only the Perle Princess can open it."

Larissa scoffed, standing aside. "Be my guest then."

"I can't do it either."

"What? But you're so"—she gestured at Lovisa's gown and general state of regality—*"obviously her."*

Considering this, Lovisa nodded, then tried her luck at the door only to share in Larissa's level of success. *"Only a part of her, it would seem. We have to do it together."*

When Larissa did not move immediately, an electric energy snapped between Lovisa's fingers. *"Do you want to know or not?"*

Startled by the abrupt change in Lovisa's tone, Larissa complied, laying her fingers on top of Lovisa's palm. While Lovisa's hands were pale, smooth, and manicured, Larissa's hands still bore the grime and wounds of battle.

Their differences were forgotten as the knob turned and the door inched open.

A surge of success flared through Larissa. She turned to share her triumph with Lovisa, but the girl was gone. Even the voice that had inhabited her mind had vanished. Larissa was truly alone.

Beyond the door lay only darkness. A twist in her stomach, the rapid pulsing of her veins, and something primal within her warned Larissa to not remember. Only pain waited within. She could choose to forget and remain in her blissed ignorance. All she had to do was shut the door.

But then, in her mind, she saw them. Darien's smile when he thought Larissa wasn't looking. Halla's freckled nose, wrinkling as she laughed. Anara's fierce eyes watching over them, protecting them. Larissa touched the scar on her face, gathering strength from it. She couldn't hide anymore. For them, she would face this fear.

Her feet crossed the threshold as she plunged into the darkness of her past.

40

Sacrifice

Lovisa

GLASS SHATTERED, FOLLOWED BY *gunshots and screams. The painful stitch in Lovisa's side demanded that she stop running, but she couldn't slow down. The attack on Perle had come suddenly in the night, but if Lovisa guessed correctly, she knew exactly who was behind it. Her family had planned for this possibility, and thus she had one goal: to reach her mother. Lovisa's feet flew like the wings of the Valkyrie down the hallways of the palace, only to stumble and stop around the next corner.*

A group of men blocked her escape. On their chests, they wore the emblem of three linked diamonds.

Shiko! her mind screamed. *She's here.*

Guns were pulled from holsters and pointed at her heart as the men spoke to each other.

"Is that her?"

"How should I know?"

"We have to be certain. The Empress wants her alive."

Lovisa raised empty hands. "I'm going to ask you once to get out of my way."

"The ring! That's her!"

"Take her."

Lovisa's mind overflowed, not with fear, but with sorrow, thinking of the funeral they'd held for Aeron without the courtesy of a body. Anger boiled over the warning of her mother's words as Lovisa raised her shimmering hands.

Energy pulsed from her palms, resounding off the stone walls and shoving the men back with the force of a tidal wave. Their bodies crumpled onto the ground, unmoving. But Lovisa's sense of triumph gave way to exhaustion. She swayed on her feet, hearing her mother's voice.

Be careful of overdoing it, Lovisa. You might hurt yourself more than your target.

Her knees cracked on the tile beneath her as she fell to her hands. In front of her, the men already stirred. Her idiotic mistake had cost her freedom. Any moment now, they would wake and take her to Shiko.

Broad arms wrapped around her chest, yanking her to her feet. A deep, familiar voice scolded her. "Lovisa, you know better."

Angry golden eyes captured hers, but under the anger, Lovisa saw fear in her father's face. He grabbed her arm, and they were running again, away from the men who were struggling to their feet. King Mikkel held his sword in one hand, and with the other, he clasped his daughter's hand. The gun at his waist shocked Lovisa; her father believed so strongly in the use of ancestral weapons. He rarely bore anything apart from his father's sword.

"What's happening?" she asked in between breaths.

"Shiko came through the passageways," Mikkel said. Sweat streaked his forehead and cheeks, and Lovisa saw flecks of blood on his cuffs.

"But no one knows about the passageways."

"They do now." He took another turn, guiding Lovisa up a second staircase. "I know we don't like your mother's plan, but it's the only option left."

A shard of ice lodged in her heart. "What about Darien? We have to find him."

"Darien knows if anything were to happen, you were both to find your mother. We can only hope that he'll be there when we arrive."

He didn't have to say what it would mean if Darien wasn't there. Another funeral without a body.

The clomping of booted feet came from the hall in front of them. They spun, but more footsteps came from behind them as well. Losing no time, King Mikkel yanked a large portrait off the wall, revealing the gaping hole set in the wall four feet up. They could only hope Shiko did not know about all of the passageways, or this would be a short escape attempt.

Lovisa pressed her palms on the ledge and clambered into the hole, scooting in to make room for her father. The light vanished as King Mikkel refitted the portrait over the hole.

"Faðir!" she cried out.

"Go, Lovisa. I'll stall them; get to your mother."

"Please, you have to come too! I don't care about the prophecy!"

"I don't either," he murmured, his voice muffled through the painting. "All of Evrópa can burn in Hel as long as you are safe." The footsteps drew closer. "Go, Lovisa!"

"It's the King," an unfamiliar voice shouted. "Kill him!"

Lovisa knew she should obey her father's orders, but she froze behind the portrait, listening as shots rang out. Then came the sound of steel on steel, grunts, howls, and the gurgles of dead and dying men. More than once she wanted to join her father in the battle. More than once she knew she should flee into the passageway as he had ordered, find her mother, and get to safety—but she could not leave.

A bullet tore through the portrait, embedding itself in the wall next to Lovisa's shoulder. She flinched, cracking her head against the wall, but still she could not leave. A thin stream of light filtered through the minuscule tear in the portrait. Her father's last words echoed in her mind. Then all was silent.

Lovisa scrambled to her knees, pressing one eye against the ripped canvas. Blood sprayed the once spotless walls. Bodies were strewn across the floor. Her father knelt in the middle of them, having fallen to his knees. His robes were torn, pierced, and stained not only with the blood of others.

A young woman stood before Mikkel, holding his sword. Petite, with black hair tucked into a smooth bun, the woman looked harmless. Until she turned. Disdain and disgust shone from sharp eyes. There would be no mercy. A tall, five-pillared crown dripping with diamonds adorned her head, the gems reflecting the blood from the walls. Lovisa had only ever seen the young Queen in passing, across ballrooms, but Lovisa knew it was her. Shiko, the Diamant Queen who'd plunged their nation into chaos.

"Where is she, Mikkel?"

"Gone," he spat. Droplets of blood splattered the hem of Shiko's black gown. She hadn't even bothered to wear armor to the fight. "You won't find her until she's ready for you, and then you'll wish you hadn't."

Shiko smiled, cocking her head to the side as though listening to a friend whispering secrets in her ear. Then she lunged, driving Mikkel's sword straight through the King's chest. Lovisa shoved her fist into her mouth, biting down hard on her knuckles to muffle the scream clawing up her throat, but nothing could stop the tears.

She fled, crawling away from the Diamant Queen, away from the bloodshed in her halls, away from the sound of her father's body hitting the floor.

In the pitch black of the passageway, Lovisa rose to her feet and fled by memory. How often had she snuck around the palace in these passageways during her youth? How often had her mother and father scolded her after losing her in them? Her father would never scold her again.

A small whimper slipped past her lips, but she shoved it down. This wasn't the time to allow her feelings to consume her. She crawled on, ripping her pants and scraping her palms, only stopping when she bumped into heavy fabric. Lovisa knew it was the curtain on the fourth floor. She waited for a moment, listening for the sound of intruders. When nothing but silence met her ears, she pulled the curtain back and slid out of the passageway, crouching low to the ground, her eyes scanning in all directions. She slipped into the room beside her, praying that the Æsir would hear her.

In the room, Queen Stjarna rose from her chair, relief chasing the worry from her eyes. "Lovisa!"

Lovisa locked the passageway door behind her, then collapsed into her mother's arms. Through her sobs, she praised the gods that had heard her.

Stjarna's hands rubbed Lovisa's back, brushing back the hair from her daughter's face. "Where is your father?"

Lovisa couldn't meet her mother's eyes. "She killed him."

Queen Stjarna's hands froze. Daring to look up, Lovisa saw her mother's face holding a mixture of desperation and determination, even as her eyes filled with tears.

A low moan revealed Darien, who lay unconscious on the couch with a large bloody welt at his temple. Lovisa scrambled to his side, her fingers lightly brushing over the wound. She pressed her lips against his forehead, not caring that her mother was watching. She praised the Norn that he was alive. "It's okay, Dar, I've got you."

"If Shiko is already here, then our original plan won't work." Stjarna paced away from her daughter, speaking more to herself than to Lovisa. "There's no way out of the palace. Verðandi, I summon you!"

Lovisa's questions died in her throat at the sight of a young red-headed girl who emerged from behind the dressing screen. Her freckled face was alight with excitement, but her skin glowed as though fire raged beneath it. Lovisa sucked in a breath.

"I knew you would call for me," the girl said, a smile playing on her lips. "Skuld told me so."

Lovisa rose to stand beside her mother even as her legs shook. This was no mere child before them; this was a goddess.

"Can you hide them both?" Queen Stjarna asked.

The child-goddess ran a hand along Darien's temples, brushing over the inflamed and bruised skin. "He's pretty, if you look past all this."

Lovisa clenched her fists but stayed where she was. Galdr radiated from the child-goddess, but it was not any type that Lovisa had ever felt before. Wild and untamed, it seized Lovisa's attention. She could focus on nothing else. Beneath the girl's hands, Darien's skin knitted itself back together. The girl tilted her head at her own handiwork. "Much better."

"Can you hide them?" Queen Stjarna asked again.

"Yes, but remember our price. We're not sure you can pay it for them both. It might be more than even you can withstand, Queen of Dreams."

Lovisa's trance broke at the goddess' words. "What price? Móðir, what is she talking about?"

Queen Stjarna cupped Lovisa's cheeks in her hand. "This is the only way. Verðandi will hide you and Darien. She'll bring you back when it's safe again. You must be brave, my love."

The three of them turned at the sound of yelling and running feet outside the chamber door. Their time was up. Queen Stjarna kissed her daughter's forehead. Lovisa felt the tremble of her mother's hands on her cheeks. Then her touch was gone.

"I'm ready, Verðandi." Queen Stjarna held out her hands to the child, who grinned from ear to ear.

As if playing a game, Verðandi placed her hands on the Queen's palms. With closed eyes and a low voice, she chanted, "Urðr, Verðandi, Skuld, Urðr, Verðandi, Skuld, Urðr, Verðandi, Skuld."

Lovisa's skin tingled at the names of the goddesses of fate.

Other voices rose, one gravely and the other deep, mingling in with Verðandi's high, sweet tones. The goddesses' voices rose; the words melded together until Lovisa could no longer distinguish the names. Overwhelming surges of galdr robbed Lovisa of her breath and burned her skin. The names of the goddess were like blows raining down on Lovisa's mental walls. There could be no resistance.

Lovisa fell to the ground as the floor shook. She held onto Darien's body, for her sake and his, to keep him from falling to the floor.

Pounding erupted against the door, which cracked and splintered. Queen Stjarna's hands shook under Verðandi's. A white-hot glow enveloped them. Lovisa shielded her eyes from the sight. A flash of light revealed the truth of her mother's actions as galdr *flowed from Queen Stjarna's body and into Verðandi's.*

"Móðir, stop!" Lovisa screamed. "It's killing you!"

Drops of blood fell from Stjarna's nose and gathered at the corners of her mouth. The pounding on the door intensified as Shiko's guards attempted to break through, but Lovisa could not look away. Even as the flush fled Stjarna's cheeks, even as the light died in her mother's eyes, Lovisa could not look away.

At last, Stjarna turned toward her daughter. A small smile crossed her face, but her eyes were already unseeing. "I love you, Lovisa. I don't regret my decision."

The door collapsed, but that was nothing compared to the shattering of Lovisa's heart as she watched her mother's body fall at the feet of the child-goddess, who glowed with new light. Lovisa knew the coming footsteps meant death, but she welcomed them. There was nowhere left to run. A gun was cocked, its barrel pressing against the back of her head.

Just let it be over, *Lovisa prayed.*

Before she shut her eyes, Lovisa glimpsed the child-goddess she'd nearly forgotten. The girl's eyes burned with the same glow from her mother's hands. Her wild red hair danced in the still air as though on fire. She turned hard eyes toward the men behind her and spoke a word.

Then the world went quiet.

There was nothing but a field and a tree and a well.

Lovisa felt nothing, thought nothing. She did not exist.

For a long time, there was nothing but the nothingness.

ᚾᛁᛘ᚛ᚄᚾᛁᛘ᚛ᚄᚾᛁᛘ᚛ᚄᚾᛁᛘ᚛ᚄᚾᛁᛘ᚛ᚄ

ONE DAY, THERE WAS a voice in her ear, telling Larissa to rise.

It was time to start her day. She pushed past the grit that coated her eyes. A young girl with pigtail braids and bright green eyes hovered over her bed with a wide grin.

Halla.

Awakening

Larissa

LARISSA GASPED; HER BODY sagged into waiting arms.

She swam through the memories that assaulted her mind. Darien murmured soothing words in her ear; Anara rubbed a hand over her shoulders. She closed her eyes at their questioning glances. Waves of anger and grief assailed her. Her father's murder. Her mother's sacrifice. For her.

All the loss and pain had been for her.

No wonder she hadn't wanted to remember. The recollection was like the destruction of a dam. Irreversible.

She was drowning in the flood of memories. She was Lovisa, Princess of Perle, daughter of King Mikkel and Queen Stjarna, heir to the throne of Perle, and bane of the Empress. She was also Larissa, daughter of Dal and Vern, sister of Halla. She could be both. Halla had been right. Larissa shook her head, smiling through the pain.

Of course Halla had been right.

"Larissa? Lara, talk to us."

A coaxing hand lifted her chin, and storm-battered blue eyes that she had known since childhood bore into hers. Another wave of emotion crashed over her. How could she have forgotten *him*?

"Darien, give her a moment."

Anara's expressionless face watched her, but Larissa caught the stifled hope hiding in Anara's eyes, weighed down by dark circles of exhaustion. Everyone had believed Aeron was dead. Lovisa and Darien had vanished for years without a trace, but Anara had been left behind. In all that time, Anara never gave up on them. Even when she was forced to search on her own.

Fifty years was a long sentence in isolation.

Larissa wiped her tears on her sleeves. She'd been so lost in her own guilt and fear; she hadn't considered Anara's sacrifice. Even now, having remembered the past, Larissa felt nauseous thinking about the devastation she'd brought to her father, her mother, Anara, Dal and Vern, and Halla. Not only to them, but to her people.

Halved, they'd told her. The population of her people had been *halved* in Shiko's anger over her escape. Their blood was surely on her own hands as well. Lovisa, too, had been halved. Larissa didn't know if either her people or herself could ever be made whole, but she had to try. She sniffed, pushing back the hair that fell in her face. Her fingers trailed over her scar, and Larissa was glad for it. It was fitting that she would carry this wound to forever distinguish herself from who she used to be.

Larissa was done crying, and she was done running. "I'll do it. I'll inspire the Viðnám."

Darien's eyes rounded. He shared a hesitant glance with Anara. "Does this mean—"

"I remember, Dar."

His face paled even as his eyes shone. Larissa wasn't sure if it was the return of her memories or Darien's reaction that caused it, but she felt her *galdr* rise to greet her like an old friend. From the corner of her eye, Larissa caught Anara's feral smile. No doubt, she could sense the increasing *galdr* in the room. Larissa spotted her gun on the bedside table, imagining it in her hand. The air around her fingers crackled with golden energy. It took nothing to shape the *galdr* this time. It responded to her as easily as wiggling her toes. The gun flew across the room, nestling happily in her hand. Anara howled in victory.

Larissa tucked the gun into her waistband, thinking of Halla, of her parents, and of her people.

There were no windows in the room, yet she could feel the arrival of dawn. Anara and Darien had kept their watch throughout the night, but now it was Larissa's turn. King Torsten and Speaker Skaði would be waiting for her answer.

Hang in there, Halla. We're coming.

Epilogue: Fate's Design
Verðandi

Urðr sat on the edge of the well. The threads that wound around her fingertips dipped into the water that swirled at the old crone's touch. Beneath Urðr's wrinkled fingers, images danced across the water. There was a burning palace, blood on the cliffs of Safír, and swirling dark mist that wove around gates made of black stone covered in ice.

"The Queen's plan is playing out," Urðr said.

Verðandi glanced up from where she sat on one of *Yggdrasil*'s mighty roots. Under her fingers, the new runes she had carved into the bark burned with the power of the gods. Although Verðandi missed her sleepers, it was awfully fun anticipating their next move.

"It's exciting!" she squealed.

"It will be what it will be," was the crone's only reply.

Both the old woman and the young girl looked up from their respective places as the third woman strolled across the clearing. Her fiery red hair drifted in a nonexistent breeze. When she reached the well, she looked up into the lofty branches that circled higher than

the eye could see. Time and time again, she maneuvered something hidden within her hands that rattled with each flick of her
fingers.

Verðandi could no longer stand the silence.

"What will happen to them, Skuld? Can they change what is to
come?"

"We shall see." Skuld unclenched her fist, revealing several carved
stones. Runes of power, luck, destiny, wisdom, revival, anguish,
and death were etched into them. Skuld rattled them once more
before examining their lines.

"They are challenging Fate's design."

Letter to the Reader

THANK YOU FOR READING *Well of Dreams*. I began writing this book in my middle school years. Would you believe it if I told you this story was originally set in a boarding school and Halla didn't exist? It's amazing to see how my book has grown since I first started passing chapters to my friends under our desks (sorry Mr. Doerksen!).

Larissa's and Halla's stories will continue in Book Two.

Until then, you can get updates and exclusive behind-the-scenes on your favorite characters and my writing process by joining my newsletter or following me on social media (@KaylaAnnAuthor). Those who sign up for my newsletter will receive sneak peeks at upcoming character art and ARC reading opportunities!

If you loved *Well of Dreams*, you can make a huge impact by leaving a review!

Supportive readers like you make all the difference when you leave a review, even if the review just says, "Good stuff." Reviews left on Amazon, Goodreads, and social media help to share this book with others and increase its visibility.

Keep reading for a sneak peek at Book Two!

Acknowledgments

First and foremost, I give all glory to God. It is through Him that I have the ability and the passion to write.

To my husband who believed in me when I didn't, supported my decision to borrow from our own "bank" to pursue this dream, and soothed my midnight doubts, thank you! Even though you are not a reader by any means, you supported me whole-heartedly, and I love you so much for it. To my family who encouraged me and allowed me to shove every book update in your face, thank you (although, you kind of have to put up with me anyway).

To my critique partners, Morgan and Michelle, you know that this book would not have been possible without your insights. Morgan, I think you've literally read over a dozen drafts, and yet you never responded with anything besides enthusiasm and support. Thank you for joining me from start to finish and for your keen eye during proofreading! Michelle, thank you for the spur of the moment Marco Polos and all those early mornings and late nights when you let me work through my bookish thoughts. I am so grateful for each of you. Thank you for encouraging me to chase my dreams when I felt selfish. Thank you for being my book's biggest champions!

To Amanda and Angela, y'all are my author support group, and you know it! I'm so grateful for the (literally countless) hours we spent on Marco Polo discussing everything from Kickstarter, to publication, to marketing, to raising children, and especially our talks about the Lord. Thank you for taking this newbie Indie author under your wings and showing her the ropes!

To my mom and Pappa, the first readers of *Well of Dreams* who knew it before as *The Awakening*, thank you for encouraging me to pursue my passions. Thank you for setting me on the path to authorship with your absolute belief that I would one day publish my story.

To my beta readers, thank you for being brutally honest with me in the kindest way possible. To my Street Team, thank you for encouraging me along the way by sharing my work and spreading the news. To my coworkers (Joanne and Alesa) who not only read my book, but let me babble on and on about it during our lunches, you guys rock! To my readers, thank you for allowing me to share this world with you.

To 12 year old Kayla, thank you for starting us on this journey. We did it.

Kickstarter Acknowledgements

Thank you to every single person who backed my Kickstarter campaign. It is because of my generous backers that I was able to create the book of my dreams including professional maps and illustrations. Thank you so much.

A.
A. A. Briggs
Abby A.
Addison Horner
Adelle Williams
Adrienne Hiatt
Alana M.
Alesa Shifflett
Alexander Parker
Alexandrine D.
Alyssa Pressley
Amanda Auler
Amanda Reynolds
Amanda Siri Hill
Amber Staples
Andie Vargas
Angela Morse
Anna L.
AnnMarie Q.
Anthea Sharp
Ava Kodah
Benjamin Weaver
Billye Herndon
Bonnie Anne
Brendan Pease
Brianna Welch-Martin
Brittany Mack
Brooke J Katz
Brownwing Family
C. J. Milacci
Carissa V.
Cassi Krotzer
Cassy
Catherine Maxwell
Chloe Hey
Christina G.
Corinne Brucks
Dale
Damon
Danielle
Doug Parker
E. A. Hendryx
Ellen Pilcher
Ellie R. Tran
Emily and Dalton Thompson
Emma Hill
Emma Shelford
Erika Gfeller
Esapekka Eriksson
Fleur DeVillainy
Francesco Tehrani

Geoff M.
Georgianna Myers
Gerald P. McDaniel
Haley Aita
Haley B.
Hannah H.
Hannah Pennington
Heath Baker
Heather
Heather C.
Heather Renee
Heiko Koenig
Holly
Hunter Beatty
Indigo Armstrong
Isabel K.
Isabella Wade
J. C. McKenzie
Jakob Baker
Jason Lovell
Jayme Jo Waltz
Jeff & Angela Mooney
Jen Woodrum
Jennifer Corry
Jennifer H.
Jeremiah Daniel Sater
Jessica McCarthy
Jessica Ness
Jill Okey
Joanne Long
Jordan Rivet
Judy Liu
Julia N. White
Justin R. Vera
Kaitlyn Deann
Kambria
Kandle Ynostrosa
Karen Brown Weaver
Karen Feldman
Karyne Norton
Kass McInteer
Kate M.
Kayla Cotrell
Kelsey
Kit Aldridge
Kristin Roberts
Kristina
Krystina Roupe
Kylie Burrage
Lanie Mores

Laura Edwards
Licia Moss
Liesl West
Linda Moss
Lindsey Petrucci
Lindsey Robison
Lindslee
Liz DuRoss
Lori Parker
Louise Davis
Lukas Baker
Lydia Baker
L.Z.
Mackay Long
Maddie Jaymes
Madison Lee Parker
Mariah J.
Marie-Helene A.
Mary Crauderueff
Mary Locke Jolley
Megan Astell
Megan Young
Melissa Hill (Bergsma)
Meredith Carstens
Michelle Baker
Michelle Forman
Michelle Frohman
Michelle Hagler
Mike McCue
Morgan G.
Morgan Rither
Moriah
Mrs. Cat Gardner
Myra Danvers
Narya A. Vicens
Natasha Rueschhoff
NekoTina
Nicole Sanders
Paige Schultz
Patricia Bowman
Patricia Parker
Paul Jacques
Paul Smith
Penny BroJacquie
Phil Proctor
Priscilla Arias
Qavee
R. Jensen
R. A. Morley
Rachael Jakubowski

Rachel A. Carter
Rachel Strehlow
Rachelle Degoumois
Rachelle Leblanc
Rain Sullivan
Raphael Bressel
Rebecca Hill
R. L. Sarty
RosieDragon
Ryan Scott James
S. W. Eon
Sabrina Nilsson
Samantha Ghormley
Samantha M.
Sanguine Kitty
Sara Francis
Sarah F. Frederick
Sarah Osborne
Sarah Schroeder
Scott Casey
Scott Reynolds
Seamus Sands
Shannon Addison
Sharon Tabb
Shavonne Clarke
Shiloh I. Reeves
Sierra Schnell
Silvver
S. J. Reed
Steff Martin
Stephanie Combs
Stephanie Meredith
Sue Frecker
T. Perry
T. L. Shaw
T. J. Smith
Tabby Clancy
Tara Hundley
Tedra Trimm
Terri Hernandez
Terry S.
Terry Twyford
The Oganessian Family
Tiffany Goldman
Tzvia V.
Valerie Galderisi
Vicki Hsu
Victoria Clemm
Whitney Cook
Yevheniia Kreimeier

Sneak Peek at Book Two

Book Two Sneak Peek
Halla

Halla's eyes focused on the dark curl that plastered itself against Darien's forehead.

Having awakened from the fog, she found herself being jostled about in Darien's arms. The memory of the pale-eyed man and the *draugr* quickened her heartbeat as she stared at the sweat beading against Darien's hairline. They were weaving through the streets of Lystheim, the cables swaying in the darkening sky above them. The sound of footsteps pursued them, just a block behind. Darien's breaths came in short gasps, and, as her vision cleared, Halla watched in morbid fascination as blood dripped from a nick in Darien's neck.

"Darien," she said, testing her voice.

"Halla!" His widening eyes glanced at her for only a moment, the relief evident on his face, before refocusing on the street ahead of him. "I'm glad you're awake."

"Is someone following us?"

"Yes," he huffed.

She remembered the warehouse, the blond man with Darien's voice, and the *draugr.*

"Where's Lara? And Anara?"

"Split up."

Her chin bumped into his chest as they barreled around the corner. Darien's chest heaved for air, but he pushed forward, adjusting Halla in his arms.

"Darien, put me down," she insisted. "I can run."

He frowned, but his feet didn't slow. Halla could feel the muscles in his arms trembling.

"I can run!" she protested again.

The battle in Darien's face was brief. His arms shuddered as he lowered Halla to the ground beside him. She had no chance to regain her footing or situate herself before Darien's hand grasped hers, and they were running again. Her side cramped up immediately, but Halla ignored it. She would not complain. She would be strong like Larissa.

They turned another corner, only to find a group of sentries ahead of them.

"There they are! In the name of the Empress, stop them!"

Darien pushed Halla behind him. "Run, Halla!"

Darien's sword clanged as he blocked a sentry's knife. Halla did not know when he had drawn it. She so desperately wanted to stay, to help, but she had promised Lara. She had promised her that if it all went wrong, she would run. Halla cursed her size, knowing she was too weak to be of any help. Tears gathered in her eyes as she turned and fled.

The sound of the commotion behind her grew louder, loud enough that she had to look back. There were more sentries now, but these new sentries seemed to be fighting *with* Darien, not against him. One of the original sentries drew his gun and pointed it at Darien who, engaged with another man, didn't see it. Just as the sentry pulled the trigger, a giant of a man tackled him to the ground. The bullet intended for Darien whizzed so close to Halla's face, she swore she could feel the heat.

The sentry was already rising from the ground, scowling at Halla and raising the gun again.

Halla fled, her small feet pounding hard down the alley. The corner was in sight, but before she could turn it, she found herself tangled in someone's arms instead. On the upper bicep, Halla saw the flash of a white and black armband. *Thræll.*

"Well, what do we have here?"

Halla thrashed against the man, then whimpered as he wrenched her back by her long blonde braids. Yanking her head, he forced Halla's head to tilt up to meet his lifeless gray eyes.

"Where's your identification, second-born?"

Halla froze in fear. She knew his voice. She'd heard it in the forest the night before.

"Halla!" Darien cried out, his voice muffled by the fighting.

Halla struggled against the *thræll's* grip, her nails scratching at the hands that held her hair. "Let me go!"

"Fenris, those aren't all sentries."

Only then did Halla realize the slaver was not alone. There were several more men sporting the white and black armbands grouped behind the leader, Fenris, who still clutched her hair. They stood uneasily, watching the fight at the other end of the alley with their hands on their weapons. Fenris' eyes never left Halla; he seemed unfazed by her feeble attempts at freedom. With his other hand, he grasped Halla's face, pinching her chin between his fingers.

"What do I care about sentries? We've got our prize."

Halla then did something very brave and very stupid. Her teeth found their mark with a swift snap. Immediately Fenris howled, curses streaming from his mouth as he drew back his bloodied finger. His other hand clutched Halla's hair more tightly, winding his fingers in what was left of her braids, refusing to let go no matter how she struggled to turn back to Darien.

She never saw the fist that hit her.

(End of Sneak Peek)

Sign up for my newsletter or follow @KaylaAnnAuthor for updates on Book Two.

Bonus Chapter

Skaði's Vengeance

FOUR YOUNG CHILDREN SAT at the shoreline's edge, oblivious to the adults that observed from farther away. They looked out at the fading sun that reflected off the rushing waters of the Klarälven River. Lovisa curled her bare toes against the pebbles on the beach.

"Who knows a good story?" she asked.

"I do," the young blond-haired boy replied.

"No more about the *Volsungs*, Aeron." The girl beside them rolled her copper eyes. "If I hear one more story about Sigurd, I'll drown myself in that river."

"No need for such drastic measures, Anara," the dark-haired boy added. He nudged Lovisa's shoulder. "I know of one."

Lovisa smiled at Darien. Behind him, Anara and Aeron glanced at each other from the sides of their eyes.

Darien fiddled with a pebble in his hand, then looked back out to the river and beyond at the snow capped mountains. "There once was a lovely giantess named Skaði, born to the *Jötnar* family. They were proud and strong, but also selfish and self-seeking. Skaði's father, the giant Thjazi, was loved by his daughter, but not by the neighboring *Æsir* gods. Thjazi was envious of the *Æsir*'s garden of golden fruit that was cultivated by the ever-youthful Iðunn. Thjazi would often sneak into the *Æsir*'s land to stare at

Iðunn as she plucked the fruit for the *Æsir* to eat. This fruit was special; it gave the *Æsir* everlasting youth and beauty.

"One day, Thjazi sent the trickster god, Loki, to steal not only the fruit, but Iðunn as well, and to bring them both back to him. Without Iðunn, the remaining fruit would wither, and the *Æsir* would die. Thjazi ate the fruit for himself and returned to his homeland with Iðunn. When the *Æsir* discovered her absence, they were outraged. Finding the trickster, the *Æsir* threatened to kill him unless he returned Iðunn to them. And so the trickster had no choice but to go and rescue the very maiden he had stolen. This trickster had *galdr* of his own and changed himself into a great hawk to enter into the Jötunn's mountains unseen. When the trickster found Iðunn, he transformed her into a nut so that he could carry her in his talons and escape.

"When Thjazi returned to his home to find his prize gone and the hawk flying away in the distance, he transformed himself into an eagle so that he might recapture his prey. Thjazi followed the trickster all the way back to the home of the *Æsir*, but, so focused on his prize, he did not see the trap the *Æsir* had set. The oldest and wisest of the *Æsir*, known as Óðinn, emerged and struck Thjazi down with fire. All rejoiced at the return of Iðunn and their golden fruit. All rejoiced, except, of course, for Thjazi's daughter Skaði.

"Skaði mourned his death. Not wanting to bring dishonor to his memory, she traveled across the high and snowy mountains to the land of the *Æsir*. Skaði demanded an audience with Óðinn and requested that the *Æsir* make amends for her father's death. Although Óðinn knew that it would be well within his rights to turn her away, he saw the opportunity for what it was. It was a chance to unite the *Æsir* and the Jötnar and to prevent further fighting. So Óðinn offered Skaði the option to take for herself a husband from any of the *Æsir* as a sign of good faith between the families. He also gifted Thjazi's body to her so that she might return him to their homelands. Before Skaði took the body, Óðinn took Thjazi's eyes and planted them in the sky. It was both to honor his memory and to signal an end of the fighting between the Jötnar and the *Æsir*. That is why, every winter, when the twin stars shine brightest in the sky, we celebrate how Skaði's loyalty and bravery put an end to further death and destruction."

Lovisa nudged Darien's shoulder with a small smile. "I liked the story, but you should have included more about Skaði's wedding."

Anara rolled her eyes. "Loki was the best character, if you ask me.

"Sure." Aeron threw a pebble into the waters. "But the *Volsungs* are still better."

"That's 'cause you want to be the hero some day, don't you Aeron?" Anara asked.

He looked out over the water. "The Norn will decide."

Bonus Chapter
Baldr the Invincible

IT WAS A COLD winter night. Even with the flames roaring in the fireplace, Larissa shivered at the cold. Beside her, Halla cuddled in closer, pulling their shared blanket tighter around them. Pappa and Mamma sat on the couch, cradling their cups of cocoa. The girls had long since finished their own. Halla had requested a story, and Pappa was all too happy to oblige.

Their book of stories was sprawled across Pappa's lap—not that he needed it to share the stories he knew from heart. "Let me tell you the tale of one of the most beloved *Æsir* that ever lived. Baldr the Beautiful was considered one of the greatest of the *Æsir*, the beloved son of the high chief of the *Æsir*, Óðinn, and the high chieftess, Frigg. One day, the *Æsir* heard rumblings amongst all living things. Frigg was visited by the *mara* who foretold the death of her beloved son, Baldr. Unwilling to accept this fate and being well versed in *seidr*, Frigg set out to save her son's life. She journeyed across the lands. Everywhere she went, she greeted each living thing—mortal, animal, and even the plants. She made each swear an oath to never harm her son. Once she covered all the lands, convinced that Baldr was safe, she returned back to the grand halls of the *Æsir*.

"When she arrived home, the other *Æsir* were delighted by the news, for they too loved Baldr. He was now invincible, unable to be subjected to harm or death. They invented a game of sorts. The other *Æsir* could throw whatever they wanted at Baldr—swords, fire, arrows, rocks—and he would not dodge. They could not harm him. The *Æsir* took delight in this new game; they rejoiced at his invulnerability. But it did not last."

Halla's eyes widened, her hands clenching the blankets in her lap as if she had not heard this story a dozen times before. "Frigg forgot something, didn't she, Pappa?"

"That's right, little one."

Halla leaned in closer, nearly upsetting the cup of cocoa at her side.

"Frigg forgot to request an oath from the lowest plant of all, mistletoe," Pappa continued. "Her oversight would not have been so unfortunate if not for the trickster living within the midst of the *Æsir*. He discovered this flaw in Frigg's perfect system. A potent of chaos and mischief, the trickster god Loki created a pointed shaft made of mistletoe. One day, during the game, this trickster handed the spear of mistletoe to Baldr's blind brother, Höðr, and encouraged him to take part in the merriment. When Höðr threw the shaft, Baldr was killed instantly."

Halla threw the blanket over her head, as she did every time she heard this story. Larissa reached to right the mug Halla had upset in her dismay, setting it farther away from her sister.

Pappa leaned forward, tugging down the blanket. "It is sad, Halla, but remember there is a point, as there is in every story. The *Æsir* and even the feuding *Vanir* mourned Baldr's death. It brought together the warring families as they honored his life. Frigg blamed herself for overlooking the small mistletoe. So each winter, we hang mistletoe as a reminder of Frigg's tears that became the berries on the leaves, for mistletoe did not have berries before Baldr's death. We remember how Frigg did not take her vengeance on mistletoe, but rather how it would become a symbol of hoped-for peace between the *Æsir* and the *Vanir* in the midst of a violent world."

Halla sighed in contentment. "Do you think people will ever tell stories of me one day, Pappa?"

Pappa's eyes met Mamma's. "Maybe one day, Halla."

Pronunciation Guide

Verðandi (Verr-thawn-dee)
Urðr (Orrth-thr)
Skuld (Scoo-ldt)
Larissa (Lah-ris-ah)
Halla (Hah-la)
*Vern Askdóttir (Vern)
*Dal Oginson (Dale)
Helga (Hel-gah)
Lovisa (LOH-vee-sah)
Darien (Dare-ee-in)
Anara (Ah-NAR-a)
Rúna (Rroo-nah)

Stjarna (Shtar-nah)
Mikkel (Mee-kell)
Shiko (Shee-koh)
Jon (Yawn)
Aeron (Airr-ron)
Aagen (I-gin)
Calder (Kahl-der)
Nia (Knee-ah)
Torsten (Tour-ston)
Halvor (Hal-vore)
Jari (YAR-ee)
Haki (Hah-kee)
Skaði (Skah-thee)

**Last names are determined by the father's first name. Then either the suffix -son or -dóttir is added based on the gender of the child.

Commonwealths

Diamant (Dee-ah-mont)
Perle (Pur-la)
Safír (Sah-fee)
Smaragd (Smear-ogd)
Rubin (Roo-bEEn)

Capitol City: Ishjem (Eess-yem)
Capitol City: Lystheim (Lies-tee-im)
Capitol City: Havsiden (Hahv-sy-din)
Capitol City: Treheim (Tray-Highm)
Capitol City: Brannsiden (Brahn-sy-din)

Glossary

Æsir (Aah-seer)	A branch of gods/goddesses in the Norse tradition
Bebe (Bay-bay)	Baby (term of endearment)
Evrópa (Ehv-rope-a)	Continent Name
Faðir (Fah-theer)	Father
Galdr (Gal-der)	Ancestral Magic
Hálfviti (Har-vit-ee)	idiot; half-wit
Hrun (croon)	Collapse
Jötnar (yot-nar)	Race of giants
Jötunn (yo-ton)	Singular form of giant
Kafteinn (Calf-tay-in)	high-ranking member of the Empress's soldiers; captain
Mara (mar-rah)	demonic creature of nightmares
Móðir (Moe-theer)	Mother
Norn (norn)	Three goddesses of fate
slápr (SLAHP-uhr)	a good-for-nothing, lazy person
Skogsrå (Scohgs-ra)	mythic cow women
Tæpəstrɪs Friðarsamningur (Tae-pas-tree-ars Free-thar-sam-ming-geer)	Peace Treaty Tapestry
Thræll (thra-eyetch)	slave traders
Viðnám (Vith-nam)	Resistance
Víti (Vee-teh)	Hell (curse word, not to be confused with Hel the place)

About the Author

Kayla Ann is a traditional and self-published author. Her traditionally published book, *Agency in the Hunger Games*, explores the importance of personal agency in a world determined to strip away individuality. Her debut self-published YA novel, *Well of Dreams*, explores similar themes of fate versus free will. Kayla Ann writes in her limited free time when she is not teaching the next generation of readers, playing board games with her husband, or serving as personal chef, hairdresser, playmate, and story-teller to her young son.